QUEEN OF THE DEAD

D0106933

TY DRAGO

sourcebooks
jabberwocky

Published by Sourcebooks Jabberwocky, an imprint of Sourcebooks, Inc.
P.O. Box 4410, Naperville, Illinois 60567-4410
(630) 961-3900
Fax: (630) 961-2168
www.jabberwockykids.com

Library of Congress Cataloging-in-Publication data is on file with the publisher.

Source of Production: Versa Press, East Peoria, Illinois, USA.
Date of Production: September 2012
Run Number: 18499

Printed and bound in the United States of America.
VP 10 9 8 7 6 5 4 3 2 1

For Susan Drago McDevitt,
a loyal fan, a great sister…and an even better friend.

I love you.

"The first casualty of any war is innocence"
—Anonymous

CONTENTS

1. Crossing Over 1

2. Recon 8

3. Prison 17

4. The Deader and the Barfly. 29

5. Good Will Hunted 36

6. Totally Worth It 44

7. Message in a Bottle 56

8. Battle Plans 66

9. Breaking In 81

10. Number Eleven. 96

11. The Tide of Battle. 106

12. Lilith's Morning 116

13. Spitting Image. 128

14. Opportunity Knocks. 141

15. Agent Ramirez 151

16. Monkey Business. 160

17. The Burgermeister and Helene 168

18. Grown-Ups 181

19. Darkness 191

20. Getting the Band Back Together. 200

21. Invasion of the Body Snatchers 210

22. Floor Plan 218

23. The Demonstration. 235

24. Dueling with the Dead 246

25. Swapping Stories. 257

26. The Last Straw 269

27. Desperation 276

28. Power Drills and Olive Branches 284

29. The Mom Trap 293

30. Bitter Truths 299

31. The Phone Call 307

32. Will's New Mission. 315

33. Haven's Librarian 322

34. Friends 330

35. Breaking In Again 336

36. The Dirt Tube. 342

37. Rescue. 355

38. Juggernaut 368

39. Life after Death. 383

40. Resurrection. 396

41. Eulogy 405

42. The Eyes of the Enemy. 416

CHAPTER 1

CROSSING OVER

T he Queen crossed the Void between worlds on Halloween, and the dead welcomed her.

She arrived without escort, emerging through the Rift without form—an entity of seething dark energy.

Her minions were already assembled, dozens of them, as many as would fit into this arched, windowless chamber. Being here was, of course, a tremendous honor—and only the most highly ranked had been invited. They stood at patient attention, a vanguard for the Army of the Dead, lit only by the Rift, which resembled a wide, fiery crack in the chamber's rear wall.

This "crack" did not close once the Queen's "Self" had fully entered this human realm.

The Rift never closed.

In the midst of the welcoming dead, resting atop a steel hospital gurney, lay the body of a young woman. The cadaver was the freshest available, as suitable a vessel as the legions could find. For the occasion, she had been dressed in tailored clothes and adorned with gold jewelry.

No expense was spared.

Nor was time wasted. No sooner had the Queen emerged from the Void than her dark energy leapt into the waiting body. This is essential, as their kind couldn't exist in this world without a host.

The eyes of the woman on the gurney, which had been respectfully shut, snapped open. She sat up, moving stiffly with muscles that had begun to decay, and gazed down at her hands. In life, they had probably been long and delicate. Now they appeared purple, the fingers stiff with rigor mortis.

Seeing them, the Queen felt disgusted but resigned.

She rarely traversed the Void personally. But the sudden and inexplicable death of her predecessor, the late Kenny Booth—so well respected and accomplished a conqueror—had made it necessary.

Oh, how she wished she could make that overrated fool pay for his failure. Sadly, his destruction made that impossible.

But someone would pay. Oh yes. Someone would most *definitely* pay.

"How long has this host been deceased?" she demanded, speaking English for the first time, wrapping her unfamiliar tongue around the unfamiliar language.

"Six hours!" came the reply, barked by a dead man in a tailored suit who stepped dutifully forward.

The Queen eyed him. His cadaver, she noted, was nearly as fresh as her own. But while his host was of interest, she also examined his Cover.

They all had Covers, the illusions that allowed them to move unchallenged among the bald monkeys populating this revolting planet. Each Cover, each false persona, had been meticulously crafted to suit the individual. His was of an Earth male in his fifties, his smooth face distinguished and his hair pepper gray. To humans, he would appear as the picture of respectability, of professionalism, of thoroughly human prosperity.

The *Malum*, after all, were masters of disguise.

The Queen slid herself off the cot and stood, testing her new legs.

They would do.

The man before her smiled. "Welcome, mistress." She noticed with some approval that he spoke English, as was the protocol.

"What is my name?" she asked.

"You're Lilith Cavanaugh," he replied. Then he held up a folder of papers. "Your dossier is here: education, employment history, personal references. You have tax records going back twenty years. It's as perfect an identity as has ever been fabricated. I handled it personally."

The Queen accepted the paperwork and scanned it. Later, when she was alone, she would read it through several times. Embracing a Cover, making it part of yourself, was important. One had to *believe* the lie. It had been a long time since she'd personally harvested a world, but there could be no forgetting the Old Rule: a successful Cover was as much bluff as illusion.

"Acceptable," she pronounced, dropping the folders casually onto the gurney behind her. "And you are?"

"James Dye, mistress," the man replied. Then he smiled, his Cover showing perfect white teeth, while the ones in the cadaver he inhabited were yellow and visibly loose.

"Dye…an amusing name and one with which I'm familiar. You were Kenny Booth's personal secretary, were you not?"

Did his smile falter slightly? She wasn't sure. It didn't matter either way.

"I had that honor, mistress. Yes."

"And what became of Booth while he was under your care?"

This time, the smile *did* falter. "Mistress, I wasn't—"

She took a step toward him. His smile vanished completely.

"Wasn't…what?" the Queen asked, closing the distance. "Wasn't in the television studio when your master was poisoned using the candies he so greedily and obsessively consumed? Wasn't on hand when his home was invaded? Weren't you laid low, along with the rest of his staff, while a collection of children…*children!*…bested you all?"

She was very close to James Dye now, enjoying the fear that shone in his eyes—not his dead eyes or the more expressive eyes of his Cover. No, it was the being within, his Self, that quaked before her—and with good reason.

"Mistress…please…"

The Queen reached up with her dead purple fingers and cupped the trembling man's head between them.

"Shhh," she cooed.

"Mercy," the man whimpered. "Mercy."

"No."

Then, in a single hard motion, she twisted and pulled, roughly ripping Dye's head from his shoulders.

There was no blood, as the host's heart hadn't been beating. But there *were* juices, and some of these trickled out as his body fell heavily to the stone floor.

Lilith held the head a moment longer, admiring the way the illusion closed its eyes, as if in sleep. A human witness wouldn't have seen the decapitation. Blinded by the Cover, a typical bald monkey would have thought the well-dressed man had collapsed, perhaps fainted. They might even have come forward to offer aid, never knowing that the only aid available to James Dye now was a new host into which to transfer his trapped Self.

The body he currently occupied—being suddenly and decidedly headless—was no longer usable.

"He doesn't transfer," the Queen announced to the rest of the assemblage. Then, growling with only partially spent anger, she hurled Dye's head into the open fissure between worlds.

Her minions murmured fearfully.

"He doesn't transfer!" And this time, she screamed it. Then, reaching down, she picked up the rest of the decapitated cadaver, and with a tremendous heave, she cast *that* into the Void too.

The *Malum* who had called himself James Dye was, like Kenny Booth, forever dead.

More murmuring, and the Queen noticed with irritation that none of their lips moved. They were speaking the Old Tongue.

"English!" she declared, her words reverberating off the arched brick ceiling. "Under my command, no one speaks the Old Tongue. You get one warning! Then you follow this fool! Is that understood?"

The murmurs ceased. Dozens of pairs of dead eyes locked on her, their Selves as well as their Covers looking suitably terrified.

Better.

"In time, one of you will attend me," she said. "The way James Dye attended Booth. If that Self fails me as Dye failed his master, he or she shall meet the same fate. As you have no doubt heard, I'm neither patient nor forgiving, and the necessity of my visit to this wretched world has done nothing to improve my mood. But I *can* be generous…if served with loyalty and competence. Is that understood?"

None spoke. None had to. Silence was assent.

"Good," the Queen said.

She briefly scanned the first page of her dossier. Lilith

Cavanaugh was five feet ten inches tall, with shoulder-length blond hair and green eyes. There were, of course, no photographs since, before tonight, Lilith Cavanaugh had never truly existed. But starting tomorrow, her face—or rather, her Cover's face—would begin to appear in local newspapers and on local television. The *Malum* were expert publicists. Soon the entire city would recognize her on sight.

Time to select the face they will see.

Smiling thoughtfully, the Queen centered herself—

—and donned her Cover.

In moments, a beautiful, blond-haired woman stood in place of the purplish cadaver, wearing the tailored suit and gold jewelry as if she'd been born in them. She touched her face and once again examined her hands, which no longer appeared dead but were smooth and elegant, with alabaster skin and polished fingernails.

Acceptable.

Then Lilith Cavanaugh addressed her minions. There was much to do, and she knew exactly where to start.

"One of you will now escort me to my new home," she commanded. "Once there, I will rest and study and ready myself to begin living the new life that has been prepared for me. But before that happens, will someone please explain to me about these…Undertakers?"

CHAPTER 2

RECON

What do you call it when you're running for your life from a rotting, animated cadaver wearing a cop uniform who—if he catches you—will savagely rip you limb from limb with his maggot-riddled hands?

Me, I called it "Thursday."

Well, "Friday," I guess. Because it was after midnight.

But I'm getting ahead of myself.

I could say all this trouble started about twenty minutes ago, but that wouldn't be true. It really started four months before that, on the day I stepped out of my house and discovered that my next-door neighbor had become a walking dead man rotting inside his JCPenney bathrobe. After that, it was my assistant principal and then my math teacher. Suddenly, they were everywhere—cops (like the dude chasing me now), store owners, and even TV news anchor guys. Thousands of them, with more showing up every day.

Corpses, with a capital "C." That's what we call them.

Not "zombies." Zombies are staggering, moaning morons. Corpses, on the other hand, are fast, smart, and organized. To the rest of the world, they're normal-looking people. Only kids can see them for what they really are—and only some kids. Guess I'm one of the lucky ones.

Since that morning, I haven't been home.

My name's Will Ritter, and I'm an Undertaker.

"How many are there?" Helene asked me twenty minutes ago.

I peered through the telescope at the goings-on at the prison gate across the street. The night vision turned the world a sickly green, but it penetrated every shadow. With it, I could clearly make out a small group of Corpses. They were doing something at the back of a Philly police car that stood idling at the curb, its headlights and flashers off.

"Four," I replied. "And whatever they're up to, they're being pretty low key about it. One's standing watch. Another's opening the gate, and the last two are pulling something out of the trunk."

"What is it?"

"Wait a minute." I peered closer. "A body!"

"Maybe one of them wants to transfer," Helene suggested.

"No…he's moving." I frowned. "I think they've got a person there…I mean a living person. Looks like he's handcuffed. Hands and feet. Gagged too."

"Lemme look," Helene said, her misty breath clouding

her face. It was freakin' cold on this dark street—just past twelve o'clock on a clear February night in Philadelphia. We'd stationed ourselves on Fairmount Avenue, hidden in the shadow of a storefront awning across from the enormous front façade of Eastern State Penitentiary.

I handed her my pocketknife—my weird, amazing pocketknife. It'd been given to me by a mysterious, nameless woman who'd visited me in a dream. I'd been pretty badly injured at the time and would have assumed that my battered head had conjured her up if I hadn't found this gift under my pillow.

It had taken me a while to fess up to the story, but most of my friends now knew the gist of it: I'd been visited by an angel.

Sounds crazy, doesn't it?

Well, my life over these past few months has kind of redefined "crazy" in my personal dictionary.

For example, take the Corpse Invasion—an army of the walking dead who somehow projected the illusion that they were ordinary men and women, an illusion that stayed put no matter how many slowly decomposing bodies they inhabited, wore out, and then replaced. For the past three years, long before I got involved, they'd been worming their way into city government, planning to take over. Last fall, one of them—a news guy called Kenny Booth—even tried to run for mayor.

He didn't win. We stopped him. The Undertakers.

Each of us is a Seer, somehow able to look right through the Corpses' illusions and spot the festering, stolen cadavers underneath. We *could* blow the whistle on them. We *could* stop these creatures in their tracks. Except, we're kids; the oldest of us is only seventeen.

And nobody believes kids, not about stuff like this.

Ever.

So we fight the war that no one else can. A guerrilla war. We hide in the shadows, only coming out at night. We watch the Deaders, and when we see an opportunity, we hit them. We hit them hard. Then we disappear.

Pisses them off no end, believe me.

Tonight, Helene and I had been quietly following a bunch of Corpse cops. To anyone else, they'd look like normal, up-standing members of the Philadelphia Police Department. To us, they were a pair of "Type Twos" and another pair of "Type Threes." That was a kind of rating system we had based on how far along a particular cadaver was in its decomposition. Type Ones were freshly dead, still fast and strong, though sometimes a bit juicy. Type Fives were dry husks that didn't move well, fought worst, and tended to fall apart.

These were in the middle.

Four Deaders in one cop car were rare. Normally, they liked to spread themselves pretty thin, infiltrating as much of the city's infrastructure as possible. Whenever we spotted more than two of them together at one time, it was a real red flag.

And almost always meant they were up to something.

After tailing them through the city streets for maybe half an hour, we'd wound up here, on Fairmount Avenue between Twenty-First and Twenty-Second streets, spying on them from a reasonably safe distance.

"They're carrying him inside," Helene reported, my pocketknife pressed to her one eye, the other eye squeezed shut. She was looking, as I'd been looking, through its night vision telescope.

Yeah, it's got a night vision telescope.

"Three are going in," she added. "But the fourth is staying put. Probably a lookout. Hold it!"

"What?" I asked.

"Looks like something fell out of the guy's pocket while they were carrying him through the gate. It's lying on the street. I don't think the Corpses noticed it."

"Can you see what it is?"

She shook her head.

"Zoom in."

"I'm as zoomed-in as this toy of yours goes. It's square and dark. A wallet maybe."

Interesting.

"We should get it," I suggested.

She lowered the pocketknife, frowning at me. "Forget it. No way."

"It could be important," I pressed.

"We're on recon. No direct contact, remember?"

It was true. Helene and I were "Angel" trainees. Angels was the name given to Undertakers crew responsible for most of the guerrilla war stuff I mentioned earlier. They were bossed by a girl named Sharyn Jefferson, the Chief's sister, and she ran it like an army general—by the book. Trainees were allowed to go out and scout for suspicious Corpse behavior, spy on them, and report back to Haven, the Undertakers' headquarters.

But we were *not* to go toe-to-toe with Deaders. It was part of the "rules and regs" that we lived by or, more to the point, survived by.

Still—

"Helene, they've snatched a living person…and an adult, not a kid. Not a Seer. Don't you think it's worth a little risk to maybe find out why?"

She considered, still frowning. Her brown hair was tied back and hidden under a heavy wool cap. Her pale face and hazel eyes shown in the dim light. For a long moment, she didn't answer.

Then she did. "Not tonight, Will."

"Not tonight? Why not?"

"Just…not tonight."

Now it was my turn to frown. "That's stupid."

"Yeah? Well, those are the rules and regs. You know them as well as I do. Plus, I'm senior on this mission. So, stupid or not, you're not going anywhere."

I bristled, giving her a look that I hoped conveyed how I

felt about her pulling rank on me. "So if I go out there on my own, you'll…what? Kick my ass?"

"Wouldn't be the first time," she said.

True enough.

"Come on. I'll keep it low and quiet. Nothing crazy. You cover me with your Super Soaker. Once I'm close enough, I'll tag the guard with my pistol, grab the whatever-it-is, and be gone before the rest of the Corpses even know I'm there."

Helene wavered. "Will…I don't think…"

"You don't trust me?"

She swallowed. "You know I do."

"Then trust me when I tell you I can do this!"

I watched her forehead wrinkle with consternation. Finally, with an exasperated sigh, she gave in. "Fine. But I swear…if you get yourself killed, I *will* kick your ass!"

"Deal. Um…I'll need my pocketknife."

Her expression turned suspicious. "What for?"

"Just in case."

She shook her head. "Uh-uh. I'll need it to keep an eye out…'just in case' *you* get into trouble. Play it slow and smart, and you can nail that Deader before he even sees you. Just make sure you turn your radio off. You know how those things have a habit of beeping or chirping at just the wrong time."

I looked from her to my pocketknife and back again. That strange gadget was my most prized possession, and the idea of going into battle without it felt wrong.

"Helene…"

She gave me one of those looks, the one with a single eyebrow raised sharply—Mr. Spock-style. "You doing this…or not?"

I gave up and peered across the street. The prison lights were still off, its walls dark. But enough illumination shone from nearby streetlamps to give me a good view of the Corpse lookout. He stood at his post, maybe fifty yards away, his stolen body as stiff as a tree trunk and big enough to snap my neck like a pretzel stick.

But something told me this was important, and lately, I'd learned to trust my instincts.

A car rolled by, heading east. I ducked back into the shadows and instinctively covered my eyes so the headlights' glare wouldn't blind me. Fairmount Avenue could be a fairly busy street, but it was late, so traffic was pretty thin. Still, I'd have to be careful crossing, as much to avoid getting pinned by highlights as run over.

Another car passed, this one going west, toward where the guard stood. Then the street quieted again.

Now! I thought. *While the Deader's got the glare in his eyes!*

But just as I tensed to run, a hand caught my arm. Annoyed, I looked back to find Helene staring pointedly at me.

"It's past midnight," she said.

"So?" I asked.

"So…don't die. Not today. I don't need the irony."

Surprised, I nodded. She let go, and I made my move,

keeping low as I hurried across Fairmount Avenue, using the patchwork of shadows for cover and the noise of the retreating car to mask my footfalls.

So...don't die. Not today.

Helene knew it was my birthday.

CHAPTER 3

PRISON

E astern State Penitentiary wasn't a prison—at least not anymore. When it was built back in 1829, it was the largest structure in the United States. The outer walls, with their towers and parapets, had been designed to be imposing, kind of an early crime deterrent. The whole thing looked like a huge medieval castle. All it lacked was a moat.

In its day, Eastern State hosted big-name prisoners like Al Capone. Then, in the 1970s, it was closed as a prison and reopened again in the 1990s as a museum. Years ago, I went there on a field trip. Most Philly kids do, sooner or later.

The place is huge and creepy, kind of like Dracula's castle, only surrounded by restaurants and microbreweries.

But now, it was closed again by order of the city as part of a restoration effort. They said they were going to make the old prison "prettier." And in the meantime, the Corpses were apparently using the place for their own reasons—reasons that involved bringing a bound, living human through its gate in the middle of the night.

I dropped into a crouch beside a brick landscaping shelf—maybe four-feet-tall—that skirted the sidewalk all the way from the eastern corner of the prison to the front gate. Atop this shelf, which was maybe ten feet deep, decorative shrubbery, most of it little more than sticks this time of year, filled the space between me and the thirty-foot perimeter wall.

Looking west, I once again spotted the Corpse guard standing just outside the gate. If he'd noticed me crossing the street, he gave no sign.

So far, so good.

There weren't a lot of hiding places between me and him—not if I stayed on the sidewalk. So I waited for another westbound car to pass and then climbed up onto the landscaping shelf, pushed through the web of plants, and pressed my back against the cold stone of the prison's outer wall.

The shadows were deep here, especially with the prison's exterior lights unlit. I started inching forward, careful not to make too much noise, staying close to the wall. After a couple of minutes, I finally neared the gates, which stood tucked away inside a brick structure that jutted out from the rest of the prison, giving me a perfect corner to peek around.

So I peaked around it.

The Corpse guard was a big one and definitely a Type

Three. His bodily fluids were draining freely now, leaving the skin shriveled and tight over muscles that were rotting out from the inside. His eyes, partially hidden beneath a policeman's hat, were sunken and milky. Dead eyes. Corpses always had dead-looking eyes—so dead you could almost make yourself believe they couldn't see you.

You'd be wrong.

This was an animated cadaver, and the invader inside of it could you see you just fine; though thankfully their night vision wasn't any better than ours.

But whose cadaver? That was the part that always bugged me when I saw these guys. That body had once belonged to a living, breathing person, one who deserved better than to end up being worn by some evil, otherworldly thing. Worse, this one wore a cop uniform.

My dad had been a cop. Karl Ritter had in fact founded the Undertakers before a particularly clever and nasty Corpse had tricked and murdered him. That Corpse—Kenny Booth, former news anchorman and Philly mayoral candidate— was toast now. I'd handled that myself.

Nevertheless, seeing one of them wearing Philly blues always ticked me off.

This particular dead cop was facing the street, his lipless mouth spread in a permanent sneer. His weight kept shifting from foot to foot, squishing about in a deepening puddle of noxious fluid that dribbled out his pant legs and over his police-issue shoes. Cadaver juice.

There'd been a time, not long ago, when such a sight would have sent my stomach into somersaults. Now all it did was make me happy. This Deader was clearly bored.

And a bored Corpse was a Corpse off his guard.

On the sidewalk about three feet to his left, between him and me, lay the small black square that Helene had spotted.

It *did* look like a wallet.

But getting it wouldn't be easy.

I edged closer, wrinkling my nose against the stench. Type Twos and Threes smell the worst of all of them. The newer ones don't reek too bad yet, while the older ones have pretty much lost their smell. It's the ones in the middle that really make you want to vomit.

A little Corpse fact for you.

Moving west, the landscape ledge tapered downward, meaning that I had only a one-foot drop to the sidewalk instead of a four-foot drop. Another break. I took it very slowly, being careful not to stumble. I was in full view now, crouched just behind and to the left of the dead cop.

Close enough.

Reaching into my coat, I pulled out my pistol and leveled it at his ear.

For you, Dad.

Then I squeezed the trigger.

The stream of saltwater caught the Corpse right in the temple. For a moment, he just stood there. A moment after that, his limbs started twitching, then jerking, then spasming wildly. He collapsed to the sidewalk, helpless, his whole stolen body wracked by convulsions.

I stepped forward and scooped up the wallet.

Nothing to it.

Corpse hands—swollen with rot—were on me half a second later.

Not the fallen guard but another one. He'd leapt out of the shadowy tunnel that led to the prison gate and wrapped his cold, sticky hands around my neck before I even knew he was there. I barely had time to gasp in surprise before he yanked me off my feet so hard that I almost left my sneakers behind. Suddenly I was inside the gatehouse tunnel, pinned against the brick wall and dangling a foot off the ground, face-to-face with a purplish Type Two whose hair had begun to fall out in shriveled clumps.

"What. This? Little. Mouse?"

Deadspeak. Talking without moving his lips. They all do it. An Undertaker I know, a science geek named Steve Moscova, thinks it's the way Corpses naturally talk to each other—their native language, so to speak. Seers can hear it more or less the same way we can penetrate their illusions. "An advantage," he called it.

Maybe. But that didn't keep it from being creepy as hell.

Gasping for air, I forced myself to stay calm. Undertaker training. Be as scared as you want, but don't panic. Right now, he was holding me helpless at arm's length. I'd dropped my pistol when he'd grabbed me.

But if I could get him to pull me closer—

"Wait…" I stammered. "Please…"

He grinned. He had rotting yellow teeth, and don't even get me started on his tongue.

"*What. Mouse. Taste. Like?*"

This dead cop was going to bite me. They do that. It's crazy because they have no working digestive systems, but they do it anyway—and they do it, well, *savagely* is the only word I can think of to describe it. I'd seen with my own eyes what kind of damage Corpse teeth can do.

Sometimes, I still dreamed about it.

"Wait!" I coughed. "I…know a…secret." This last word was hard to get out past his tightening thumbs.

The Deader frowned at me. "Secret?" he asked, this time in English. Then he pulled me closer. "Tell me, mouse. And maybe I'll kill you fast."

Bingo.

I let go of his thick wrists and let my arms dangle, as if I were getting weak. Then I turned my hands into tight fists but with my thumbs stiff and pointing up at a sharp angle. More Undertaker training.

"Tell me!" he snarled.

I drove my thumbs into each of his armpits, seeking—and finding—the place where the nerves met. His expression turned slack with surprise as his arms went numb and he unceremoniously dropped me. My knees buckled, and I slid down the wall of the tunnel, landing on my butt.

"*Here!*" he called in Deadspeak, both his arms flopping uselessly at his sides. "*Undertaker! Quick! Here!*"

In seconds, the remaining two Corpses would come running from inside the prison, answering their buddy's call for help.

Time to go.

I scrambled up and headed for the street end of the short tunnel, but one of the Corpses was faster, putting his big body between me and the only way out.

"*You. No. Leave. Boy!*"

"Will! Catch!"

Helene appeared at the mouth of the tunnel, her own pistol pointing at the fallen lookout, who still lay twitching on the pavement. At the same time, her free hand swung in a smooth arc, tossing me something.

Yes! I thought.

My pocketknife sailed over the second Corpse's shoulder. I snatched it out of the air, barely dodging the armless Deader's teeth as he snapped at my hand. Then I hit the *2* button on the face of the closed knife. Two small steel prongs snapped out one end. Holding the button down, I shoved the Taser against the Corpse's broad chest.

His milky eyes widened. His whole body shuddered. Then he collapsed.

A hundred and fifty thousand volts will do that to you.

I love my pocketknife!

At the same moment, Helene fired point-blank into the face of the Deader in the street just to make sure he stayed put. His convulsions worsened. Saltwater. It messed up the neural receptors or something—more Steve-speak. A good shot in a leg made a Corpse walk in circles. A good shot in the face put this one down, at least for a few minutes.

Unfortunately, it didn't do anything permanent.

Footsteps sounded in the courtyard beyond the closed gate at my back.

"Let's go!" Helene snapped.

The two of us bolted across Fairmount Avenue and around the corner of Twenty-First Street, where we'd stashed our bike. Yeah, I said "bike"—singular. We were trainees, you see, not true Angels, which meant we had to share a bike when out on recon missions. Sharyn said it was because the cool saddle-seated Stingrays the Angels rode were in short supply. Really, I suspected it was her way of making sure we didn't get too cocky.

Kind of like I just had.

Helene pedaled because, well, she was almost a year older—and just a little bit stronger—than me.

It bugged me sometimes, but at least she didn't rub it in.

"Hold on!" she exclaimed completely pointlessly. I leaned back on the long seat and reached behind me to grab the chrome safety handle. I could have wrapped my arms around her waist instead. It might even have been safer.

But I never did that with Helene. I didn't really know why not.

Behind us, the prison's iron gate ripped open. Deadspeak

doesn't have curse words—at least none that I've heard. But these dudes did their best anyhow.

As Helene kicked at the pedals, taking us out onto Twenty-First, heading toward Center City Philly, I heard the cop car rev up.

They were coming after us.

"Tell me you got the wallet!" Helene yelled.

"I got it," I said. "It's in my pocket."

She nodded and pedaled harder as behind us, in a squeal of tires, a Philadelphia police cruiser turned sharply onto Twenty-First Street, no doubt driven by an enraged cadaver with murder on his mind.

Bikes are slower than cars. But they're also smaller and much more maneuverable. So for a biker to stay ahead of a pursuing car is less about pedaling hard—though that's part of it—and more about picking a route that has as many turns as possible. Some parts of Philly make this easy, offering short blocks intermixed with nice, tight, shadowy alleys for shooting down and disappearing.

Unfortunately, this wasn't one of those parts.

And such maneuvers generally required only one person on the bike. After two blocks of lumbering turns, I knew this one wasn't going to work.

"Drop me off!" I called.

"What?"

"We can't make it…not with both of us riding! Drop me off! I'll find a place to hide and call Haven for help!"

"Forget it!" she snapped. "I'm not leaving you here!"

"Then they'll kill us both and get the wallet! Trust me! I can lose them—at least until backup gets here!"

She wavered, unhappy.

Behind us, the cop car was bearing down like the two-ton wall of metal it was. The Deader had his siren and flashers off. Even his headlights were dark. One of the big risks in going against dead cops was that they often radioed for backup. This worked for them because even if it was a human cop who eventually caught us, the Corpses could always arrange something nasty later.

You see, they knew, like we knew, that regardless of what story we told while in custody, no one would believe us.

But this Deader stayed dark, which suggested that he didn't want us falling into "official" police custody.

He just wanted to kill us.

Helene clearly saw what I saw. More than anything else, it convinced her.

"I'll cut around the next corner," she said, sounding very unhappy about it. "You jump off!"

"Okay!"

If she'd cut the corner of Wallace Street any closer, we'd have both ended up splattered against the brick wall of the neighborhood bar. But her move was a good one—so sudden and perfectly timed that the dead cop overshot the intersection altogether, buying us precious seconds that were punctuated by the squeal of breaks.

"Take the wallet!" I told Helene as she stopped the bike in the tavern's shadowed doorway.

"You keep it," she replied.

"Take it!" I said again, shoving the small black square of leather at her. "In case they catch me!"

"Just make sure they don't!" she snapped. Then, before I could argue further, she kicked off and headed down the street in the direction of Center City. Glancing the other way, I saw the cop car right itself and come after us. His lights were still off.

I slipped the wallet into my coat pocket and stepped back in the shadows of the entrance to the bar, pressing myself against its heavy wood door. Light shone faintly from within, and I could hear music playing. But I didn't dare go inside. For one, I'd get thrown out immediately for being underage. For another, if a dead cop followed me, the bartenders and customers would hand me over without a second thought.

Because, of course, to them he wouldn't *be* a dead cop. The Corpse's Mask would show them a perfectly normal police officer just out doing his duty. Their noses wouldn't burn with the reek of his putrefying flesh. Their ears wouldn't hear the squish of his decomposing feet inside his shoes. And their eyes—well, they just wouldn't see the truth.

It was the Corpses' greatest weapon.

The cruiser rolled noisily past me, chasing after Helene. His lights stayed off, and he didn't slow. He hadn't seen me. The trick had worked—so far.

I raised my wrist to my lips and whispered, "Haven. This is Angel Four."

For a few seconds, there was no reply, and I felt a sudden stab of panic. Had I broken the makeshift gadget during the fight with the Corpse? It wouldn't have been the first time.

"This is Haven, Angel Four. That you, Will?"

"Hey, Justin. Yeah, it's me," I said. "Listen, we ran into trouble. I'm on foot, and Helene's coming in hot."

"What? Oh, barnacles! Hold on…"

I thought, *Barnacles? SpongeBob? Really?*

The wait felt like hours but was probably half a minute.

"Will, I'm showing you at Nineteenth and Wallace. Helene's a block away. She's moving fast."

You just gotta love GPS.

"She'd better be," I said. "There's a Deader in a cop car on her butt."

"Barnacles!" he said again. "One sec…"

I rolled my eyes.

It was more like fifteen "secs," but who was counting?

"Marlee's already talking to her on another line," Justin told me. "We're setting something up. I've also radioed Sharyn. She's on her way. Stay put."

And as he said that—I mean *right* as he said that—another Corpse came around the corner of the building and bumped right into me.

CHAPTER 4

THE DEADER AND THE BARFLY

Like the one in the car, this Deader wore a cop uniform. Seeing him clearly by the light of an overhead streetlamp, I realized this early Type Three was big, solid—and familiar.

He was the Corpse I'd zapped back in the prison entrance.

"Undertaker," he snarled.

"Dead guy," I replied.

I went for my pocketknife, but he was faster. Corpses are often a lot faster than they look. His first swipe knocked the golden gadget from my hand, sending it flying across Wallace Street. His second swipe sent *me* flying. I slammed into the side of a mailbox, the impact knocking the wind out of me. Worse, I actually heard the crunch of plastic as my water pistol shattered. I'd shoved it into the rear waistband of my pants, and now it was leaking cold saltwater into my underwear.

This Deader had just disarmed me in the space of maybe two seconds. And he knew it.

He grinned. I always hated it when they grinned.

"My. Turn. Boy."

Behind him, the bar door suddenly opened and a man—a nice, human-looking man—staggered out. He looked blearily at the Corpse. "'Scuse me, Ocifer," he said in a slurred voice. Then he noticed me in a heap on the sidewalk with my back against a mailbox. He blinked. "There some poblem here?"

The Deader glared at him, and for one horrible moment, I thought he might go for the guy's throat. But Corpses are smarter than that, and their Masks are important to them, usually more important than the condition and safety of whatever body they're wearing.

"No problem, sir," he said in English. "Just caught a vandal."

Ever get the wind knocked out of you? It isn't painful so much as scary. Apparently, your diaphragm—that's the big muscle in your chest that helps your lungs expand and contract—gets hit and kind of seizes up, making it very, very hard to breathe. You can't talk. You can't get air.

Scary.

Well, that was happening to me, and while I knew from bitter experience that it wouldn't last, I simply didn't have time for it. I needed to shout something right now, or this drunken dude was going to wander off, and then Dead Cop would kill me.

With my chest heaving, I slammed my elbow into the side

of the mailbox. It made a loud, low, metallic thump like a drum beat.

The Corpse's glare turned my way. The other guy looked skyward, as if he'd heard thunder.

I did it again.

This time, the bar dude looked at *me*.

"What's ee doin'?" the man slurred.

"Ignore him," Dead Cop said. "Just go about your business, sir. I have this covered."

I did it a third time.

"He's gonna wake the neighbers," the drunken guy observed.

"I'll stop him," the Deader said. Then he took a step toward me, his decaying feet making squishy noises inside his Philly police-issue shoes. I wasn't sure exactly what "stop him" meant, but I figured it couldn't be good.

Fortunately, I'd just caught my breath.

"Help!" I screamed. "This guy isn't a cop! He's crazy, and he wants to kill me!"

The Corpse hesitated. Then he made a bad mistake. He turned and glanced back at the drunken bystander in a way that even from my vantage point looked really guilty.

The guy in the bar doorway narrowed his eyes.

"'Ang on a second..." he said. "Lezzee some ID... 'officer'..."

"Of course, sir," the Corpse said. And why wouldn't he? After all, he *had* ID. He *was* a cop!

But his back was to me, his attention fixed entirely on the suspicious bar dude, and that was all I'd wanted.

In one reasonably smooth motion, I found my feet, stepped up, and punched Dead Cop in the back of his neck right at the base of the skull. Corpses have a vulnerable spot there, the place where the spinal cord meets the base of the brain, and a good shot paralyzes them. It doesn't last long.

But it lasts long enough.

Dead Cop went stiff—no pun intended. Then he fell forward, right into the drunken dude, and they both went down in a heap against the door of the bar. Though he couldn't see it or smell it, the poor human guy got himself lathered up pretty good in cadaver juice. I wondered if, tomorrow morning, his wife would notice that he smelled like roadkill.

Time to disappear. The drunken guy was struggling under the weight of the fallen cop and at the same time staring at me in bleary confusion. Wherever I ran now, he'd report to the cop. Worse, the Corpse atop him was already twitching. This Deader was a strong one and would be back on his feet in a minute, maybe less.

Fortunately, while I'd been flopping around on the sidewalk beside the mailbox, trying to catch my breath, I'd also picked out my hiding place. Well, the building anyhow.

Empty buildings come in two flavors in Philly: boarded up and not boarded up. How many of each you find depends on the neighborhood. This particular street was mostly row homes and small corner shops. While I had been fighting to breathe, I'd managed to spot one house in particular that looked like nobody lived there.

How could I tell? It wasn't a lack of lights on in the house; it was after midnight after all, and the whole neighborhood was dark. But something else was missing from its windows.

Curtains.

In Center City, Philadelphia, everybody lived on top of everybody else. Privacy was hard to come by. So curtains and blinds were usually kept closed, especially after dark.

And a house that didn't even have curtains pretty much *had* to be empty. Or so I hoped.

I leaned over the Deader and yanked the baton from his belt. Like his shoes, it was a Philly police-issue weapon. Wood on the outside and lead on the inside. He had a gun too, but those were pretty useless against Corpses. This, however, might do some damage—if it came to that.

Then I made for my target building, crossing Wallace Street at a run.

"Hey!" the drunken man slurred after me. "Come back eere!"

Right, I thought. I wondered if, in all the history of the world, any fugitive had ever obeyed that command.

I wanted to look for my pocketknife, but I hadn't seen where the Corpse's blow had sent it. It might have been under a car, buried in a clump of sparse shrubbery, or down the sewer for all I knew. But I just couldn't risk the time. Instead I made right for the first-floor window and smashed it with the baton, keeping my face averted. Then, mindful of the jagged glass in the frame, I climbed inside.

The living room was dark and empty. No furniture. No carpets. It smelled of mold and rat poop. Yep, definitely empty.

It looked like a pretty standard Philly layout. Living room leading to dining room leading to kitchen, with a staircase on the left. Upstairs, there were likely three bedrooms: a front, middle, and back. It would be the back bedroom I wanted.

I headed that way, taking the stairs two at a time and almost kicking the door in. The bedroom, like the rest of the place, was empty and deserted. Two dark, rectangular windows filled the rear wall. Beyond them would be a twelve-foot drop into an alley or, if I was lucky, a fire escape.

I was lucky.

From downstairs came a heavy crash. Evidently, the Corpse had recovered. He'd be searching the house for me, not skipping a room. Time to be a little quieter.

On tiptoe, I crossed the bedroom's hard wooden floor to the windows and pulled one of them open. It was old and creaky, but at least it wasn't painted shut. Then, glancing back toward the hallway door, I listened furiously.

Nothing. No footfalls. He was being quiet down there, probably hoping to surprise me.

Swallowing, I climbed out onto the fire escape. A quick look up showed that there was no roof access. A quick look down revealed the expected alley. A retractable ladder hung at the far end of the iron scaffold. Before I went to it, however, I took a moment to peer—one last time—back into the darkened house.

Dead Cop was there.

I mean *right there*—grinning at me.

"Hello. Boy."

CHAPTER 5

GOOD WILL HUNTED

C orpses were like that, lumbering one minute and cat quick the next. How this wormbag had come up the stairs and into the bedroom so fast and quiet was a puzzle I had no time to solve. Before I could react, before the chill that ran down my spine even had time to freeze my backside solid, he bent at the waist and lunged his upper body through the open window, his big purple-gray hands like claws.

I think maybe I screamed. To this day, I'm not sure.

I recoiled, catching myself just before I upended over the fire escape railing and went tumbling down to the alley floor the hard way. The Deader was all over me in a heartbeat, his fingers smearing stinking fluid all over the front of my coat as they scrambled their way up toward my neck.

Undertaker training kicked in. Rather than retreating, I leaned forward over his shoulders and slammed the window closed, pinning him at the waist. He felt nothing, of course, but the pressure held him in place, and the angle kept his rotting paws away from my throat. Better still, the move earned me a few spare seconds—long enough to raise the baton.

I brought it down with all my strength, slamming it across the side of the Corpse's head. He grunted. Then he bared his blackened teeth and surged forward again. I hit him a second time. Then a third. And all the while, I was making noises—either warrior cries or terrified sobs—again, I'm not sure. My mind felt fogged over by fear, desperation, and more than a little rage.

I *hated* these things.

With the fourth hit, I thought I heard something—like a dull crack. Had I broken the Corpse's neck? If so, he'd go limp immediately.

He did, his heavy arms flopping to the latticed floor of the fire escape. His kicking feet, still inside the bedroom, dropped like twin bags of sand.

Panting and sweating despite the winter's cold, I stepped back. My eyes felt as wide as dinner plates as I stared at him, still clutching the baton, ready to use it again if I had to.

I spared a moment to cross my eyes and take a quick peek at Dead Cop's Mask. It was a Seer's trick, something that most Undertakers picked up pretty fast. If you held your eyes a certain way, you could sort of see a Corpse the way the rest of the world—the adult world—saw him.

Not surprisingly, this Deader's illusion was of a pretty

big guy, with dark skin and dark hair. He hung motionless, pinned by the window sash, his Mask hovering almost ghost-like over his true worm-food body. I switched off this trick of vision almost at once, partly because it tended to give me a headache and partly because doing it was a little depressing. It seemed to drive home—at least for me—just how alone the Undertakers were in this war.

This dude wasn't dead, of course. You couldn't kill a Corpse with a gun or a knife, much less a lead baton. Stakes through the heart were useless. So were silver bullets, sunlight, garlic cloves, and wishes.

But you *could* damage their stolen bodies badly enough that they became useless to the entity inhabiting them. With his spine crushed, this Corpse was down for the count. He wouldn't be able to move until another body became available to him. And *that* wouldn't happen until his undead buddies found him and were able to discreetly move him to a more secure location.

Thing was, Corpses had this weird link that let their friends know when one of them was in this kind of trouble.

Which meant there'd be more on the way.

Time to go.

I staggered over to the retractable ladder and wasted half a minute trying to figure out the release mechanism in the dark. Finally, with the jerk of a lever, the metal ladder crashed downward, stopping three feet from the alley floor. The noise of it made me jump—nerves.

I descended as fast as I could and dropped onto the concrete. The alley was a blind one, and on three sides of me, the darkened backs of row homes rose like canyon walls. The fourth side was the only obvious exit, and it opened onto a lit city street.

I blew out a sigh. It steadied my pounding heart—a little. Then I raised my wrist and said into my radio, "Haven? This is Angel Four."

Nothing.

I peered at the watch, but it was too dark to see if its LCD screen was working. Chances were I'd busted it either climbing into or out of the empty house. Stupid things were always breaking.

With another sigh, I turned toward the mouth of the alley—

Just as a figure leaped down from the fire escape to block my path.

"Hello. Boy."

My heart nearly exploded in my chest—I swear.

The Corpse towered over me like a pillar made of rotting flesh, once again wearing his black-gummed grin. His head was bent at a slightly odd angle. But as I watched, horrified, he reached up with one hand and shoved it roughly back into alignment. There was a sound like chalk breaking. His grin widened.

"Fooled you," he sneered in English.

And he had. He'd known I'd effectively trapped him in

the window, so he'd faked going limp. And I'd been just scared enough and desperate enough to buy it.

And now I was going to die for it.

Standing there, rooted by fear and exhaustion—frozen in place despite all my training—I whispered a silent good-bye to the mom I hadn't seen in four months.

Happy birthday, I thought.

Then the Corpse's left arm came off.

One minute, it was there, attached to his beefy shoulder, and the next, it was on the ground at his feet, a useless lump of dead flesh. Together, we both looked down at it. Then we both looked up at each other, and I could see he was every bit as perplexed as I felt.

"Hey, big dude!" a voice called. "You dropped somethin'!"

Dead Cop whirled around.

Sharyn Jefferson, boss of the Angels, stood right behind him.

In her hands, poised to strike, was Vader, her Japanese wakizashi sword. "Hi, Red!" she said to me, once again using the nickname I was sure all redheaded people despised. Her lips wore a wry smile, but her dark eyes were as hard as granite.

The Corpse growled—actually *growled*—and then it went for her, reaching out with his remaining hand.

Big mistake.

Sharyn was a tall girl, dark-skinned and athletic, with kinky black hair done up in dreadlocks. At seventeen years old, she and her brother, Tom, ran the Undertakers—and had ever since my dad had been killed by the Corpses.

She was also the best fighter I'd ever seen. Well, maybe the *second* best.

Moving with catlike grace, she sidestepped the attacking Deader. Her sword slashed in a silver blur. And this time, it was his right arm that hit the concrete.

The Corpse swayed on his feet, his milky eyes literally radiating hatred. In English, he hissed, "Stupid girl! You can't kill me!"

Sharyn smoothly sheathed her sword, and from inside her coat, she produced a mean-looking hypodermic. The needle had to be ten inches long, and its syringe was filled with clear liquid. Grinning, she held it up. The Corpse's eyes followed it.

"Wanna bet?" Sharyn chirped. Then, in one fluid motion, she turned on her heel and backhanded the needle into the Deader's chest, slamming the plunger home. "Watch this, Will!"

Dead Cop peered down at the big hypodermic sticking out a few inches below his collarbone. For a moment, the menace left his expression, and he looked as befuddled as a dead and desiccated face was capable of looking.

Then he exploded.

Once second, the mutilated, walking cadaver stood rooted on the alley floor, and the next, pieces of him went whizzing off in every direction. There was very little blood; the cadaver had probably been embalmed weeks ago. But the parts themselves were plenty gross, and I ducked and threw up my hands to keep from getting smacked by chunks of flying dead guy.

In Dead Cop's place—for only a second or two—stood a human-sized figure of dark energy that glared savagely at Sharyn. I could almost feel the evil radiating off the alien thing as, without a host body to sustain it, it shriveled up and vanished with an odd little pop.

"Ta-da!" Sharyn declared.

Then she bowed. There was Corpse stuff all over her.

"What *was* that?" I asked.

"Later," she replied. "For now, let's split. There might be more of 'em on the way." She started to turn, but I put my hand on her elbow.

"Is Helene okay?" I asked.

Her smile widened, as if I'd just passed some kind of test. "Yeah, she's cool. Lost the Deader cop about eight blocks from here. Would have come back looking for you, but I called her off. I was closer."

I might have asked how she had found me, but I already knew. My wrist radio had a built-in GPS chip that apparently still worked despite the rest of the gadget being toast. Thank God for Steve Moscova, who made each one of them by hand.

"Sharyn…" I stammered awkwardly. "I know we broke the rules and regs. But don't blame Helene. It was my idea."

"That right? 'Cause when I radioed Helene a few minutes ago, she told me it was *her* idea. Funny thing, huh?"

"She's just trying to cover for me!" I protested.

"'Course she is, little bro. By the way, here's a little something of yours I found on the street." She pulled my pocketknife out of her coat and handed it to me. "Figure you dropped it while you was playing around with Big, Dead, and Ugly."

"Thanks," I said with relief, welcoming the familiar weight of the gadget in my hand.

"No sweat. Now...you got something for me?"

"Huh?"

She chuckled. "The mystery wallet, little bro...the thing that might just make this stunt of yours worth it. You got it?"

For a mouthful of bitter seconds, I was afraid that I *didn't*, that it had been lost somehow during the fight with the Deader! But then my shaking hands found it right where I'd put it—in the inside pocket of my coat.

I handed it to her, and she opened it, holding it up to the meager light from the street.

After a moment, her face split into a wide grin. "Oh yeah, dude. Totally worth it!"

CHAPTER 6

TOTALLY WORTH IT

C ome on," I begged. "What was that trick with the needle?"

Sharyn only grinned, steering the bike we both rode right off Sixteenth Street and down the ramp of an underground public parking garage beside Love Park, leaving behind the night, the open air, and—overhead—Philly's massive city hall, which loomed like a dark fortress.

The largest municipal building in America, Philadelphia City Hall occupies four full acres of land in what the town's founder, William Penn, named Centre Square. It's a huge, seven-story structure more than a century old, topped by a five-hundred-foot tower featuring a thirty-seven-foot likeness of Penn himself—the biggest statue on any building in the world.

All this appeared in the tour books. What didn't, however, was the Philly that hid below the streets. Down there, tunnels connected subways to shops and food courts. Some of these tunnels were generations old, and together, they made a labyrinth that few people knew of and even fewer knew well.

This was *our* city.

At the lowest level of the parking garage, tucked away in a shadowed alcove, stood a heavy steel access door. This opened into a long, unlit passage that smelled of dust and urine. The passage ended at another door, which Sharyn opened with a key. Beyond that lay a flight of stairs and a hanging plastic curtain carefully painted to resemble a brick wall—an effective illusion that she brushed aside with a wave of her hand.

Haven occupied a subbasement sixty feet below City Hall. Before Tom Jefferson, Sharyn's twin brother and the chief of the Undertakers, had discovered it a few months ago, it had been long-abandoned and forgotten.

Except by the cats.

Yeah, I said cats—that had been introduced down here decades ago to deal with the rat problem. Now, after countless generations of living their whole lives in darkness, these "kitties" had left cute and fuzzy behind in favor of ugly, scary, and mean.

Since moving in, we'd run into our share of what Helene sometimes called "devil cats." Eventually the Monkeys—the Undertakers crew responsible for building and equipment maintenance—had whipped up some traps. They snagged about three cats a week and then relocated them to a part of the basement we weren't planning on using. It was a tricky job and even a bit dangerous—but I suppose it beat wrestling with Deaders in alleys in the middle of the night.

After we walked our Stingray through the "brick wall," Sharyn and I were immediately greeted by Helene. She took one look at us—at me—and the relief on her face made me just a little bit uncomfortable. Beside her, a hulk of a boy with short-cropped blond hair and a neck as thick as a watermelon occupied the only chair. He was on guard duty.

This small, dimly lit room marked the gateway into Haven. There were three such gateways.

"Will!" Dave said, jumping to his feet. "Heard you guys had some trouble."

"Hi, Dave," I replied.

"Nothing we couldn't handle, Hot Dog," Sharyn said, breezing past him. "Will, get that bike put away, and let's talk to my bro. He's in the caf. You got five minutes."

And just like that, she exited into the hallway, leaving behind only the three of us.

"I hate it when she calls me that," Dave Burger grumbled.

"Which is probably why she does it, Burgermeister," Helene replied, smiling.

Dave immediately cheered up. "Burgermeister" was a nickname he *did* like. "Ran into a Deader, huh?" he asked.

I nodded. "Type Three. A big one. Dressed like a cop."

His eyes lit up. "Yeah? What happened?"

"What usually happens," I replied, feeling tired

and—yeah—a little grumpy. "Sharyn showed up in the nick of time. Only this time, she actually killed one."

"Killed a Corpse?" the Burgermeister blinked. "You mean 'killed him' killed him? Like Booth?"

I nodded.

Helene and Dave swapped identical looks of astonishment. "How?" they demanded in perfect unison.

"Sharyn wouldn't tell me. She stuck him with some kind of needle."

"Yeah?" Helene said, smiling. "Some new weapon maybe?"

"Maybe, but to use it, you gotta get real close!"

Dave's big, round face darkened. "Wish I could've been out there with you."

I punched his big shoulder, a gesture I knew he appreciated. Dave had been wanting to get into the Angels crew since we'd both been recruits.

Notice I said "recruits," not "volunteers." Nobody "volunteers" to live in a dank, cold, subterranean dungeon, fighting for their lives against an ever-growing invasion of the reanimated dead. No, every kid in Haven was here because he or she had to be, not because they wanted to be. Each was a Seer who'd been lucky enough to escape the Corpses and get found instead by the Undertakers.

If we went back to our homes, the Corpses would find us and kill us for what we could see—and probably kill our families too.

We stayed and fought because, really, what else could we do?

"I wish you could too," Helene told Dave. "But keep up your training. Sharyn'll hold another tryout in a couple of months."

"I'm too big," he said, still looking sour. "And too slow."

"Big's not a bad thing," I replied. "And some more training will help speed you up."

He looked pointedly at me. "Not *that* kind of slow."

"Oh."

Helene gave me a glare. "I'm sure it's nothing like that," she said to Dave. Then, glancing at her watch, she added, "Come on. Let's get to the cafeteria. Time's up."

The Burgermeister brightened again, his blues apparently forgotten. He was like that. "Yeah! Come on, Will! Tom wants to see you!" He took my arm in one of his beefy paws and pulled me toward the open doorway.

"Hold up, Dave! Aren't you on gatekeeper duty?" I protested.

"The gate can keep itself for a couple of minutes," he said.

"But the bike…"

"Leave it!" Helene exclaimed. Then she was behind me, pushing. Together, they half-carried me around a corner and along one of the main corridors.

These two seemed awfully determined to get me into the cafeteria in a big hurry.

What in the world was going—

Oh no.

"Surprise!"

The single word was shouted by almost a hundred voices. Though it was the middle of the night, pretty much every on-site Undertaker was in the cafeteria, a lot of them wearing stupid pointed party hats. Balloons had been tied to the ends of the long tables, and a big banner covered the back wall, blocking most of the dirty bricks.

HAPPY THIRTEENTH BIRTHDAY, WILL!

"Oh crap," I muttered.

Helene and Dave started laughing. Someone took my picture, the flash blinding me. Then Sharyn stepped up and pulled me into one of her long, uncomfortable hugs. I squirmed. She didn't care. Finally, she released me and stepped back, holding me at arm's length. "Happy birthday, little bro," she exclaimed. "Come on! We got cake!"

They dragged me over to the nearest table, where a big white sheet cake waited. Looming protectively over it stood a tall, slim kid wrapped in a soiled apron. This was Nick Rooney, boss of the Moms, the crew responsible for the cooking, the cleaning, and—well—picking up after everybody else.

"Hasn't been easy," Nick told me, grinning, "to keep everyone away from this cake until you finally showed up! Gather 'round, everybody. We got some singing to do!"

They gathered—the Undertakers—and as they did, I couldn't help but notice their faces. Some, like Sharyn,

Dave, and Helene, wore smiles. But others had more vacant expressions, and I could tell they were feeling what I was feeling. Celebrations didn't belong in Haven. There wasn't anything about our life here that warranted celebrating.

We just wanted to go home.

Helene was good at hiding it, but I knew she felt the same way. And the Burgermeister too, who talked about his grandmother—his only family—more and more these days. Tom and Sharyn had been orphaned young, so *maybe* they had an easier time accepting the situation. But for those of us who'd abandoned our families to live in this dank basement and fight our lonely war, the last thing we felt like doing was singing "Happy Birthday" to anyone.

"Please don't…" I muttered.

They did.

The Undertakers were a resistance group, fighting the Corpses any and every way they could. As an organization, they were smart, resourceful, and brave.

But they couldn't sing.

"Happy birthday to you" seemed to take a really long time, and when it was over, Sharyn yelled for me to make a wish.

So I wished.

I wished the same wish I wished every night when I closed my eyes—the same thing that I knew every kid in the room wished.

I wished to go home.

For four months, I'd been living as a runaway. Thanksgiving had come and gone. Christmas had come and gone. New Year's had come and gone. Heck, I'd even missed Groundhog Day. Somewhere out there, my mother and my sister carried on without me. Not a day went by when I didn't think about them. It was like a black hole in my gut, a big emptiness from which nothing could escape—certainly not joy and especially not on special occasions.

Like my birthday.

Then I halfheartedly blew out the thirteen candles.

Everyone clapped. Some of them even looked like they meant it.

It should have been a good moment. It wasn't.

It sucked.

"That's enough," a voice said. "Give the man some air."

A tall figure—taller even than Nick—pushed his way through the crowd and came to stand beside Sharyn. Side by side, it was easy to see the resemblance between the two of them: the same coffee-colored skin, the same intelligent dark eyes. But where Sharyn Jefferson gave off this air of reckless adventure, of finding fun in any situation, no matter how scary—her brother gave off something else altogether.

Tom Jefferson, the Chief of the Undertakers.

"Happy birthday, bro," he said to me, smiling knowingly. And in that smile, I saw—with relief—he knew what I was feeling. Tom "got it." He usually did.

"Thanks," I replied.

"Nick," he said. "Why don't you start doling out the cake and ice cream? Will, Helene, and me got something to talk about."

"Ease up, bro," Sharyn protested. "It can wait until after the party."

"No, it can't," Tom and I replied at the same time, which Sharyn seemed to find hilarious.

"Two of a kind!" she laughed. "Okay, we all can party without you for a bit!"

Tom nodded to Helene, and then he led the two of us out of the noisy cafeteria and down to his office. It was near the west entrance, the one we'd come in only minutes ago. Bigger than most of Haven's chambers, it served as Tom's sleeping quarters and command center.

There were no doors in Haven, mainly because when we'd found this place, all the doors had either been long since removed or had rotted into nothing. Instead, we used curtains or heavy blankets draped across the thresholds for privacy. Tom held his open for us, and Helene and I ducked under his big arm and stepped inside.

Tom kept the place pretty sparse—just a desk and a few folding chairs set up around a small conference table. On one wall was a bulletin board that someone had scrounged up. It was layered with printouts and newspaper clippings about the Corpses and their goings-on around town. On the opposite wall hung another curtain, this one leading to the adjacent room, where Tom did his sleeping and dressing.

"Spill," he said, facing us. "I want to know everything that happened, moment by moment, from the start of your recon to the minute you got back."

It was a familiar drill.

Helene, as senior trainee, spoke first. She told him about us spotting the four Corpses in the cop car and following them to Eastern State Penitentiary. She described watching the Corpses carry their human captive through the prison gate and about the "something" that was dropped.

Then she looked at me.

With a sigh, I explained my decision to retrieve the mysterious something and about how I got spotted and almost caught. Then I related our escape, the decision to split up, and my one-on-one battle with the big Deader. Like Helene, I left nothing out. There's been a time, not too long ago, when I might not have told Tom everything.

Those days were over.

"I know we broke the rules and regs…" Helene began.

"*I* broke them," I said. "Helene tried to talk me out of it."

Tom nodded, considering. Then he said, "Look, you two. I ain't saying it wasn't an acceptable risk—" Helene flashed me a smile. Then Tom continued. "—for *experienced* Angels." Her smile disappeared. "But for a couple of trainees, it just wasn't a smart move. Gettin' that wallet wasn't worth your life, Will, or yours, Helene, and that was almost the price tag. So here's how it is: You two are still on the

Angels crew, but neither of you will be going out alone. For the rest of your training, you'll each do your recon gigs partnered with an experienced Angel."

"But don't you need the others for combat and rescue missions?" I protested. "Isn't that the reg? Angels for rescue, trainees for recon?"

"Regs sometimes need to change," Tom replied evenly. "If this is what keeps you both from taking risks you ain't ready for, then this is how it'll be."

I started to argue further, but Helene elbowed me in the ribs.

I shut up.

"All that said and done," Tom added, "my sister gave me the wallet just now. Do either of you know what it is?"

We both shook our heads. "Sharyn took it from me back in the alley," I said. "She looked at it and told me what I'd done had been 'totally worth it.'" I paused a moment to give Tom a pointed look that he firmly ignored. "But she wouldn't show me what it was."

"Yeah, well, that I can fix." He reached into the back pocket of his jeans and pulled out the narrow square of leather. "'Cept it ain't a wallet."

And it wasn't.

My father used to call them "badge folds." One half might hold a silver badge, and the other displayed an official-looking identification card. When he'd made detective, he had gotten one just like it.

Except *this* ID card didn't come from the Philadelphia Police Department.

Instead, it read:

SPECIAL AGENT HUGO RAMIREZ
FEDERAL BUREAU OF INVESTIGATION

"Sorry, bro," Tom said to me. "But I think the party's over. We've got work to do."

CHAPTER 7

MESSAGE IN A BOTTLE

The doorbell rang at 8:30 in the morning on Will's thirteenth birthday.

Susan Ritter, Will's mother, had been hurriedly dressing for work. It was Friday, so her daughter, Emily, the only remaining member of Susan's once whole and happy family, would soon be heading to school. Because kindergarten is only half a day, around one o'clock, she'd have to take the bus to her aunt's house. There, Susan's sister, Angela, would watch the little girl while her mother finished her nursing shift at Philadelphia's Jefferson Hospital.

It was an arrangement Emily didn't like. Angela, though a sweetheart, was single, childless, and not very good with kids. Unfortunately, without Will around, Susan had no choice. She had a dead husband and a missing son, but the bills still needed to be paid.

At the sound of the doorbell, she uttered a low curse and

marched downstairs with her hairbrush still in hand. Emily, she noticed, hadn't even looked up from her breakfast. The five-year-old had become increasingly detached these last few months—from her mother, from her kindergarten, from the world as a whole.

It was her way of coping with all the loss she'd suffered in her young life.

Susan worried about her.

In fact, "worry" was just about the only feeling Susan had left.

She opened the door.

A grim-faced man regarded her from the stoop. He was dressed in a tailored suit and wool overcoat. "Ms. Susan Ritter?"

"Yes?"

"Ms. Ritter. My name is Edward Scanlon. I'm an attorney at law. Is your son, William Karl Ritter, at home?"

Susan blinked. "Will? Why?"

"It's a bit difficult to explain, Ms. Ritter. May I come in?"

"Let's see some ID," Susan said.

The man produced a business card bearing his name and declaring his partnership in a Center City law firm she'd never heard of. Susan frowned. "Let me see your driver's license."

"Excuse me?"

"I'm a policeman's wife, Mr. Scanlon. Anyone can print up a business card. Let me see your license."

He looked a little put out, but he reached into the back pocket of his trousers for a wallet and then fished out a Pennsylvania driver's license complete with picture. Susan examined it. "Okay," she said finally. "Come in. But I only have a few minutes. I need to get my daughter to school and me to work."

"I understand," Scanlon replied, stepping inside the Ritters' small row home in the Manayunk section of the city. "My condolences on your loss, by the way."

Susan glared at the man, thinking he was referring to Will—who was definitely *not* dead and thus didn't need "condolences." After a moment, however, the lawyer cleared his throat and added, "For your husband, Detective Ritter. A good man."

"Yes, he was," Susan replied, softening. "It's been more than two years now."

"I'm sorry."

"Thank you. Did you know my husband?"

The man nodded. "Briefly. A few months before he was…before he died, he hired my firm to keep something for him. A package."

"What kind of package?" Susan asked.

"We've never opened it. Your husband was very explicit about that. The package was to be locked away somewhere secure and then delivered to this address on the occasion of his son's…*your* son's…thirteenth birthday. Which is today, I believe?"

Susan nodded, trying to make sense of this. "My husband gave you something to give to me when Will turned thirteen?"

"No, Ms. Ritter. Not you. The package is addressed to William. Is he here?"

"No, he isn't," she replied. Then after a long pause, she sighed and added, "My son disappeared four months ago. The police have classified him as a runaway."

Scanlon processed this. "I see. And the authorities have been unable to find him?"

Susan thought this a strange question. After all, if they *had* found Will, he'd *be* here, wouldn't he? But people, she knew, leaned toward awkward, even stupid comments when confronted with someone else's tragedy. As she'd learned after first Karl's death and now Will's disappearance, it was a quirk of human nature to trip over your tongue when offering comfort to someone who can't really *be* comforted.

It was tiring sometimes—but Susan could forgive it.

She shook her head. "No, they haven't found him."

The lawyer shuffled his feet uncomfortably. "I see. I'm sorry to hear that. Well, then, as you are William's parent and legal guardian, I'm within my rights to deliver the package to you."

Scanlon reached into his briefcase and withdrew a small brown envelope. It was square, about eight inches to a side, and there were words on the face of it, written using a heavy felt-tip pen. They had clearly been written by Karl's hand; Susan would have recognized his handwriting anywhere.

To My Son, Will:
  Happy Birthday
  Dad

Susan turned it over in hands that had suddenly started to tremble.

What is this?

"Sign here, please?"

She looked up. "What?"

Scanlon was holding a sheet of paper. "I need you to sign this form confirming receipt."

"Oh." She took the paper and signed with his proffered pen. Then she accepted the envelope. It was very light. "And you say you don't know what's in it?"

"No, Ms. Ritter. My firm's duties on your late husband's behalf are now concluded. On a personal note, may I say that I liked Detective Ritter, and I'm sure he had his reasons for wrapping this business in such mystery."

"Yes. Thank you." Susan showed the man to the door and watched him walk purposefully down the stoop toward the street. At the last moment, however, he looked back. "Ms. Ritter?"

"Yes?"

"I hope you find your son."

She managed the very barest of smiles. "Thanks." Then she shut the door.

"Who was that, Mommy?" Emily asked from the living room.

"Nobody, sweetheart. Are you ready to for school?"

"Do I have to go to Aunt Angie's after?"

"You know Mommy has to work, Em."

"I know." Then after a pause, "Mommy?"

"What, sweetie?"

"Is everything ever going to go back to the way it was?"

Susan stood motionless at her front door. "I don't know, Em," she said. Then she held up the package, looking again at her husband's handwriting.

Karl... I miss you.

"Em...I'm going to go upstairs and finish getting ready. You eat your cereal, and we'll leave in a few minutes, okay?"

"Okay, Mommy."

Susan went to her room, closed the door, and used nail scissors to tear open the package. Turning it over, she let out a little gasp when an unmarked DVD dropped onto her bed. For several seconds, she stared at it. Then, moving as if in a fog, she picked it up and inserted it into the player mounted atop her small television. It was the first time that either the TV or DVD player had been used in longer than she could remember.

At first, there was just static—and then Karl's face filled the screen.

Susan felt her throat close up.

Her first thought, crazy as it might be, was: *My God! He looks so much like Will!*

The resemblance had always been there: the same red hair,

the same freckles. But in the two years since Karl's death, Will had grown taller, his face thinner. Even the pictures of Karl that she had around the house didn't quite capture—

"Hello, Will."

Susan put a hand to her mouth.

"I've arranged for this DVD to reach you when you turn thirteen. That fact that you're getting it means that something has happened to me. I'm sorry for that—more sorry than I can ever say.

"Will, by now, I'm guessing you've started…seeing things. I don't know who it will be. A neighbor. A teacher. Maybe you're a late bloomer and don't even know what I'm talking about, but something tells me that isn't the case. You're my son, and I'm the only adult who's ever had the Sight. That's what we call it. Capital 'S.'"

Susan wiped the tears from her eyes and stared at her husband's face. He looked earnest, even a little desperate, leaning in close to the camera. He was sitting—*my God*—he was sitting right where she was now on this very bed. The camcorder had probably been set up on the dresser.

What had she been doing when he'd filmed this?

And what in God's name was he talking about?

"Son, if none of this has happened yet…it will. Just put this DVD away, hide it from everyone, even your mom. Then you can pull it out again when you need it. But if it *has* happened and if you're Seeing them, then you're probably scared to death. I don't blame you. I was scared too the first time. Then, later, when I found out more about what they were and what they wanted and how the ability to See them was given to only a few seemingly random kids…well, that scared me even more.

"And I knew I had to make this recording.

"Son, you're not crazy, and you're not alone. The important thing now is not to tell your mom or anyone else what you've Seen. She won't believe you. I'm sorry to say it, kiddo, but it's true. She'll love you and try to get you help, but that will only alert them, and then they'll find you and your mom and your sister, and they'll…"

Karl visibly swallowed, and for the first time, Susan read the fear in her dead husband's eyes.

"We're at war, Will. Most of the world doesn't know it, but we are. I have no idea where they come from or how they do…what they do. But I know what they want. First the city. Then the state. Then the country. And then the world. They're careful, and they're taking their time, but in the end, they'll be the death of us all.

"You need to go into Center City. I wish I could tell you exactly where, but I can't risk this DVD getting into the wrong hands. You'll have to ask around. But don't go to the police. Don't go to any city officials. Ask if anyone's heard of the Undertakers. Remember that name: the Undertakers. Ask every kid you see…on the street, in the stores. Don't worry if you don't find them right away. Believe me, son, they'll find you. And they'll help you.

"Making this recording is like putting a message in a bottle. I have no idea if it'll end up in the right hands. If it does, then remember that I love you.

"I guess I don't have much else I can say. I'm beginning to think this whole idea was a long shot at best. But I'll go through with it. It's the only way I'll be able to sleep at night, the only way I'll be able to face Sue, knowing what I know and knowing I can't tell her.

"Will…good luck. I love you."

The DVD ended.

Susan sat on her bed, her hands clasped so tightly that her knuckles went white. Tears rolled down her cheeks.

A war? Invaders bent on world conquest? My God…was Karl unbalanced? Maybe even insane?

Susan went to her bedside table and pulled out the familiar white envelope. Though she'd read it a thousand times, all but memorized it, she read it once again—and once again struggled to make sense of what it said.

Will was alive and had "friends." There were "scary things" happening, and he had to "fight" them.

The letter had arrived, without a return address or even a postmark, a few weeks after Will's disappearance. Susan had shown it to no one, afraid that her sister or the police would dismiss it as a heartless prank, thereby bursting the bubble of hope she managed to build around it. But now, she had the DVD too. And Karl's words, while vague and deeply unsettling, seemed to support the letter's contents.

But what did any of it mean? What were these "things" that Will might or might not have started seeing? Teachers? Neighbors? It sounded like a crazy conspiracy theory. Had Karl been *telling* their son to run away from home?

It was unthinkable!

The Undertakers.

She'd heard of them—a gang that had been somehow associated with the death of television anchorman Kenny Booth last year. Booth himself had mentioned the name just before he'd died on camera. The papers had run with the story for a while—and why not? Nobody could even explain exactly what had happened to the telejournalist and mayoral candidate. He'd just *exploded* on live TV.

But in the end, the whole thing had sort of faded away. Nobody knew who the Undertakers were or if they even existed.

All that had happened about a month after Will had gone missing.

Scary things. Invaders.

Friends. Undertakers.

My God...

For months now, years if you counted from Karl's death, Susan had been fighting to stay afloat amid a flood of disasters and heartbreak. Well, her husband was forever gone, but Will was still out there. Maybe it was time to stop wallowing and feeling sorry for herself.

Maybe it was time to take some action.

Maybe, she thought, *it's time to find my son.*

CHAPTER 8

BATTLE PLANS

astern State Penitentiary," Tom explained, "has been closed to the public for three months. This came down from the Community Affairs Office 'round the same time *she* showed up. Now…since Sharyn and me know some of you ain't as up to speed on her as the rest, I'm gonna take a minute to review."

The entire Angels complement had gathered in the rec room, occupying a loose assortment of folding chairs that were the furniture of choice in Haven. One of the Hackers, the Undertakers' answer to the Geek Squad, had hooked a laptop computer to an old twenty-five-inch TV. The girl was now displaying a slide show of sorts that her crew had hastily put together at Tom's request.

The screen showed the prison frontage, with the big gate where Helene and I had gone Deader-fighting clearly visible. As we watched, this image changed to that of a woman's face, a Dead woman's face. A Type One—very fresh. The hair was mostly still there, though the skin had gone purple with clotted blood and her lips had begun to thin and pull back from her teeth. She didn't even look embalmed, a process the Corpses often used to help their stolen bodies last a bit longer.

"Lilith Cavanaugh," Tom said. "Philly's new director of community affairs. If you read her creds, she sounds pretty cool: got most of her schooling in Europe; spent the last five years doing public relations for Euro Disney. She even speaks with an English accent. To be honest, it's the best job the Corpses have ever done at setting up a backstory for one of their own. She showed up a little over a month after Kenny Booth died on live TV—"

A few feet away, Sharyn chimed, "Pop goes the weasel."

Everybody laughed. Yeah, it's a pretty stupid joke. But if you'd known the guy, you'd have appreciated the humor.

Tom pressed on. "Cavanaugh has wasted no time taking over where Booth left off. She's already got the police and most major city departments in her back pocket. Officially, she answers only to the mayor's office. Unofficially, I figure she's got the new mayor either completely charmed or completely scared. Either way, he and the city council let her do pretty much whatever she wants.

"More'n once, we've heard Cavanaugh referred to by Deaders as 'Majesty' or 'the Queen.' As we figure it, Booth's failure has convinced the Corpses...*Malum*, as they call themselves…to send in the 'big gun.' A member of the Corpse royal family maybe. But whoever she is in her world, in *ours* she's the new boss of the invasion."

I looked at the face on the screen, with its slack skin and bloating features. Then I did what I figured the others were doing and crossed my eyes. The Mask trick also worked on photographs—better, actually, because a photo didn't move. Instantly, a second face materialized over the first, kind of floating atop it. It showed a woman in her late thirties, with long blond hair and a movie-star face. While her real smile was grotesque, this one was dazzling, all white teeth and red lips.

The Chief said, "Cavanaugh makes a lot of public appearances, opening shopping centers, visiting schools, stuff like that. In just a few months, she's become respected and well liked. Some folks are already seeing the mayor's office in her future."

I had to force my eyes to relax. The image of the Queen's Mask was eerily captivating. No wonder she'd taken the city by storm.

Tom continued, "She's better organized and…in my opinion…a bit smarter than Booth was. She's already expanded Corpse influence throughout the city. She's also the one who closed Eastern State to tourists. We don't know why, but from Will and Helene's recon last night, it looks like she may be turning it back into a prison. Which brings us to our current situation."

He nodded to the Hacker, and the screen changed again, this time showing the wallet ID photo of Hugo Ramirez, special agent for the FBI. Ramirez had a square face, short-cropped black hair, a neatly trimmed goatee, and heavy-lidded brown eyes. He wasn't smiling.

"Looks like the Corpses have caught themselves a pretty big fish," Tom explained. "Now, we don't know why they would've taken the risk of snatching a Fed, but they did, and it seems pretty clear that we need to do something about it."

Another nod, and this time, the screen showed an overhead view of the prison's layout.

"Agent Ramirez is in *here*…somewhere. We need to find him, boost him, and get him back to Haven. Then we need to find out what he did that spooked Cavanaugh into pullin' this stunt."

Chuck Binelli—a veteran member of the Angels—yelled out, "How do we know they haven't moved him? I mean… the Deaders must figure Will and Helene grabbed the ID."

It was Sharyn who replied, "We know he's still there 'cause we been watching the place ever since Will called it in. Nobody's come in or out."

"But that probably won't last," Tom added. "Which is why we need to go in now…today."

"In the daytime?" Burt Moscova, another Angel, asked. "Talk about risk!"

"I know," the Chief admitted. "This one's gonna be particularly dangerous, but I think it's worth it. A small team led by Sharyn will hit the place hard, find Agent Ramirez, and hopefully make it to the streets again before the Corpses even know what happened."

"Hopefully?" Chuck muttered.

"Yeah," said Sharyn, grinning. "That's the bad news. The good news is that we got us a new trick to stick up our sleeves. And you dudes are gonna *love* it!"

Tom motioned to the back of the room.

Steve Moscova stepped forward.

A small, skinny kid with dark hair and a round face hidden behind thick glasses, Steve was the science geek who dreamed up our weapons and other gadgets. He was also Burt's older brother, though he'd gotten his Eyes later, a point of some embarrassment for him. In truth, every Seer was unique, though the ability was often shared by all the children in a given family.

Seeing the Moscova brothers together always made me think of my little sister, Emily. She was only five years old and wouldn't get the Sight for another six years—if she got it at all.

The Corpses *had* to be gone by then.

It was a quiet vow I'd made to myself.

Steve carried a bath towel, clean but worn, which he laid out atop the television and unrolled.

Inside were six syringes.

Each was identical to the one I'd seen Sharyn use back in the alley, and each was filled with the same clear liquid.

"I call these 'Ritters,'" Steve announced, smiling, "in honor of the first person to ever kill a Corpse."

As the room broke into applause, I felt my face redden. Helene, who was sitting behind me, playfully elbowed my ribs.

Still grinning, Steve waited until the noise died down. Then he started talking again—now all business. "A single Ritter contains fifteen cubic centimeters of concentrated saltwater. If fully injected into the chest or abdomen of a Corpse, the result is a sudden and violent disruption of the host body's tissue structure."

"English?" Burt suggested.

Steve sighed. "It makes the Corpse blow up."

Another round of applause, this one mixed in with assorted whoops and shouts of "yeah!" and "awright!"

Then one of the girls, an Angel named Katie Bell, called out in her especially high-pitched voice, "How does it work?"

"We don't really know," Steve replied. "There's no real physiological reason for saltwater to have such an effect on a cadaver, so it must be linked to the nature of the invaders themselves. But there's no denying that it *does* work. Sharyn tested a Ritter on a Corpse just a few hours ago, and the results were...compelling."

"Compelling!" the Boss Angel exclaimed. "That ain't the word for it! That Deader popped like a balloon! Pieces of him are probably *still* rainin' down all over that alley!"

This brought another round of cheers.

"We can kill 'em!" Chuck shouted. "We can *finally* kill 'em!"

"But…" Steve said. "There's a catch."

The cheers died down.

"Always is," Chuck muttered.

"Depending on the size of the host body, full effectiveness can take up to ten seconds, during which time the Corpse remains dangerous."

Burt raised his hand, an old classroom gesture that he seemed to be the only one to bother with. I suspected he kept doing it because he knew his big brother liked it. "So…we gotta get in close enough to stick a Deader and then back away fast enough so he doesn't kill us before the stuff can work?"

"Well…" Steve stammered. "I wouldn't put it quite that way."

"Ain't as bad as all that," Sharyn assured us. "You hit the dead dude with a few shots of juice from your Super Soaker or pistol. Then, when he's down, you let him it have it with the…Ritter."

As she said this last part, Sharyn winked at me.

Inwardly, I groaned.

"Just don't hit bone," Steve warned. "You can snap the needle. The best spot is right here." He pointed to his stomach, roughly where his navel would be. "The soft abdominal tissue. It'll take some force…I'm using large gauge needles… but once you penetrate the skin, the plunger only needs a second to empty the barrel."

"Each of you gets one of these," Tom announced, "along with your usual equipment. But use it only as a last resort. I'd be happier if none of you has to get that close to a Corpse. Now Sharyn's gonna walk y'all through the plan we've worked out, so listen up. We don't know what the Corpses got in mind for Agent Ramirez, but we can make some pretty good guesses. Be ready to split in an hour. Good luck, Undertakers."

Then, with a nod to his sister, the Chief left the rec room.

Sharyn grinned broadly. "Dudes, this mission's gonna *rock*! This here's the first time y'all might get the chance to actually waste a Corpse! Well...except for Red, of course."

More applause.

"Come on," I muttered. "Enough."

"'Fore we split," the Boss Angel continued, holding up an empty Ritter, "I'm gonna walk y'all through how to use one of these and how not to get bit, beaten to death, or strangled in the process. Hot Dog...that's your cue!"

Dave's here?

This was supposed to be an Angels-only meeting, with the exception of the Hacker running the laptop. The fact that the Burgermeister had been invited was an interesting surprise, especially because I knew how badly he wanted to join Sharyn's crew.

Under the circumstances, I'd have thought he'd be grinning, glad to be a part of an Angels' mission in any way at all. But he wasn't. In fact, he looked resigned, maybe even grim,

as he rose out of a chair in the back and trudged forward
to stand beside Sharyn. Once there, the giant kid towered
over the Boss Angel—at least half a foot taller and maybe a
hundred pounds heavier.

But I knew she could kick his ass.

Fact was, we probably all could.

Before he had gotten his Eyes, Dave Burger had been
a force to be reckoned with in his neighborhood. A local
fighter, even a bully. But here in this world of the walking
dead with its very real dangers, he'd found out quickly that
he lacked the speed and—sorry, Dave—the smarts to stand
up against kids half his size who'd been trained in what
Sharyn called "street karate."

But here he was, and I couldn't help but wonder why.

Eyeing the Burgermeister up, Sharyn hastily screwed the
needle off the end of her syringe.

"There!" she announced, showing everyone her handi-
work. "Harmless. Hot Dog, stand right there. Now turn a
little so's everyone can see your front. Cool! Just like that.
Now…"

The Boss Angel addressed us, "Last night, I had old Vader
with me and used that to convince the Deader's arms to be
elsewhere. That made stickin' him a whole lot easier. Y'all
won't have that advantage, so there's a number of ways you
can play it.

"First, you can come up at 'em from the front. Hot Dog,
I want you to do your best to tag me. Don't hold back, dig?"

"I guess," he muttered. Then, as if reaching some internal decision, he came forward suddenly and swung his meaty fist at Sharyn's head.

She ducked smoothly under it.

He swung the other fist, a sweeping haymaker that, if it had landed, would probably have knocked the girl's head right off her shoulders.

Sharyn moved as though made of liquid, weaving under the arcing arm, sidestepped, and, with Dave momentarily off balance, drove her fist—with the syringe in it—hard into the Burgermeister's belly. Then she made a show of hammering down the plunger with her thumb.

He gasped and doubled over as Sharyn jumped back about six feet.

"Kill!" she announced. "Stick, plunge, and back off. It's that simple."

Dave straightened, more surprised than hurt by the blow.

"Thanks, Hot Dog. Y'all see where that hit? Right above the navel. Nothing behind there but soft stuff. Now let me show you the rear attack." She motioned to Dave, twirling her finger.

Sighing, he turned obediently around.

"This is trickier," she admitted. "From the front, you got this whole section here...from the solar plexus to the pelvic bone. From the back, though, the sweet spot's smaller and a little harder to nail. You want to hold the Ritter like this"— she flipped the syringe over in her hand so the business end, needleless, stuck out of the top of her fist instead of the bottom—"then it's about quiet. Don't count on a Corpse showing you his back in combat. The only way you're likely to get a chance like this if you sneak up on his smelly butt."

She made a show of creeping up on Dave, who fidgeted nervously, knowing what was coming.

"When you hit, use both hands—one to stick and one to plunge. Like this."

Sharyn rammed the syringe into Dave's lower right side, making him wince. Then, shifting her weight, she hammered in the plunger with the heel of her other hand. A second later, she was six feet away again.

"You want to make the hit just above the kidney. Too high and you scrape a rib. Too low and you hit the hip bone. You can go for the butt, but Steve-O says the juice needs a lot longer to work in fat than it does in muscle or tissue." She grinned. "Questions?"

Chuck asked. "How many Deaders have you nailed this way?"

"Four," Sharyn replied. "That's what I spent last night doin', riding around the city and wasting Corpses. The last one was with Will in an alley near the prison. For all the others, I was alone."

"Why alone?" Helene asked, "How come we didn't know about it until now?"

"Top secret," the Boss Angel replied. "We're turning up the heat here, brothers and sisters. For the first time, we got us a practical yet lethal weapon to use against the Deaders. Until we were sure it worked, Tom and I figured we'd keep it quiet…just in case somebody…" Her words trailed off.

But we all knew what she meant.

In case somebody got grabbed by the Corpses, who had this God-awful way of getting someone to talk.

"Any other questions?"

"How big a group is going?" Burt asked.

Sharyn considered this. "I'm going. So are Will and Helene because they've had a look at the place…at least from the outside. I'll take three others."

Every hand went up, including Dave's—though, of course, his was ignored.

Shouts of "Sharyn!" and "Ooo! Ooo!" flooded the room. There were between ten and twelve Angels at any given time. While a lot of kids like Dave itched to join, others tended to transfer out after a particularly close call. Well, either that or—

Enough said.

Sharyn scanned the room, looking a lot like a teacher panning for student volunteers. "Chuck," she said at last. "Burt. And Katie."

Groans of disappointment followed the announcement.

The Boss grinned. "What? Y'all that eager to get yourselves killed? Chill. If this was a night job, I might take the whole crew. But because it's daytime, I want to keep this small and quick. Next go 'round, dudes. I promise. For now,

I need the team to meet me in Tom's office. We got some stuff to look at 'fore we hit the streets."

The meeting broke up. Helene and I stood and looked at each other. She grinned. "'Ritter,' huh? Face it, Will—you're famous! You just can't get away from it!"

I didn't reply.

Want to know why I was so uncomfortable at that birthday party earlier? It wasn't the surprise party itself. It was the sad fact that in the four months I'd been living at Haven, that was the *only* such party I'd ever attended. And this despite the fact I knew a half-dozen kids who'd had birthdays come and go unnoticed during that time. Why me and nobody else?

Because I was Karl Ritter's only son.

And that wasn't the end of it. Now I had a weapon—a brand new Undertakers weapon—named after me! They could say it was because I'd killed Booth, and I felt sure that was part of it. But it wasn't *all* of it.

Again—Karl Ritter's only son.

A lot to live up to.

And it was a rare day when I felt equal to the challenge.

Helene read my face. "Jeez. Cheer up! At least we didn't get into too much trouble over last night's mess."

"We can't recon together anymore," I complained.

She shrugged. "I was half-expecting Tom to put me back into the Schoolers and you back into the Moms! He's not big on kids ignoring the rules and regs."

The Schoolers was Helene's old crew, the Undertakers who infiltrated area middle schools, looking for and rescuing new Seers. That was how Helene and I had met. She'd found me, alone and terrified and Seeing the walking dead everywhere I looked, and had gotten to me before the Corpses had. After that mission, she'd graduated from Schooler to Angel trainee.

The Moms were Nick Rooney's crew. Usually filled with the greenest recruits, the Moms did the cooking, cleaning, laundry, and basically every other duty that nobody wanted. I'd never spent a day on that crew, having moved right from First Stop, the Undertakers' boot camp, to Angel training.

But that's another story.

Besides, I knew Tom would never have demoted me like that. After all, I'd done far stupider things as an Undertaker than going after that wallet, and I'd always managed to stay in his good graces.

Bulletproof, I thought.

Because I was Karl Ritter's only son.

"Come on," Helene said. "Let's get to the briefing."

As I followed her out of the rec room, I glanced around and spotted Dave. He still stood near the front, motionless as a statue—a big statue. He wore a strange expression on his face—sad and kind of wistful. Maybe he wished he was going with us to the prison. Maybe he wished he could just get himself into Angel training.

I half-expected him to meet my eyes, maybe toss me

a silent plea for help. *Talk to the Chief for me*, that look might say.

Except the Burgermeister wasn't looking at me at all.

His eyes were on Sharyn.

CHAPTER 9

BREAKING IN

Undertakers prefer to move about in the city at night.

As far as we've been able to tell, Corpses don't see in the dark any better than we do. To be honest, we're not really sure how they "see" at all, given that their eyes are rotting out of their heads. Like with a lot of other Deader abilities, they just do it. Still, we've learned that it's easier to run, easier to hide, easier to keep from getting beaten to death or eaten in the dark.

Occasionally, though, the shadows just aren't an option. Occasionally, we need to confront Deaders with the sun in the sky.

At night, it's about stealth, about hitting them hard and fast and then disappearing.

During the day, it's about being smart.

The signs read:

TY DRAGO

THE SCHOOL DISTRICT OF PHILADELPHIA SPONSORS "BREAKING IN" WHERE PHYSICAL FITNESS MEETS HISTORY!

The Hackers had photoshopped two of them in less than an hour, printing them out on poster paper and glueing them onto a couple of those plastic folding "Wet Floor" signs you can get at any office supply store.

Our Angel strike team was dressed in sweats and sneakers, including Sharyn. The five of us stood at loose attention on the sidewalk as she strutted back and forth, wearing a hard gym-teacher expression that made her look older than she was and carrying a big silver whistle that she blew—well—a lot.

"We don't got all day, boys and girls!" she announced. "Let's get this party started! Fetch the ladder!"

A small crowd had gathered—all nicely human. They were clearly amused by what they were seeing: a handful of kids struggling to pull a heavy aluminum extension ladder from the rear of an unmarked white van. We moved in formation, making little "hup hup" sounds with each step, per Sharyn's instructions. Frankly, the whole thing felt ridiculous, but it *did* seem to have the desired effect.

As we hauled the ladder across a narrow strip of landscaping and stood it up against Eastern State Penitentiary's thirty-foot outer wall, the crowd's only reaction was to watch and laugh. Dressed in sweats and "hupping" like soldiers, the operation felt more like street theater than what it was: breaking and entering.

82

But at least between our performance and our printed signs, no one was challenging us.

The great city of Philadelphia was always doing dumb stuff like this.

"Ladder in place, ma'am!" Chuck Binelli barked, saluting Sharyn. She saluted back, the action stiff and military precise, as if she saluted people all the time.

"Head on up!" the Boss Angel barked.

Chuck went first. Then Helene. Then Katie. Then Me. Then Burt.

Sharyn saluted the crowd, blowing the whistle one last time. The small audience actually applauded.

Then she followed us up.

Sharyn had parked the white van on Corinthian Avenue, a narrow side street that ran along the penitentiary's eastern wall. The prison entrance was on Fairmount, the southern side, which meant our "ladder bit" had gone down around the corner and out of view from the gate. Hopefully, the Corpses—none of whom were in sight—wouldn't know we were here despite all the "hup hups" and the whistle-blowing.

Making so much noise in the name of surprise was a risky tactic but a necessary one. We needed to get into that prison, and nobody figured the Deaders would just open up if we knocked.

Sharyn joined us atop the wall. This time, she didn't blow her whistle. From here, the crowd couldn't see us; Corinthian Avenue was too narrow.

Which meant the show was over.

Eastern State Penitentiary lay sprawled out below us like a huge, many-legged spider. The design had been pretty unique in its day: a central hub topped with a guard tower, with cell blocks radiating out from it in all directions. The wheelhouse design had been copied by a lot of other prisons around the country.

"Red," Sharyn commanded. "Check the towers."

I pulled out my pocketknife and tapped the 7 button, springing the telescope. Peering through it, I scanned the prison's tall central structure. Then I turned my head and studied the smaller guard towers mounted on the outer wall at each of the four corners.

"Clear," I reported.

"Not real big on security, are they?" Helene remarked.

"Yeah," Sharyn admitted. "I'm surprised. After you two hit the gate last night, Tom and I kind of figured they'd have posted at least a few lookouts. Maybe they're tryin' to keep a low profile. But don't trust it. If any of y'all sees a Deader pop up, signal the rest."

"Then what?" Chuck asked.

"Then I'll take him out before he can give the alarm."

"How?" Burt asked.

But Sharyn only grinned and changed the subject. "Listen up. Burt, Chuck, and Katie to hit the north side of the prison. Helene, Will, and me'll go south. With the guard towers empty, I don't figure they got too many

Deaders in here. But that might change fast if we get spotted. Keep to the rooftops of each cell block and see what you can see through the skylights. Careful, though…some of the blocks were under repair when they closed this place down. Don't want nobody falling through a weak spot. Everybody dig?"

We all dug.

"Burt, your team gets the ladder. You can use it to bridge over to the nearest cell block. And keep your radios on. If you spot a Corpse, radio the rest of us. And if you spot Ramirez, even better. Let's do this, Angels."

With that, we split up. Sharyn went first, balancing her way along the crumbling, three-foot-wide battlement, with Helene and me following close behind. Below, on Corinthian, most of the spectators had moved on. The few that remained looked more bored than suspicious.

Good.

It struck me that I wasn't scared to be doing what I was doing—well, not *really*. Here, I was trotting atop a wall with a three-story drop on either side of me, and the only thing running through my mind was tactics. In the four months since I'd stepped outside my family's house in Manayunk and been hit with the Sight, most of things that used to scare me had lost their power.

When did I get so brave? I wondered.

We neared the southeast corner of the prison. The original stone watchtower had been updated with a more modern brick guardhouse that jutted outward along the wall just enough to keep us from getting around it.

We stopped, crouching low and studying the prison grounds. The courtyard remained empty.

That was the good news.

The bad news was that the gap between us and the roof of the nearest cell block looked at least fifty feet wide!

"So…how do we get over there without killing ourselves?" I asked.

"Like I told you back in Haven," Sharyn replied, "it's a surprise!"

Then our dreadlocked leader reached into her backpack and withdrew what looked like a small steel crossbow.

"What's that?" Helene asked, her eyes lighting up.

Sharyn grinned. "Say hello to Aunt Sally!"

Helene looked blankly at her. I didn't. I'd seen it before— or something like it. Steve had shown it to me during my early days with the Undertakers—a crossbow that shot grappling hooks. Back then, however, it hadn't been called "Aunt Sally" or anything else. In fact, it hadn't worked at all.

"She's the first of her kind…what you call a 'prototype,'" Sharyn explained. "Check this out."

She pointed the crossbow toward the cell block roof—

—and fired.

With a soft *twang*, a steel bolt shot across the intervening space, digging deep into the hard tar that layered the roof. In its wake ran a thin black cable, barely as big around as my pinky, that Sharyn immediately pulled taut, leaning back on it with all her weight. Perched as she was atop a thirty-foot wall, if the cable snapped or the bolt came loose, she'd have likely gone tumbling down onto Corinthian Avenue.

But it didn't, and neither did she.

"Sweet," she muttered. "Dead-on accurate and with the power of a bow twice its size. Steve's the man! You gotta love that little nerd. But this…" Sharyn twisted a lever on the side of the crossbow, detaching the entire crank assembly, the black cable included. Then she knelt and fastened this rig firmly into the mortar at our feet, turning the crank until the cable was as tight as a guitar string.

Finally, she stood up and pulled another crank assembly out of her backpack, fitting it onto the crossbow, bolt and all. And just that quick, she was ready to fire again.

"This bit was Alex Bobson's idea," she continued, referring to the Boss of the Monkeys, Haven's construction and maintenance crew. "He improved on Steve's design. That dude may be a jerk, but he delivers. Zip line, anyone?"

Helene chuckled. I felt my stomach knot up. Nobody'd mentioned this part of the plan to me.

"You don't gotta get all green, little bro," Sharyn said. "I know it's your first zip, which is why I kept this part of the plan to myself until now. But trust me. It's easy!"

She slid her legs over the side of the wall, heedless of the drop. Then she pulled out three more lengths of cable, these about nine inches long and capped on both ends with thick leather loops. She handed one to each of us. "I'll go first. Do what I do. Just slip your wrists through one end, toss it over the wire, and then do the same with the other end. After that, you just push off…"

And she did.

As we watched, Sharyn dropped away from the wall, and hanging from her leather loops, she rode the tight cable all the way down to the cell block's roof. There, she landed lightly, freed herself, and waved for us to follow.

"Me next…or you?" Helene asked.

"You ever done this before?"

She shook her head.

"Me neither." I swallowed.

Helene eyed me. "You gonna be okay?"

"Sure," I replied, wondering if I meant it.

"I'm willing to go next," she said. "But not if you're gonna freeze."

I felt my face flush. "When did I ever freeze?"

She shrugged. "Okay." Then, with hardly any hesitation at all, she dropped down as Sharyn had, looped herself over the cable, and pushed off. She hit the roof seconds later, sticking the landing perfectly.

Helene always made everything look so easy.

I swallowed a second time. My turn.

I sat down, inching forward until my legs dangled over the courtyard. It was a *seriously* long way down. Taking a deep breath, I put one wrist through one strap and hung my cable over the zip line. Then I put my hand through the other strap.

My eyes found Helene's. She looked expectantly at me from the rooftop. Beside her, Sharyn flashed her trademark grin.

I felt my stomach tighten further. I ignored it.

Just be brave, I told myself. That had been the motto of an Undertaker named Tara Monroe. A friend.

A dead friend.

Undertakers tended to have a lot of dead friends.

I pushed off.

It wasn't half as bad as I thought it would be. In fact, if it hadn't been so cold, I might have enjoyed it. Wind bit at my face as all my weight suddenly hung from my arms. The wire between my fists skittered down the cable—sounding a bit like a big zipper sliding open.

Guess that's where the name comes from.

I hit the roof more clumsily than the girls, forcing Sharyn to scoop me up before I could stumble and break my nose on the edge of a skylight.

"Not so bad…was it, little bro?" she asked.

As she said this, our radio watches suddenly chirped.

Helene answered. "What's up, Burt?"

"There's a Corpse in the central guard tower!" the boy's voice hissed. "He's looking our way, but we ducked behind some barrels! I don't know if he saw us!"

When she heard this, Sharyn turned all business, yanking

me to my feet and then spinning around and snatching up her crossbow. "Tell 'em to stay hid," she told Helene, who conveyed the message.

"What are you going to do?" I asked.

"Been practicing," Sharyn replied. "Check *this* out."

She raised Aunt Sally to eye level, pressed the stock into her shoulder, and sighted the watchtower. Maybe a hundred feet away and twenty feet up, a dark figure stood motionless behind the glass windows, facing away toward the northeast corner of the prison—where Chuck, Burt, and Katie were huddled.

Sharyn's finger found the trigger.

Twang!

She *had* been practicing.

Her bolt cut the air in a sweet, true arc. It broke the watchtower window with an audible crash of glass, followed an instant later by a wooden thump.

Through my wrist radio, I heard Katie exclaim, "Got him!"

Then Chuck added, "Man, what a wicked shot!"

Sharyn raised her wrist. "Meet up at the base of the watchtower!" she exclaimed. "I'm going to take 'em out!" Then she said, "Come on!" to us and took off running along the cell block, careful to avoid the skylights that dotted the roof like potholes.

Helene and I followed, struggling to keep up.

At the base of the watchtower, Sharyn seized the cable

that dangled from her fired bolt, tested it for a second, and then climbed, walking up the side of the building. "Stay here," she whispered back. "Don't know how much weight this thing'll handle at once."

So, feeling frustrated, we watched as the Boss Angel scaled the watchtower, scrambled over the catwalk railing, kicked in the rest of the already broken window, and climbed inside. Then, after a long bunch of seconds, she waved for us to come up.

"She makes it look so easy," Helene sighed.

"Yeah," I agreed.

I was thinking the same thing about you a minute ago.

"You first this time," she told me.

It's pretty hard to climb a cable, even if you do have good gloves and a wall to brace your feet against. The skinny twelve-year-old I'd been even two months ago could never have managed it. But the slightly less skinny thirteen-year-old I was now could and *did*—with some effort. At last, winded and my arms aching, I let Sharyn help me through the broken window.

Then, as she signaled Helene to follow, I looked around the watchtower.

There wasn't much to the place. No furniture. Just bare walls, windows on all sides, and a stairway that led down into the prison proper.

Between two of the windows, with her back to us, stood a Corpse. She was a solid Type Four. Pretty well decomposed, she'd had lost most of her bodily fluids. Any bloating was done, leaving her sunken and dried up. Her skin, gray and flaky, hung off long, thin bones, and her hair had little more than dark wisps peeking out from beneath an oversized police-issue cap.

Beetles crawled all over her. The Corpse's body was literally being eaten away from the inside out.

I never got used to that.

Dead Lady Cop's arms and legs twitched spastically—and with good reason: Sharyn's crossbow bolt has caught her at the base of the skull, gone all the way through, and pinned her head to the wooden window frame.

Chuck had been right: a wicked shot.

But then that was Sharyn.

"Hey, Deader!" Sharyn chirped as Helene climbed through the window. "Having a bad day or what?"

The cadaver's lips moved. Unfortunately, with the steel bolt sticking through its open mouth and into the wood, there wasn't much it could say in English. So it switched to Deadspeak.

"Others. Coming. For. Me."

"Yeah, I'll bet they are," Sharyn agreed. "But I think we got us a minute or two. So I'm gonna make you a one-time offer. You tell me how many Deaders you got on-site...and I just might let you live."

The Corpse looked sideways at her. *"You. No. Can. Kill. Me."*

Sharyn laughed. Then she held up her syringe. "Know what this is? Any of your buddies happen to get iced last night...maybe in ways you can't figure?" Her smile vanished, and she leaned close. "So, one last time—you spill and maybe I leave you here to transfer when your Holmes find you. Otherwise, I stick you with this and cap your sorry dead ass."

I suddenly saw something flash through the Corpse's milky eyes—a look I'd I never expected: terror. She squirmed frantically against the bolt that pinned her to the wall, but it was no good. She wasn't going anywhere, and we all knew it.

"Well?" Sharyn pressed. "I need an answer, bag o' bones."

"*Six.*"

"Six more Corpses downstairs?"

Dead Lady Cop nodded as much as the bolt through her face would allow. "*Six,*" she repeated. But as she said that, there was something in her expression—at least insofar as a dead body pinned through the mouth to the wall can *have* an expression—that I didn't like.

She looked cagey. Not like she was lying, but—

"Six," Helene echoed.

I knew what she was thinking: There was one of us for each of them. Not great odds but better than we'd had last night!

"Cool!" Sharyn said. "Thanks, Deader!"

Then she tossed her Ritter—*oh God, that name!*—to Helene, who smoothly snatched it out of the air.

The Boss Angel said flatly, "Waste her."

Helene looked from Sharyn to me and back again. "But you said…"

"I said 'might.' Fact is, one less Deader is one less Deader. If we switched places, you can bet she wouldn't be cuttin' us no slack. Do it."

Helene wavered.

Sharyn said, "We got no time. She's stuck in a useless body, and that means the others have been called. Do it now."

Helene stepped to the Corpse, who struggled desperately, making low growling sounds in her rotting throat.

I considered saying something—protesting—maybe making some comment about how keeping our word was one of the things that made us better than them. The moral high ground, I guess you'd call it.

But I didn't.

Helene found my eyes. I shrugged.

Then she slammed the Ritter into the small of Dead Lady Cop's back, emptying it with one push of her thumb.

"Everybody down!" Sharyn commanded. We dropped to the dusty floor.

At first, nothing happened.

Then it did.

The Corpse exploded but not like the one in the alley had, spilling guts everywhere. This one's guts had dried up weeks ago. Instead, it erupted in a cloud of gray dust that filled the watchtower and covered everything, including us.

Helene and I struggled to our knees, coughing and trying not to puke. But Sharyn seemed more or less unfazed, standing up and looking over at where the Corpse had been. The figure of dark energy was there but only for a second. *Pop!*

"Okay," the Boss Angel said. "Let's get into position. I'm callin' a Number Eleven."

CHAPTER 10

NUMBER ELEVEN

The Angels have moves, and some of these moves have numbers.

A Number Eleven involved covering multiple exits to a building—and then hitting the Corpses inside from different directions at once. Being shaped like a big pinwheel with cell blocks sticking out from a central hub, Eastern State Penitentiary was a solid candidate for this approach.

Better still, because it was a museum these days and not a prison, its layout was easily available on the Internet. So back at the briefing, we'd all studied it. The cell blocks, some one-story and some two-story, had been built at different times during the penitentiary's long history. Each had a number; the one Helene, Sharyn, and I had zipped to and then run along had been Cell Block One. Katie, Chuck, and Bert had spotted the watchtower Corpse from the roof of Cell Block Three.

Because there were something like fourteen cell blocks off the hub and only six of us, Sharyn modified the Number Eleven. She and I would attack from above while Helene and the rest would go down into the prison yard and pick cell blocks at each compass point. Then, on a signal, we'd hit the hub all at once.

Hopefully, the Corpses would be so busy responding to Dead Lady Cop's call for help that they'd focus on Sharyn and me, giving the others the element of surprise.

A workable plan.

What could go wrong?

Helene left the watchtower the same way she'd come in— via the cable. Sharyn and I took the stairs. These led down into a big, round, empty room that once upon a time had been the prison library. From here, a lone door opened onto a railed walkway overlooking Cell Block Seven.

We could already hear noises from downstairs.

They were coming or getting ready to come.

The dead.

"See them steps?" Sharyn whispered, pointing to a couple of metal staircases that led down from the walkway to the floor of the cellblock. "That's how they'll hit us. You take the top of one. I'll take the other. Wait until they're halfway up before you start shootin'."

I nodded and went to the indicated spot. Sharyn did the same, raising her radio to her lips. "Sound off, Angels."

"Angel Two in position," Chuck radioed.

"Angel Three in position," Burt radioed.

"Angel Four in position," Katie radioed.

"Angel Five in position," Helene radioed.

In case you're wondering, I was Angel Six. Low rung on the seniority ladder.

Sharyn's manner turned thoughtful. When she next spoke, her voice had softened, with much of its trademark mischief gone. "Listen up, Undertakers. We're about to go into combat. I ain't gonna ask you if you're scared. I know y'all are scared. *I'm* scared. We got even numbers in this fight...one-on-one. But we also got surprise, and that can make all the difference. We're gonna *do* this, Undertakers. We're gonna remember *what* we're fightin' and *why* we're fightin' them. Then we're gonna turn our fear into anger and use it to hit these wormbags harder'n we ever hit 'em before."

I listened. We all listened.

The Boss Angel said, "This time...for the first time... some of these Deaders won't be goin' home. Use your anger, Undertakers. Let it make you sharp. Let it make you ready. Let it make you *mean*."

"Mean," I echoed.

Then, one by one, the rest of the Angels repeated this one-word mantra.

We'd all heard this speech before or some version of it. Sharyn used it a lot—and with good reason: it worked.

Still, my heart had begun to hammer, and my throat felt desert dry.

"We do this right," Sharyn concluded, "and chances are the Corpses won't know what hit 'em. Y'all dig?"

"Angel Two digs," Chuck radioed.

"Angel Three digs," Burt radioed.

"Angel Four digs," Katie radioed.

"Angel Five digs," Helene radioed.

The Boss Angel gave me a pointed look.

"Angel Six digs," I replied, though I *could* have told her nobody said "dig" anymore. At least not since disco had died.

But this was Sharyn.

"Cool," Sharyn said. "Stand by…"

Ever seen zombie movies where the monsters come shambling along, moaning and with their arms extended, like they want a hug? Well, that's what I was expecting, moment by moment, as I stood atop that staircase with my Super Soaker poised and ready. It was one of the small Super Soakers, as the big ones were hard to conceal and wouldn't have worked well with our ladder trick.

A calculated risk—trading firepower for the all-important element of surprise.

Except the surprise-ees weren't showing up for the party.

A full minute passed.

"Somethin' ain't right," Sharyn muttered.

"We heard them," I whispered to her. "Didn't we?"

"Yeah," she said. She frowned down at the archway leading from Cell Block Seven into the hub. Both of us listened hard. Nothing.

Sharyn's wrist radio cracked. Chuck's voice sounded edgy and impatient. "Hey, Boss. We doin' this or what?"

"Hold up," Sharyn told him, told us all. Then she gestured for me to stay put and headed down the staircase. She moved slowly, with catlike grace, her sword poised and rock steady in her hands. I covered her with the Super Soaker, ready to fire the moment one of the dead appeared.

None did.

Six of them, Dead Lady Cop had said.

I still didn't think she'd been lying, but she'd definitely held *something* back.

Sharyn passed through what had once been the security gate at the mouth of the cell block. Then she pressed herself against the cold concrete archway that marked the hub's threshold. Her eyes flicked to mine.

I swallowed dryly and gave her a nod. "I've got you covered."

She nodded back. "I know, little bro."

Then she peered around the corner and into the hub.

"Oh fudge!" I heard her yelp.

Then something grabbed her, yanking her out of view.

Something *big*.

It happened so suddenly that for a second or two, my mind barely registered it. But then, panic—cold and electric—laced down my back. Barking Sharyn's name, I took the stairs three at a time, bounding down and out through the gate in the span of a few heartbeats.

Beyond it, the hub was brightly lit—a circular room about

thirty feet across, with pipes and electrical cabling running across the ceiling and a polished tile floor. Its walls were lined with numbered doors, each one leading to a different cell block.

And the dead were here.

And they *weren't* surprised.

There were six of them, just as promised, all in various states of decay. Some were moist, like the cop in the alley. Others were flaky, like the one in the watchtower. Every one of them had milky eyes set into rotting skulls—eyes that focused on me as I entered. Empty eyes, except for the hatred that radiated from them.

And all of them wore yellow raincoats.

These were of the heavy vinyl variety, like the kind firefighters wear, with hoods that covered most of the wearer's face. The moment I saw the Deaders, I instinctively fired, blasting a hard stream at the nearest of them, a tall Type Two who stood right at the door to Cell Block One.

The saltwater bounced harmlessly off the thick vinyl.

The Corpse grinned at me, maggots dribbling out from between his teeth.

I froze where I stood, rooted in place by shock and horror. I knew I couldn't afford it. Angel training: In combat, keep moving. No matter what happens, never stop moving. But seeing a Corpse in what amounted to anti-saltwater armor had shaken me down to my shoes.

Then a voice called, "Watch it, little bro!"

Instinctively, I ducked as an arm, draped in yellow vinyl, whipped through the air where my head had been just a moment before. I pivoted and fired at the second attacker. He was shorter than the first one and flakier, his sunken eyes and desiccated gray skin barely visible beneath his hood. My stream of water bounced off his chest as he came at me again, batting away my Super Soaker. It flew from my grasp and hit the stone wall, cracking and spilling its contents.

We're gonna die here.

I pushed the thought away and retreated, putting some breathing room between me and my two attackers. At the same time, I looked for Sharyn.

She was on the other side of the hub, surrounded by four Corpses. They all had guns, being dressed as cops and all, but of course they'd never draw them. Deaders don't use weapons ever. Tom thinks its a culture thing. Like the others, these wore raincoats too, and they circled the dreadlocked girl like a pack of wolves. The Angel Boss brandished Vader, its blade glinting in the artificial light, her dark eyes darting everywhere at once. Most of the Deaders were Type Threes—smelly, with tissues halfway melted into putrid ooze that drained off them like sweat.

They were pretty nasty.

But the *fourth guy*.

Now I knew what had grabbed Sharyn back at the archway to Cell Block Seven. And I finally understood why Dead Lady Cop had seemed so coy.

She'd known what was waiting for us down here.

He was a Type Two—and he was a *giant*; there's just no other word for it. Seeing him, I couldn't image where the Queen had found such a body. He had to be six-eight at least—maybe more. Three hundred and fifty pounds of purple, bloated dead man, squeezed into a raincoat meant for someone half his size. His legs were tree trunks, his arms as thick as my whole body. He towered over the rest of us, his massive, yellow-hooded head nearly touching the ceiling.

And, from Sharyn's expression, she was way more worried about this dude than the others.

I didn't blame her.

Where in God's name are Helene and the others?

Then I remembered: they hadn't been called! Sharyn's last order to them had been to "hold up," and given her current circumstances, I guessed she hadn't found an opportunity to radio anything different.

So, with my own two Deaders closing in, I raised my wrist and called into the open channel: "Angels! Get in here! Now!"

Someone replied, "On our way!" I thought it might be Helene, but I wasn't sure. And I suppose it didn't matter.

At the same time, one of the Threes surrounding Sharyn spotted an opening and surged forward, his sloppy hands reaching for what he assumed to be the girl's unguarded back. What he didn't know was that Sharyn had twice as many eyes as anyone else. She spun on her heel and slashed with Vader. The Corpse's body took two more steps, but his head went the other way.

Then, before he'd even hit the ground, the Boss Angel ducked a swing of the giant's arm and drove the point of her sword through the throat of another of the Type Threes. A quick twist later, and his spinal cord was severed.

He went down like the lifeless lump of meat he was.

Neither of them was dead, of course; only a Ritter could do *that*. But both Corpses were down for the count and would stay that way—completely immobile—until their Deader buddies came to their rescue.

Good news for Sharyn.

But I still had my own problems.

Two Corpses—sticky and flaky—came at me, taking their sweet time about it. And why not? I was unarmed as far as they could see. I retreated until my back met stone. Then I scrambled through my coat and came out with my pocketknife and my Ritter. With my pocketknife in my left hand, I pressed its *2* button, activating the Taser.

The syringe was in my right.

An image of Dead Lady Cop in the watchtower flashed through my mind. Helene had killed her—forever and always. That's what Ritters did.

Could *I* do that? I mean, it was one thing to *cripple* them the way Sharyn had done with her sword just now. But it was another to kill—really, permanently *kill*—the being inside them. Wasn't it?

Shouldn't it be?

But I'd killed Booth.

I swallowed.

The flaky guy came in first, reaching for me with hands like bones wrapped in parchment. As they got close, I could see the flesh on them ripple weirdly.

Picking my moment, I dodged under his arm and pressed my Taser into his pit. For a second, I worried that the raincoat might protect him. It didn't. His entire body jolted from the shock.

Then the skin on his hands split, and beetles tumbled out. Dozens of them. Hundreds. A fountain of small black bugs. They poured over me, tumbling over my neck and shoulders and getting into my hair. As the Deader toppled forward, I leapt clear, yelling my head off and slapping at the insects with both hands.

In my revulsion, however, I stupidly dropped my Ritter and my pocketknife.

And the other Corpse fell on me.

CHAPTER 11

THE TIDE OF BATTLE

H e brought me down, wrapping his arms around me.

I hit the floor hard, slamming my head against the tile. Immediately, the room seemed to tilt. Then dead hands, sticky with juices I didn't want to think about, snaked around my neck. The Corpse's rotting visage loomed before me, his eyes gleaming and his mouth opening insanely wide, like shark's jaws. My head was spinning, and it was all I could do to brace my forearm under his chin, trying to keep him from biting me.

The Deader's black tongue lolled out from between receding lips. His teeth, dripping maggots, snapped downward toward my face.

Then he stopped.

His expression turned bewildered—right before he exploded.

"Ugh!" I heard Chuck Binelli exclaim as bits of dead guy covered us both.

For fleeting seconds, I stared up into a different face, a face wholly alien, wholly evil. It had no weight, no solid matter at all, but it *did* have eyes, which seemed to burn me with their gaze. There was hatred there. But there was also terror. Awful terror.

Whatever this thing was, it knew it was dying.

And then it was gone.

Leaving pieces of his stolen body up my nose and in my mouth.

Rolling over, I pushed myself up onto my hands and knees and vomited. My head pounded, and the world seemed to spin worse than ever.

Across the room, Helene, Katie, and Burt rushed to Sharyn's aid—though I saw each of them hesitate, just for a moment, when they caught sight of the giant.

Fear flashed across their faces.

"I hit the sweet spot!" Chuck exclaimed. "First time! Hey…you okay?"

I nodded. Then I vomited again. I felt like I'd been hit with a hammer and then dipped in a bucket of chum.

"Zapped…the other one…" I sputtered. "My…Ritter."

"I'm on it," he said. Then, sounding apprehensive, he added, "Will…these dudes are wearing raincoats!"

Are they? I thought bitterly. *I hadn't noticed.*

Burt went for the giant, his own Ritter out and ready. But the big guy saw him coming and moved with surprising speed, swatting the boy aside as if he were a pesky mosquito.

Burt crashed to the tile floor, momentarily stunned. The giant advanced on him, but Sharyn sprang between them, brandishing her sword.

Meanwhile, Katie and Helene focused on the remaining Type Three, cornering the smelly cadaver against a large bronze plaque that was mounted into the stone wall of the hub. Both girls had their Ritters out. As Helene feigned a thrust, drawing the Deader's attention, Katie moved in and smoothly planted hers into the Corpse's belly, right through the raincoat.

Hissing—yeah, they hiss sometimes—he swiped at her, forcing her to jump back, leaving the syringe's plunger unplunged. Seeing this, Helene stepped up and executed a solid roundhouse kick, slamming her sneakered foot into the Type Three's middle section.

Both girls jumped back.

"Watch this, Katie!" I heard Helene say.

The Corpse exploded—a wet popping sound.

A moment later, I heard a similar sound—though drier and raspier. I looked back to see that Chuck had found my fallen Ritter and used it on the flaky guy I'd zapped.

Apparently, the only one who had a problem killing these things was me.

But the good news was that five of the six were down.

For one glorious moment, I actually thought we had this battle locked up.

Wrong.

The giant, maybe reacting to what had just happened to his buds, went completely off the rails. He threw himself at Sharyn, who lifted her blade to meet him. Vader went right into the big guy's chest, undoubtedly piercing his heart. But what good was that when the darned thing wasn't beating anyway?

Cursing, Sharyn tried to pull it out. But once again, the enormous Type Two proved himself to be amazingly fast. He snatched up the Boss Angel, wrapping his bloated, putrid hands around her upper body and pinning her arms. Then, lifting her off her feet, he squeezed brutally.

Sharyn cried out and dropped her sword. The giant kicked it away.

Then he *threw* her.

This wasn't the offhand slap he'd given Burt, who still lay dazed on the floor. This was vicious and deliberate, and it had all the monster's strength behind it. Sharyn flew across the room, her arms and legs flailing.

Then she slammed headfirst into the far wall. I actually heard the *crack*, and the sound of it made my blood go cold.

Katie screamed, "Sharyn!" Then she ran around the giant and toward where the Boss Angel's broken body lay in a heap on the tiles.

The huge Type Two whirled on Helene.

He spoke in English, his voice as deep as thunder. "What did you just *do*, girl?"

Helene stared up at him, her face pale. Bravely, she

raised her Ritter. "The same thing I'm gonna do to you!" she exclaimed.

She jabbed at him, but he knocked the syringe from her grasp with a single swat of his massive paw. Then he grabbed her by the throat.

"No!" I screamed. I tried to rise to my feet only to lose my balance and fall back. I didn't vomit this time, just heaved a little, which I suppose was a sign of improvement. But my head still swam.

Fortunately, Chuck and Burt were in better shape. They closed in on the giant from behind. Chuck delivered a well-placed kick to the monster's lower back that he completely ignored. Then Burt pushed Chuck aside and slammed his Ritter into the Corpse's unguarded kidney.

An instant later, he stepped back, his face reddening.

The plunger was gone from the syringe and all its salt-water drained off. It must have broken when he'd been knocked down.

"Crap," I heard him mutter.

The giant lifted Helene off the floor, one of his bloated, snow shovel–sized hands locked around her slender throat. At the same time, his other arm swung like a baseball bat, catching Burt in the side of the head and knocking him into Chuck. Both of them went down hard, the wind knocked out of them.

Then the Type Two looked over at me, and reading the horror on my face, he grinned.

There were no bugs in his teeth. In fact, he had no teeth at all. His mouth looked like a twisted black pit that had been dug into the purplish, slimy surface of his face.

In Deadspeak, he said, *"Watch. Girl. Die."*

Helene!

The word filled my mind, pushing away everything else. Sharyn lay unmoving near the entrance to Cell Block Six, with Katie cradling her head. Burt and Chuck flopped on the floor like landed fish, their chests heaving as they tried to convince their lungs to expand and let in air.

And Helene hung helplessly in the giant's grasp, her eyes wide, her face going purple.

Again, I tried to find my feet. My head felt twice its normal size.

You just got a bad bump! I told myself. *Most of it's shock. Move!*

I staggered a step. Two. It was like navigating one of those moon bounces.

Move! Or she's gonna die!

I moved, one foot in front of the next, with the prison hub pitching and yawing around me like a boat on rough water. Finally, I saw the giant's huge, broad back looming before me. Only then did I realize I had no weapon. My pocket-knife was God knew where, lost someplace in the room. My Super Soaker was history. And something told me my fists weren't going to do a thing to this Dead Superman.

Then I spotted Vader.

It lay where Sharyn had dropped it, just a few feet away. I reached for it, leaning over, struggling to keep my churning stomach in line as my trembling hand closed around its hilt. When I straightened again, the room was still spinning, though not quite as badly.

At least I could keep my balance, which was good because I needed it.

Helene had stopped gasping. I couldn't even hear her struggling anymore.

Oh God...

I raised the sword, and with a great heave, I drove its point into the base of the giant's skull. I heard a *scrape* that set my teeth on edge as the blade glanced off his collarbone. But I kept going, getting my shoulder under the sword's guard and pushing upward with my knees.

Corpses don't feel pain. That's both an asset *and* a liability. Pain, you see, has a purpose.

It tells you when you're in trouble.

But this giant felt nothing at all as Vader drilled all the way into his brain.

I heard rather than saw Helene fall to the floor, felt rather than saw the giant topple sideways. He hit the floor so hard that the impact vibrated up through my shoes. I almost fell too, but after some struggle, I managed to step forward over the helpless giant and catch the wall with one hand. It steadied me.

"Sharyn's hurt bad!" I heard Katie yell. But at that

moment, I didn't care. Well, I cared. I mean, of course, I cared. It was just that—

"Helene?" I croaked.

I slid my back down the wall until I sat right beside where the girl lay. Trembling, I put a hand on her shoulder and shook her.

She didn't move.

Oh God. Please...

"Helene!" I coughed, a bit louder this time. Then I shook her again.

With a loud gasp, she sat bolt upright and drew in a mighty lungful of air. Her face, despite the cold, appeared soaked in sweat, and the eyes that found mine looked glassy.

"You okay?" I asked—pleaded, really.

When she replied, her voice sounded raspy. "Think so."

My heart started beating again.

"Jeez!" Chuck moaned as he and Burt finally caught their breath. "What a freak *that* dude was!"

I managed a nod. "My pocketknife's...over there," I said, pointing to where I thought it might have fallen.

"I'll look for it," Burt said.

Chuck came over to us. "You two okay?"

"I'm good," I said. And I was. My stomach had settled, and the room wasn't spinning anymore. Well, not much. "Helene?"

"I'm good too," the girl replied. Then she fixed me with her hazel eyes. I noticed that one of them had some blood in its white part, probably from the near strangling. "Thanks, Will."

I nodded, feeling vaguely uncomfortable and almost faint with relief. We helped each other to our feet and staggered over to where Sharyn lay, her head resting in Katie's lap. The younger girl looked up. There were tears on her cheeks. "She's hurt bad. She won't wake up."

"We gotta get her out of here," I said.

"Where's the FBI dude?" Helene asked.

Burt, who was dutifully scanning the hub floor, pointed toward the doorway to Cell Box Three. "He's in there. I passed him as I was coming in. I think he's unconscious."

As Helene helped Katie, I went to look.

Just beyond the archway stood a wheeled gurney, the collapsible kind like paramedics use. On it laid a man in his thirties, with short, dark hair and a neatly trimmed goatee. His eyes were shut, and his mouth hung slack. Definitely alive, though he looked heavily drugged.

"Hey," I said, shaking his shoulder as I had Helene's. It had worked then, so maybe it would work now.

It didn't.

I checked his pulse. It was strong. At least the guy wasn't likely to die on us. But moving him out of here was going to be a problem. A bunch of kids didn't just wheel a gurney out onto Fairmount Avenue without drawing some stares.

Frowning, I returned to the hub.

Helene, Chuck, and Katie were huddled around Sharyn. Burt had found my pocketknife. Seeing me, he tossed it over. "Wish I had one of those," he said wistfully.

"Yeah?" I said, surprised by how smoothly I caught it. "Considering how much I've been losing it lately, maybe it'd be better off with somebody else."

"I think Sharyn's in big trouble," Katie reported, sounding miserable. "I checked her eyes. One pupil's big. The other's small."

"Is that bad?" Chuck asked.

"It's not good!" the girl snapped at him.

Helene said, "We gotta get her back to Haven."

"And Ramirez too," I added. "He's out cold. Drugged maybe. No way he's walking out of here."

Chuck muttered, "What a screwup."

"At least we're all alive," I told him. That thought made me risk a glance at Helene, hoping I wouldn't catch her looking at me. I did. She smiled, and I turned away again. My stomach shuddered strangely—probably still a little queasy. "But we're not going to be able to get Ramirez and Sharyn into the van. Not carrying them. Not in broad daylight."

Helene added, "And with all these Corpses down for the count, you *know* there are more on the way…and soon!"

"What do we do?" Burt asked.

I didn't know. Then I did.

"Check these Corpses for cell phones," I said. "I've got an idea."

CHAPTER 12

LILITH'S MORNING

An ambulance?" the Queen of the Dead asked incredulously. "They stole an ambulance?"

"*Yes. Mistress,*" the big fool from the prison answered in the Ancient Tongue.

"English!" she cried, rising from behind her chair. She slammed one fist against her desktop, and when she lifted her hand away, she noticed that some skin and fluid had stayed behind, smeared against the heavy varnish.

This body is withering. I'll have to arrange for another.

The two of them were alone in her office on the fifth floor of City Hall. The fool standing across from her was wrapped in a new body. His old one, a particularly large specimen— difficult to find—had been rendered useless that morning at Eastern State Penitentiary. Apparently a sword had been driven through his brain pan.

The Undertakers.

"Yes…sorry, mistress," the fool stammered. "English."

The Queen sneered at him. "And just how did a handful of human schoolchildren go about stealing an ambulance?"

"After the boy incapacitated me, he used my mobile phone to call an ambulance. He told the emergency dispatcher that they'd been part of a school field trip to the prison and that a part of the ceiling in the hub had collapsed. Then he and one of the girls went to open the gates while the others arranged the room."

"Arranged?" Lilith demanded. "What does *that* mean?"

The fool explained, "They cleaned up the mess as best they could and dragged the remaining bodies into one of the old prison cells."

"Including you?"

"Yes, mistress…though in my case, it took three of them. My host body was somewhat large."

Unlike your intellect. "Go on."

"Well…once we were all piled up in the cell, I could no longer see what was happening, but I heard the boy and girl return a few minutes later with two emergency medical technicians. The EMTs were pushing something on wheels, a gurney probably. The Undertakers' manner immediately changed. They started to all talk at once…and they sounded frightened, shaken, very different from what they'd been in battle."

Clever, Lilith grudgingly admitted to herself. "And the EMTs accepted this story?"

TY DRAGO

"It appeared so, mistress. There was a good deal of noise as they examined the girl I'd injured and put her on their gurney. That was when the Undertakers produced the guns."

"Guns?" Lilith demanded. "What guns?"

"Well...*our* guns, mistress," the fool replied, shuffling uncomfortably in his new body. It wasn't a particularly good specimen, much smaller than his last one. And being at least a month dead, the bones cracked noisily under the layers of rotting skin and muscle. But it was the best the idiot could have hoped for under the circumstances. "The Undertakers took our human weapons and hid them under their coats. This was while the boy and girl were away fetching the ambulance."

"You're telling me that these...children...threatened two adult EMTs with firearms?"

The fool nodded. "They unloaded them first."

"Did they?"

Lilith frowned. Her people at the prison had been "wearing" police officers. As such, each had carried a standard-issue pistol—loaded. But these were just a part of the disguise, never intended to be drawn from their holsters, much less used. In her native world, weapons were considered cowardly, even blasphemous.

It was a cultural inhibition that could be...inconvenient.

Still, it had never occurred to her that these props could be taken by the enemy and used against them. After all, bullets couldn't kill the dead.

And yet, these…brats…had stolen and made good use of them!

Something to consider.

"I believe they forced the EMTs to remove their jackets before handcuffing them. Finally, two of the boys, posing as EMTs, loaded the injured girl and the FBI agent into the ambulance and drove off, leaving behind the redheaded boy and the two girls."

"And what did *they* do?" Lilith asked.

"As near as I could determine, mistress, they…apologized."

"Apologized?"

"Yes, mistress. I heard him. I think it was the redheaded boy."

"Apologized to whom?"

"To the EMTs, mistress. He explained that they needed to get their friends to safety and that they meant no harm. Then he apparently showed them that the guns they carried weren't loaded and promised to call the police as soon as they were clear of the prison."

"I see," the Queen remarked thoughtfully. "And how did the captured men react?"

"Not well. They uttered a good many human curses and threats. But finally, they went quiet, and the Undertakers left. Apparently, they kept their word because a short time later, the police *did* come, with some of our brethren among them. They found us and saw to our safe removal and transfer. Then I was summoned here."

Resourceful, these Undertakers. Children, yes—but clever and courageous.

And dangerous.

After last night's encounter outside the prison had ended with one of her minions missing, Lilith had decided to increase the guards on the FBI agent. Excessive, certainly, to ensure the security of one drugged prisoner—more than enough to discourage any intruders.

And yet, the Undertakers had come in anyway.

Ramirez's abduction had been a risk but a calculated one. Now, however, thanks to this redheaded boy and his friends, that risk had blown up in her face.

Where have you taken him, you meddlesome brats? And where are you hiding?

Their last lair had been in an old warehouse on Green Street in the Callowhill section of the city. But that had been abandoned months ago. Where were they now? Somewhere in the city surely.

Perhaps close.

Then the fool said, "I thought he meant to…end me, mistress."

Lilith looked up. Her minion was trembling. "What's that?"

"End my existence," he explained. "With those needles. You assigned seven of us to that prison. Only three returned. And after what I did to their leader…"

"Sharyn Jefferson." She'd recognized the description.

"Yes, mistress."

"Did you at least manage to kill her?" the Queen demanded.

"I'm not...certain," the fool stammered. "But she was critically injured. I'm sure she'll die."

Lilith's glare made him shrink back in fear. "Oh... you're sure, are you? So, tell me, why *did* the Undertakers spare you?"

"They didn't want to," he said, visibly cowering. "Most of them wanted to use their last remaining needle to finish me." The fool actually shuddered. "But the redheaded boy...he stopped them. He said he'd let me live...so I could deliver a message."

"A message...for who?"

"For *you*, mistress."

"What message?" the Queen demanded.

"He said, 'Tell the Queen that Will Ritter, the dude who iced Kenny Booth, says hi...and tell her *she's* next.' Those were his exact words."

Will Ritter.

The boy who killed Booth.

"Did he really?" Lilith remarked. "Such bravado."

The Queen tapped a button on her desk phone with one red-lacquered finger. "Come in here!" she commanded.

Within seconds, her assistant appeared.

His name was Gerald Pierce, and she'd chosen him personally from among the rabble who'd welcomed her through the Rift. Since then, Pierce had demonstrated enthusiasm, loyalty—and relatively high intelligence for a Warrior Caste. Also, his host was always fresh. Like herself, Pierce preferred frequent changes, never occupying a single cadaver for longer than two weeks.

Lilith appreciated such fastidiousness. So many of her minions wore their bodies until the flesh literally fell off their bones.

Very uncouth.

"Pierce," Lilith said. "Please take this minion somewhere and amputate his arms and legs. Then leave him in a morgue drawer somewhere…alone in the dark. In a month or two, I'll decide whether to let him transfer."

"Yes, Ms. Cavanaugh," Pierce replied. He always used her human title, never "mistress." It was something else about him that she appreciated.

"What? Wait!" the fool stammered. "Mistress, please! I—"

"You…what?" Lilith demanded. "You allowed a band of children to sneak into *my* prison, kill…not incapacitate, not overcome, but *kill*…four of my minions and make off with a prisoner who holds extremely dangerous information? Is that what you were going to say?"

"No. Mistress. Please…"

The Queen sneered at him. "Consider yourself fortunate that I don't destroy you myself here and now. As it is, I'll give you two months solitude to consider your failure. Then we'll see. Consider that punishment merciful…certainly more so than you're worth."

She faced Pierce. "Get him out of here. Then come right back. It appears the Undertakers have discovered a method for killing us."

Pierce looked stunned. And she couldn't really blame him. Real death was rare among the *Malum*.

"Yes, it's…disturbing," Lilith said. "Let's discuss it when you return."

"Certainly, Ms. Cavanaugh."

Pierce left with the fool following, looking downcast and terrified but obedient. Good. No struggling. No further protests. Perhaps she'd let the idiot live after all. While blind obedience was a weakness, it was one that she could use.

Sometime later, Pierce returned as ordered. But he wasn't alone. With him came Martin D'Angelo, Philadelphia's chief of police. He, like Pierce and the fool from the prison, was of the Warrior Caste and had served Lilith's predecessor, Kenny Booth. D'Angelo's Cover was that of a fat human male, and he seemed to favor hosts that matched. The body the chief now wore was at least a month old but large-boned and still thick with rotting meat.

The Queen frowned. "What's this?"

D'Angelo stepped forward and held out the thing he carried. It looked like a shoebox.

Her first thought was that this was some sort of attempt at humor. Part of her own Cover was Lilith Cavanaugh's reputation as a staple of fashion, which in this world included the acquisition and collection of "stylish" footwear.

Had the idiot brought her a pair of shoes as a joke?

But, no. The Warrior Caste *had* no sense of humor.

"Am I supposed to know what that is?" she asked impatiently.

D'Angelo replied in English, "We were able to secure an anchor shard, mistress."

The Queen's eyes lit up—at least her Cover's eyes did. The eyes of her host remained as dead as ever. Without a word, she snatched the shoebox, took it to her desk, and hurriedly opened it.

What she found inside inspired her first genuine smile of day.

Slowly, reverently, she withdrew the shard. It was perhaps ten inches long and an inch wide. Any human who happened to look upon it might call it "quartz," but in truth, this particular substance, native to the *Malum* homeworld, had no Earth equivalent. Much harder that diamond, far clearer than glass, and glowing as if powered from within, the anchor shard was a treasure indeed.

"How many of our people did we sacrifice to get this?" she asked D'Angelo.

"Only a hundred and fifty."

"All worker caste?"

"Yes, mistress."

The Queen nodded. Perfectly acceptable losses; a bargain

really, when one considered the cost and difficulty involved in bringing even ordinary solid matter through the Rift. And an anchor shard was nothing like "ordinary."

She handed the shard to Pierce, who accepted it without hesitation. "Keep this on your person at all times," she commanded. "Guard it until we're ready to use it."

"With my life, Ms. Cavanaugh," her assistant said.

She faced the Chief. "D'Angelo, I want you to send your best men to the prison to begin preparing it. I want the anchor shard in place and functioning by the middle of next week."

"Of course, mistress," D'Angelo replied. Then the fat fool bowed low, a *Malum* gesture of respect, as he departed.

I need to break him of that.

With Pierce watching, she went to the window and gazed down at the courtyard. Philadelphia's city hall was an imposing structure, more fortress than office building—with a five-hundred-foot central tower that offered an impressive view. The base of that tower stood directly across from her office window.

Lilith visited the tower's observation deck quite often. Perhaps she'd do so later today. Few tourists would risk the bitter winds this time of year, but the cold was not a problem for her. She liked the view. It sparked her imagination.

It was up there that her most recent plan had formed.

"The acquisition of the shard is an unexpected windfall," she told Pierce without turning. "It means we can accelerate our plans. And the more aggressive our schedule…the more rapidly our people are able to infiltrate the layers of human government…the faster we can prevail.

"And the faster I can abandon this filthy world, mistress?" Pierce added.

"Exactly so. Unfortunately, it seems the Undertakers have developed a weapon to use against us. A *lethal* weapon. I need to understand more about it."

Pierce replied, "I've already put the right brethren to work on it."

He'd anticipated her. "Good work."

"Thank you, mistress."

"You're excused."

Pierce left her alone. She continued gazing out her office window, down at the scurrying humans in the courtyard, going about their pointless lives, huddled against the cold.

I'm going to kill you all. And I'm going to tear down every-thing you have ever built.

So far, this had been a fortuitous day.

Her desk phone buzzed. Pierce said, "Ms. Cavanaugh. You have a visitor."

Lilith's eyes fell to her daily calendar. It was noon, and her first scheduled appointment wasn't until two o'clock.

"A visitor? Who?"

"Ms. Susan Ritter," Pierce replied. "She's the widow of Detective Karl Ritter. She'd like to talk to you about her son…Will."

Will Ritter.

The *Malum* had a saying: "When the prey falls into your jaws, you don't stop to say thanks or ask why. You just eat."

"Please send her in," Lilith said with a smile.

CHAPTER 13

SPITTING IMAGE

I'm not going to tell you exactly how we got Sharyn and Ramirez back to Haven. Frankly, I'm not real proud of it. We did what we had to do. Let's just leave it at that.

Katie saw to the van while Helene and I rushed to the infirmary. There, we found Tom standing over his sister, who lay on the ambulance gurney. Agent Hernandez occupied the next one over, still heavily drugged.

Tom met my eyes. I'd never seen him look so worried. "How is she?" I asked.

"Still unconscious," he replied. "What happened back there, bro?"

I told him everything, finishing with, "I'm sorry, Chief. If I'd moved faster…"

"Ain't your fault," Tom replied, sounding like he meant it. I felt relieved. "How's your head?"

"Okay," I said. And it was, more or less. At least the

dizziness and nausea were gone, though I had a killer headache.

Tom turned to Helene. "Come here."

She went to him, and he put his hands on her shoulders and examined her throat. The Corpse's fingers had left huge bruises that had begun to turn purple. "Your throat hurt?"

"Yeah," she croaked.

"Ian!" Tom called.

Leaning over Sharyn's gurney was Ian McDonald. Ian was Haven's medic, the son of a big shot Philly surgeon, who'd gotten the Sight and been forced to go on the run like the rest of us. He wasn't a real doctor, of course, being only fifteen, but he was smart and did his best to do the job. The infirmary was crammed with textbooks as big as cinderblocks that were all about all things medical. Ian spent hours studying them. I didn't envy the kid.

Ian hurried over and lifted Helene's chin. "Still having trouble breathing?" he asked her.

"A little."

"It's swelled up some…inside…constricting your windpipe. Could be worse. If he'd pressed any harder, he might have done permanent damage. Lucky."

"Yeah," Helene whispered. "I feel lucky."

"Go get some ice cream. Maybe a Popsicle. The cold'll help with the swelling. And I'll give you some ibuprofen for the pain. You'll be okay."

"I'm okay *now*," the girl replied, pushing his hands away.

"Have a look at Will," Tom said. "Got socked in the head."

The medic fingered the lump on the back of my skull. Unsurprisingly, it hurt. "Ow!" I exclaimed.

"Skin's not broke," Ian reported. "Did you get dizzy?"

"Yeah," I admitted.

"Still dizzy?"

I shook my head. At least it didn't hurt to do *that*— probably a good sign.

"How long did it last?" he asked.

"I dunno. A minute or two."

"What's that stuff all over you?"

I felt like I was being interrogated. "Corpse juice. Chuck stuck one of them while it was on top of me, and it kind of exploded in my face."

The medic grimaced and looked carefully in both my eyes. Then he pulled my nose up uncomfortably and peered up my nostrils. "Swallow any of it?"

"Yeah," I admitted, and my stomach rumbled a little at the memory. "But I puked it back up."

At that, he almost smiled. "I'll bet you did." He turned to Tom. "He's okay. Cadaver fluids are toxic, but it sounds like his body evacuated them."

"How about his head?"

"A bad bump. Maybe a very minor concussion. He's fine."

Tom nodded.

"What's going on with Sharyn?" Helene asked.

Ian looked at her, then at me, then at Tom, and then over his shoulder at the gurney. "She's a different story. She's also got a concussion…but hers is a lot worse."

"What *is* a concussion…exactly?" I asked.

Ian replied, "Well, your brain kind of floats inside your skull…surrounded by fluid that acts like a shock absorber. That's why just banging your head doesn't instantly kill you. But Sharyn was hit harder than the shock absorber could handle, and her brain got knocked around. Will, yours only got knocked a little bit. No big deal. But Sharyn—"

"How much worse is it?" asked Tom, looking miserable.

"That depends. Without an X-ray…and somebody to read it…it's hard to know. If she wakes up, she should be fine."

"If?" Helene gasps.

Ian looked at Tom, who seemed to age ten years before my eyes. "Yeah. I'm sorry. If."

The Chief of the Undertakers slowly nodded. "Ian…will you stay with her?"

"All day and all night," the medic replied.

"Thanks, man." He visibly swallowed. "How's Ramirez?"

"He's okay," said Ian. "I think the Corpses chloroformed him at first and then kept him out…probably with sodium pentothal. I don't know when they last dosed him, but from the look of him, I'd say he's going to be out for hours and—"

Then the guy on the gurney said something that froze us all where we stood.

"Karl?"

Hearing my father's name sent a shock dancing up my back. With a gasp, I stared at Hugo Ramirez of the FBI.

And he stared right back at me.

"Karl?" he repeated. The word was slurred. Then his eyes rolled back in his head, and he slumped again, going limp.

"He's be doin' that on and off for a while," Ian remarked. "That's the first time he talked though."

Tom said, "Ian, I want you to move Agent Ramirez's gurney into my office…and I want you to handcuff him to it."

We all looked at him in surprise.

"Please just do it," Tom said. "And…Ian…let me know when my sister wakes up." That was the way he said it. Not if. When.

"Sure, Chief," said Ian.

"And make sure Helene gets her ice cream and her pills. Helene, you're off duty for the next eight hours. Rest up. I need you at your best."

Helene looked ready to protest. But then she closed her mouth and nodded.

Ian called, "Amy?" And from a corner of the room, a petite blond girl appeared. She'd been sitting at an old wooden school desk, involved in some task. Inventory maybe? Patient records? Did Ian even *keep* patient records? In any event, the girl had been so quiet and her movements so slight that I hadn't even noticed her.

"Yes, Ian?" she asked in a tiny voice. Then her eyes touched mine. "Hi, Will."

"Hi, Amy," I said. Then, as a matter of habit, I smiled at her.

Not many people smiled at Amy Filewicz. She'd had it worse than most. The Corpses had caught her early and had brainwashed her with the *Pelligog*, these disgusting ten-legged spiderlike things they imported from their native world. Once one of these spiders bores into you, your free will turns to mush. The Deaders had used them on this poor little girl, and then they'd sent her to join the Undertakers as a spy. In the days that followed, Amy killed one boy and almost killed me too before she was finally released from *Pelligog* control and rescued.

Now, despite the fact that she'd been used as a tool, her mind twisted, most of Haven still treated her coolly. They couldn't forget the boy named Kyle, who'd died by her hand. Only Nick, the Boss Mom, and now Ian were really kind to her. Well, them—and Helene and me. We both knew what the *Pelligog* could do and how helpless you were against its influence.

Those spiders still made guest appearances in my nightmares.

"Amy," Ian said, "could you take Helene to one of the first aid benches and get her ice cream for her throat and a supply of ibuprofen?"

"Sure," Amy replied. "How many pills?"

"Eight should do it. Helene, that's one every six hours until they're gone."

"Got it," Helene said. Then, giving me a quick smile, she let Amy take her hand and lead her off into the shadows.

"How long has Amy been working for you?" I asked the medic.

"Her first day," he replied. "Nick's idea. He thinks she needs to get more involved. But it's actually been pretty cool having her around. Never had an assistant before. She's been doing some of the stuff I've never had time for."

"Solid, Ian," Tom said, a little distractedly. "Will…with me."

Then he turned and left the infirmary. I gave Helene a final wave, pointed a worried look in Sharyn's direction, eyed Ramirez nervously, and then hurried after him.

"Wait up," I called.

Tom was walking really fast down the corridor in the direction of his office. The Chief's back was ramrod straight, and he uncharacteristically ignored the hellos and questions about Sharyn he got from the kids we passed along the way.

"You okay?" I asked, catching up to him.

He didn't answer me. Instead, he stopped outside of a particular curtain I knew well and pushed it aside. Then, as I followed him inside, he switched on the lights.

Finally, he said, "No, bro. I ain't okay."

The room was small. Like the rest of the Undertakers' headquarters, it had brick walls, a dirt floor, and a low ceiling. The only light came from a bare hanging bulb, one of hundreds that the Monkeys had strung up throughout this old subbasement. What set this particular room apart was that while there was a cot, complete with pillow and blanket, no one lived here.

No one ever had.

This was Tom's memorial to my father, Karl Ritter, the founder of the Undertakers. He'd been dead for more than two years, a victim in the early days of the war with the Corpses. At the time, Tom had set aside Dad's old room at Haven, decorating it with pictures and mementos until it looked a bit like a shrine. My first day as a raw recruit, he'd shown it to me.

Except *that* Haven wasn't *this* Haven.

A few months back, circumstances—*me*, to be honest— had forced the Undertakers to abandon the warehouse that had been their lair and move to this more secure if less comfortable headquarters. And Tom had moved his Ritter Memorial too.

"You added some pictures," I said.

"Yeah," he replied. His voice was always softer, more subdued in my dad's shrine. "Found them in an old box of Karl's personal possessions that turned up after the move. Look at this one."

He pointed to a three-by-five of my father cradling a baby. My mother stood beside him. Both were smiling.

Looking at it, I felt that old familiar ache kick in.

Tom said, "I'm guessing that's you in his arms."

"Guess so," I said, swallowing dryly. The shameful truth was that I didn't visit this place nearly as much as Tom did. I sometimes asked myself why this shrine, which was managed and maintained with such love and respect by the Chief of the Undertakers, held so little appeal for me.

But, of course, I knew the reason.

Being here *hurt*.

"Sharyn's gonna be okay, Tom," I said.

"Is she?"

"Of course she is."

"Ain't no 'of course' about it, Will. Was Tara fine? Or Kyle? Or your old man?" He sat heavily down on the cot. "This is war, and wars got casualties. Soldiers die. And because…except for Karl…all our soldiers are kids, kids die. It happens, and wishing it didn't ain't gonna change it."

"But Sharyn's different!" I protested. "She's—"

He silenced me with a gesture. "Sharyn's tough, and if anyone can get through this okay, it's her. But I've been doing this job too long to have any illusions about her chances. She's my sister, and I love her. Losing her would be like losing my right arm. No…it'd be worse than that. It'd be like losing half of myself.

"But it *can* happen, bro…at any time. That's war."

I tried to come up with something encouraging to say. But Tom was right. As amazing as his sister was, she remained as mortal as the rest of us.

Instead, I asked, "Is that what you brought me in here to talk about?"

He uttered a small, humorless laugh. "Nope. I guess part of it is that right now, I need to be in here. And I kinda wanted you with me. You know what I mean?"

And I did. My father had been Tom's father's too—in a way. Karl Ritter had rescued Tom and Sharyn from the streets, kept them out of prison, and helped them find purpose in their lives. Then, when the Corpse Invasion began, he'd been their leader, their general, and their inspiration. His death had broken Tom's heart as much as it had broken mine.

So why did Tom *like* coming into this room while I didn't?

"The memories in here keep me strong," he said, as if reading my mind. "Not just the personal memories...the times he spent with me. But all his past. Just knowing that he lived, that he was real, helps sometimes." Then he shook his head. "That don't make no sense."

"Yeah, it does," I replied. Then, "Tom?"

"Yeah, Will?"

"Why do you think Agent Ramirez said my father's name?"

He shrugged. "Could be a coincidence. There are a lot of Karls in the world."

"You believe that?" I asked.

"Nope."

"He was staring right at me when he said it," I pointed out.

"I know. That's the other reason I brought you in here. I

want you with me when Ramirez wakes up. I want you in the room when I talk with him. Just the three of us."

I blinked. "What for?"

Tom smiled gently. "Look at that picture of your dad. The one where he's holding the baby."

I looked. The photo had to be a dozen years old—my father appeared younger than I remembered him but still recognizable. His shock of red hair, like mine. His green eyes, like mine. His thin, angled face and broad smile.

God, how I missed him.

"You don't see it, do you?" Tom said, rising from the cot to stand beside me. "Ramirez did. Even as out of it as he was, he saw it."

"Saw what?"

"You look like your dad, Will. So much so that it some-times startles me. Lately, I'll turn a corner in this cat-infested pit and see you and…just for a split second…I'll think I'm looking at him. Gives me quite a shock."

"Used to feel that way right after he died. Even though I knew he was gone, a part o' me still kept expecting him to come strolling into Haven…the old Haven…with that cocky smile on his face and quoting Mark Twain."

"Mark Twain," I echoed. Dad's favorite writer. He'd read *Tom Sawyer* and *Huckleberry Finn* to me when I'd been very young. And he quoted Twain all the time.

"News of my death," Tom recited, "has been greatly exaggerated."

"I wish," I muttered.

"Me too, bro."

Actually, I found out much later in school that this wasn't the original wording of the quote. What Twain *really* said was, "The report of my death was an exaggeration." My dad got it wrong.

But I like his version better.

For a couple of minutes, we stood in silence, side by side, studying the old photo.

I looked like my father? Mom had always said so, but the idea that the resemblance could be so strong that someone would mistake us—well, that had simply never occurred to me.

Tom said, "It ain't just a physical resemblance. When you came to us four months ago, you were a scared kid…and with good reason. But since then, you've gotten tougher day by day. We all seen it. It's why me and Sharyn made you the youngest-ever Angel trainee. You're a born leader, like your dad. And like him, you don't really know it."

I stared at Tom, trying to make sense of what he was saying.

He tilted his head and regarded me, "You still don't get your role around here, do you, bro?"

"My role?"

But then the Chief waved his hand, as if dismissing the whole topic. "I think Ramirez knew your dad, and maybe that's connected to why the Corpses took him. Anyway, when he wakes up, I need to make him understand that the dudes that got him now ain't the ones who originally took him. That's he's been *rescued*. That'll be the easy part. But then I gotta tell him stuff he *ain't* gonna want to hear. And I'm hopin' that you being there might make some things a bit easier for him to take…because you're Karl Ritter's son. It's a shot in the dark."

"What is it you have to tell him that he won't want to hear?" I asked.

Tom laughed again. As with the last one, it sounded sad and hollow. "That after saving his butt from the Deaders…I can't let him go."

CHAPTER 14

OPPORTUNITY KNOCKS

Two hundred feet directly above Karl Ritter's memorial, Lilith Cavanaugh checked her reflection in the small, tasteful mirror that hung on the wall beside her office door. Her Cover was perfect, her blond hair expertly styled, her dress flawlessly tailored, her makeup impeccably applied—the very picture of professional, political womanhood.

Then, for a moment, she examined the body underneath. *Definitely time for a replacement.*

The skin was turning from gray to splotchy purple. Her hair had begun to fall out, and two of her teeth felt loose.

I'll have to have Pierce make arrangements for a new host.

She'd lost count of how many she'd occupied since that first night when she'd crossed the Void. At first, obtaining replacements had been fairly easy. Her minions controlled the city morgue and made sure to notify the Queen each time a young female body in good condition reached their tables.

Better still, once a particular body had decomposed beyond its usefulness, it was a simple thing to have it cremated at the city's expense.

Convenient.

Unfortunately, young female deaths—at least the right sort of deaths—had proven difficult to come by. Fire and car crash victims, after all, just wouldn't do. Too gauche.

So toward the end of last year, Lilith had instituted a new "policy." She'd ordered carefully selected minions to go out into the city night in search of promising candidates—young women who lived alone and would not be missed. It was a radical approach and not without its risks, but the flow of fresh hosts had proven worth it—for a while.

But over the last few weeks, she'd been forced to abandon it. Despite all their best efforts, the human media had begun to take notice.

This left Lilith in the deplorable position of having to wear these loathsome human bodies far longer than she would have liked.

It was degrading!

Still, life went on. Pasting a broad smile on her painted lips, the Queen opened her office door.

"Mrs. Ritter?" she asked.

Her visitor looked up. The woman's face was awash with complex emotions: desperation, terror, despair, hope. It was really quite amusing.

Ritter was tall, almost as tall as Lilith's Cover. Her long

hair was blond and her skin smooth and flawless, though her makeup was minimal. She wore department store clothes that seemed chosen more for comfort than style. But she wore them well, and when she stood and approached, the Queen couldn't help but admire the grace with which this human creature moved.

Interesting.

"Yes," she said. "Susan."

"Very nice to meet you, Susan," Lilith offered her hand, which the woman accepted. "I'm Lilith Cavanaugh. Please, come into my office."

Susan Ritter followed her. "Thanks for seeing me like this, Ms. Cavanaugh...without an appointment, I mean."

"Not at all," the Queen gestured to one of her visitor chairs. Then she settled herself beside her desk. "As it happens, you caught on me a slow day. Only six hours of meetings between now and five o'clock."

Ritter did her best to laugh but didn't quite manage it.

Too much on her mind perhaps.

Poor thing.

"What can I do for you, Mrs. Ritter?" she asked.

"Susan," the woman repeated.

"Yes, of course. Susan."

"You can help me find my son," Susan said.

"Your son?"

"Will. He disappeared from school back in October. He and a girl named Helene Boettcher. Nobody's seen them since."

Oh, they've been seen. Just not by you.

"I see," Lilith replied. "I'm sorry, but I'm not familiar with the case. Missing persons are, of course, a police matter."

"I've been to the police," Susan insisted. "Called all of my husband's old friends on the force when it first happened. They promised to move heaven and earth to find Will. That's a direct quote. And maybe they did. But it didn't help. They never found him…and lately, I've come to think they've stopped looking."

"I'm sure that's not the case." In fact, Lilith knew the opposite to be true. Her minions on the police force were very eager to locate young Mr. Ritter.

But the boy, like all the Undertakers, seemed very good at staying hidden.

"Well…maybe not. But I'm done waiting," Susan said firmly. "I took a day off work. I've just spent my entire morning walking around Center City…looking for him. I knew it was crazy. I knew it made looking for a needle in haystack look easy. But I did it anyway."

Susan rubbed her perfect face with her perfect hands.

"I never really expected to find Will, but it was worse than that. I saw him *everywhere*. Every time a boy in a hoodie went by, I was convinced it was him. A couple of times, I was so sure that I actually grabbed a stranger by the shoulder before I realized my mistake."

"This must be terrible," Lilith said.

Susan fidgeted and nodded. "Finally, it occurred to me to

come here…to you. I know that finding lost kids isn't your job. And I know all this happened before you even came to Philadelphia. You didn't know my husband, and you certainly don't know Will. But I've seen you interviewed, Ms. Cavanaugh. Time and again, you've talked about your 'open door' policy and about being the city's 'friend in need.' Well, I'm in serious need."

It was a public reputation the Queen had carefully cultivated. The formula was a simple one: the more the people of this city trusted her, the more damage she could do.

"Of course, Susan. And I'd like you to call me Lilith."

"Do you have any children, Lilith?"

"I'm sorry to say I don't," the Queen replied. "I've never married. Too career-minded, I suppose." Then, after a moment's calculation, she added, "I can't pretend to understand your pain, Susan. First, your husband…yes, I *am* new to the city, but Detective Ritter's reputation lives on…and now your son."

Susan's face twisted up, and for one delicious moment, Lilith thought she might cry. But she steadied herself. "I have a little girl. Emily. She's five. That's just old enough to understand what's happened to her brother but too young to be able to make any sense of it…not that I've been able to make any sense of it. And after what happened today…"

The Queen said, "And if I may ask, what exactly *did* happen today?"

Susan reached inside her jacket and produced a DVD, which she laid on the desktop. "This happened."

Lilith picked up the unlabeled disk and examined it.

"A message from my husband. He apparently left it with a lawyer two years ago to be delivered to my son on his thirteenth birthday. That's today."

The Queen's manicured brows knitted. "Really? Detective Ritter must have had a flair for the dramatic."

"He may have had a 'flair' for more than that," Susan replied, sounding almost bitter. Then, sighing, she added, "I think Karl may have been delusional."

"Delusional?"

"Unbalanced? He talks about some kind of secret invasion. And about 'seeing' things that most people can't see."

If Lilith had possessed a living spine, a chill might have run along it. As it was, all she felt was surprise—and anger. This Ritter family was proving to be quite a nuisance. No wonder Booth, vain fool that he'd been, had taken such an interest in them.

Now across from her sat the wife and mother of two of the *Malum's* most troublesome enemies. Susan looked half exhausted from worry and grief. But despite all that, she remained poised and resolute, a perfect specimen of human womanhood.

I could launch myself across the desk…right now. I could take her throat and apply just enough pressure to kill her. No broken neck. A broken neck would render the body useless. It would require precision and a certain delicacy of touch. But in five minutes' time, no more, I could be wearing that fine body.

No one knows she's here.

"Unbalanced?" Lilith asked gently. "I may be a relative newcomer to this city, but the idea of Detective Ritter having some kind of mental illness seems...unlikely. Can I see for myself what's on the disk?"

Susan nodded.

Lilith loaded it into the player beside her office's television.

The mother and the monster watched the short recording together in silence.

Karl Ritter spoke calmly. He looked directly into the camera lens, his tone frank and almost apologetic as he left this message for a son who, if Lilith had her way, would never live to see it. As Karl spoke, Lilith thrilled to see a single unconscious tear roll down Susan's cheek.

Human suffering was so...tasty.

When the DVD ended, Lilith said, "I can understand your concern."

Susan replied, "I lived with that man for eleven years. I loved him. But now I'm wondering if I ever knew him at all."

"I can appreciate that," the Queen said. And she meant it. Lilith *always* appreciated human closed-mindedness. It shielded her people.

It made things so easy.

"But that's not the half of it," Susan went on. "My son's been missing for four months! And the only word I've received is this." She produced a folded sheet of paper, which she handed across the desk to Lilith. "It came about a month after his disappearance. The handwriting is Will's. I'd swear to it!"

Frowning, the Queen unfolded the paper, noticing as she did the splotches of decomposition fluid her finger left on the table. The stains posed no danger, of course. Unlike her husband and son, Susan could neither see nor feel them. But they were irritating nonetheless.

The paper was a brief letter. It read:

Dear Mom,

I'm okay. I'm sorry I can't come home yet. I'm also sorry I can't tell you where I am. There's this stuff I have to do—important stuff. I know you're sad. I'm sad too. I know you're probably real worried about me. But I really really want you to trust me. Scary things are happening, and I have to fight them. It's a fight that Dad started before he died, and now it's my job to finish it. I know you don't understand, but it's really safer if you don't.

I'm not alone. I've made some good friends, and we're all working real hard so I can come home.

Until then, you've got to be real careful, so burn this letter. Take care of my sister and try not to worry *too* much. I know I used to tell you to stop babying me. That I wasn't a kid anymore. Well, it wasn't true then. It's true now.

I miss you.
Love,
Will

How sentimental these humans were. The child's letter warns his mother to be careful, warns her to burn the letter. And yet, here she sits, showing it off to a person she's only just met.

"My son's joined some kind of…cult, Lilith," Susan said, her voice cracking. "Karl mentioned the Undertakers. I've heard of them. They're supposed to have been involved in Kenny Booth's death last fall."

"Yes," the Queen remarked thoughtfully. She read through the letter a second time. "I'm going to need to keep this, Susan. And the DVD. For analysis."

The woman visibly paled. "Do you have to? They're all I've got. I…didn't think to make any copies."

"I'm sorry, but if you want my help, it's important that we find out as much as we can about your husband and your son…and their involvement in this street gang."

"So…you'll help me? I know this isn't in your job description. But—"

The Queen went to the woman and rested a reassuring hand on her shoulder. Susan looked up and offered Lilith a small, grateful smile. Tears glistened in her eyes.

It would be easy. Do it correctly, and her neck won't break. So easy.

"Susan, my 'job description' is to be whatever the good people of this city need me to be," the Queen said, smiling. "Of course, I'll help you. I'll do everything I can. I promise you. For now, go home to your little girl…Emily, was it?"

"Yes," Susah sighed. "Emily."

"Go home to her and wait. It may take a little time. But I'll call you the moment I know something."

Susan rose from her chair and hugged Lilith, the gesture as sudden as it was unwelcome. Lilith actually heard some of the bones in her current body crack, felt the tendons tear. The Ritter woman had just cost her two or three further days of use. Thanks to this ridiculous display of gratitude, the Queen would require a new, proper cadaver by nightfall.

Nevertheless, she smiled.

"Thank you. Oh God…thank you," Susan said, crying openly. Then, collecting herself, she let Lilith show her to door.

Karl Ritter's widow was smiling when she left.

As soon as the door to the outer office closed, Lilith said to Pierce, "I need a new body…right away."

"Yes, Ms. Cavanaugh."

"And have D'Angelo come see me. I have a mission for some of his better minions."

"Of course, mistress."

The Queen of the Dead considered chastising her assistant for using her *Malum* title. But right now, she simply felt too good.

A fortuitous day indeed!

CHAPTER 15

AGENT RAMIREZ

As I've said, Tom kept two rooms for himself. The outer one included a desk, a conference table, a bulletin board, and a few chairs. This was where he did his "Chief" stuff. The inner one, separated by a blanket hung across the opening, had a bed and small dresser in it.

It also—now—had a gurney.

We both sat in silence, Tom on his bed and me on a folding chair, waiting. Just waiting. Something I'd never been good at. Agent Hugo Ramirez stirred and murmured. He even rolled over a couple of times, but it was almost sixty minutes before our—what? Guest? Prisoner?—finally came around.

Ramirez swallowed dryly. His eyes settled on me. He blinked. I half-expected him to call me Karl again. But instead, he whispered, "Water?"

I got up and offered him a plastic bottle, holding it to his lips. He drank some and then nodded and lay back.

"Mi duele la cabeza," he muttered.

"Huh?" I said.

"Usted va a estar bien," Tom replied.

I looked at him. "You speak Spanish?"

"A little," he replied with a shrug.

The sounds of our voices seemed to rouse the FBI guy a little further. The next time he spoke, it was in faintly accented English. "Who are you?"

"I'm Tom Jefferson," the Chief said. "This here's Will Ritter. He's Karl's son."

Ramirez digested this news. His dark eyes regarded me thoughtfully. "Where am I?"

"Someplace safe," Tom replied.

Ramirez's laugh turned into a cough. He tried to sit up on the gurney. That was when he noticed the handcuffs fastening his right wrist to the gurney rail. He scowled at Tom. "What's *this*?"

"I'm sorry," the Chief told him. "We...need to keep you here for a while."

"We? Look, kid..."

"Don't call me 'kid,'" Tom said flatly. "I'm the Chief of the Undertakers."

"The Undertakers," he echoed, as if he knew the word.

Tom nodded. "We're the ones who saved your life today, Agent Ramirez. You'd been snatched by a group of cops who are part of an...organization...we call the 'Corpses.' Getting you away from them wasn't easy, and my sister got herself hurt doin' it. So I'm looking for a little respect from you."

"Respect?" Ramirez snapped. "I'm chained to the wall… Chief. Now I don't know what kind of game you boys are playing, but this is what's called abducting a federal agent, and it's a crime!"

Well, he sure seems wide awake now!

"I got that in the back of my mind," Tom said. "Now… how's about telling me what happened to you last night?"

"I'm not here to answer questions, son," Ramirez replied.

Tom slowly stood, his eyes flashing. Whenever he did that, he seemed to fill the room. "I'm not your son, Agent Ramirez. Right now, I'm your jailer. I'm the man who decides when you eat and when and where you get to use the toilet. This is my place, and these are my people. You'd best remember that."

Ramirez studied him—more curious, I thought, than intimated. "Chief of the Undertakers," he mused.

"Straight up."

"And what *are* the Undertakers? A street gang?"

"No, agent," replied Tom. "We're what you'd call a resistance group."

"Resistance," Ramirez echoed. "Against who? These… Corpses?"

Tom nodded.

"And the Corpses are an organization, you say. One made up of Philadelphia police officers?"

"Partly. The Corpses have wormed their way in to key positions all over the city. Teachers. Local officials. There are even Corpse doctors working at some of the hospitals. They're everywhere."

Ramirez didn't respond to that right away. Instead, his gaze grew distant, inward. After a few moments, we heard him mutter, "There's no way it could be *that* big."

Tom regarded him. "That ain't the kind of response I expected, agent. Makes me think you know a little something about all this. Care to share?"

"Not with you…Chief," Ramirez replied. Then, after he tested his chains again, he added, "What do I have to do for you to let me go?"

Tom sat back down on his bed. "You could start by understanding that we're on the same side. Karl Ritter founded the Undertakers more than three years ago to fight the Corpses. He died in that fight. So have a lot of us. Now, from the way you reacted to Will earlier, I'm guessin' you knew his old man. True or false?"

Ramirez's eyes slid to mine. "Are you really Karl's kid?"

"Yeah," I said. It was the first word I'd uttered during this…interview? Interrogation? From the onset, Tom had asked me to keep quiet—at least at first. "He's gotta get that *I'm* the dude he needs to deal with," he'd told me at the time.

"Your dad was a good man," Ramirez said. "I'm sorry we lost him."

"Thanks," I replied. "Except he wasn't 'lost.' He was murdered...by Kenny Booth."

This was probably more than I should have said. Tom gave me a sharp look. He seemed about to speak, but then the FBI guy said something that shut us both right up.

"I know."

Tom and I stared at him.

"Well...I suspected," Ramirez added. "That's how this whole thing got started."

The Chief said, "Sounds to me like we got a lot to tell each other."

Ramirez regarded him. "Maybe so, Chief. But if you want me to trust you, then I think I'm due a little of that in return. Uncuff me."

Tom shook his head. "Can't. Not yet."

"Why not? What are you afraid I'll do?"

"Fact is...you're an adult, and that means I got no idea what you'll do. I got the safety of my people to consider."

"What?" Ramirez asked. "No grown-ups in the Undertakers?"

Tom replied, "Plenty of grown-ups, agent. But no adults...not since Karl died."

"That doesn't make sense."

"We're real, agent. And you're here. Now, you'll be fed well, and we'll find you some fresh clothes. Ain't nobody gonna hurt you. You got my word on that. But until I'm convinced you either can't or won't make trouble for us, you'll *stay* here."

"You're committing a federal crime, son."

"You said that already," Tom replied.

Ramirez dropped his head back down on the gurney, clearly frustrated. "I don't believe this…"

"You're mad, agent. I get that. But I got no choice. So here's a suggestion that might speed things up."

The FBI guy eyed him. "I'm listening."

"Tell us what went down between you and the Corpses last night."

Ramirez rattled his right wrist. "And…if I do…will you unlock this thing?"

The Chief replied, "It'd be a step in the right direction."

"Not good enough," Ramirez said. "If I'm going to compromise an active federal investigation, I'm going to need a gesture of trust."

"Federal investigation," Tom echoed. "That may be what *you* call it. But my people, we call it a war. Now I don't know nothing about your 'active investigation,' but I guarantee this much: You know *less* than nothing about what's really going down in this city…and you wouldn't believe most of it if you *did* know."

"You keep talking about your people…these Undertakers. How many of you are there?"

Tom hesitated for a moment, not because he didn't know the number—quite the opposite; he probably saw it in his sleep—but because he didn't know how much he should reveal. Finally, he replied, "Almost a hundred and fifty."

Ramirez blinked. "A hundred and fifty…kids? All kids?"

Tom nodded.

"And where do you find these soldiers of yours?"

Tom said, "No."

"No, what?"

"If you want to hear more about *us*, you're gonna have to tell me more about yourself."

Ramirez's face darkened. "This isn't a game. If you really do have that many minors in this gang of yours—"

It was out before I could stop it. "We're not a gang! We're an army! One that my father started and ended up dying for!"

I could almost feel Ramirez taking in my slender thirteen-year-old frame, my freckled face, my shock of red hair—and dismissing me. "You're kids," he muttered.

"Kids who just saved your life," Tom replied flatly. "Get some rest, agent. I'll be in later with food and clothes." Then he unsnapped the radio watch from his wrist and tossed it onto the gurney. "If you feel like talking, just hit the button on the side and you'll get one of our Chatters. Ask for me." Then he stood, and with a nod in my direction, he started toward the curtained doorway. I followed.

Ramirez picked up the watch with his free hand, looking it over as if it were from Mars or something. "What is this? Now just wait a minute! You're in a lot of trouble here, Jefferson!"

Tom paused and looked back at him. In that moment,

his eyes seemed about a thousand years old. "Trouble, Agent Ramirez? You don't know the meaning of the word."

Then he led me out through his office and into the corridor. When I started to speak, he touched a finger to his lips and kept walking until we were a good distance away. "Listen, bro. I need you to go see the Monkeys and get them to build me a door...a big, heavy, bolted door...that we can use to seal that room up. And see if they can put a little window in it—about eye level. Make sure it's thick glass. Tell Alex I'll need it soon...no later'n dawn tomorrow."

"Sure," I said. "No problem." Except it *was* a problem—sort of.

The Monkey Boss wasn't exactly a fan of mine.

"What's the door for?" I asked. "I mean...we got that dude chained to the wall!"

Tom replied, "It ain't that. But we can't keep him forever, and I think maybe I got an idea about how we might convince him."

"What idea?"

"Later, okay? I need to worry over it a little longer 'fore I share."

"Okay," I replied.

"In the meantime, nobody talks to Ramirez. Not without me being there. Spread the word for me? Tell all the bosses."

"Sure. Where you gonna be?"

"In the infirmary," he replied. "With my sister."

As he walked off, I saw that Tom's shoulders were

slumped. He looked tired. "You think you *can* convince him?" I asked suddenly.

He glanced back at me. "Fifty-fifty," he sighed. "To his eyes…we're just kids."

Then he headed off down the corridor, leaving me standing there, trying real hard not to think what I was thinking.

We are *just kids.*

CHAPTER 16

MONKEY BUSINESS

In the old Haven, most of the daily Undertaker business had been conducted in this giant space called the Big Room. There'd been a high ceiling and lots of square footage that let each of the crews spread out and do their thing.

The new Haven was very different.

In this forgotten subbasement of cobwebs, wild cats, and crumbling bricks, each crew had been forced to lay claim to a space to make its own. The Hackers kept their computers all in a single dark, cavelike room with more monitors in it than lights. The Chatters set up their telephone tables in a spot near Haven's geographic middle so they could tap into the city's phone lines.

On first moving in, the Monkeys had spent days setting everything up—stringing electrical wire and tapping into the city's utilities to get us power and water. On top of that, they installed space heaters to keep us from freezing to death and bathroom facilities—but, trust me, the less I say about *that*, the better.

It isn't pretty.

To accomplish all this, the Monkeys claimed the biggest spot they could find. Their room was really three rooms linked by wide, crumbling archways—jungles of work benches, supply shelving, and tool racks that had somehow earned the nickname the Monkey Barrel.

Overall, it wasn't any more or less comfortable than the rest of headquarters. The ceiling was low. It smelled of cat droppings and old mold, and from all the activity in here, the air always seemed half filled with dust.

But despite all that, it was actually a pretty cool place. There were always interesting happenings, some new project in the works. Hammers hammered. Saws sawed. Welding torches welded. It was easily the noisiest place in Haven.

I'd probably have liked coming if it wasn't for one thing. Or really, one person.

Alex Bobson.

One of the first people I'd met at Haven had been Tara Monroe, the old Monkey Boss. I'd been a scared twelve-year-old back then—had it really only been four months ago?—and she'd taken the time to be nice to me. I'd liked her.

Then, a couple of weeks later, Tara had died saving me and a bunch of other recruits from the Corpses. She'd been sixteen years old.

Alex, one of her crewers, became her replacement. Like

Tara, I'd met him on my first day as an Undertaker. Unlike Tara, he *hadn't* been nice. I'd disliked him from the start, and nothing had happened since to change my opinion.

The kid was a first-class jerk.

Alex was taller than me, three years older, and he had muscles where I wished I did, though he was nowhere near as big as Tom or the Burgermeister. Helene sometimes joked that Alex needed those broad shoulders to rest his "chip" on.

It always seemed funnier when I didn't have to talk to the guy.

"Hey, dudes!" Alex called when he noticed me. "The birthday boy's decided to pay us a visit!" As some of his crewers laughed, the Monkey Boss abandoned the bike he'd been servicing and sauntered over to where I stood, a few feet inside the Barrel's doorway. "So…what are you now? Twelve?"

"Thirteen," I said.

He made a show of eyeing me skeptically. "Thirteen? You sure? You look more like eleven to me." This sparked more crewer laughter, though I noticed it sounded a little forced. Not every Monkey was as big a jerk as their boss.

I said, "Tom sent me to tell you he needs a door built between his office and his bedroom. He wants it as strong as you can make it."

"That right?" Alex replied, smirking.

I nodded. "And he wants a window in it at eye level. Thickest glass you can find…but small."

"Does he?"

"Yeah. And he needs it by dawn tomorrow."

"Uh-huh. Got somethin' in writing?"

"What?" I asked.

"Something in the Chief's handwriting that proves you're telling the truth."

I glared at him. "Why would I be lying about something like this?"

He shrugged. "Some kind of joke maybe. Busy work for my crew. You celebrity types are always ordering people around for the fun of it. It's a power trip."

"I'm not a 'celebrity,'" I said.

His smirk turned into a humorless grin. "Sure you are, Ritter. Heck…you're probably the closest thing the Undertakers got to a mascot."

I hoped, in the uneven light, my reddening face wouldn't show. But one look at Alex indicated otherwise.

Then, from somewhere behind him, someone called, "Will ain't nobody's mascot!"

Alex whirled around, scowling. He didn't like it when one of his crewers contradicted him. Behind him now, I peered over his shoulder into the shadows that filled the back of the Monkey Barrel.

A huge, hulking form emerged from the darkness.

"Burger!" Alex snapped. "I'm pretty sure I gave you a ton of machine parts to organize and stack."

"Yeah," Dave said. "I'm done."

"Done? That's a load of crap! There were something like thirty crates!"

The Burgermeister shrugged. "Took me a little longer than I expected."

Alex frowned, his fists on his hips. "After that, you were supposed to haul that equipment down to the cafeteria."

Dave stopped in front of the Monkey Boss, towering over him. His thick blond hair was matted with sweat, and his face wore its "coming storm" look—the one I felt sure had struck fear into the hearts of many a kid from elementary through high school.

Back in the old days. Before the war.

"That's done too," Dave said, his voice rumbling like thunder. "Just got back in time to catch you dissing Will."

"It's cool, Burgermeister," I said.

"And it's not your business!" Alex snapped. He was trying to appear in charge, but I noticed he kept shifting nervously from foot to foot, like a man facing down a bull about to charge.

"It *ain't* cool, Will," Dave replied. Then he fixed Alex with eyes like blue granite. "And you messing with my friend *makes* it my business."

"Your friend," Alex echoed. "Oh, I know all about your friend. The great Will Ritter! The prodigal son of Karl Ritter himself! Tom's golden boy! The kid who made us abandon our perfectly good headquarters for this dank, smelly sewer hole. The kid who thinks nothing of sticking his neck out— and anybody else's neck for that matter!"

Dave's hands rolled up into fists the size of river rocks.

"It sucks down here," he said in that low, rumbling voice. "We all get that. But that don't mean I gotta listen to you insult Will."

"What you gotta do," Bobson said, "is whatever I *tell* you to do! You're lucky I even let you on my crew. You don't know one end of a screwdriver from another, and you're about as good with tools as a two-year-old!"

Dave took a step toward Alex, his eyes blazing. As I watched, the considerable muscles in his right arm tightened, announcing the coming blow like the hush before a storm.

This is about to get bad.

So Alex, being Alex, decided to bring it home. "As for your 'friend'...as far as I'm concerned, Will Ritter is a skinny, no-talent show-off with more luck and name recognition than value!"

That did it.

Standing as I was behind the Monkey Boss, I did the only thing I could: I kicked him in the back of the knee.

The thing about a kick behind the knee is that if it's done right, you're going down. It doesn't matter how big you are or how good your balance is. Unless you're a flamingo, you're hitting the dirt.

And I did it right.

My timing was good too because the very moment that Alex tumbled backward, his arms pinwheeling, Dave was delivering a roundhouse punch with just slightly less force behind it than a ballistic missile.

Alex fell, and Dave swung, overbalancing due to his sudden lack of target and nearly toppling over himself. Then, as he staggered a few steps, trying to recapture his balance, I stepped forward and placed one of my own feet squarely on Alex's chest, leaning down just hard enough to make it look good.

The Monkey Boss lay stunned, staring up at me from the dirt floor.

"Just make the door," I told him flatly, "and keep your opinions to yourself."

Dave came to stand beside me. He looked disappointed and maybe a bit confused by the sudden turn of events, but he recovered quickly and added a hearty "Yeah!"

Alex glared at both of us. He didn't say a word. Around us, the Monkey Barrel had gone uncharacteristically quiet. This little incident had cost their boss some face. That wasn't going to improve our relationship—but at least he still *had* a face.

The Burgermeister patted me on the back at bit harder than necessary. "Come on, Will. I could use some food."

Then he headed for the Monkey Barrel exit.

I gave a three count before I removed my foot from Alex's chest. Leaning down, I whispered sharply, "I just saved you from having your jaw broken. Remember that."

Then I straightened and followed Dave.

From behind me, I heard the Monkey Boss shout, a little hoarsely, "You know what I remember, Ritter? I remember that surprise party you got last night. How many of them you been to since you joined up? None, right? My birthday was last month. I turned sixteen. Where was *my* cake?"

Dave muttered something under his breath about Alex's possible parentage.

I ignored him.

Though deep down, I knew Alex was right.

CHAPTER 17

THE BURGERMEISTER AND HELENE

rap!" Dave yelled.

We froze in our tracks halfway along an empty corridor as something skirted around us and ran down the hallway—a fuzzy blur—before it disappeared around a corner.

A cat.

"That was a big one!" the Burgermeister exclaimed.

"Yeah," I said.

"Wouldn't want to pet it," he added with a nervous laugh.

"Nope," I said.

"Probably take your arm off!"

"Yeah," I said again. I had more on my mind than wild cats.

And with that, my friend and I continued on our way, heading for the room we shared.

In the old Haven, there'd been only a boy's dorm and a girl's dorm, with army surplus cots for beds and footlockers for dressers. In the new Haven, the cots and footlockers were still here, but the dorms had given way to two-person bedrooms. On first realizing this, most of the kids had paired up pretty automatically, with the stragglers getting thrown together by lots. Only Tom and Sharyn each had private quarters.

Our space was small, about eight by six, just big enough for our cots and lockers. The only light came from a candle because, so far, electricity hadn't made it as far as the private rooms. Also, the lack of ventilation meant we couldn't use kerosene heaters. True, the subbasement's thick walls helped insulate us.

But still, going to bed in Haven meant chilly darkness. And a lot of blankets.

My side of our little cave was pretty sparse, though Dave had managed to spruce his up with a poster he'd found somewhere. It showed an old, worn-out, button-eyed teddy bear sitting in a dark gutter, looking lonely. The band was called the Mopey Teenage Bears. I knew nothing about them, but my roommate seemed to consider that poster his most prized possession.

We'd come here on our way to the cafeteria because Dave wanted to change his shirt. What I hoped that meant was he wanted to spray his sweaty pits and *then* change his shirt. The Burgermeister had some great qualities, but under-developed sweat glands weren't among them.

"Can I ask you something?" I said as he rummaged through his footlocker. "Whose idea was the party last night?"

Dave frowned. "Bobson's a scumbag. Ignore him."

"Who?" I pressed.

"Helene. She told me, and then we both told everybody else. Once we got Tom's okay, she and Nick set it up."

"How did Helene know it was my birthday in the first place?"

"I dunno. She just did. Why? Didn't you like the party?"

"No! It was cool. It's just…nobody else around here ever gets a birthday party."

Dave's yellow eyebrows knitted. "So?"

"So…you're fifteen, right?"

"Um…yeah."

"But when we were back at First Stop together, you were only fourteen. I heard Sharyn say so."

Did his face redden a little? In the bad light, I wasn't sure.

I pressed on. "So you must've had a birthday, and nobody knew it. You never even mentioned it."

"Look, dude!" he snapped. "All we wanted to do was give you a fun night! I'm sorry you hated it so much!"

Then, giving me a hard look, he turned and stormed out through the curtain.

"Hold up!" I called after him. But he'd already gone.

I stood alone in the dark, trying to make sense of what had just happened. I replayed our conversation but couldn't figure out what had made him so mad. Outside our room, other kids hurried by, talking among themselves and going about their daily business.

I gave the quiet darkness another five minutes, hoping the Burgermeister would reappear. He didn't. I briefly considered going after him. He'd probably be in the caf. When the Burgermeister was upset, the Burgermeister ate. But then I rejected the idea. Dave tended to get sullen when he was pissed. It would be a couple of hours at least before any apology would penetrate that thick layer of sulk.

So, partly because I wanted to tell Tom that he'd be getting his door and partly to check on Sharyn, I headed for the infirmary.

Tom wasn't there, but Helene was. So were Burt and Chuck. Both were sitting on one of the patient cots, with Amy ministering to nasty-looking cuts on their shoulders, elbows, and knees. Burt had a shallow gash across his forehead too. It looked eerily like a second smile.

Sharyn lay where I'd last seen her, still on the ambulance gurney. Her head was wrapped in white gauze, her eyes were shut, and her skin looked ashen and sunken. Just seeing her like that made my heart sink. She was one of the founding Undertakers, and I doubted there was a kid in Haven whose life she hadn't saved at one time or another. She was our best fighter—with the possible exception of Tom—but more than that, she was this beacon of optimism and good spirits in the midst of a pretty bleak life.

A world—especially *this* world—without Sharyn Jefferson in it didn't bear thinking about.

Helene and Ian stood vigil beside the gurney, looking every bit as worried as I felt.

"Any change?" I asked.

They shook their heads.

Ian said, "That's not necessarily bad. With injuries like this, the biggest risk is always brain swelling—"

"Brain swelling?" Burt exclaimed. "Sick!"

Ian ignored him. "Thing is, without an X-ray, I can't really know what's going on inside her skull. The best we can do is watch her, hour by hour. If the swelling gets worse, there'll be signs. So far, though, she seems to be holding her own."

Burt offered, "Sharyn's tough. Nobody tougher." Then, "Ow! Watch it with that thing, Amy!"

The little girl, who'd been administering what looked like a butterfly bandage to the boy's torn forehead, jumped back in alarm, her eyes wide. "Sorry!"

"Ignore him, Amy," Helene told her. "He's being a wuss. Burt, it's not her fault you bumped heads with a brick. Let her do her job."

Burt glowered but didn't object when Amy resumed her first aid.

"What if Sharyn's swelling *does* get worse?" I asked Ian.

Haven's medic shifted uncomfortably. "Well…she'll die. Unless I risk a shunt."

Helene asked, "What's a shunt?"

"The swelling is caused by blood. It fills the inside of the skull and starts cutting off oxygen to the brain. Usually, the blood reabsorbs over time...no problem. But in really bad cases, a small hole is drilled into the skull. Then a thin tube is stuck through it to drain off the excess blood and relieve the pressure on her brain."

"Cool!" said Burt.

"Cool?" Helene exclaimed, whirling on him. "This is Sharyn's life we're talking about, you insensitive pig!" Her throat still sounded hoarse but much better than it had. I suppose the pills and ice cream had helped.

Chuck reached over and punched him on the arm. The younger Moscova brother looked immediately sheepish. "Didn't mean it like that! Sorry...it was stupid."

Helene looked about to say something more. Then she turned back to Sharyn, impatiently wiping at a tear on her cheek. "Forget it."

I suppose I should say something, maybe tell her that the Boss Angel would be fine, that she'd be swinging Vader around again and lopping Deaders' heads off in no time.

Except I wasn't sure I believed it.

So I asked, "Where's Tom?"

"You just missed him," Ian replied.

Helene added, "I'll bet he's in your father's room."

Yeah, I'll bet he is.

Burt said, "Before he split, Tom put Chuck in charge of the Angels. Temporarily, I mean."

Chuck, who hadn't had much to say, offered me an unhappy wave.

"Okay," I said. "Why are you guys here anyway? What happened?"

"Remember the half-pipe we had back at the old Haven… for skateboarding?" Burt replied. "Well, Chuck and me were trying to build one in one of the empty rooms along the east wall."

That was a part of the subbasement that hadn't been completely explored yet, much less made usable. Tom had issued orders for everyone to stay clear of there for safety's sake.

Apparently Chuck and Burt had other ideas.

"Almost got it done too," Burt continued. "But then a piece of the ceiling came down and tripped us off our boards. I slammed my head on some loose brick, and Chuck here bit through his tongue pretty bad. Ian's just stitched it up. That's why he's not talking."

Beside him, Chuck uttered two thick, uncomfortable syllables that I translated to mean "bad luck."

"You shouldn't talk," said Amy in her quiet voice.

Helene groaned. "Bad luck? You were where you weren't supposed to be, doing something you weren't supposed to be doing, and you got yourselves hurt!"

Burt glowered at her. "Will does it all the time!"

The girl's eyes flashed my way, as if it was my fault these two were dorks. But then she said, "Will breaks rules and takes risks when he feels he *has* to…when there's something serious at stake. It's not the same thing!"

Helene paused, as if waiting for my confirmation.

I just shrugged.

"But this *is* serious," Burt protested. "We're Angels, and biking and boarding are big parts of what we do! And since we moved to this dungeon, there hasn't been any place to practice."

This time, Chuck uttered four syllables that I took to mean "we're getting rusty."

"You heard Amy!" Ian barked, an uncharacteristic sharpness to his voice. "No talking! Not for at least a couple of days."

Chuck's lips snapped obediently shut.

Helene exclaimed, "You're both lucky you didn't break your necks!"

"I'm going to find Tom," I said.

Burt and Chuck offered little waves. "Could you...you know...put in a good word for us?" Burt asked. "We really do gotta get back to work on our boarding. The Chief'll listen to you."

Will he?

As I left the infirmary, heading back in the direction of Tom's office, Helene caught up with me. "You okay?" she asked.

"I guess," I replied.

She touched my arm and a little inexplicable shock of *something* flashed from the point of contact and warmed my stomach. "No, you're not," she said. "I know Will Ritter when he's okay, and something's definitely bugging you. What's up?"

"You mean besides the war with the Corpses, Sharyn's coma, missing my family? Besides all that?" I said it with a smile she didn't return.

"Yeah, besides all that."

"Your voice sounds better," I noticed.

"Thanks. Ian's great. Now quit stalling."

I sighed. "Dave and me had a fight."

"A fight? About what?"

"It's not important."

She eyed me. "Come on, Will. Spill it!"

I dished up another sigh. "I asked him who set up my party last night. He said it was your idea, but that…once you got Tom's approval…everybody got involved."

"Something like that. Why?"

I'd known Helene Boettcher for about six months, ever since she'd appeared in my math class at Towers Middle School. For the first several weeks, I'd been completely incapable of stringing three words together in her presence. Her long dark hair and vivid hazel eyes just seemed to close my throat up.

Then I'd started seeing Corpses, which included Mrs. Yu, our math teacher.

And Helene Boettcher had saved my life, spiriting me away from everything I'd known and making me an Undertaker.

Since then, we'd been through a lot together, risking our lives in the war. It was a toss-up as to whether she or Dave was my best friend.

And a couple of hours ago, I'd almost watched her die.

The memory of it was like a festering wound.

"How did you even find out it was my birthday?" I asked. "I never said a word about it."

"I always knew," she replied. "When I was sent into your school to watch out for you, Tom gave me your file, and I pretty much memorized it. Not much else to do in the evenings as a Schooler. I was living in a sewer pipe in those days, remember? Wanna hear your social security number?"

"No thanks."

"Will, what's wrong?"

"It's not important," I repeated. "Forget it."

She studied my face. "You didn't like it...the party, I mean." Not an accusation; just a statement of fact.

I shrugged. "Sorry..."

"Don't be. I didn't do it for you."

"Huh?"

Helene laughed. I felt my cheeks redden. She saw it and laughed harder. "I'm sorry!" she stammered. "But you should see your face!"

"You threw a surprise party for me that wasn't for me?" I asked.

"Well, of course it was for you. I mean, it was your birthday...but it could have been anybody's."

That did absolutely nothing to ease my confusion.

"Look," she said. "Dave's got it a little wrong. The party was actually Nick Rooney's idea. Ever since we moved to the new Haven, morale's been at an all-time low around here. I mean, look at this place! It's dark. It smells. It's infested with cats, for God's sake! Cats that look more like giant rats than anything in a Friskies commercial."

"Yeah. So?"

"So, nobody likes it here, and it's been starting to show. Nick figured what we needed was a party. We haven't had one since you killed Booth last year. But now, like then, we needed a reason...something to celebrate. So they went to Sharyn, and Sharyn came to me. I remembered that your birthday was coming up, and it just kind of...ballooned... from there."

A coincidence? I'd gotten the surprise party because my birthday happened to be the next one on the calendar? I wasn't sure if I was relieved or disappointed.

"After you and Tom left, it kept going, you know," Helene told me. "It went on pretty much all night. Everybody needed it."

"Yeah," I said. "But..."

"But what? What's so bad about giving you a party?" Then realization flashed across her face. "You're worried that it made you look too...special!"

"Sort of."

She shrugged. "Some kids probably think that. Who cares? The point is that there were some smiles around here for a change." Then her own smile faded. "Until Sharyn got hurt. Jeez, Will...what if she dies?"

Tara died. So did Kyle Standish. And there were other Undertakers, including my father, who'd given their lives for the war effort long before I'd ever even *heard* of Haven.

Undertakers died. Nobody liked it, but it happened.

And I was all worked up about a party?

"We keep fighting," I replied quietly. "What else *can* we do?"

Helene nodded. "So…you're okay?"

"Fine," I said.

Except every time I close my eyes, I see that Corpse…almost killing you.

But I couldn't tell her that. Even if I wanted to, I lacked the words.

"Stupid stuff," I explained. "No matter how bad things get, I always seem to be able to find time to worry about stupid stuff."

"Yeah, we all do that. You should go talk to Dave. Settle it. He's pretty shook."

"Shook?" I asked. "About what?"

Helene treated me to a pitying look. "You know, for a smart guy, Ritter…sometimes you can be such an idiot! I'll see you at dinner."

"Sure," I replied, perplexed.

She took a half step toward me, and for a terrifying second, I thought she meant to hug me. She'd done that once before, right after I'd managed to rescue us both from a Corpse trap. It had been awkward then. If she did so now, given the thoughts that were churning around in my head, I felt sure I'd squirm right out of my skin.

And Helene seemed to sense that because she checked herself. Then, with a shy little smile, she headed up the corridor back toward the infirmary.

I blew out a shuddering sigh of—what? Relief? Disappointment?

Silently, I cursed myself. Everything that was going down around me, and I was getting all worked up about…well, stupid stuff.

Except that wormbag almost killed her.

I shuddered.

CHAPTER 18

GROWN-UPS

When I got back to Tom's office, Ramirez was screaming. Not shouting or yelling or even hollering—but screaming as if half blind with rage. The dude was so loud I actually paused in Tom's office, hesitating. Was Tom even *in* there? If not, who on earth was the FBI guy screaming at?

I inched toward the bedroom curtain and peeked through.

Tom *was* there, standing with his back against the far wall, his expression carefully neutral. Across the room, Ramirez sat atop his gurney, straining against his handcuff chain. The forefinger of his free hand was pointed accusingly—even threateningly—at the Chief's passive face.

He wasn't using a lot of words that my mom would have approved of, but the gist of it seemed to be this: "Let me go or every evil thing that has ever happened in the history of the world will happen to you times infinity."

I considered leaving. Crazy as it sounded, given everything

I'd been through, the idea of having an adult lay that much hate on me felt a little scary. I honestly didn't know how Tom could handle it so smoothly.

But then, of course, I did.

He was Tom.

I worked up my courage and pulled aside the curtain, hoping to catch the Chief's eye.

Instead, I caught Ramirez's.

"Case in point!" he exclaimed. "How old is this boy? Eleven?"

Shades of Alex Bobson. I felt my face flush. "I'm thirteen."

The FBI guy ignored me. "It's obvious he idolizes you! And I'm sure the rest of them are the same way. They do what you say, think what you tell them to think. I was wrong before! This isn't a street gang! It's a cult! The Cult of Jefferson!"

"That's stupid!" I exclaimed. "Tom's the reason I'm still alive...the reason we're all still alive!"

This time, Ramirez didn't ignore me but instead directed his fury at me like a flamethrower. "So you 'see' these things too? These walking dead men?"

Now I understood all the yelling. Tom had decided to risk the truth, and the FBI guy had reacted the way grownups always did.

"Yeah," I muttered.

"What did you say?" he snapped.

I took a deep breath.

Enough.

"Yeah," I said again, louder this time, matching his glare

with one of my own. "I See them. I've been hunted by them. I've watched friends of mine die because of them." Then, after a long pause, I added, "Kenny Booth was one of them."

Ramirez's mouth opened and closed. For the moment, at least, his anger cooled. "Booth," he echoed. His voice sounded hoarse, probably from all the screaming. "Booth," he repeated.

"He was their boss," Tom explained calmly. "And he was eyein' up the mayor's office. We had to stop him."

"Kenny Booth is dead."

"Straight up," Tom replied. Then he looked right at me—*hard*—like he was trying to tell me something.

Unfortunately, I didn't get the message.

"I killed him," I told Ramirez defiantly. Out of the corner of my eye, I saw Tom's shoulders slump.

"What?" the FBI guy gasped.

"Will..." Tom began.

"Booth died on live television," Ramirez remarked. "Exploded. But nobody was ever able...I mean...the cause of death was never fully..."

"The Corpses got this thing about salt," I said. "Like an allergy, I guess...but worse. I got Booth to swallow a salt pill I'd tricked out to look like this candy he liked. I wasn't even sure it would work until it did."

Across the room, Tom rubbed his face with his hands.

Ramirez sat back on the gurney. "Karl Ritter's kid," he muttered. "My God..."

Tom pushed off the wall and came to stand beside me.

"Agent, I get where you're at. This *can't* be real. This city *can't* be infested by legions of animated cadavers. And the thirteen-year-old sons of police detectives *don't* go around murdering TV journalists."

"What have you done to these kids?" Ramirez demanded. "What is it? Drugs? Hypnosis?"

Tom nodded, not in agreement but more like he understood the FBI guy's viewpoint. I had to admire the Chief's patience. I wasn't sure I'd let a stranger tear into me like this without getting seriously pissed. Especially when my sister might be dying—a casualty of the war this dude denied even existed.

"How's about I make a deal with you, agent?" Tom said. "You give me twenty-four hours. I'm going to set up a kind of demonstration…something that I hope'll convince you I'm tellin' the truth. If that don't work, then tomorrow night, my people will knock you out and drop you off anywhere in the city you want…within reason."

The agent studied him. "How do I know you won't just kill me?"

Tom shrugged. "You're a problem…one I ain't sure how to solve. We can't keep you chained up forever. You need food, water, bathroom breaks. And never even mind the fact that this is *my* bedroom. Now, given all that trouble, if we was killers, you'd likely already be dead. Whatever you think of me, you gotta see the truth of *that*."

Ramirez seemed to calm somewhat. "Let's say I buy that for now. What kind of demonstration are you talking about?"

"I'm still working on the details," Tom replied. "In the meantime, I suggest you chill. I'll make sure you get some water. All that hollering must've burned your throat pretty bad."

Then, before the FBI guy could reply, Tom put an arm around my shoulders and led me through the curtain and out of the room.

Once we were in the corridor, he stopped and gave me a hard look. "That wasn't smart, bro."

"You were straight with him about the Corpses," I replied defensively. "So was I."

"*I* didn't confess to wasting a public figure on live TV. *You* did."

I looked at him, my mouth hanging open. He looked right back at me.

"So what's gonna happen when we *do* let him go?" Tom asked me. "You think...even when this war is over...that he's just gonna forget you said that? He's a *Fed*, Will! That's like a super cop! No way is he gonna let you off the hook for what he figures was a cold-blooded murder!"

I actually felt the blood drain from my face. "I...didn't think about it that way," I stammered. "I just wanted to... convince him..." The words trailed off.

"Yeah, I know," the Chief said. "And at this point, that's about your only shot. We *gotta* convince him! It's the only way you'll ever be able to go back to your life."

Now it was my turn to rub my face with my hands. "I messed up, Tom. I'm sorry."

He shrugged. "What's done's done. Now we just gotta deal with it."

"How?" I asked, wishing I didn't sound quite so desperate. "I mean…how *do* we convince him? He's a grown-up! He can't See the Corpses! What can we possibly do that won't make him just shake his head and call us crazy again?"

"That's what the door's for," Tom remarked.

"I told Alex about it," I said.

At that, he almost smiled. "Yeah, I heard about your visit to the Monkey Barrel. Alex came to me a while ago. Complained every which way about you. Said you and Dave ganged up on him and hit him."

"That's not what happened!" I snapped.

But he raised a hand. "I can guess what went down. Alex got outta line, Dave's temper cracked, and you did something to keep it from turning ugly. Am I close?"

"Yeah!" I exclaimed, astonished. "How did you know?"

"Let's just say I'm familiar with the parties involved. Know why I sent you down there in the first place? I could have sent anybody to order me up that door."

"I dunno," I replied. "I figured it was 'cause I was there at the time."

"That's part of it but not most of it. Will, Alex's got a lot of anger. He's a solid Monkey and a decent enough Boss, but that chip on his shoulder is more like a plank. And he seems to point a lot of that your way."

"I've noticed," I muttered.

"It's a situation that needs to be handled," he continued. "And I sent you down there because the only way it *will* be handled…for good and all…is if the two of you handle it yourselves. I know you try to steer clear of Alex, and I don't blame you. But that won't solve the problem."

"What will solve it?" I asked.

"Making him see you like I see you…like most of Haven sees you."

I grimaced. "Most of Haven sees me as Karl Ritter's kid… and figures you treat me special because of that."

"That's Alex talking."

"But he's not wrong, is he? I *do* get special treatment because of who my dad is!"

Tom folded his arms and studied me. "What special treatment exactly?"

"Well…" I paused. "You put me on the Angels way younger than usual."

"I did the same thing with Helene. Know why?"

I shook my head.

"'Cause she's *good*, Will. We're an army, and an army is made up of soldiers. But not all soldiers are combat material. Helene is. She proved that when she pulled you out of your middle school on the day you got your Eyes. Half the city was looking for you, but she kept her head and got you both to Haven safely. So I asked her to join the Angels."

"And me?"

Tom rolled his eyes, something he didn't do very often.

"Will, you got more courage than most kids years older. Sometimes it's a reckless kind of courage that gets you into trouble...but more often than not, it works out for you. And half the time, you don't even know it. Where else would I put you *but* the Angels?"

I stared at him, speechless.

Then he added, "But that ain't all of it."

"Huh?"

"You got a serious mind."

I blinked. "A what?"

"A serious mind. Once you committed to the Undertakers, you gave it all you got. You don't just suffer this war the way most of the others do. You come at it like a challenge, a problem to be solved...like something that stands between you and your family."

"Well...it is!"

"Sure, it is," he agreed. "What's more, it's a challenge every kid in Haven faces. 'Cept most don't handle it like you do."

"How *do* I handle it?" I asked, feeling uncomfortable and not sure why.

"Let me ask you something," Tom said. "When's the last time you played?"

"Played what?"

"Anything. Cards. Monopoly. A video game. When was the last time you dropped yourself in front of one of the TVs in the rec room and just watched cartoons for a couple of hours?"

I started to say something but stopped myself. The fact was that I couldn't remember. In all the months I'd been living this life, hadn't there been a single moment of good old-fashioned fun?

No. Of course not. Haven wasn't about fun. Being an Undertaker wasn't a game.

"So?" I asked, a little defensively.

"So, you said just now that you get special treatment," Tom replied. "Well, I say you get treated the way you *should* get treated. A while ago, I told Ramirez that there were grown-ups in the Undertakers but no adults. Remember?"

"Yeah."

"I like to think I'm one of those grown-ups," Tom said.

"You are," I admitted.

"And guess what, bro? So are *you*."

I stood there in that cold, dank corridor, trying to take it in. I'd been a kid once, just a normal middle school kid worried about homework and friends and crushing on the girl who sat beside me in math class. I'd had friends that I'd hung out with in the evenings and a mom who nagged me to pick up my dirty clothes and put my shoes away. I'd owned an Xbox, a PlayStation, and a Wii.

Back in those days, I'd whined when there was nothing worth watching on TV or if the dinner menu didn't suit my liking. But I'd also laughed at my baby sister when she said or did something cute, at my friends when they cracked a joke or tripped over their own feet. I'd made fun of Old Man

Pratt, who lived next door and was probably the meanest person on Grape Street.

But then I'd gotten the Sight, and Old Man Pratt had turned out to be much meaner than I'd ever imagined.

Old Man Pratt had been a Corpse.

These days, I didn't whine, and I didn't laugh. Games held no interest for me. All I wanted to do was work, push the cause forward, fight the Corpses—so I could someday see my mom and sister again.

But would they even recognize me? Would I even recognize myself?

Tom said, "An eye-opener, ain't it?"

I nodded wearily. All my discomfort and irritation was gone. Suddenly, I felt tired. Very tired.

"You've been up for almost twenty-four hours, bro," the Chief said. "Go and get some sleep."

"I want to see the demo for Ramirez," I protested.

"You will. But there's stuff to be done first to prep for it, and I need you for that. I'm calling a meeting of the Angels in"—he checked his watch—"four hours. That'll make it around eight o'clock tonight. Be there, okay?"

"Okay," I replied.

"Good. Get going now. Think on what I said."

"I will," I promised, a little reluctantly. Just what I'd needed—one more thing to think about!

CHAPTER 19

DARKNESS

The dark alley in the Callowhill section of the city stank of rotting food, urine, and human despair. Against one grimy wall, a man dressed in rags lay in a drunken stupor, clutching a near-empty bottle in one gnarled hand. His face, barely visible in the light that leaked in from the street, was twisted in half-conscious despair and pain—a mask of suffering.

Lilith Cavanaugh reveled in it.

She stood amid the filth, wrapped in a stylish blue pants suit and fine wool long coat, and waited.

Just coming here was a risk, of course, but a worthy one.

Also, as it happened, a necessary one.

Pierce stood at the mouth of the alley, eyeing the street and repeatedly checking his watch. The host he wore was new, barely a week dead. He'd transferred his Self into it just before they'd come out here. But Lilith's own body was in desperate need of replacing. Unfortunately, male cadavers were easier to find than females.

It was unbearable.

For the hundredth time that day, the image of Susan Ritter filled her thoughts.

What a fine replacement she would make.

"He's late," Pierce said. A pointless observation.

"He'll be here," Lilith replied.

"Ma'am…" her assistant remarked hesitantly. "I'm…uncomfortable with this arrangement." He looked at her. Then, reading her irritation, he immediately turned away again.

"Do you have an alternative suggestion to make?" she asked coldly.

"No, ma'am."

"Are you willing to take on this man's task?" Lilith pressed.

"No, ma'am."

"Can you imagine any one of our people who would be willing to assume the duty? Any at all?"

"No, ma'am," he replied.

"Then tell me—what choice do I have?"

Her assistant hesitated again, perhaps weighing whether his next words were worth the danger or not. Finally, steeling himself, he said, "We could find another way."

Lilith had to admire his courage. Speaking truth to power wasn't something she encountered very often. Her opinion of Pierce rose a little higher.

Nevertheless, she replied flatly, "This is the *only* way."

Pierce looked as if he might say more but then thought better of it. Apparently, his courage didn't extend to pushing the matter further.

Wise as well as brave.

"He's late," Pierce said again.

Fool.

Then a voice spoke from behind her, "Your assistant should learn some patience."

Lilith spun around, experiencing a sensation she hadn't known for longer than she could remember: shock.

And she didn't care for it—not one little bit.

The man in rags stood before her. He still reeked of alcohol, but his desperate, empty expression was gone. The eyes that now held hers looked clear, their gaze steady.

He spoke again, "Sorry if I scared you, Ms. Cavanaugh."

"Startled," she corrected, working hard to hide her annoyance.

"Sure." He smiled, showing white teeth that gleamed in the dull light.

Pierce appeared at her side, his manner protective. Another small point in his favor, Lilith thought, though unnecessary. The stranger wasn't a big man, barely five-foot-eight, with a slight frame. She could snap his spine in seconds with her bare, manicured hands.

And she still might, considering the "startle" he'd given her just now.

Instead she said, "Mr. Dashiell, I presume?"

"Just Dashiell."

"All right then, 'Just Dashiell.' First, let me compliment you. A very effective disguise. Should I assume that you've been waiting here for us all this time?"

He nodded. "I like to get to know my potential clients, observe them for a while. See what sort of people they are."

The Queen smiled inwardly. *If you only knew.*

But of course, this human's mind was as limited as the rest.

Then she corrected herself with some irritation: *well, not quite all the rest!*

"And what sort of people are we?"

Dashiell nodded to Pierce, who glared silently at him. "Your man here is the nervous type. They tend to make mistakes."

"I see," Lilith replied coldly. "And me?"

"You're a little harder to figure," the man admitted. "You're not the all-smiles, super-friendly civil servant I've seen on the local news. No, the fact you're even here proves you've got a darker side. And the way you stand in this rat-infested alley, looking not only like you own but *like* owning it…well, let's just say I haven't been able to categorize you yet."

"Charming," Lilith remarked, though inwardly, she was pleased. This human, while as blind as the rest, seemed not entirely inobservant. Even that infuriating prank he'd pulled—sneaking up on her that way—suggested a level of resourcefulness that would suit her immediate needs.

I'll use him...then I'll kill him.

"Charm," Dashiell said, "is not usually what my clients are looking for."

"I suppose not," the Queen replied. "Still, I think we can do business. Are you clear on the particulars of the job?"

He nodded. "Are you clear on the particulars of payment?"

"Of course," she said. "Money. Always money. That's what it's all about to you people, isn't it?"

Dashiell stared blankly at her. "I'm a professional, Ms. Cavanaugh. I have no interest in politics and no loyalty to any particular religion, creed, or country. I thought you understood that about me."

"Your reputation makes that plain."

"Then it also makes plain my motivation. I work for payment." Then, with a sneer, he added, "As you do, I'm sure."

"My people aren't profiteers, Dashiell," Lilith told him. "We're artists."

"I don't understand," the man said, sounding impatient. "Are we doing business or not? I don't like having my time wasted."

The Queen of the Dead replied, "Neither do I."

Then she dropped her Cover.

And suddenly, it was Dashiell's turn to be "startled."

The Queen knew full well what she looked like and saw that image reflected in the eyes of the terrified man. He staggered back a step, his face going instantly pale. He didn't scream. Instead, bile rose up in his throat, making him gag.

Then he whirled around to run.

Lilith threw herself upon him, clutching his throat with bloated purple figures and turning him back to face her. His horror shone brightly on his features.

She grinned broadly, displaying her blackened, receding gums and rotting teeth.

"This isn't about money," she hissed.

Then she kissed him, pressing her cold, dead lips against his trembling ones. *Now* Dashiell tried to scream, but the sound was muffled. He struggled wildly, a victim in full panic, but the hands on his neck were too strong.

Then Pierce was there, his own Cover still in place. He seized Dashiell from behind, lifting up the man's coat and shirt, exposing the bare flesh of back. Then her minion produced a small metal tube.

With Lilith still kissing the terrified human, Pierce wordlessly uncapped the tube and pressed its open end against the bare flesh of Dashiell's thrashing lower back.

The helpless man screamed again, the sound going nowhere except into Lilith's gaping mouth. His flailing intensified for a few moments. Then it stopped.

The terror in Dashiell's eyes turned to confusion.

The Queen released him and stepped back.

He stood there, swaying a little, with Pierce still behind him. The human's face, though still pale, was no longer twisted in fear.

"Feel better?" Lilith asked.

He nodded. "What…did you do to me?"

"I'm sorry, Dashiell. But it was necessary. You see, the sad reality is that we don't have the funds necessary to meet your usual fee, so we were forced to do something I don't like to do—show you who we are."

"You're…dead," he whispered, more in wonder than in fear.

"Not exactly," she replied. "We're travelers. We come from a place far away. So far, in fact, that bringing our actual bodies would be impossible. So we unfortunately require human corpses to use as hosts."

"Hosts," the man echoed.

"Yes. My face…the face you've seen on television and in the newspapers. The one you saw when we met just now…" She paused a moment, steadied herself, and redonned her Cover. "*This* face…is an illusion. You see, we've come to your world to do your people a great service. But no matter how generous our motives, we would never be accepted as we truly are."

"What…service?"

"No need to concern yourself with that," Lilith told him gently. "Just answer me something: given what I've just told you, are you willing to waive your usual fee and perform this task without charge?"

Dashiell blinked several times. His mouth worked wordlessly.

He's resisting.

Humans resisted the *Pelligog* more than any race the *Malum* had so far encountered. It was one of the things that would make their eventual destruction all the more satisfying—and beautiful.

Finally, the man said, "Of course. Thank you for explaining things to me."

"No, Dashiell. Thank you. This is a selfless act you're taking on. One that will help not just my people but yours in ways you can't even imagine. You have an opportunity to do something truly great with your life. Doesn't that sound appealing?"

The man grinned his cocky grin, the first time he'd done so since being turned. "It certainly does, Ms. Cavanaugh."

"I'm happy to hear it," Lilith said. "Now please understand that this needs to happen on Sunday. And it needs to be public…preferably in broad daylight."

"I understand."

"This is Friday night," Lilith pointed out. "That allows you less than two days to prepare. How confident are you that you can make the necessary arrangements?"

Dashiell smiled another arrogant, white-toothed smile. The Queen fought the urge to kill this immodest human despite her newly established control over him. Using the *Pelligog* guaranteed a human's loyalty but sadly did nothing to make them less loathsome.

"The necessary arrangements have already been made," he replied. "Realizing that your timetable was so short, I went ahead and set it all up beforehand. I promise you, Ms. Cavanaugh…it'll happen on Sunday."

Another *Malum* edict: *The worst sort of fool is one who believes himself brilliant.*

She matched his smile. "That's wonderful news, Dashiell! Now let me explain to you the particulars of your task…and the sacrifice I'll ask of you once you've completed it."

CHAPTER 20

GETTING THE BAND BACK TOGETHER

When you're an Undertaker, especially an Angel, you learn to get by on less sleep than you're used to. Back in my old life, I could hit noon on a good Saturday, wrapped in a cocoon of blankets, dozing until lunchtime.

These days, four hours was pretty typical, and six a guilty pleasure.

That afternoon, I got around five.

I opened my eyes to find the candle lit and Dave sitting on his cot, looking at me. I noticed with relief that he didn't seem mad anymore.

"Hi," I said.

"I'm a jerk," he said.

"Tell me something I don't know."

He offered up a small smile. "You awake? Awake enough to talk, I mean?"

I nodded. "What time is it?"

"Going on nine o'clock."

"Nine!" All my sleepiness disappeared, and I sat bolt upright. "I was supposed to be in an Angels meeting at eight!"

"Chill," the Burgermeister said. "Tom sent me to get you. Told me to tell you the meeting got pushed back an hour."

It wasn't like the Chief to postpone meetings. "How come?"

Dave lowered his eyes. "Sharyn. She…um…don't look good."

I felt that familiar cold knot tighten in my gut. "How not good?"

He shrugged. "I ain't no doctor. Half the time, I don't think that Ian kid even speaks English. I was in the rec room, watching some tube, when Maria showed up and just blurted it out about Sharyn. By the time I got to the infirmary, there were something like thirty kids hanging around. After a while, Tom came out and told us she was in bad shape. I couldn't believe how…I dunno…*tired* he looked. Then he asked me to tell you the Angels meeting got pushed back. Says he's gonna have it right there in the infirmary, I guess so he can stay close to his sister."

"Holy crap…" I muttered.

"Yeah," he said. He looked as if he wanted to say more, but he didn't.

I stood up, shaking off the last bits of sleep. "Guess I need to get to that meeting."

Dave stood up too, swallowing up half the room with his size, and looked nervously at me. "Before you do…" he began.

"Yeah?"

He studied his shoes. "Sorry about before."

"Forget it."

"I was just mad…"

"I know. It's not—"

But then, he continued, "'Cause you took down Bobson before I could."

That stopped me. "Oh."

His broad shoulders rose and fell. He didn't say anything.

So *I* did. "That's what you were mad at? The whole Alex thing? I thought you were ticked off about the birthday party."

"Nah." He waved one beefy hand. "I figured you wouldn't be all that thrilled with that. So did Helene. We did it anyway because Sharyn wanted to throw a party. I only got ticked off at you when you mentioned it 'cause…well…'cause it kind of brought it home."

"Brought what home?" I asked.

"How useless I am."

I stared at my friend, trying to figure him out. He was twice my size, easily the biggest kid in Haven—even bigger than Tom. "You're not useless," I said uncomfortably. "That's just stupid."

"Yeah," he said, sounding utterly miserable. "I'm that too."

"What?"

He kept his eyes lowered. "Stupid. That's why I won't ever be no Angel. I don't have the brains for it."

"That's not true!"

"Yeah, it is, dude. Everybody knows it. I'm big and strong, so they use me for the heavy stuff around here. I'm the fork-lift, the jackhammer, the pack mule. But every time I try out for the Angels, I get my butt handed to me. That's 'cause the kind of fighting you guys do ain't about size and muscle. It's about speed…and brains."

I tried to think of something to say, but nothing came to mind. The best I could manage was a halting "Burgermeister…I…"

He met my gaze, and for half a minute, neither of us spoke. He looked like a kicked puppy, and there I stood—his supposed friend—without the slightest idea how to help him.

Some "grown-up."

"You should get to your meeting," he said. "I just wanted to tell you I'm sorry."

"Dave…" I began. But he turned away and dropped back down onto his cot. It creaked beneath him, as it always did. Since he had come to Haven, the Burgermeister had so far put two cots in the trash heap just by laying on them.

I said, "Dave…it might help if you learned how to handle your temper."

He didn't reply.

"Save all that anger for the Deaders," I suggested.

He laughed, no humor in it all. "And when do you think I'm gonna get a chance to fight a Deader? I ain't seen one in months. They never let me out of here."

I went to the curtain and paused, deciding. Then I said, "Come with me."

He didn't budge. "It's an Angels-only meeting."

"Come with me anyway. I'll smooth it over with Tom."

That got him to look at me. "He won't like it."

"Probably not," I said, though inwardly, I wasn't sure if—right now—the Chief would care all that much. His sister was badly hurt, maybe dying. And if that was twisting in *my* gut like a cold knife, what must it be doing to *his*? "But Dave…I'm going out on a mission tonight. And I want you to come along."

"What for? You don't need me. Look at how you handled Bobson. I was ready to tear his head off, but you tripped him up before I could. And you did it on purpose too. I know that. You did it to keep me from getting into trouble for wiping the floor with that crud."

I shrugged.

The Burgermeister sat up, a move that his third suffering cot didn't seem to care for. "Will, you got the guts and you got the moves."

"So do you," I said, meaning it. "Your moves are just… different than mine. It's not about brains. It's about style of combat."

It sounded good. I wasn't sure if I really, deep down, believed a word of it, but his response surprised me. "Yeah, that's what she says."

I blinked. "She…who?"

"Sharyn."

"Sharyn told you that?"

"Yeah. More or less." Then his expression suddenly turned shifty. He cleared his throat. "Um…you sure you can smooth it over with the Chief?" he asked. "If I decide to come with you to the meeting, I mean."

"I think so. Come on."

For the first time since I'd woken up, Dave "The Burgermeister" Burger grinned. He had a big toothy smile that would've looked good on Alice's Cheshire Cat.

Then he stood, and together, we headed into Haven's dark hallways.

The corridor outside the infirmary was crowded—real crowded. There had to be fifty kids jammed up there. At first, I was annoyed. Most of these boys and girls were just gawking. I'd seen it a hundred times back in school. Whenever something tragic happened, there were always those who wanted to get close to the action, ready to spread rumors or gossip.

Except, these are Undertakers…not kids.

And none of them were gossiping…or talking much at all. The faces we passed as Dave plowed us a path through the crush of bodies were still and expectant, maybe even reverent, nodding to me as I went by.

This wasn't a mob. It was a vigil.

For Sharyn.

We pushed through the curtain to find Sharyn still on her

stolen gurney, limp and ashen. Ian fussed over her, checking the IV drip plugged into her arm, shining his little doctor's penlight into her eyes, and looking generally unhappy. Amy stood at his side, handing him instruments as he asked for them, quiet and dutiful. A born nurse.

Across the room, the Angels had gathered in a loose standing circle with Tom at its center. He spotted me and waved. Then he spotted the Burgermeister and stopped waving. His brow furrowed, but he said nothing.

Dave and I walked over, taking a spot beside Helene, who looked at me, then at him, then back at me with a questioning expression.

The Chief said, "I'll be needin' two teams. The first is going into combat. Now, because my sister is…sick…and because Chuck and Burt"—he gave the two boys a pointed look. But neither saw it because they were staring at the floor as if worried it might suddenly jump up and make a break for it.

Tom continued—"are off duty with trainin' injuries, the next in seniority on the Angels crew takes command. That's you, Katie. You up for it?"

Katie glanced back at Sharyn and sighed. "I guess so."

"Thanks," said Tom. "Now this is gonna be a hard one, dudes. So I want every combat-ready crewer to go along. Here's the gig: I want y'all to bag me a female Corpse. Get that? Female. Find one, corner it, and incapacitate it. Then bring it back to Haven, blindfolded, of course, and trussed up like a Thanksgiving turkey. But it needs to be functional. No permanent damage to the body. That's important."

Nervous looks were traded around the circle. Finally, a boy named Sam, one of the newer Angels, raised his hand.

"This ain't a classroom, Sam," Tom said. "If you got something to ask, ask."

Sam swallowed. "What for? I mean…we only just started actually killing them, and now you want us to bring one back alive?"

"Not sure 'alive' is the right word," Burt murmured.

Sam glared at him. "You know what I mean!"

His question was taken up by the whole circle, except for me. I had a pretty good idea what Tom might have in mind.

"I'll get to that in a minute," the Chief said. "Now the second team. Helene, because the senior Angels are gonna all be needed to pull off this Deader-napping, I need you and one or two others to go out and get me a real dead body."

Helene said, "Huh?"

"You want a cadaver," I said. "One that's just plain dead and hasn't been transferred into."

Tom nodded. "The second team's going to play it smart and low key. I've already had the Chatters looking up the recent obituaries. They've found a good candidate at one of the nearby funeral homes. This operation is strictly 'in and out.' No combat. No direct contact at all with the enemy. Just some good old-fashioned body-snatching."

"I want Will with me," Helene said, throwing a smile my way.

"I figured," the Chief replied.

"And Dave," I said.

Helene hesitated for only a second. Then she nodded. "And Dave."

The Burgermeister pumped the air with his fist.

"Hold up," Burt complained. "Chuck and me can't go... but you're sending *him*? He's not even an Angel trainee! I mean, why is he even here?" Then, when Dave shot him a dark look, he added quickly, "No offense."

"He's here because I invited him," I said. Then to Tom, who looked skeptical, I argued, "This mission doesn't need someone with combat training. But we *are* gonna want somebody who's strong enough to carry whatever body we get. Dave's perfect!"

"Yeah!" the Burgermeister added loudly.

"I'm with Will," Helene said.

Tom studied us both. For a second, he looked like he might smile. If his sister hadn't been laid out on that gurney, I thought he might have. But she was, and he didn't. "Okay. Sharyn'll probably have my head when she's better, but...just this once...I'm cool with it. Both teams leave in two hours."

Katie asked, "Um...you said you'd explain why?"

Tom replied, "Y'all know about the FBI agent we've got in my bedroom? Well, I've decided that, the situation bein' what it is, we need to do more than just let him go. We need to *convince* him. We need to show this dude that the Corpses are real and that we're not just a street gang of delusional minors."

"How?" Burt asked.

This time, the Chief actually managed a slight grin. "I'm settin' up a demonstration for our new friend," he said. "And to make it happen, I'm going to need a Corpse…and a corpse."

CHAPTER 21

INVASION OF THE BODY SNATCHERS

Until tonight, I'd only ever been in one funeral home. That had been in Manayunk, near my house. It was called Huntington Memorial—a big white mansion just off Main Street. I didn't remember too much about it. At the time, I'd been pretty messed up.

My dad had just died.

Who knew Philly had so many other such places? Hundreds of them, all over the city.

This particular one was called Chang's, and the Chatters had picked it simply because it was close to one of Haven's three secret entrances—and it supposedly had a "good" cadaver inside, awaiting a funeral that was scheduled for the morning. A woman, apparently—which was why Tom wanted Katie's team to come back with a female Corpse.

Deaders, when they transferred, always stuck to the same gender.

Doing this felt wrong. Really wrong. If we were successful, it meant that tomorrow, a bunch of innocent people would assemble to grieve for a loved one whose body would have gone missing.

No. Not "gone missing." *Stolen*.

By us.

"This isn't right," I muttered as the three of us walked down the street toward Chang's.

"I know," Helene said. "It makes me feel heartless. Like a…I dunno…"

"Like a Corpse?" the Burgermeister finished.

We both looked at him. "Yeah," replied Helene. "Like a Corpse."

"Tom wouldn't be doing it if it wasn't necessary," I pointed out.

"I know," she replied. "But just 'cause something's necessary doesn't automatically make it right."

There was no arguing with that.

Chang's Funeral Parlor looked about as much like the one in Manayunk as a dachshund looks like a St. Bernard. I mean, they're both dogs, but that's about as far as you can take it.

Chang's sat on the west side of Ninth Street between Cherry and Arch—a three-story, brick-fronted row house set amid shops and parking garages. The three of us walked past it twice before we finally spotted the sign, which was oddly small and almost impossible to see in the dark.

"Don't look like much, does it?" the Burgermeister observed.

Helene eyed the place over. "Think you can pick the lock, Will?"

I glanced up and down the street. It was almost twelve on a cold, drizzly Friday night in February. Even so, there were people around. A couple of women were huddled together under the awning of a twenty-four-hour dry cleaner, chatting away. At the other end of the block, moving toward us, an unhappy-looking man was walking a "mop" dog.

Not many people. But too many.

"Yeah," I answered. "But we're too easy to spot. Let's go around back."

The alley that ran between Chang's and the deli next door was really narrow—so narrow that a couple of times, the Burgermeister pulled a Winnie-the-Pooh. Each time, he managed to wriggle free but only after a lot of squirming and muttered curses. Worse, the second time he got stuck, Helene nearly burst out laughing.

"Shut up!" he growled, straining like a hatching bird. "It ain't funny!"

"Both of you, shut up!" I whispered.

Helene pressed her lips together but still shivered with suppressed chuckles.

Dave finally wormed free and stumbled after us into the funeral home's tiny backyard.

"I don't care what happens in there, dudes," he muttered. "*I'm* goin' out the front!"

"Come on," I said, leading the way up a few short cement steps to the building's back door. Not surprisingly, it was locked.

Also not surprisingly, I had my pocketknife.

I knelt in front of the knob and pressed the *1* button. Then I inserted the twin prongs that popped out into the keyhole. After that, it was just a matter of holding the button down and letting the automatic picks do their work.

Within thirty seconds, the latch clicked.

"We're in," I whispered. "Only one of us should go first… check the place out."

"I'll go," Helene said. "I'm supposed to be in charge."

"That's why you should stay out here," I argued. "In case something happens that you need to take charge of."

I looked over my shoulder at her to see if she'd bought it. She hadn't.

Her hands were on her hips, never a good sign. "That's stupid. I'll go in and make sure it's clear. Then I'll radio the two of you when I find the body."

"I'm better at this than you are," I argued.

"How do you figure that?"

Behind her, the Burgermeister said, "Dudes…"

Ignoring him, I muttered. "I'm just saying…"

"Saying what?" Helene demanded.

"That…I've got some experience sneaking through dark houses at night."

She opened her mouth and closed it again, frowning.

We both knew what I was talking about—a solo mission to Kenny Booth's house to rescue her.

"You've done it *once*," she said finally.

"That's once more than you," I countered.

"Enough!"

The voice wasn't loud, but it was deep and angry. We both looked at Dave, who stood behind Helene, shadowing her like a mountain. His hands, like hers, were on his hips. But his were bunched up into fists.

He said, growled really, "You both go in! I'll stay out here and keep watch. We all got radios. I'll call you if I see something I shouldn't, and you call me when you need me to come in. Just turn the lights on if you can, will ya? Unlike you two, I ain't so good at sneaking around in the dark." Then, after a long pause, he added, "And stop acting like doofuses. You're both better than that."

Helene and I swapped guilty looks. Then, with a shared shrug, the two of us slipped through the door, leaving Dave alone on the back porch.

Inside was a kind of foyer, with yellow rain slickers hanging on pegs against one wall. The floor was carpeted, so we didn't need to worry too much about someone hearing our footsteps. Of course, it also meant we wouldn't hear *their* footsteps either.

I stopped and listened hard. The place was deathly quiet. Sorry about the pun.

"I don't think there's anybody here," Helene remarked.

"Good," I said.

Beyond the foyer was a carpeted hallway that fed three rooms of varying sizes. In each, folding chairs had been lined up to face the far wall. In one of the rooms, a big wooden casket sat atop a long curtained table.

"Think there's somebody in there?" Helene asked nervously.

"It's just for show," I replied.

"Show?"

"When someone dies, the family visits the funeral home, and they kind of show off what they can do. Like a stage set."

"How do you know that?" she asked. Then, when I gave her a hard look, she added, "Sorry."

"Besides, dead bodies need to be kept cold until right before the service."

"Right," she said. "I knew that. I guess this place has me a little spooked. Sounds weird to say that. I mean…I fight the living dead all the time. You wouldn't think that the dead Dead could freak me out like this, but they do."

I nodded.

"There's probably a morgue…or whatever they call it… downstairs," I said.

"Let's do it."

Cellar stairs in a Philly row house are easy to find. They're almost always right under other stairs, and Chang's was no exception. The door was unusual though—thick, heavy steel, cold to the touch but painted to look like wood. It was

TY DRAGO

also locked, which seemed odd at first, until Helene pointed
out that you couldn't have some dude at a funeral wandering
downstairs and finding tomorrow's dead bodies.

She had a point.

I picked the lock with my pocketknife. Helene opened it
a crack.

"There's light," she said. "I think somebody's down there."

"Figures," I muttered.

She went first, and I followed, each of us making as little
noise as possible. The cement stairwell was well lit, with a
sharp right turn about halfway down to the basement floor.

At the midpoint landing, we paused. Voices floated up
from the around the corner. I couldn't help but wonder what
sort of people would be working at midnight in the cellar of
a funeral parlor.

But then I noticed that the voices I heard weren't—strictly
speaking—voices at all.

And these weren't people.

Yellow rain slickers.

I'm an idiot.

"Crap..." Helene muttered. "We should just split."

"We need that body!" I whispered back.

"I know...but we're not set up for a fight."

Not entirely true. I had my pocketknife with its Taser.
And all three of us had left Haven with full water pistols
under our belts. That was probably enough if we were lucky
and if there weren't more than a couple of Deaders on-site.

I motioned for Helene to follow me back up the steps.

Once we'd returned safely to the main floor and had shut the heavy door behind us, I headed straight to the kitchen.

"Will!" Helene whispered sharply.

"Hang on…"

I found what I was looking for right away. The whole thing took maybe two minutes to prepare.

"What are you doing?" she demanded at first. Then, as she watched and it started to dawn on her, she asked instead, "Will it work?"

"Sure," I replied. "Why wouldn't it?" I tried to sound more confident than I felt. "But it's gonna be heavy. Give Dave a call."

She whispered into her wrist. The Burgermeister responded. I didn't catch what he said, but then Helene rolled her eyes and felt for the light switch.

The overhead lamp lit, momentarily blinding us both but giving Dave a clear path from the door. He showed up half a minute later.

"Find a dead body?" he asked.

"More than one," Helene replied. "Unfortunately, looks like some of them are…occupied."

The Burgermeister's eyes lit up. "Awesome! Let's kick some Corpse butt!" Then he noticed what I was doing, wrinkled his forehead, and added, "Hey, Will…what's with the bucket?"

CHAPTER 22

FLOOR PLAN

We didn't report our situation to Haven.

If we had, Tom would have ordered us home immediately. I was breaking rules and regs again, and I knew it. Last night's business with the wallet had gotten Helene and me split onto separate teams by the Chief, a constraint that Tom had evidently forgotten with everything that had been going on.

But another breach tonight might even see me doing a stint with the Moms!

I had two choices: I could give up this crazy idea or I could pull it off. If I came back with both my friends unharmed *and* with a female dead body in tow, Tom wouldn't ask questions. Probably.

Sometimes I wondered why I kept doing things like this.

Chang's basement was split into at least two rooms. The first one stood empty. It appeared to be a kind of filing room, with an unoccupied desk surrounded by big cabinets that were stuffed with folders. Apparently the computer age hadn't yet reached Chang's Funeral Parlor. The light came from overhead florescent bulbs.

A door stood in the center of the far wall. The Deadspeak—they were chattering up a storm in there—was coming from just beyond it. The top half of the door was frosted glass, through which I could make out vague moving shapes but couldn't tell exactly how many shapes there were.

But at least now we could make out some of what was being said.

"How. Old?"

"Three. Days."

"How. Die?"

"Drown. Kill. Self."

"Foolish. Human."

"You. Want?"

"Acceptable. Call. Van."

The three of us exchanged looks. "Flank the door," I said.

Helene took the left. I took the right. The door's hinges weren't visible, which meant that it would open away from us. The knob was on Helene's side. She tested it gingerly before she gave me a "thumbs up." It wasn't locked.

Okay…the point of no return. Am I doing this or not?

Who was I kidding?

I nodded to Dave, who came up and stood right in front of the door. In his hands was the big five-gallon green plastic pail. I'd filled it almost to the brim, which had made it way too heavy for either me or Helene to lift. However, the Burgermeister handled it with ease.

I raised one hand, displaying three fingers. Then two fingers. Then one. Then a tight fist.

Now.

Helene turned the knob and shoved the door all the way open. It swung wide before it banged against the inside wall.

The inner room was much larger than the outer one. Morgue-like metal doors were built into the left-hand wall, with cluttered shelving on the opposite side. The finished ceiling was brightly lit and seemed high for a basement, maybe twelve feet. The floor was sunken, with a ramp leading down to a cement floor. All the surfaces were painted a high-gloss gray.

In the center stood a metal table surrounded by an assortment of gadgets, with tubes and dials and wires that probably had something to do with handling dead bodies.

And speaking of dead bodies—

Four of them, two Type Threes, a Type Two, and a Type One, were all huddled around the fifth cadaver, who lay atop a shiny steel table setup in the middle of the room. This last dead body was that of a young Asian woman—genuinely deceased. In life, she'd probably been pretty. But her skin had turned gray and hung loose.

The Corpse had been right—about three days dead. Funny the things you get to be an expert on when you're an Undertaker.

Then, when I heard Helene mutter, "Oh…crap," I looked over at the Deaders.

And they looked right back at me. The Two wore a fancy suit, complete with power tie. The Threes were also in suits, but theirs looked more formal and less businesslike. I'd seen suits like that before—just once.

They were undertakers. Well, you know what I mean.

The Corpses run Chang's Funeral Parlor!

Up until now, we'd assumed the Deaders got their host bodies from the city morgue or, in rare cases, from killing living people. The idea of them taking over local mortuaries and running them as regular businesses—well, I didn't think that had occurred to anyone in Haven. A useful bit of intel.

That was the good news.

The bad news was that the Type One in the room was Lilith Cavanaugh.

"Well, now," she said in English. "What have we here?"

The Queen of the Dead. We'd been calling her that since she first popped up on the news, this well-dressed Corpse wearing the Mask of a pretty blond lady. She'd taken Philly by storm, smiling into every camera lens and showing up at all the big parties and political events. In just two months, she'd become the face of what the papers were calling "The *new* Philadelphia"—elegant, gracious, beautiful.

Except, *we* knew what hid beneath that beauty. Since her arrival, girls had gone missing all over the city. They were from different neighborhoods, different ethnic background, different walks of life. But they'd all had one thing in common. It was the same thing the poor dead woman on the metal table had.

In life, they'd all been good-looking.

"To Her Majesty," Sharyn had once joked, "'well dressed' means more'n a pretty cocktail shift!"

So, yeah, we knew Lilith Cavanaugh. Except that, up until now, we'd only known her from afar. This was the first time an Undertaker had met her face-to-face.

On either side of the Queen, her cronies tensed up, ready to charge. They outnumbered us, and they knew it.

"Dave!" I shouted. "Now!"

The Burgermeister stepped forward. No hesitation. No argument. He just pushed himself in between Helene and me and swung the big bucket he carried in his big arms.

Five gallons of water splashed across the floor, covering every inch of it, spilling over the Deaders' shoes.

For a long moment, nobody moved—not us, not them. Then Cavanaugh looked down at her expensive red pumps and smiled thinly. As she did, the corners of her mouth cracked loudly enough to hear. A bloated fly squeezed through the newly made gash and buzzed lazily around her head.

I felt my stomach flip-flop.

"Saltwater?" she asked in English. "How rude. I paid quite a bit for these shoes, and now you've ruined them." Her smile widened. More flies emerged. It was hideous. "A clever trick, Undertakers…but it can't harm us through our footwear! Your childish chemistry is useless!"

Screwing up my courage, I pushed in front of Dave until I stood inches from the edge of the wide puddle. In my hand, I held my pocketknife.

"Not chemistry, Your Deadness" I replied, offering up a smile of my own. "Physics."

Then I bent down and tapped the wet floor with my Taser.

Saltwater is great for incapacitating Deaders. But that's not all it's good for.

It's also a wicked conductor.

For half a minute, everything was light and noise. Electricity flooded the air, making every hair on my body stand at attention—a really weird feeling. Sparks flew, snapping at the metal table and the stainless steel contraptions that surrounded it. The Corpses stiffened and dropped hard, splashing and flopping about in the charged water like landed fish.

I kept tasing for most of a minute. There was a sound in the air like cloth ripping—so loud I couldn't hear much of anything else. Then I smelled something sharp and sickly, burning rubber, I suppose, or maybe burning flesh.

The lights went out.

Something in contact with the wet floor must have been plugged into one of the wall outlets because a fuse had clearly popped. Fortunately, a second later, one of those boxy-looking emergency lights mounted up near the ceiling flickered on, bathing everything in a greenish glow.

I straightened up and blinked, letting my eyes adjust.

The poor dead girl still lay on the metal table, her body covered with a sheet and her skin looking oddly healthy in the greenish light.

Bodies were sprawled across the floor all around her, eyes sightless and limbs askew in the wide puddle of water. These soaked, zapped Corpses weren't dead, of course. But they'd be trapped in their immobile hosts until rescued.

Either way, it had *worked*!

Then I heard Helene and Dave both gasp. I looked at them and then followed their shared gaze up to the ceiling.

Ever hear the term "my blood ran cold"? You hear it in old horror movies, the ones starring Vincent Price. But I'd never really gotten the concept behind it.

Until now.

The Queen of the Dead wasn't on the floor amid her fallen cronies.

She was on the ceiling.

I'd seen Corpses jump plenty of times. They were good at it, some of them better than Michael Jordan. But this had to be twelve feet straight up! And that wasn't the half of it because the ceiling in this room was, like the walls and floor, concrete. Cavanaugh had somehow jabbed her fingertips deep into the hard surface—her toes too, having leaped right out of her fancy red pumps. Clearly she had tremendous strength, much more than any Deader I'd ever seen.

But *that* was crazy!

Her host body, after all, was human. How could human bones drive into cement?

As if reading my mind—a terrifying thought—the Queen grinned her hideous grin. "Don't look so surprised, children. You're all stronger than you look. Consider the karate master who breaks a cinder block with the blade of his hand. This is no different."

I leveled my pistol at her. Helene leveled both of hers. The Burgermeister, who held nothing now but an empty bucket, just glowered. "Your dudes are down for the count," he said. "Those bodies they're in just got good and fried. Will's seen to that. No way are they getting up again until they can transfer. That means you're alone."

Cavanaugh laughed. "Others will come. In fact, they're coming already." Then she tilted her head and looked directly at *me*. Any cold, running blood I had in my face drained away.

"Will?" she echoed thoughtfully. "Will…Ritter?" Her grin widened. "I got your message. The one you left with my minion at the prison."

"Great," I replied. "Thing is, though…we need the body on that table."

The Queen studied me. "That makes two of us. But what do *you* need it for? Since when do the Undertakers have any interest in the truly dead?" Then, when I didn't reply, she laughed again. "Well, that leaves us with something of a dilemma, doesn't it? We can't both have the pretty human cadaver. A standoff."

"Except there's three of us!" Helene said sharply, her pistols rock steady. "And we got *these*!"

Cavanaugh sighed. She sounded relaxed, even casual— as if dangling like a spider upside down from the ceiling was as natural as chilling on a sofa. "I'm not afraid of your saltwater."

"Why don't you come down and say that?" Helene pressed.

I took a step forward. As near as I could estimate, Cavanaugh was in range—barely.

"In a moment, little ones. I need to decide which of you to kill first, though I suppose it hardly matters, provided I leave young Will here for last." Her eyes bore into me again. "You see, I want to tell you a few things…reveal a few surprise associations I've made of late…before I kill you. Who knows, maybe I'll wear your girlfriend there as my next host. I've never occupied a body so young."

Beside me, despite her nearly bottomless bravery, I heard Helene utter a small involuntary cry of horror.

Suddenly, the blood came rushing back to my face. Only it wasn't cold anymore.

"No way!" I screamed, the word bubbling out of me like a war cry. Then I fired.

I'd been right. Cavanaugh *had* been in range—except she

wasn't there by the time my saltwater hit the ceiling. She'd vaulted sideways with the speed and agility of a big cat onto the top of a steel cabinet at least six feet away.

I turned and fired a second time. But she simply jumped again—this time from the cabinet, off the back wall, and then onto the countertop on the far side of the room. For a moment, I managed to see through my fury long enough to wonder why she didn't just drop to the floor. But of course, she couldn't. Although no longer electrified, the floor was still layered in saltwater—and the Queen's feet were bare.

I aimed and fired a third time, but it was no good. She was too fast for me. With a final leap, she cleared all our heads and landed atop some shelving by the door. Whirling around, I took aim again, silently wondering why Helene wasn't doing the same thing. But then I noticed Helene wasn't even beside me anymore.

The Queen smiled. "This is all very amusing. But I *want* the body on that table. I need a new host."

A voice said, "You can't have her!"

I looked over my shoulder to find Helene standing beside the metal table. Her pistols were nowhere in sight. Instead, she'd snatched a nasty-looking syringe. It was almost the size of a knitting needle and *must* have been used for embalming or something like that because I couldn't image any doctor sticking anything that big into a living person.

Helene had turned the dead girl's head to the side and was pressing the needle's point against her lifeless temple.

"What game are you playing, child?" the Queen asked. All the amusement was gone from her dead eyes.

"This isn't a game," Helene replied flatly. "And this girl isn't a prize. She's a person…or she was, and she deserves better than to be used up and discarded by the likes of you. I stick this needle through her temple and into her brain, and she becomes useless. Am I right?"

Cavanaugh actually snarled—a guttural, terrifying sound that made my hairs stand up as if I were still tasing the water.

I tried to catch Helene's eye. If she did this, the body would be useless to *us* too! She *had* to know that!

But she wouldn't even look at me.

The Queen hissed, "You're playing with fire, young lady!"

Helene shrugged. "Whatever."

Then she raised her arm high, the long needle gleaming in the dull green emergency light. "Rest in peace," she said to the dead girl on the table.

With an inhuman cry, the Queen of the Dead leapt at her, her bloated purple hands—mangled from the concrete— reaching out like talons. She meant to tear Helene's throat out with those hands, to rip her head from her shoulders. I could see it in her milky, hateful eyes.

A lot of things happened fast after that.

One, Helene smiled triumphantly and raised her other hand, the one she'd kept hidden behind the body. In it was one of her water pistols, which she leveled at the Queen, who was in midair and irrevocably committed to her leap.

Two, yours truly went into full panic mode. I fired repeatedly at Cavanaugh but missed every time. Then, in desperation, I threw myself in her path—anything to keep her away from Helene.

Three, I heard Helene yell, "Will! Don't!" But like the Queen, I was irrevocably committed. I slammed into Cavanaugh just as she reached the metal table. All my weight was behind my shoulder, and I caught her midway up her torso, knocking her out of the air.

Four, the two of us crashed together, toppling a couple of wheeled carts and shoving the table hard enough to throw the body atop it into Helene. I hit the floor a second later. So did Helene—but with the poor girl's cadaver atop her. However, the Queen, as agile as ever, somehow managed to balance herself on the table edge, vault over it, and land once again atop the shelving.

"Enough of this," I heard her say, and I struggled to my feet. On the other side of the table, Helene cursed wildly, trying to get out from under the deal girl's limp form.

Frantically, aware of how badly I'd just screwed up, I spun around in a circle, trying to track Cavanaugh. She was moving around the room with insane grace, leaping from surface to surface so quickly I could barely keep up.

How can something that dead move that fast?

Then, to my horror, she landed behind Dave. The Burgermeister, who'd stood helpless in the face of this disaster, was wise to the Queen's presence at his shoulder just a moment too late. Cavanaugh seized him by the throat, lifting the huge kid off the floor with such force that the empty bucket flew from his hand.

"Look at your friend, Will!" the Queen roared. She slammed Dave against the doorframe. The Burgermeister's big hands clawed at the dead fingers digging into his neck, but her grip was clearly too strong.

No…please. Not again.

Somewhere along the line, I'd lost my pistol. I still had the Taser, but I was much too far away to use it. And this time, Cavanaugh wasn't standing in the puddle of saltwater. *I* was.

"Look at him!" she screamed, her dead visage twisted with fury. "I want you to watch his face as I snap his neck! Look at him!"

Helene was trying to get to her feet, but I could already tell she'd be too late.

I did this. I went off mission again…only now Dave's going to pay for it!

But then Dave, red-faced and all, somehow managed to grin.

"That ain't…no way…to snap…a neck," the Burgermeister gasped. Then, raising both his arms, he grabbed Cavanaugh's head in his huge hands and gave it a single hard twist.

I actually heard her spine snap.

The Queen of the Dead dropped into a heap at Dave's feet.

"*That's* how you snap a neck, Your Royal Wormbagness," he pronounced.

I'd only known of three occasions when Dave had gone against the dead. And each time, he'd lost—bad. As big and as strong as he was, *they* were stronger, with their Queen being the strongest of all. And he just wasn't that good at fighting them.

At least, I'd *thought* he wasn't.

I looked back at Helene, who'd finally found her feet. She'd recovered at least one of her water pistols, but of course, there wasn't anybody to shoot at anymore. The two of us swapped looks. Her expression was as incredulous as mine, but behind her disbelief was visible anger—anger at *me*.

And I honestly couldn't blame her.

Dave wiped his hands together with a "job well done" kind of pride. Then, grinning, he trudged across the wet floor toward us, "Hey, Will, how'd you dream up that bucket trick? That was pretty sick!"

"Huh?" I asked stupidly. Then, looking from my friend to the "broken" Queen on the floor and back again, I said distractedly, "Steve told me about it. Well, he *suggested* it *might* work, but I don't think anyone ever tested it."

Helene remarked, "Duh? Who besides you's got a Taser?"

"Just me and Tom," I admitted. "Sorry, Helene. I really blew that."

"Yep. You really did."

"Sorry," I said again.

"Whatever." It was the same thing she'd said to the Queen while she'd been baiting her trap. Same tone too. Then, gazing down at the girl's cadaver, which lay in the puddle at her feet, she added, "Well, at least she can't transfer. The body's too wet with saltwater."

"Good," I said.

"Hey, dudes!" the Burgermeister said brightly. "No harm done! In fact, looks to me like we *won*!"

Helene and I scanned around. We'd secured the cadaver we'd been sent to get. Better still, four Corpses lay sprawled out on the floor all around us. Every single one would need a new host before they got up again.

And one of them was the Queen.

It was a good score. An *Angels* score.

Helene said to Dave, "How'd you learn that...neck break...thing?"

The Burgermeister's expression turned sheepish, and for a second, I thought he wouldn't answer. Then he did. "Sharyn taught it to me."

"She did?" Helene and I asked at once.

"Yeah. She's been giving me private lessons."

"Since when?" I asked.

"About a month," he replied with a shrug.

I blinked. "But—"

"Forget it for now," Helene interrupted. "Cavanaugh was right. Others are coming. Let's get the body and split before they show up."

"I hear that!" Dave exclaimed, clearly happy with the change in subject. Then he unceremoniously stepped past us and scooped up the dead girl's cadaver like a rag doll, tossing her limp form over one shoulder.

"Let's go!" he declared.

On the way out, I noticed a fancy cell phone lying on the floor near the Queen's broken form. I pocketed it, thinking the Hackers might be able to wring out some decent intel.

Then I promptly forgot about it when one of the morgue drawers kicked open.

I honestly don't think there's a scarier sight in the world.

The three of us spun around as hands—the stiff, gray hands of a Type One—groped out of the darkness and clutched the edges of the opening. Once it found purchase, it pulled, and the drawer on which the Deader lay screeched as it rolled along its tracks.

He lay on his back under a sheet, no more than a day or two dead, an old man no doubt earmarked for a coming funeral. This wasn't the sort of cadaver the Corpses favored—too frail. But this dude evidently intended to make the most of it because he sat stiffly atop his drawer and faced us, his seemly sightless eyes alight with menace.

"I'm Gerald Pierce," he declared in English, a little over-dramatically to be honest. Probably brown-nosing for the Queen, who helpless as she was, could hear him. "And I will kill you all in my mistress's name!"

Then he swung his legs over and dropped to the floor.

Right into the puddle of saltwater.

His newly stolen body stiffened and then started twitching.

With a look of genuine horror on his dead face, he toppled over onto his back, which only got him wetter.

The three of us watched him until his twitching stopped, which meant that saltwater had done its bit and that Gerald Pierce—whoever *he* was—would need yet another host.

"What a tool," Helene muttered.

Then we got out of there.

CHAPTER 23

THE DEMONSTRATION

We walked the three blocks back to Haven's northern entrance without any problems—or much conversation. After his mind-blowing defeat of Lilith Cavanaugh, Dave looked happier than I'd seen him in weeks. And Helene... well, Helene wasn't talking to me.

At one point, we had to briefly duck into a darkened storefront to watch several Corpses hurry past going the other way back toward Chang's. The Queen's help had arrived. Soon, every single Deader we'd felled in that basement would be back on his—or her—feet, safely encased in a new stolen body.

If only I'd had a Ritter. Just one.

And this time, I think I might be able to use it.

By morning, Chang's Funeral Parlor would be cleaned up, almost as if our big fight had never happened. The floor would be mopped, the broken equipment removed or replaced. And of course, all the dead bodies would be gone.

Including several that *should* have been there.

I glanced over at Dave's lifeless burden, and I didn't think I'd ever felt so lousy about succeeding.

On our way out, I'd suggested to the Burgermeister that he might want to cradle the girl in his arms like a sleeping child rather than over his shoulder like a sack of mulch. Helene agreed, and Dave did so, which turned out to be a good thing. We didn't pass too many people while en route to Haven, but those we *did* pass didn't give us a second glance.

Four teenagers headed home after a late night, with one of them too drunk to walk. Not a pretty picture.

But certainly better than the truth!

Behind the graffiti-covered frontage of an abandoned printing house on Spring Garden Street stood an old fence, one section of which had been broken or cut. After a quick check to make sure no one was looking, we went through, doing our best to hold the chain links wide enough for Dave and his bundle of joy.

From there, we located a particular cellar window, with nails that had rusted away or been pulled out. Helene swung it open, and I climbed through, turning back so the dead girl could be handed to me.

There'd been a time when a building like this would have creeped me out. Now all I felt in this rat-infested cellar was measured relief.

"That went okay," Dave remarked.

"I guess," I replied.

Helene didn't say anything.

A concealed staircase in the cellar led to a subcellar, which led to a sewer, which led to an unused maintenance door.

And simple as that, we were home.

The sentry, who happened to be a sour-faced Burt Moscova, looked us over. "How'd it go?" he asked.

"Went fine," Helene replied. "How's Sharyn?"

"The same. Tom says you're supposed to take the body straight to his office. It's all set up. Um…you got a *girl* body, right?"

I nodded.

"Sure did!" Dave grinned. Then he pushed past Burt and marched through the door. For a moment, I thought he might start whistling.

"What's with him?" Burt asked. "He's not usually this… happy, is he?"

"At least somebody is," Helene muttered. Then she and I followed the Burgermeister into Haven proper.

Things were happening outside Tom's office.

Alex Bobson and two of his Monkeys were just pushing through the curtain, carrying tools. After a moment, Steve came out too, followed by Tom. And all the while, I could hear Agent Ramirez, still hoarse from shouting but shouting anyway. "Answer me! Who's that old woman? What are you doing with her? *Jefferson!*"

Tom sighed and said to Alex, "How tough is that door?"

"Tough enough," the Monkey Boss replied. "Ain't a

Corpse alive…you know what I mean…gonna get through without a week's worth of pounding."

"I don't need a week," Tom remarked. "Just ten minutes. But they're gonna be ten hard minutes."

"It'll hold," Alex said. "I guarantee it." Then he noticed Dave, Helene, and me coming up the corridor, and his smile vanished. Without a word, he and his guys shuffled away with their tools in hand, heading in the opposite direction.

"There you go," Dave grunted with obvious satisfaction. "Dude *can* be taught!"

Tom and Steve approached us. "You got a female cadaver?"

"Yeah," I said.

"Any problems?"

"Nope," said the Burgermeister.

"We ran into some Corpses," I replied. "But we took care of it."

Tom's brow knitted. "You were supposed to back off if you hit trouble."

"I know," I said, meeting his eyes. "But Steve gave me an idea, and it seemed like a good time to try it out. I held up my pocketknife, displaying its Taser.

Tom glanced at the Brain Boss, whose eyes widened. "A group zap?" he asked.

I nodded.

"Fantastic! How many?"

"Three at once," I said. Then, after some hesitation, I added, "Plus the Queen."

Tom's stiffened. "You ran into Cavanaugh?"

Helene said, "She was after the same body we were. Needs a new host apparently."

"You dudes *should* have backed off! How'd it go down?"

Helene told him, though she left out the part where she came up with a solid plan to goad the Queen into dropping her guard only to have the whole thing completely fouled up by me. But in leaving that part out, I saw her jaw tighten.

She's really mad at me.

Tom regarded Dave. "My sister's been trainin' you on the side?"

The Burgermeister's smile faded. "Yeah." Then he quickly added, "But Will's the mastermind."

"Is he?" the Chief asked.

"Heck, yeah! If not for him, we'd probably have turned tail and run when we found out about the Deaders being there."

Please, Dave, I thought miserably. *Don't help me.*

"Well, we'll talk 'bout that later," said Tom. "For now… why don't the three of you follow me? The night's just getting started."

With that, Tom headed back through the curtain into his office, with Helene, Steve, Dave, Dave's dead burden, and me in tow. Inside, I saw that most of the furniture had either been removed or shoved up against the wall. A wooden door had been fitted into the archway to Tom's bedroom. It looked solid and thick, just as ordered, with an eighteen-inch window built into its upper half. Two iron deadbolts, each almost a foot long, held it closed, and instead of a knob, it had a big steel pull ring.

Cuffed to this ring by both hands stood Agent Ramirez, looking sweaty and red-faced with anger. Trussed up as he was, he couldn't reach either of the bolts, but he had a nice clear view through the window.

Right now, though, he was looking at *us*—and at the Burgermeister in particular.

"Jeez, you're a big one!" he said, his voice gravelly. "What are you, son…sixteen?"

"He's fourteen," said Helene.

"Fifteen," I corrected.

"He is?" Helene asked. It was the first time she'd spoken to me since Chang's. She scowled, as if I'd somehow tricked her into breaking her silence.

Dave didn't reply at all.

The FBI guy's eyes flicked from Dave's girth to the small, limp figure in his arms. His face, if possible, went even paler. "What *is* this?" he demanded.

"A demonstration," Tom replied. He sounded exhausted.

"Is that girl all right?"

"She's dead," Tom said flatly. "But before you start off again, we had nothing to do with her death. All we did was take her body from the funeral parlor."

"All you did…" Ramirez echoed. "Are you even listening to yourself, Jefferson? First you kidnap and imprison an innocent old woman, and then you have these children break into a funeral home and steal a body? And that's 'all you did?'"

Tom sighed. "Agent, I know how all this must look to you. And for what it's worth, what we have to do to this poor girl's body sickens me. She's a human being, one of us, and she deserves respect. This kind of thing is the Corpses' game, not ours.

"But I need…absolutely *need*…to make you understand. I gotta break through that wall of disbelief that you and everybody like you has built up around themselves. That disbelief is the best weapon the Corpses got. You not only don't believe in 'em…you *can't* believe in 'em because doing so would turn your whole worldview upside down."

The FBI guy shook his head. "You're completely insane."

"Well, if you still believe that in five minutes," Tom replied, "then I'll let you go." He turned to Dave. "I'm gonna open this door. There's a Corpse in there, a Type Three female pretending to be an old lady. She's tied up on the bed with a bag over her head. I want you to carry that girl's body in and lay it on the blanket that's set up on the far side of the room. Got it?"

"Got it," Dave said.

Tom shouldered Ramirez aside and slid back the two deadbolts. Then, after he grabbed the steel ring, he pulled the heavy door open, forcing the agent to shuffle uncomfortably along with it.

All the while, Ramirez kept talking—pleading—*begging* Tom to think about whatever it was he planned to do. These were people, not monsters—just people. And this delusion of his, into which he'd somehow hooked the rest of us, had to stop before something truly awful happened.

Then he looked at me and added, "Unless it already has."

Tom ignored all of it in patient silence, standing aside as Dave began to move past him and into the bedroom. At the last minute, though, Tom stopped him. "Hold up," he said. "Dave, I know you been carrying that poor girl for a while now, but you think you can lower her so the agent here can have a look?"

The Burgermeister nodded and bent his knees until the dead girl's face was close to Ramirez's shackled hands.

"What are you doing?" the agent demanded.

"Check her pulse," Tom said.

"I can see she's dead," Ramirez replied with disgust. "I've seen my share of bodies."

"Take it anyway. In the next few minutes, you might have second thoughts…and I want you to be *really* sure."

The FBI looked down at the bloated purple face, grimaced, and then twisted one hand until two of his fingers touched the lifeless flesh of the girl's throat. He took his time about it, frowning in concentration. Then, with a sigh, he nodded.

"She's dead. No doubt about it. And God help you, Jefferson."

"I'll take all the help I can get," Tom agreed. "Go on, Dave. Take her in…but be respectful."

"I will," the Burgermeister said. Then he stepped past Tom and entered the bedroom. Half a minute later, the big dude came back out, this time without the dead body in his arms.

"Thanks, man," Tom told him, slapping him on the back. "A solid piece of work."

Dave actually blushed a little.

I suddenly realized that Tom, as a rule, didn't pay much attention to the Burgermeister. I'd always kind of taken my close friendship with the Chief for granted; it hadn't really occurred to me before how many Undertakers went through their days without seeing, much less talking to Tom Jefferson.

"Steve," the Chief said. "Got the pistol?"

Steve handed him a green plastic water gun. It was tiny, far smaller than the one I carried. Just what was he planning to do with *that* puny thing?

I started to ask, but the Chief looked pointedly at me, and I kept quiet.

He showed Ramirez the water pistol. The FBI guy studied it suspiciously but, for once, didn't say anything. Then Tom fired a squirt into his open mouth and made a sour face. "Saltwater. Tastes lousy, but it can't hurt nobody."

"If you say so," Ramirez muttered.

Tom shot him on the cheek. The agent flinched and cursed but then settled down. After a moment, his tongue flicked out and tasted a bit of the water nearest his lips.

"Saltwater," Tom said again.

"Saltwater," Ramirez agreed.

The Chief nodded. "Now here's how this is going to work. I'm going to go into that room alone. After that, Will's gonna bolt the door shut. I'll take the bag off the old woman's head and uncuff her. Then I'm going to squirt her in the face the same way I just squirted you."

"Why?"

Tom nodded to Steve, who explained, "Salt interferes with the control the Corpses have over the cadavers they inhabit. The Corpse will go into spasms and fall to the floor. The effect lasts about two minutes."

"And they usually recover in a mean mood," Helene added. "Tom, are you sure…"

He gave her a sharp look, and *she* went quiet.

"It's a trick," Ramirez said. "You've set something up."

Ignoring him, Tom addressed the rest of us. "I'm gonna put Will in charge of this room while I'm in there. I know the rest o' you probably want to stay, and I appreciate that, but I'm gonna ask that you don't. The window's small, and Will and Agent Ramirez are the only people who need to see what's happening. It'll be simpler if they're the only ones tryin' to."

Then he said to me, "Bro…you don't open this door unless I tell you to. Got it?"

I nodded.

He nodded.

Then, tiny water pistol in hand, the Chief of the Undertakers stepped into what used to be his bedroom—to face the dead.

CHAPTER 24

DUELING WITH THE DEAD

As Ramirez pressed himself up against the glass, I went and stood beside him. Helene, Steve, and the Burgermeister headed reluctantly for the curtain.

At the last minute, I called, "Dave, can you stick around?"

He and Helene looked back at me.

"Sure!" he replied.

Helene began, "Tom said—"

"I know what he said," I told her. "But I'm asking Dave to stay."

"Why?"

"In case of trouble," I replied with a shrug.

"No problem," the Burgermeister said.

Helene treated me to a hard, searching look. "What's going on?"

I didn't know how to answer that. I felt my mouth open and then close. Finally, I said, "Sorry, but I don't have time for this."

Then I turned away.

After a few long seconds, I heard Helene's rapid footfalls in the corridor, moving off. Dave came and stood at my shoulder.

"You're in deep trouble, dude," he whispered.

"Yeah," I whispered back.

Ramirez remarked miserably, "All you kids are in deep trouble."

"You got no idea," I told him.

Through the small window, we watched as Tom approached the bed, *his* bed, on which a figure lay firmly tied to the posts. There was a bag over her head, but even so, I knew it was, as Tom had explained, a Type Three. Her stench still filled the office from when the door had stood open.

Only Threes stink *that* bad.

The Chief reached down, and in one quick motion, he yanked the bag off her head. The face beneath it was almost charcoal black, dried up and starting to flake. The eyes were sunken and so milky that they looked almost pupil-less. She wore a long coat over a blue patterned dressed. Her hands were small with sharp-nailed claws.

She snarled at Tom, baring a mouthful of loose yellow teeth.

"Dear God, Will…" Ramirez breathed. "You have to let me stop this."

I crossed my eyes and saw what he saw.

The woman on the bed was maybe in her seventies, frail and silver-haired. She looked like she might snap in two in a stiff wind. A helpless, frightened old lady. No wonder Ramirez was so horrified. If I couldn't See the truth, I'd have been pretty horrified too.

Except the eyes that were fixed on Tom weren't fearful. They were angry. And calculating.

Be careful, Chief.

"Listen up," Tom said to the Corpse. "See that window in the door? See them faces? They're here for a show…so you and me are gonna give 'em one. The rules are simple: you waste me, and you get out of here, easy as you please."

The old woman—my eyes started to ache, so I uncrossed them—the rotting cadaver glared at Tom. Then she looked over at us, staring right at Ramirez and me, her expression suddenly thoughtful. Fortunately, with the lights at our back, she shouldn't be able to discern more than vague silhouettes. The window was a necessity—to let Ramirez watch the goings-on. But it was just as important that this Deader not know specifically *who* was watching her.

Thing is, Corpses are cruel and vicious and, yeah, butt ugly, but they're not stupid. If this one spotted the adult standing beside me, she might just figure out what we were up to—at least enough to convince her to play it "human." And if the "little old lady" on the bed started crying and begging, looking all small and terrified, that would be *real* bad for Tom's demo.

I waited, holding my breath.

"Undertaker," she said in Deadspeak. *"Why. I. Trust. You?"*

248

Tom pretended that he'd heard. This was also part of the plan. Ramirez couldn't hear Deadspeak. For this to work, the Corpse had to speak English.

When the Chief didn't respond, Dead Old Lady frowned, her expression wary.

"Got nothin' to say?" Tom asked innocently. "Then maybe I should just leave you here until you rot away to nothing."

Half a minute passed.

She's figured it out.

Except, she hadn't. "Undertaker," she repeated in English this time. "Why should I trust your word?"

Tom grinned. "You got another choice?"

The Corpse pulled at her bonds. "Release me then," she snarled. "So I can kill you and leave this place."

The Chief shook his head. "Nope. That body stays tied up right where it is. But 'cause I'm a good host, I've arranged another way for you to get loose." He pointed to the dead girl who lay on the blanket where Dave had left her. "It's a lot fresher than the one you got now anyway."

The Type Three's milky eyes flicked over to the body on the blanket. Mine flicked over to Ramirez. He'd stopped squirming and struggling against his cuffs and was now staring through the glass, a strange expression on his face.

"Here," Tom said. "Let me give you a little incentive."

Then he fired a some saltwater into Dead Old Lady's face.

"No!" Ramirez exclaimed, though I had no idea why. He knew what was in the gun.

The Corpse responded the way they always do. Her body went rigid and then started bucking and thrashing in helpless spasms. The ropes around her wrists held—but only just.

After a few moments, I heard a cracking sound, and one of her arms snapped free from its shoulder socket. One second, it was thrashing away with the rest of her. And the next, it just hung limp inside the sleeve of her coat.

FBI Guy's eyes blinked repeatedly, as if he were trying to focus on something.

Tom fired another squirt of water. Then another. He kept firing until the pistol was empty. I understood that was the plan, but seeing him do it still scared the crap out of me.

See, I also knew what was coming *next*.

The Corpse bucked furiously. Another loud crunch, and the second arm ripped free. The monster rolled off the bed, the coat coming with her, leaving behind both arms—now bare and still tied to the bedposts. The detached limbs were black and flaky, and bugs skittered in and around them, spilling out onto the mattress.

"Tell me you didn't see that!" I demanded.

Ramirez didn't answer. He didn't even look at me. His forehead was pressed right up against the window, his eyes glassy with horror—though what kind of horror, I couldn't be sure. Corpses were able to extend their Masks so passersby didn't see things like severed limbs. But how far did the power of that illusion really go?

We were about to find out.

Tom stepped back and dropped the now useless gun. His face remained completely calm as he watched the Corpse on the floor thrash and writhe and then finally go still.

Now, I thought.

"He killed her…" Ramirez said, but he sounded more confused than accusatory.

"Did he?" I answered.

The dead girl on the blanket sat up.

Beside me, Agent Ramirez let out a sound halfway between a gasp and a moan. I crossed my eyes and had a look at the room the way he was seeing it.

The old lady had *moved*. She no longer lay in a heap beside the bed. Instead, she was rising to her feet atop the blanket in the opposite corner of the room, her eyes fixed on Tom.

Where she *had* been, there was now a decaying lump of flesh, still wearing the old woman's wool coat and blue print dress—except that the cadaver's severed arms hung from ropes fastened to the bedposts.

The Mask had been dropped from the old body and moved to the new.

Which meant that the old woman Ramirez and I saw was now totally naked—Masks don't extend to clothing. The view wasn't pretty, so I quickly uncrossed my eyes. At least looking at dead bodies didn't embarrass me.

"No…" the FBI guy whispered.

"What's the matter?" I asked. "See something you can't explain?"

He started to answer. But then we both jumped as the newly risen Corpse launched herself at Tom.

He should have dodged. He *could* have. I'd seen him do it. One-on-one, I didn't think there was a Deader alive—so to speak—who could have tagged him. No, he *let* this one hit him. It was part of the show.

But she hit him hard. *Very* hard. One moment, he was standing in the middle of the room, looking at her, and the next, he went airborne, slamming into the opposite brick wall in a shower of dried mortar. He landed on the bed, dazed but struggling to recover.

Dead Old Lady/Girl pounced on him, clawing at his face with grasping purple fingers. Her teeth snapped forward, going for his jugular. But at the last second, Tom managed to block her with his forearm. Hissing, she bit deep into the muscle just below his elbow.

Tom cried out in agony.

He slammed his left fist into her abdomen. Her body shuddered with the blow, but her jaws remained fastened to Tom's arm like a pit bull's.

Long enough, I decided. Either Ramirez was convinced or he was an idiot. No way was I going to watch the Chief of the Undertakers die to make a point.

"I'm going in there!" I announced.

"No!" the agent snapped. "Uncuff me. I'll go in!"

I looked at him. He looked back at me. "You'll run," I said.

"No, I won't. God help me, I swear I won't. I don't

know what that…that *thing*…is in there. But it isn't"—he swallowed—"natural."

I wanted to believe him. Despite everything I'd been through over the past few months, however much I'd learned to rely on my own skills and my own courage, such as it was—the idea of surrendering this problem to the nearest adult was shockingly strong.

Unfortunately, I didn't dare.

"Sorry," I said, pulling out my pocketknife. Through the window, Tom had managed to get his feet up between himself and the Corpse and force her back, breaking her hold on his arm. A big chuck of his flesh went with her. Blood, Tom's blood, flew in every direction.

Dead Old Lady/Girl slammed into the far wall but recovered instantly. She leapt at Tom again, snarling, her receding lips sticky red and her mouth a gaping maul.

To Ramirez, I said, "Move over. I need to open the door!"

"I can't let you do this, Will!" he said, pleaded. "For your father's sake!"

Bringing my dad into this was a low blow, though Ramirez probably didn't get that. "Dave," I said. "Grab him."

The Burgermeister wrapped his arms around the FBI guy, lifting him completely off his feet. The cuffs rattled as they reached their limit, making Ramirez wince. But it gave me the room I needed to work the deadbolts and pull the door open. While it moved, Dave also moved, dragging the agent out of the way as I bolted into the room.

The Deader was on top of Tom again, her knees on his chest, one hand on his throat and the other trying to rake his face with her long gray nails. The Chief was bleeding badly from his mangled arm and a deep gash across his nose.

I couldn't risk the Taser. With the two of them in physical contact like this, zapping her would zap him too. Instead, I popped the blade and lunged at the girl, aiming for the sweet spot at the base of her skull.

However, at the last second, she spotted me. Her head twisted grotesquely and seized my wrist in an iron grip. As she squeezed, I cried out, and the knife fell from my hand, bouncing under the bed.

With lightning quickness, her hand released my arm and clamped around my throat.

It was like getting caught in a steel vise.

Almost at once, I saw stars. A terrible pressure filled my head, as if my brains were being squeezed out of my ears like toothpaste from a tube.

Then, through my blurring vision, it seemed as if the girl grew a second pair of arms—these wearing the sleeves of a man's white shirt. The new arms wrapped around her upper torso and, with a great heave, pulled her off of us. The grip on my neck fell away, leaving behind deep fingernail gashes but letting wonderful air back into my lungs.

My vision cleared.

Ramirez was holding the Corpse up much the way the Burgermeister had been holding *him* up a minute ago.

"What do I do with her?" he cried as Dead Old Lady/Girl thrashed like an enraged cat in his arms. He staggered to and fro, finally stumbled into a corner. "Come on!" he exclaimed desperately. "What am I supposed to do?"

I couldn't speak; my throat was too sore. My knife lay somewhere under the bed, but right now, I lacked the strength to find it.

However, Tom pulled himself to his feet. He'd looked beaten half to death—probably because he *was*—but he moved nevertheless, crossing the small room on legs that quivered under him like an old man's.

From the inside pocket of his jacket, he produced a Ritter. *He had that all the time?*

"Hold her steady," he said in a hoarse voice.

Ramirez did the best he could. But the Corpse grabbed his left arm in both hands and wrenched it savagely. The FBI guy cried out in pain and lost his grip. Dead Old Lady/Girl whirled on him, her teeth snapping and her fingers lunging for his eyes.

"Your turn!" she snarled.

Then Dave smacked her.

The big guy had stepped into the room just in time. His backhand blow bounced the Deader off the far wall. Then, as she was trying to regain her balance, the Burgermeister caught her in her arms, much the way Ramirez had. Except Dave's arms were a *lot* bigger. They closed like vices.

Tom shook his head a few times, as if trying to clear it. Then he drew back his hand and drove the syringe deep into the Deader's bare abdomen, using his thumb to slam the plunger home.

"Let her go, Dave," he said.

"You sure?"

The Chief nodded. Beside me, Ramirez was cradling his left arm, his face sweaty, his eyes wide.

The Burgermeister shoved Dead Old Lady/Girl aside. She stumbled a few steps before she whirled around, ready to attack again.

Then she exploded.

For a second or two, the thing inside of her glared at us. Then it was gone too—forever gone.

For half a minute, nobody said anything. Tom stood rigidly in place while beside him, the FBI guy cradled his injured arm. His eyes were glassy.

Finally, with a sigh, the Chief spoke—coughed really.

"Welcome to the Undertakers, Agent Ramirez."

CHAPTER 25

SWAPPING STORIES

I believe you," Ramirez said. "But who in the world's going to believe *me*?"

We were back in the infirmary, and it struck me that I'd been spending a lot of time here lately. Most of that, of course, was because of Sharyn, who lay where she'd been laying for more than a day now, doing exactly what she'd been doing all that time. Nothing.

Except maybe dying.

But I tried not to think about that.

Helene was here. So were Steve, Dave, and Chuck Binelli, who'd been on hand when we arrived, getting his stitched tongue checked. As we'd come stumbling in, a ragtag procession, I'd fleetingly wondered if Helene was still mad. When I caught her looking at me, it was only with worry. She was seeing the purple bruises on my neck—so much like her own.

"I'm fine," I assured her.

"I didn't ask," she replied. Then she turned away.

Yep. Still mad.

Tom sat on one of the patient cots, with Ian stitching his arm. He wasn't using any anesthetic, just working carefully with surgical thread and a curved needle. The Chief would wince every so often but otherwise didn't seem to notice. Amy stood at Ian's shoulder, watching carefully.

Maybe he was training her. Not a bad idea.

Across from him, the FBI guy had plopped himself down on another cot, his hair matted with sweat. His left arm hung in a sling, the shoulder—according to Ian—badly sprained.

To Ramirez, Tom said, "Getting other people to believe you ain't the issue. I don't expect you to run back to DC and start telling your bosses at the bureau all about the Corpses. I just need to know that you won't run to the local cops and tell 'em all about *us.*"

Ramirez ran one trembling hand through his hair. "That girl was dead," he muttered—more to himself, I thought, than to any of us. "I took her pulse…took my time about it because I expected a trick. But no, she was dead. I swear she was."

He looked up at Tom. "And you kids have been living like this…for years?"

Tom shrugged. "Some of us longer than others. But, yeah." He motioned toward Sharyn's gurney. "That's my sister. She got herself hit by a Corpse during the raid to rescue you. A big one…much bigger than the female I just fought. Sharyn's been in a coma ever since. Ian…he's our medic…" Ian paused in his stitching long enough to offer FBI Guy a completely ridiculous wave.

Tom continued, "Ian don't know if she's gonna wake up at all." His face was calm, his voice rock solid with control.

"You should get her to a doctor," Ramirez said.

The Chief shook his head. "Not an option. This world is being *invaded*, agent. It's been going down for three years, and you and all your fellow suits ain't had a clue about it. We don't get why we can See 'em and you can't. But this war is real, and the only ones who can fight it is *us*. We're soldiers…and in war, soldiers die. Sharyn wouldn't be the first, and she won't be the last."

He looked at Ian, who'd just finished the last stitch. "I'll bandage it," the medic said.

"In a minute," Tom replied. Then he stood and crossed to Ramirez's bunk. Sitting beside the trembling man, he continued, "I need to hear you say it: you gonna keep quiet about us or not?"

Ramirez visibly swallowed. Then he nodded.

"Out loud, agent," Tom remarked.

"I'm not going to say anything, I swear it. But…how far does this go? How many of them are there?"

"Thousands. With more coming in all the time. We don't know how they get here or where they come from, but it's pretty clear what they're after. Power. They move slowly, worming their way deeper and deeper into society. It's kind of like a spreading stain…small but getting bigger day by day."

"Just here?" Ramirez asked. "In Philadelphia?"

"As far as we know."

The FBI guy shook his head. "It's…unbelievable."

"But you *do* believe it," the Chief pressed.

"Yeah," Ramirez replied. Then, meeting Tom's eyes, he added, "Yes, I do."

Helene and Chuck actually applauded. Dave pumped the air, making a "woof woof" sound that I made a mental note to tease him about later.

"Thing is," the agent continued, "Karl came down to Washington to see me just weeks before he died. We'd known each other for years. We met when, a long time ago, I tried to recruit him for the bureau. His record was *that* good. But he wasn't interested. Philly was his home, he said. He'd been born here, lived here, and he'd die here. I guess…" He looked at me. "I guess he did. I'm sorry, son."

I didn't reply.

Ramirez cleared his throat. "Now when a man like that tells you he's on to something…something big, a conspiracy so terrifying he doesn't quite yet dare reveal the particulars, you have to take notice. And when that man ends up dead less than a month later…well, I couldn't ignore it."

He stared at his shoes, which still had some bits of dead body on them. "I couldn't open an official investigation because Karl hadn't come to me in an official capacity. The FBI can't get involved in local crimes except under very particular circumstances…like a state line being crossed."

Steve asked, "How about a dimensional line?"

Ramirez paused, looked at him, and then continued, "But I have…had…my contacts in the local PD, and Karl was well respected. I brought a few of these cops into my confidence, asked them to nose around a little but to keep my name out of it. This went on for the better part of a year and had just started making some progress. Then my contacts started reporting rumors involving a local newsman. Kenny Booth. But then…" his voice trailed off.

For a long moment, no one said anything.

So I did. "But then they died."

He regarded me, as if surprised I'd figured that out. "Yes, they died. Tragic accidents…one or two months apart. A fire. A car crash. A fatal heart attack. Coincidence, right? What else could it be? Who could murder four police officers, your father included, without someone besides me taking notice?"

It was Helene who answered. "Kenny Booth, that's who."

The FBI guy nodded. "Kenny Booth. Karl mentioned him that time he came to me. Just a passing remark, like he didn't quite believe it himself. But now I think he was trying to plant a seed in me, to start me wondering. He knew full well what Booth was, but there wasn't any way he could convince me, so he just dropped enough of a hint that…after he died…"

He sighed. "Then later, when those cops died too, I started investigating Booth, quietly and on my own time. He was clean…squeaky clean. *Too* clean. Nothing on his record, not even a parking ticket. In fact, before he came to Philly, he didn't seem to have existed at all, except on paper. I mean, I've seen my share of phony IDs, but this one was a work of art, so nearly perfect that I knew there was no way I could convince my superiors that Booth was anyone but who he said he was."

"Booth came to Philly three and a half years ago," Tom said. "He died just last October, two years after he killed Karl. Two years. That's a lot of investigating, Agent Ramirez."

Ramirez looking dejected. "I did everything I could. I knew in my heart that Booth had been involved somehow. But he was so careful, so smart. I couldn't touch him, couldn't even get enough on him to start an official investigation." He faced me. "I'm sorry, Will."

"It doesn't matter," I replied, meaning it. "I got him for both of us."

He took that in, looking me over with fresh eyes. "Saltwater," he said. "Like that syringe Jefferson used on the old lady just now."

"We call them 'Ritters,'" Steve said.

"For Karl?"

The Brain Boss shook his head. "For Will…the first person ever to kill a Corpse."

I kept my face neutral, but inwardly, I groaned.

"What Will came up with was a little different," Tom explained. "But it worked the same way. Get salt into a Corpse's body, and the body explodes, leaving the invader inside unprotected. It dies within seconds."

Ramirez asked, "And how many of them have you gotten?"

The Chief shrugged. "The technique's only about four months old, and the Ritters have been around for just a few days. But it's a start."

"It's a start," the agent agreed.

"Listen," Tom told him. "You know something about us, and we know something about you. Was your investigation into Booth the reason the Corpses grabbed you the other night? Did they figure out it was you behind all the questions?"

Ramirez shook his head. "No. They didn't come after me because of Booth. They came after me because of Lilith Cavanaugh."

Everybody went suddenly quiet. The agent remarked, "You know her, I guess?"

"Yeah," replied Tom. "Cavanaugh's the new Boss Corpse. She replaced Booth. We call her the Queen of the Dead."

"Lilith Cavanaugh is…one of *them*?"

We all nodded.

"But she's…"

Dave finished his thought. "Hot?"

"Wicked hot," Chuck added. It was the first time he'd spoken. The word sounded pretty clear to me. Either his tongue was healing, or he was getting used to the stitches.

"Her *Mask* is," Helene corrected. "But Cavanaugh's probably the worst of them. She goes through like a body a week…apparently doesn't care for it when they start to rot around her."

Tom said, "Most Deaders hang onto a host body long as they can…until it literally starts falling apart. It's a security thing…transferring risks exposure, like we showed you in the demo. But not Cavanaugh. We have reason to believe she might even murder women she thinks are good-looking… just so she can wear their skin."

Ramirez muttered an oath in Spanish. I didn't know what it meant, but I could guess.

"So…yeah," the Chief concluded. "We know her."

"She's a lot like Booth in some ways," the FBI guy explained. "Same squeaky-clean past, same 'too perfect' paper trail. Like Booth, she just showed up one day with all these credentials and references and…just like that"—he snapped his fingers—"got herself appointed the city's new community affairs director. I guess you could say it was a red flag that only I could see."

"Your own personal Sight," Dave quipped. He laughed and then looked a bit embarrassed when nobody joined him.

Ramirez continued, "I decided to reopen my investigation…all on my own this time. No more putting others at risk. No more dead cops. Just me."

"Good idea," remarked Helene.

"Honorable," Tom added.

The agent sighed. "I made some phone calls, asked some questions. The wrong questions as it turned out. I ended up getting a call from someone in Cavanaugh's office, a guy named Pierce."

"Pierce," I echoed. "We met him last night at the funeral parlor."

"Guy's a tool," Helene added.

Ramirez regarded us, a sour expression on his face. "He sounded scared but said he had information for me and asked if I'd meet with him at an all-night diner in South Philly. I agreed. But when I got there, they were waiting. Four cops."

"Corpses," Steve remarked unnecessarily.

Ramirez said, "Pierce had set me up. I never even got into the diner. They grabbed me, cuffed me, and hustled me into their cruiser. Once inside, I was chloroformed, and the next thing I knew, I woke up here."

"They had you for something like nine hours," I told him. "And they didn't ask you any questions?"

"If they did, I don't remember them."

Tom, Helene, and I exchanged looks.

"Amy," the Chief said quietly. "Could you fetch a magnifying glass?"

I saw the little girl go pale. She, of all people, knew what we were thinking. "Okay," she whispered.

"What now?" Ramirez asked. He looked suspicious all over again.

"We gotta make sure you ain't a mole," Tom said.

"A mole? You mean a spy?"

We all nodded.

"The Corpses got a way to control you," I explained. "They call it the *Pelligog*...and it's just about the scariest thing I've ever seen."

"*Pelligog*," Ramirez repeated, as if testing a new word. "Look, kids...I admit my eyes have been opened, but this..."

Tom said, "Don't be tryin' to take it in all at once, agent. The bottom line is that we need to see the small of your back—just for a second. So, do you mind liftin' your shirt?"

The FBI guy stared at him. "This has been the craziest couple of days of my life."

None of us replied.

Amy returned, carrying a big magnifying glass. Ramirez saw it, uttered a nervous laugh, and pulled up his shirt.

"Dave," Tom said. "You get on his left, and I'll take his right. Sorry, agent. Just a precaution."

"Protocol," Ramirez said.

"We call 'em rules and regs...but, yeah."

With the Chief and the Burgermeister flanking the FBI guy, Amy leaned over the cot, peering through the magnifying lens at Ramirez's bare back.

Why her and not Ian, you ask?

Because Amy knew all too well what she was looking for.

She took her time about it. I felt like I was standing on pins and needles.

"Nothing," the little girl finally reported in her whispery voice.

"Well, that's a relief," the agent remarked, straightening up and pulling down his shirt. "What…exactly…were you looking for?"

Steve said, "We recently found out that the *Pelligog*, when they enter a host body, leave a tiny cut on the lower back."

"It looks like a check mark," Amy said.

Ramirez absorbed this. "And I don't have it?"

She shook her head, offering him a small, surprisingly pretty smile.

Tom and Dave stepped back. The Chief said, "But it still don't explain why the Corpses took you but didn't ask you no questions."

"Maybe they were gonna *Pelligog* him," I suggested. "But we got there before they actually did it."

"Then you're lucky," Helene said to Ramirez. "I've had one of those things on my back. So has Amy. We both know what it does to you."

I went over and stood beside her. I wasn't sure why; it just seemed like something I should do.

Ramirez said, "I need to get out of here. I need to tell somebody…something. I don't know what yet. Obviously, the truth won't work."

"And who can you tell?" Tom asked him. "You don't have the Sight, and without it, you may as well be a blind man. How can you even know who to trust?"

"I can't just do nothing!"

"Sure you can…for now. Go back to DC. I doubt the Corpses'll risk nabbing you again—at least not there. Keep your head down and wait. We'll make sure you stay in the loop."

But the FBI guy shook his head. "You don't understand. There's a time limit here. That's what brought me to Philly."

"A time limit?" I asked.

He nodded. "The governor of Pennsylvania is visiting Philadelphia this weekend…and I'm pretty sure Cavanaugh plans to assassinate him."

For several long seconds, nobody said anything.

Finally, Chuck muttered, "How—"

But that was as far as he got before Sharyn started dying.

CHAPTER 26

THE LAST STRAW

Pierce flew across the office, striking the far wall hard enough to shake it and topple a case full of books the Queen hadn't and would likely never bother to read. He fell in a heap, his new host body broken in several places.

Lilith staggered across the room and loomed over her personal assistant. He raised his head and looked feebly up at her; evidently, that last blow apparently hadn't broken his host's spine.

Unlike what had happened to *her* a few hours ago.

"There were three of you," she said, keeping her tone level. "Three. That should have been enough to protect me. But instead, you were bested by three children wielding toys. Worse, they took my new host, leaving me trapped in a worthless shell, helplessly awaiting rescue!"

She seized Pierce's collar, lifting him effortlessly off the floor.

"And when my minions finally arrived and carried me to my home, did a new host await me? No, they hadn't found one! So I lay on my human bed, stranded inside a rotting husk, for hours. Hours!"

She cast his body like a rag doll the width of her office. He slammed into the door with such force that the wood cracked and plaster rained down from the ceiling.

This time, when he hit the floor, he didn't move at all.

Lilith Cavanaugh crossed to him, shuffling on legs that popped and creaked with each step. The body her minions had finally found was at least two months old—the bones brittle and the muscles thin and weak. It required all her considerable Self to imbibe it with the strength necessary to punish her underling in this manner.

In fact, it took all her will to tolerate being inside of it at all.

The Queen glowered down at Pierce, toying with the idea of driving her foot through his skull, smashing it to powder. But doing so would likely shatter her own leg, and given the circumstances, she simply couldn't risk that.

But oh how she wanted to!

Then Pierce's eyes met hers. "I'm…sorry…Ms. Cavanaugh," he wheezed.

Despite his situation, her assistant continued to address her by her human name.

Until that moment, she'd been on the fence. But that simple gesture of respect had convinced her to let him live.

Lilith sighed. "It was *our* funeral parlor, Pierce. Why would there be salt there?"

He struggled to reply but couldn't manage it. She knew the answer anyway: because Chang's was a recent acquisition and her minions had been too afraid of the salt to risk touching it, even to throw it away.

Idiots. I'm surrounded by them.

"You need a new host," she told Pierce.

And this one's simply less foolish than most.

Lilith shuffled over to her desk and picked up the phone. With Pierce incapacitated, she was forced to look up the number in the Philadelphia City Hall directory and dial herself. One more indignity.

After the third ring, the chief of police answered, "Pierce?"

"No."

"My Queen?"

Idiot.

"Is that how you want to address me, Chief D'Angelo?"

"No. I'm sorry. What can I do for you, Ms. Cavanaugh?"

"I need a host brought up to my office immediately." The Queen frowned at her withered black claw of a hand and added, "A male."

Then she hung up and sat down in her desk chair.

"Pierce," she said thoughtfully. Then, when he didn't respond, she added, "Look at me when I'm talking to you."

To his credit, he tried, his broken body twitching uselessly around him. He looked feeble—ridiculous.

"Pierce," she said again. "Last night's fiasco has convinced me that these Undertakers have grown entirely too bold. Tomorrow is an important day, and I refuse to risk it being ruined by a ragtag collection of human hatchlings!"

"Yes…Ms. Cavanaugh," Pierce wheezed.

The Queen brooded.

Finally, D'Angelo showed up. The police chief wore his uniform, as did the minion who followed him, carrying a sack over one shoulder. Lilith motioned wordlessly at Pierce's broken body. Wordlessly, the chief nodded to the minion, who just as wordlessly delivered the sack.

"How fresh is it?" the Queen asked.

"Sixteen days, mistress…er…Ms. Cavanaugh. Unmarked. A drug overdose."

"Acceptable. Well, Pierce, what are you waiting for? Applause?"

Pierce's body went still. At the same instant, the sack began to move. For half a minute, they watched him struggle to open the canvas from within. D'Angelo moved to help, but Lilith waved him off.

Lessons needed learning.

Pierce's fingers, swollen and deep purple, wiggled out through the top of the tied sack and tore downward. At last, it fell away, allowing the body to rise stiffly to its feet. It wasn't a particularly good specimen—the skin showed signs of faster than normal decay. Probably died in the sun.

Disgusting, these human forms.

"Go and dress yourself properly, Pierce," the Queen commanded. "Then return here. We have work to do."

"Yes, Ms. Cavanaugh," her assistant said. Then he walked past D'Angelo and the minion, disappearing through the door.

"Thank you, chief," Lilith said. "Are we fully prepared for tomorrow?"

"Of course, ma'am."

"Any word from the morgue?" she asked.

The chief of police squirmed inside his uniform. "No, Ms. Cavanaugh. I'm sorry."

"That will be all."

"Yes, mistress."

Lilith glowered as her minions departed.

This host of necessity she wore annoyed her on every level. It was much older, in fact, than the one she'd hoped to replace last night at Chang's.

Humans might have called that "ironic."

Unfortunately, no other suitable candidate was available. If only she could order her minions out among the rabble to find her something suitable. But, no. However bad her need, caution was paramount. Nothing could be allowed to upset tomorrow's timetable. After that, a great many things would be changing—*if* she could keep the Undertakers out of her way.

The Undertakers.

The Ritter boy had stolen her cell phone as she lay helpless. Its loss didn't overly concern her; aside from contact numbers, there was little of value on it. But the theft *was* galling—especially given what else had been taken!

But what did Karl Ritter's band of whelps need with a human cadaver?

Lilith stopped brooding and started analyzing.

Half a minute later, she sat up in her chair, found her notepad, and ran one sticky purple finger down its length until she found the phone number she was looking for.

Then she dialed, doing her best to ignore the bits of skin left behind each time she tapped a number.

"Hello."

"Susan," the Queen said. "It's Lilith. I'm sorry to call you so early on a Saturday."

"I was up."

"I may have some news for you."

"Really? Tell me!"

"Well, it's rather complicated, and with everything that's going on this weekend, my schedule's full this morning. Can we possibly meet in person? Maybe this afternoon?"

"You tell me where and when, and I'll be there!"

"My office," Lilith said. "Two o'clock. And feel free to bring your daughter."

"That's all right. I can ask my sister to watch her for a couple of hours."

"This might take longer than that, Susan."

"Emily gets fussy on the train. It'll be easier if I can let her stay home."

Lilith almost argued but stopped herself. While inconvenient, the obstacle was manageable. "All right. If you're sure. I'll see you at two o'clock."

"Lilith?"

"Yes, Susan?"

"Should I be...hopeful?"

The Queen of the Dead grinned into the phone. "Oh yes. I think you should definitely be hopeful."

Then she hung up...and smiled.

CHAPTER 27

DESPERATION

Laying atop her cot, Sharyn's body jerked. Then it jerked again. Within seconds, she was flopping about wildly, her eyes wide open and sightless.

Tom made a sound that was very nearly a whimper. Then he, Amy, and Ian rushed to his sister's bedside.

"Hold her down!" the medic commanded. "Amy, get me the stick!" As the little girl hurried off to obey, Tom wordlessly threw his weight onto Sharyn's struggling form.

As he did, Ian barked, "Come on, guys! Help!"

We all rushed over. Helene took one leg and I took the other while the Burgermeister—his face pale—grabbed the girl's upper arms. "'S'okay, Chief," he said to Tom. "We got her!"

Chuck and Ramirez were the last to arrive at the gurney, and seeing no obvious way to help, they apparently decided to ask dumb questions instead.

"What's going on with her?" Chuck asked.

"Is it a seizure?" the FBI guy wanted to know.

"Not a seizure," Ian replied. "She's convulsing. We'd better strap her down."

"With what?" I asked.

"There's a bag of rags in the corner. Can one of you get it?"

It struck me as odd that of all of us, Ramirez was the one to obey. He came around the gurney and held the bag open for Ian, who pulled out a fistful of worn but clean rags, passing them around. "Wrists and ankles," he told us.

"Do we have to?" Tom asked him, looking miserable.

"If we don't, she could throw herself off the gurney... maybe even break a bone."

The Chief nodded. We went to work tying the girl down. It wasn't easy. She was strong and struggling like a panicked animal. But we managed it. With a sigh, Ian stepped back.

Ramirez looked worried at Sharyn's restless body, bucking against her restraints. "What if she swallows her tongue?"

"That's a myth," Ian told him offhandedly. "You can't actually swallow your tongue."

FBI guy frowned. "Are you sure?"

It was Tom who answered—a little impatiently, I thought. "He's sure."

"What exactly happened to her anyway?" Ramirez asked.

"Head trauma," Ian replied, "I think maybe it's a vasogenic edema."

"A what?" Dave demanded.

"I know what it is," the FBI guy answered. "Her skull cavity is filling up with fluid, cutting off the oxygen to her brain." He faced Tom, who wore an expression I'd never seen on him before.

The Chief looked terrified.

"Jefferson," Ramirez said. "She *needs* to go to a hospital."

Tom shook his head.

The agent came around the gurney and squared off with him, toe-to-toe. When he spoke this time, he wasn't gentle. "She's your sister, and if she doesn't get treatment, she's going to die! Don't you get that?"

Tom tore his eyes away from Sharyn's sweaty face. "No hospital," he croaked.

"For God's sake, kid," Ramirez snapped. "This isn't a game—"

I knew that the Chief of the Undertakers was fast. I'd seen him in combat. But until that moment, I hadn't known *how* fast. He seized the agent's collar with the speed of a striking cobra. Ramirez was cut off mid-sentence as Tom spun him around and slammed him against the brick wall next to Sharyn's gurney. The man winced.

Beside me, Helene yelled, "Tom! Hold up!"

But Chief ignored her, his eyes locked on Ramirez. When he spoke, his voice carried more menace than I'd ever heard there. "You figure I think this is a game? That's my twin sister there. It's been her and me, *just* her and me, for almost the whole of our lives. She's my family, the only family I *got*!"

"Look," the agent said, struggling to sound like a responsible grown-up; we *were* just kids, after all. "I'm sorry if I upset you. But you have to look at this maturely—"

It was the *way* wrong approach.

Again, Tom shook him, this time so hard I thought his head might hit the bricks and we'd end up having two of them tied down on gurneys. "The Deaders *watch* the hospitals!" he exclaimed—screamed almost. "All the time! And especially now 'cause they know they hurt her! They'll watch for her to show, and if she does, they'll *kill* her. Quick and quiet so nobody suspects a thing!"

Ramirez stared at him. "That's…not possible—"

"They've done it before! More times than I can stand to think about!"

"But they can't just murder children in a—"

Tom groaned and released Ramirez's collar, eyeing the guy like he was the biggest idiot on the planet.

"They're an army of animated cadavers," he said flatly. "I know you can't See that, but *we* do. An army of rotting, sticking, maggot-riddle wormbags. But you know what they ain't? They ain't zombies, and this ain't the latest chapter of *The Walking Dead*. The Corpses are smart. Smart as us. Smart as you. And they know what they're doing. They got a hundred ways to take us out, the kids who can See 'em. They make it look natural…illness or accidents. And they don't get caught. They don't *ever* get caught!"

Ramirez gaped, speechless. Tom uttered an unmistakable "I'm done with you" grunt and returned to Sharyn's side, taking his sister's hand. "Do we got any options, Ian?" he asked.

Haven's medic looked pale, but he nodded. "One. Maybe. I've been icing her skull—at least as much as I think I can get away with without risking hypothermia."

"What's hypothermia?" the Burgermeister asked worriedly.

"It's when your body gets too cold and stops functioning," I replied.

"Oh," he said.

Ian cleared his throat. "There's something called a ventriculostomy," he said. "But, Tom, it's risky. Seriously risky. Even if we had the right equipment and a sterile place to do it, it'd be long odds."

"And what if we leave her like this?" the Chief pressed.

Ian shrugged miserably. "She'll die. Probably by the end of the day."

"So...what choice we got? What...exactly...is a ventriculostomy?"

I was quietly astonished that Tom had been able to repeat the word so smoothly. I couldn't seem to wrap my tongue around it or my mind around what was happening. True, I'd seen death since becoming an Undertaker. More than once.

But this was Sharyn.

Ian said, "Well...it's pretty common in hospitals. Basically, you drill a hole through the skull at just the right spot. Then you stick a catheter…a plastic tube…into the brain to drain off the excess fluid."

"Jeez…" Chuck muttered. "And that's supposed to *help*?"

The medic nodded, though he didn't look convinced.

Tom said, "I don't gotta ask if you ever done this before. Of course you ain't."

From behind him, Ramirez whispered, "This is crazy." He faced Ian. "What do you even know about surgery?"

"My dad's a surgeon at Jefferson Hospital here in Philly," the boy replied. "I was kind of raised with a scalpel in my hand."

"What does that even mean?" Ramirez snapped. "The fact that your father's a surgeon doesn't make *you* one!"

"No, it don't," Tom said. "But *this* does." He lifted his shirt, displaying a jagged scar that ran across the lower right side of his midsection, maybe six inches long. I'd seen it before but had assumed it was a battle wound.

"Ian took out my appendix," the Chief said. "Almost a year ago now."

Ramirez stared incredulously at the scar. "Even so, there's a big difference between an appendectomy and brain surgery."

"Yeah…but we don't got no choice. Bottom line, agent, this is happening, and Ian's gonna do the job. The only remaining issue is: are you gonna try to stop me?" There was no threat in the Chief's words this time. Just a question from a desperate brother.

The FBI guy looked at each of in turn. I could almost read his mind.

You're kids.

But he said nothing.

"What do you need?" Tom asked Ian.

"I think I've got something I can use for the shunt…the tube that actually gets stuck into her brain. And I've got some flexible hose to drain off the stuff that comes out. But—"

"But what, Ian?"

Haven's medic lowered his eyes. "Tom, listen. I'm gonna need a power drill, something small but with enough kick to get through her skull. Then…I'm gonna need somebody to use it."

We all looked at him.

Ian swallowed. "I…I don't think my hands are steady enough. Not for this. I'm sorry."

"It's cool, Ian," the Chief said. "I'm glad you told me now instead of later. You walk me through it, and I'll handle the drill."

Without even knowing I was going to do it, I stepped forward. "No."

Tom faced me. "Will?"

"Not you. Not me. Not anybody else in this room," I said. "We need somebody who's good at this. Somebody with experience."

The Chief frowned. "Who do we got with experience at something like *this*?"

"Ian," I said. "Is there stuff you gotta to do to get ready?"

The medic nodded. "First, I'll find the right medical book and review the procedure in detail. After that, I'll have to shave her head and sanitize it. Then I'll mark the right spot on her skull and lay out some clean towels. I'll also need to boil some water to sterilize the equipment."

"I can do some of that," Amy said quietly.

"Thanks, Amy," Tom told her.

"Okay," I said. Then to Tom, "You sure you want to do this? I mean, *really* sure?"

"It's a chance, bro. Leave her like this…and she's dead."

"Then stay with her. Keep holding her hand. Let her know you're there. I got this."

Tom hesitated, and then his broad shoulders slumped. He gazed down at his sister, stroking her sweaty, convulsing face. When he looked back me, it was with a truckload of gratitude.

Right now, he didn't have to be Chief. He didn't have to be a leader.

Just a brother.

"Thanks, Will," he whispered.

CHAPTER 28

POWER DRILLS AND OLIVE BRANCHES

The Monkey Barrel was as noisy as ever.

At first, no one noticed me. Then, all of a sudden, it seemed as if *everyone* did. The sawing and hammering stopped at once.

I pasted on what I hoped was a friendly smile. "Is Alex around?"

"What do you want?" More a snarl than a question.

Alex Bobson emerged from the shadows. He wore a heavy canvas apron, rubber gloves, and a pair of thick plastic goggles. I had no clue what he'd been doing, but from the smell, I guessed it hadn't been the highlight of his day.

"Hi," I said.

"You got no friends here, in case you ain't figured that out. So if this is a social call—"

"Sharyn's dying," I said. "And I think you're the only person in Haven who can save her."

That stopped him. He stared at me. They all stared at me. I felt myself squirm. It was like being on stage during a school play and discovering you'd worn the wrong costume.

"What are you talking about?" Alex asked, still nasty but wary too.

"Sharyn's brain is swelling from the hit she took," I explained. "It's gonna kill her unless we can do this procedure to relieve the pressure."

"What procedure?"

I shrugged. "Ian said the name, but I didn't catch it. Started with a 'V.' The point is that we need to drill a hole through her skull without hitting the brain and insert a tube to drain out all the extra stuff. You know, to get the swelling down."

Alex absorbed this. "So…what do you want *me* for?"

"Sharyn once told me that you're a jerk—" I replied.

"Look, Ritter—"

"—but that you get the job done. That crossbow you made her…Aunt Sally…is some serious equipment. Bottom line, you're great with tools, the best we got. Now Ian's a solid medic, but even he doesn't believe he's steady enough to drill that hole without killing Sharyn. I think maybe *you* are."

Now it was Alex's turn to squirm. Every eye in the Monkey Barrel moved from me to him. "You want me to… drill a hole in Sharyn's head?"

"Yeah."

"That's nuts."

I shrugged. "Ian's getting her ready in the infirmary right now. You need to bring a small power drill, the smallest you got. Plus a clean bit."

"What kind of bit?" he asked.

"Kind?"

He growled again, "Wood bit? Metal? Masonry? Ceramic? Jeez, Ritter!"

"I don't know," I replied. "Something that'll make a clean hole through bone, I guess."

"What size? Do you at least know that?"

"Nope."

"You're useless," he told me.

"Whatever."

"Okay," he said, thinking aloud. "I'll bring a half dozen standard and half dozen metric…all ceramic and all different sizes. One of 'em's bound to work. Gimme a minute."

"Does this mean you'll do it?"

He glared at me. "What? Did you figure I'd say *no*?"

Then off he went, cursing me under this breath.

Someone asked, "Is Sharyn really dying?"

I replied, "I hope not."

I heard Alex in a corner of the room, searching through drawers, the contents of which rattled noisily.

Another Monkey asked, "And drilling a hole in her head's gonna save her?"

I replied, "That's what Ian says."

A third voice added, "But Ian ain't a doctor."

I replied, "He's more doctor than anybody else around here."

Nobody had any comment to make about that.

Alex returned a minute later with a beat-up canvas backpack over one shoulder. "Let's go. The rest of you stay on schedule!"

"Good luck, Boss!" somebody called.

"Save her!" another kid added.

Alex didn't reply. Instead, he headed out of the Monkey Barrel at a fast trot, with me chasing after him, keeping pace.

"Thanks," I said.

"What for?"

"For doing this."

"I'm not doing it for you."

"You're doing it for all of us," I said. "That includes me."

He looked about to say something but thought better of it and increased his pace. We were nearly running now, maneuvering through Haven's shadow-laden corridors with the ease of long practice. The crowd outside the infirmary had grown heavier, maybe sixty kids deep. Alex called, "Make a hole!" And they did, their expressions ranging from curious to terrified.

Inside the infirmary, things had been happening in my absence. An old wooden podium had been set up beside Sharyn's gurney. A ridiculously thick book lay open atop it.

Ian was hurriedly scanning its pages.

Sharyn's body continued to convulse against her

restraints. I noticed that her head had been turned to the left and another cloth fastened across her temples to keep her still.

The girl's eyes rolled in their sockets, unseeing.

Ramirez was shaving Sharyn's bare skull. Her dreadlocks had already been cut off and lay like coiled black snakes on the floor. He worked with a cheap disposable razor, carefully removing the stubble left behind by what must have been the girl's first haircut in years.

Tom stood right where I'd left him beside the gurney. Beside him was Amy, her small hand resting gently on the Chief's forearm.

Helene looked surprised as we entered. Nearby, Chuck frowned, as though perplexed.

Dave scowled.

"Alex?" Helene asked. "What are you—"

The Monkey Boss marched right up to Tom and spoke, cutting Helene off in mid-sentence. "I've got a drill and every bit I even thought might work."

The Chief didn't reply. His face was drawn, his skin ashen. Sharyn lay on her deathbed, and he looked like he might check out right along with her.

Ian said, "Good. Thanks, Alex. I've got some water boiling in a pot on the hotplate. You'll want to drop the bits into it for a few minutes."

Wordlessly, Alex went to the counter with the hotplate and did as instructed. Then he returned and held up the power drill he'd brought. It was small, not much bigger than the water pistols we used—for detail work, I suppose.

"Might be okay," the medic pronounced.

Ramirez looked at Alex. "You know what we're planning to do here?"

The Monkey Boss nodded.

"And you're okay with it?"

He nodded again.

"That drill," the FBI guy said. "Are you any good with it?"

"Yeah," Alex replied. No bragging. Just a statement of fact.

"You need a very steady hand," Ramirez pressed. "Steadier than *I've* got. Otherwise, you'll kill her."

Alex raised his right hand, palm down. He had long fingers, calloused from the work.

It was also absolutely motionless.

Ramirez nodded slowly. "Looks good. But this isn't a two-by-four you're drilling into. It's a person's skull. There's going to be blood. Can you handle that?"

Alex glared at him. The infirmary was cemetery quiet.

"I watched both my parents get killed in front of me," he said, his tone stone-cold. "My mother was bitten to death. My father was ripped limb from limb. Then the Corpses blew up my house to cover their tracks, faking a gas leak. But before that, one of them came at me, and I took my dad's chainsaw to him. We were in the garage when it happened, and I painted the walls with that Deader's guts. When I ran out of my house that night…just seconds before it went up in flames…my family was dead, and I was soaked in the blood of at least one of their killers.

"So," he added into the awkward silence that followed. "I'm pretty sure I can handle whatever stuff comes out of Sharyn's head."

Ramirez blanched—seeming, if possible, even more shaken than he'd been after the demo.

"We got a saying around here," Tom muttered without looking up from Sharyn's face. "There are children in the Undertakers but not a lot of childhood."

Chuck added, his stitched-up tongue garbling the words but not much, "What the Chief means is that this isn't the yearbook committee, and we don't need a 'faculty advisor.' For two years now, we've been fighting this war and looking after ourselves. We're good at it."

"Yeah," Dave Burger piled on. "So back off, man."

Ramirez looked utterly defeated.

"Why don't you go sit down?" Ian suggested. "We can handle this."

"Yeah," Ramirez—the only adult in the room; the only adult in Haven—replied quietly. "I suppose you can."

Then he went and sat down, dropping into one of the folding chairs lined up against a nearby wall.

Ian said, "You too, Tom."

"I'm staying here," the Chief replied.

Ian looked at me for help.

I went to Tom's side. "Come on," I told him. Then I put my arm around his shoulder—a gesture he'd done to me about a hundred times. For a second or two, he resisted, but then he let go of Sharyn and let me lead him away from the gurney. Amy went with us, holding the Chief's big hand in her small one.

Helene, Dave, and Chuck followed us.

Agent Ramirez sat hunched over, his eyes focused on Sharyn's gurney. He looked miserable but resigned.

I motioned Tom into a chair beside him. Helene took the next seat over. "She's gonna be okay," she told him, pasting on a smile.

"Sure she is," said Dave.

Well-meaning words. But empty.

Then Amy whispered, "She'd want you to stay strong."

Tom looked at the little girl. There were tears in his eyes. "Yeah…she would."

"Amy," Ian called. "Why don't you stay with him? Will, I could use another set of hands, if that's okay."

I nodded and turned away.

Tom caught my wrist. "She's all I got, bro," he whispered. The expression on his face was like an open wound.

Four months ago, such a display of raw emotion—especially coming from another guy—would have thrown me for a loop. Back in Towers Middle School, you didn't open yourself up like this, no matter what was happening. You just didn't.

But Towers Middle School was a million miles away.

"No, she's not," I told him. "But I hear you."

Tom nodded, let go of my wrist, and buried his face in his hands. Helene and I swapped a look that had about a hundred things behind it. Then I went to stand at Ian's left shoulder. Alex, I saw, had positioned himself on the medic's right.

"Okay," Ian said. He sounded scared, but his voice was steady. "Let's do this."

CHAPTER 29

THE MOM TRAP

Susan Ritter's first thought as she stepped into Lilith Cavanaugh's office at two o'clock on Saturday afternoon was that it didn't look all *that* "hopeful."

There were a half-dozen people waiting for her and all of them, except for Ms. Cavanaugh herself, were uniformed police officers. They studied her, stone faced, as Lilith made the introductions. One of them, Susan was astonished to discover, was none other than Martin D'Angelo, Philly's chief of police. She'd never met the man, but she knew what the media said about him—that he was a hard cop, difficult to work for, but competent.

If anyone can find Will, he can.

Except that there was something about D'Angelo's expression, the way he regarded her.

Something almost, well, predatory.

"Nice to meet you, Mrs. Ritter," Chief D'Angelo said,

smiling with his mouth but not his eyes. "I never had the… pleasure…of knowing Detective Ritter personally, but I knew him by reputation."

"Thank you," Susan replied, shaking the big man's hand. Except she wasn't sure exactly what she was thanking him for. What he'd said about Karl hadn't been a compliment— not quite.

"Have a seat, Susan," Lilith purred. Susan sat and watched with growing apprehension as Lilith settled into her own desk chair and the men, D'Angelo included, positioned themselves behind her. It was odd. The way they stood made them seem somehow subordinate, as if Cavanaugh were their boss.

But Lilith was the city's community affairs director, and Susan felt pretty sure the chief of police didn't report to the Community Affairs Office!

Then she noticed that one of the uniformed policemen had stayed behind and now stood with his back to the closed office door, his expression stony.

Her apprehension deepened.

"What's going on?" Susan asked.

Lilith smiled. "Where's Emily?"

Susan licked her lips. "What?"

"Your daughter. Where is she right now?"

"With my sister," Susan replied. "Why?"

"Your sister Angela?" Lilith said. Then she glanced down at the piece of paper on the desk and recited Angela's address. "Is that correct?"

Susan blinked. "Yes. Ms. Cavanaugh...I don't..."

"Lilith," the other woman corrected. "I asked you to call me Lilith."

"Lilith," Susan whispered. Her mouth felt suddenly dry.

"A pity you didn't bring her with you." Cavanaugh wore her smile, but the warmth had bled out of it. What was left reminded her of D'Angelo.

Predatory.

Lilith continued, "I've shared your husband's DVD with these gentlemen. They found it as interesting as I did... though most of what poor dead Karl had to say was already familiar to us."

"Poor dead..." Susan began, feeling her anger rise. What kind of way was *that* to talk?

"You see, Susan, three years ago, about a year before his death, Detective Ritter founded an organization called the Undertakers. You've heard of it, of course...though you made the mistake of calling it a street gang. Actually, it's more of a children's army, a small legion of runaways who have banded together to fight a common foe."

"Common foe?" Susan echoed. She felt sick to her stomach.

"An invasion from another world," Lilith said. "Another universe actually. These invaders can't travel physically but instead arrive here as pure energy. As such, they must possess human hosts in order to interact in this society. Unfortunately, these hosts can't already be...occupied. Rather, the host body must be quite dead."

Susan's mind reeled. This was insanity! A madman's fantasy! And her confusion was made all the worse by the calm, matter-of-fact way in which Lilith spoke, as if she were teaching arithmetic to a first-grader.

"Now strolling around wrapped in rotting flesh isn't much use to an invading force. So these beings have developed the ability to project an illusion, an image of normalcy for the world to see. That way, no matter how many of their hosts rot out…and they rot so terribly quickly…the world at large still sees them the same way. Clever, wouldn't you say?"

Susan opened her mouth to answer, but nothing came out.

Lilith's smile widened. "It's not a perfect system. But it works." She examined her perfectly manicured hands resting atop lightly on her desktop. For a moment, her smile faltered. But then, it was back, her eyes once locking on Susan's. "Except for the Undertakers."

"The Undertakers…" Susan breathed.

"You see, that little army didn't fall apart when your husband died, as one would expect. Instead, they grew larger, stronger…and smarter. They went deeper underground, learned how to hide, how to fight back, how to become first an annoyance to these invaders and then a genuine threat."

Susan's apprehension was morphing into alarm. She felt as if she were walking through a shifting dream.

Nothing about this makes sense!

Lilith said, "The Undertakers, for reasons no one understands, are able to penetrate these beings' illusion, to see them for the 'borrowed' cadavers they truly are. Karl had the same peculiar talent. So does your son. I'm afraid Will has fallen in with these wayward children. He appears to have dedicated himself to their cause."

"What…cause?" Susan asked.

"Why, defeating the invasion, of course!" Lilith replied with a totally inappropriate laugh. "By thwarting the plans of the beings they call 'Corpses' and…I suppose…sending them back where they came from."

Then all the men started laughing too, except there was no humor in their collective laughter. It sounded more like anger.

Susan felt her blood go cold. "My God…"

"And these beings are quite determined *not* to be thwarted," Lilith continued after a moment. "Which brings me back to my original point. It's a pity you didn't bring Emily with you to this meeting today. You see, Susan…we need her. And I'm afraid now we're going to have to go and get her, even if that means killing your poor sister Angela to do it."

"What are you talking about?" Susan exclaimed, jumping to her feet. "Are you crazy?"

Lilith rose too, slowly, as if she had all the time in the world. "No, Mrs. Ritter. I'm not crazy. In fact, let me show exactly what it is I am."

Susan watched in mute horror as Lilith's perfectly made-up face and elegantly styled hair shimmered and melted away. An instant after that, the same thing happened to the men behind her.

And when she saw what was left behind, Susan began screaming.

And didn't stop.

CHAPTER 30

BITTER TRUTHS

Sharyn's body, which had been hammering against her bonds throughout the operation, finally quieted. Her eyes closed. Now instead of her familiar dreadlocks, she was shaved bald and had a plastic tube sticking out of her head. A reddish mixture of blood and "shock absorbing" brain fluid was oozing through the tube and into a bucket.

Ian took Sharyn's blood pressure with one of those upper-arm cuffs.

"I think it worked," he said.

Tom, Amy, Helene, and the Burgermeister came and stood around the gurney. Only Chuck and Ramirez stayed in their chairs.

The Chief took his sister's hand. "She's sleeping?"

"Still in a coma," Ian said. "Though I think we relieved the pressure on her brain. But, Tom…there's no guarantee here."

"I know. Ian…you're a genius."

The medic shook his head. "All I did was read a medical book and follow the instructions. Alex did the work."

Tom turned to the Monkey Boss. "I owe you big."

"No, you don't," Alex replied. "I'm an Undertaker."

Then, without another word, he collected his drill and bits and left the infirmary. We all watched him go.

"Thanks, Alex!" I called after him. If he even heard me, he gave no sign of it.

Strange kid, I thought.

"Strange kid," Dave remarked.

Then, from his chair, Agent Ramirez said, "That…was amazing."

Tom looked over at him. Then, as we all watched, the Chief of the Undertakers gently released his sister's limp hand and crossed the room to stand over Ramirez.

"Do you get it now, agent?" he asked flatly.

The FBI guy nodded.

"We're not kids," Tom said.

"No, you're not."

"We don't need carin' for, lookin' after, guiding, or parenting," Tom said.

"No, you don't."

"We're soldiers," Tom said.

"Yes, you are."

"And because we got the Sight and you don't…we're the only soldiers there *are* in this war."

Ramirez said, "I understand that, Jefferson."

Now it was Tom's turn to nod. He waved the rest of us over, except for Ian and Amy, who stayed with their patient. We all settled into a loose circle of chairs. Then the Chief said, "Okay, you were telling us about Cavanaugh…and her plans to kill the governor."

"You want to do this *now?*" the FBI guy asked.

"If not now," the Chief replied, "when?"

Then, as if reaching some internal decision, Ramirez started talking. "The governor and his wife are arriving in Philadelphia this evening for a dinner with the mayor and city council. Then tomorrow…Sunday…they both have some public appearances to make before they go back to the state capital in Harrisburg. The governor's wife is speaking to some school kids at JFK Plaza while the governor and the major will be at the opening ceremonies of the new public pier on Penn's Landing."

I pictured both spots in my mind.

John K. Kennedy Plaza was a cement square with a big fountain in the middle of it that sat across the street from City Hall, maybe a hundred yards—and sixty feet up—from where we now sat. Except nobody called it "JFK Plaza." Instead, it got its nickname from a big piece of modern sculpture that stood near its southeast corner. Four giant letters: an "L" and an "O" perched atop an equally big "V" and "E."

Love Park.

Penn's Landing was called that because, according to tradition, that was where William Penn, the guy who founded

Philly, first landed with his ship back in the seventeenth century. These days, it was a fancy waterfront area with lots of expensive shops and restaurants, many located on big piers that stretched out into the Delaware River.

"What makes you think Cavanaugh's gonna try to ice the governor?" Tom asked.

"Nothing concrete," Ramirez admitted. "Remember that network of cops I mentioned? Well, they started whispering to me about Cavanaugh having her eye on the governor's mansion. From what I could tell, they seemed to think it was funny…the beautiful and popular community affairs director having such big ambitions."

"But she ain't even an elected official," the Chief said. "Just a mayoral appointee. How can she just jump from that to *governor*?"

"She can't," Ramirez admitted. "And if all I had was the rumor, I'd probably dismiss it. But then, from inside the bureau, I got the word that Dashiell had gone to Philly."

"Dashiell?" Helene asked.

"He's an international assassin…a contract sniper. More rumor himself than actual person. Nobody knows who he really is. But over the past ten years, he's been linked to dozens of assassinations. Corporate big wigs and industry leaders mostly. A few political figures. They say he's an American, maybe ex-Army Special Forces. But again, nobody knows for sure. No known photos of him exist."

"And you think this dude's come *here*?" Chuck exclaimed.

"A report crossed my desk suggesting that Dashiell may have turned down a job in Budapest because he has a contract in Philadelphia. He tends to work fast, so it's likely that whoever he plans to kill, it'll happen soon. Add that to the fact that the governor's in town…"

"A big coincidence," said Tom.

"I don't believe in coincidences," the agent remarked.

"Neither do I. Okay, let's go with the assumption that, for whatever reason, the Corpses have decided to kill the governor."

"But why hire this Dashiell guy?" I asked.

Helene added, "Yeah! The Queen's got thousands of Deaders. Couldn't they just arrange one of their famous accidents?"

Chuck suggested, "Maybe knocking off a Seer and making it look accidental is one thing. But killing the governor, who's got to be surrounded by guards, is something else."

"The Queen's got her reasons," Tom added. "If she hired a sniper, then it probably isn't an 'accident' that she's after. Maybe a political assassin fits better with her long-range plans…the governor's mansion and all."

"That's why one of the Corpses can't do the job," Helene said. "Corpses won't use guns!"

The Chief nodded.

"Crap," the Burgermeister remarked.

"So what do we do?" I asked. "How do we stop it?"

Tom turned to Ramirez. "Any idea when and where this

is gonna go down? The dinner tonight? Penn's Landing tomorrow? Somewhere in between?"

The FBI guy shook his head. "None. I wasn't even completely sure the threat was real. I certainly had my suspicions about Cavanaugh…that she was corrupt, that some of the cops in this city were on her personal payroll. But that's a long way from killing the governor. Besides, as you say, what's her motive? But then something happened that convinced me."

I said, "The Corpses took you."

Ramirez nodded. "Probably to find out what I knew… and who I might have told."

"But they had you so long," Helene remarked. "And didn't even question you?"

"Maybe they wanted you out of the way," Tom suggested. "They couldn't risk an 'accident,' not with a federal agent, not this weekend. So they planned to keep you on ice until Monday…then waste you."

"It's possible," Ramirez admitted.

The Chief said, "So we gotta assume that either today or tomorrow, this Dashiell dude's gonna make his play. Because he's a sniper, the play'll likely be outdoors."

"I have to call the state police," Ramirez said. "Warn them."

"Then what?" Tom asked. "Cavanaugh's smart, agent… and she's had time to prep for this. You already know that the Corpses have infiltrated City Hall. What makes you so sure they ain't already in Harrisburg? Maybe a lot of 'em."

"Crap," Dave said again.

"What are you telling me?" Ramirez asked.

"I'm *asking* you: How do you know you can trust whoever it is you call?" the Chief replied. "Or whoever it is *they* call? One thing we've learned: the system ain't our friend. And you got it double bad, Agent Ramirez. At least *we* can See who we're dealing with."

We all watched the FBI guy absorb this. "I'm useless," he said, sounded resigned. "My country…my whole world's… being invaded, and there's absolutely no way I can help."

"Ain't true," Tom told him.

"I can't fight an enemy I can't even recognize."

"No, you can't," the Chief agreed. But you *can* help *us* fight 'em. We're an army, and an army needs supplies and intelligence. Sitting in your DC office, you can help with both. We'll work it out. You're one of us now…kind of an Undertakers 'irregular'…the only adult to know what's really going on. That can't be nothing *but* an asset!"

Ramirez studied the floor for half a minute. "That could work." Then he shook his head sadly. "I'm so sorry, kids. It's not fair you've all had to suffer through this alone."

At first, none of us spoke. Sitting beside Helene, I felt my chest tighten up. The FBI guy was right. It *wasn't* fair. I was thirteen years old. So was Helene. Dave was fourteen—or maybe fifteen. I wasn't really sure. And Tom, the oldest of us, wouldn't turn eighteen for another six months.

Not fair at all.

"Life ain't always fair, agent," Tom replied flatly. "But we play the hand we're dealt…and we play it pretty good. I think you've seen enough to know that."

Ramirez nodded. "You people know what you're doing. I'm done denying that. But that doesn't make it just."

Tom shrugged. "A great man I knew once said, 'Sometimes crying for justice is only another way of complaining.'"

"Who was that?" I asked. But I already knew the answer.

"Your dad."

Tom and I shared a brief smile.

"So," I said. "I guess my question still stands. If the Queen really *is* out to kill the governor, what do we do about it?"

Tom asked, "The governor's got guards right? State cops?"

Ramirez nodded.

"Well, we can't trust 'em," the Chief said matter-of-factly. "So we'll just have to do their job for them."

CHAPTER 31

THE PHONE CALL

In Haven, when the Chief says it's time to do something, stuff happens quickly.

Katie, the current active Boss of the Angels, hadn't been at the impromptu meeting in the infirmary. But as soon as she was notified, she called the Angels together in the rec room.

At that gathering, she laid out the plan.

Three teams would take up positions close enough to the governor to be on hand if something happened while far enough away that—hopefully—they wouldn't get spotted, either by the governor's security team or, worse, by the Corpses.

"And the Deaders'll *be* there," she said. "No doubt about that! Dead cops. Dead politicians. Dead whatever. But Agent Ramirez says that Cavanaugh's assassin is a sniper. That probably means a rifle and a rooftop. Teams One and Two will take the tall buildings around Penn's Landing. Use binoculars and look for people…*any* people. Remember, this guy isn't a Corpse. Any single person on a rooftop is a candidate. Team Three will be on the ground—as close to the governor as possible."

"Then what?" Burt asked.

Katie replied, "If either Team One or Two reports anything suspicious, Three's job will be to make some trouble. Break a store window. Trigger a car alarm. Anything to alert the governor's security that something bad's happening."

"They'll come after us," Chuck pointed out.

"Yeah," Katie agreed. "But first, they'll secure the governor, get him out of the open air and into the nearest car or building. That's all we're after. Three's job at that point will be to scatter. Disappear."

"Risky," said Zack Perkins, another of the Angels.

"Yeah," added Tina Woo. "But no worse than the Eastern State gig the other day, and I didn't even get to go on that one. So I'm totally up for this!"

Chuck declared, "Me too!"

"And me!" said Burt.

"Zack's right," Katie said. "This is a risky one—and not just for Team Three. Teams One and Two could maybe get themselves shot at by a human assassin, someone who's *real* good with a rifle and who won't be fazed by saltwater. So Tom's told me to say that if anybody wants to beg out of this one, it's cool."

"No way!" Tina exclaimed.

Everyone looked at Zack. "Hey, I just said it was risky! No chance am I walking away from this!"

"Cool," Katie replied.

"What about us?" Helene asked. "Will and me. The trainees?"

I didn't like Katie's answer. "Don't worry. You're in. We need the bodies. Helene, you're on Team One. Will, you're on Team Two. Rooftops."

Helene glanced at me, an oddly satisfied look on her face. "Okay," she said.

"Okay," I echoed—muttered really.

Because it *wasn't* okay. Not at all.

"Good," the acting Boss Angel said. "Now, the governor won't get into town for another seven hours. Tom wants everyone in this room to rest up and get themselves fed. Let's all grab some sleep, guys. I think most of us need it. By the time we're up again, mission maps will be drawn up and ready. Let's go."

The meeting ended with everyone talking animatedly— all except me and Helene. We just stood there, three chairs apart, eyeing each other. After a moment, Katie excused herself between us and followed the rest of the crew out of the rec room.

We were alone.

Helene looked at me.

I looked at her.

"I'm sorry," I said.

She eyed me. "What for?"

"Freezing you out before…during Tom's demonstration."

"Uh-huh," she said. Her eyes blazed. I hated it when her

eyes did that. But I kind of liked it too. I wasn't sure why. "And before that, back in the funeral parlor?"

I didn't say anything.

"I *had* her, Will! She wanted that cadaver bad, and she was coming for me, and I'd have nailed her between the eyes with my pistol! But *you* had to throw yourself in the way and almost got Dave killed in the process!"

"I—I know…" I stammered. "I just…um…"

"You just…um…*what?*"

I shrugged miserably. "I was afraid…"

Her eyes stopped flashing, like throwing a switch. "Afraid of what?"

"I didn't want Cavanaugh to…you know…"

"Hurt me?" she finished.

"I guess so."

She stared at me like I'd just changed colors. And from the warmth in my cheeks, maybe I had. For most of a minute, neither one of us spoke.

Then, quietly, she said, "This is 'cause of what happened at the prison, right?"

"I guess so."

"So…what?" she demanded, and just that quick, her eyes were flashing again. "You saved my life and now you're responsible for me or something?"

"No!" I exclaimed. "It's nothing like that! It was just… you know…" My mouth inexplicably filled up with cotton, like a magic trick.

"No, Will. I *don't* know. What's up with you?"

I swallowed repeatedly, but the cotton stayed right where it was.

"You almost…died." I replied.

"I know. I was there. But you saved me. So?"

And then, wishing I was facing a hundred Deaders instead of having this conversation, I blurted, "The way it made me feel…you almost dying." I felt like an idiot. "I…don't ever want to feel like that again."

Helene blinked. A moment passed—painfully long. Then another.

Finally, with a very slight smile, she said, "Well, that's about ten percent kind of nice."

"Helene…"

"And the other ninety percent pisses me off!" she added.

"Oh," I said.

"Will, you're pretty good in a fight."

I frowned. "Um…thanks."

She nodded. "But you also know I can still kick your sorry butt from one end of Haven to the other, right?"

I didn't answer. I didn't have to. We both knew it was true.

Then Helene did a funny thing, a thing that was terrible and awesome at the same time. She took my hand. Her skin felt warm. No, more than warm. It felt hot, almost as hot as my face.

"Get this straight," she said. Her words were hard, but

her tone was soft. "I'm nobody's damsel in distress. What we do is dangerous…and no matter what happens, I've got your back and you've got mine. But I'm *not* your responsibility, and you're *not* my knight in shining armor."

"This isn't stupid crap like that," I snapped.

"Then what kind of stupid crap is it?" she pressed. Her anger had morphed into patience, which was somehow worse. "Did you feel this way about Dave last night when the Queen grabbed him?"

"No."

"You figure he's better in a fight than I am?"

I flashed back on the way the Burgermeister had snapped Cavanaugh's neck like a pretzel stick. At the time, Helene had been sprawled across the wet floor with a fallen cadaver.

But I answered, "No."

"Do you worry about any of the others? Chuck, Burton, or Zack?

"No."

"How about the girls. Katie? Tina?"

"No," I repeated, this time a little defensively.

"So what's different about me?"

My face felt like it was on fire. I looked sheepishly at Helene, who stood there—so close—her face calm, her hazel eyes bright and intense. Suddenly, the cotton in my mouth felt like cement.

"Do I gotta say it?" I muttered miserably.

For about an hour—or maybe it was a few seconds—she

didn't answer. Then she did. "No, you don't. Just...knock it off."

Then she walked purposefully out of the rec room, leaving me alone.

My knees went wobbly, and I sank into the nearest chair. It was cold in the rec room. Heck, it was cold *everywhere* in Haven. But I was sweating anyway, beads of it burning on my forehead. I tried to make some sense of what had just happened and whatever it was that I felt about what had just happened.

Finally, because I couldn't think of a better thing to do, I went to my room. The Burgermeister wasn't there. With a sigh, I kicked off my shoes and stretched out on my cot. It was cold, so I pulled up the blanket and—as I sometimes did—closed my eyes and pretended I was home.

Even though I knew I wasn't.

I didn't think I'd sleep, not with everything that was churning around in my head, but I did. I slept long and hard. If I had dreams, I don't remember them—which, in Haven, is usually just as well.

This time, it wasn't Dave who woke me. It was a ringing phone.

I almost jumped out of my skin, leaping off the cot as if it were on fire. I didn't have a cell phone. No Undertaker did. They were too easily traced. But then the stupid thing rang again, and there was no doubt it was coming from me. I ran my hands all over my clothes, kind of a self pat down until I found it and fished it out of my pants pocket.

It was Cavanaugh's phone—one of the clamshell kind, black and shiny and expensive, but no iPhone. Probably paid for by the city. I wondered how often the Queen had used it.

It rang a third time.

Weirdly, I sniffed it, half-expecting it to smell of death. But instead, it smelled of sweat. Mine. It had been a long night.

I didn't dare answer it, of course. That was against the rules and regs because doing so might give the Corpses a chance to—what was the word Steve used?—"triangulate" the signal. The smart thing would be to turn it over to the Hackers or the Brain Factory. Somebody in one of those crews could analyze it, maybe get some good intel. That was why I'd taken it in the first place, only to forget all about it in the midst of the chaos since.

I popped open the phone and almost hit the "Ignore" button. Then I saw the caller ID and stopped cold.

I knew the number. Of course I did.

But that's crazy!

Without consciously deciding to do so, I pressed "Answer" and put the phone to my ear. "Mom?"

A voice spoke and the sound of it—the *implications* of it—scared me worse than I'd ever been scared in my life. And that's saying something.

"Your mother can't come to the phone, William."

Oh, God.

CHAPTER 32

WILL'S NEW MISSION

I ran through the corridors of Haven even faster than I had when Sharyn was crashing and I'd gone looking for Alex Bobson. Kids stared at me as I went by, most wearing tired, blank expressions. Nobody threw a joke or snide remark at my back. Maybe they were getting used to seeing me tear down these dank, narrow halls.

Or maybe, like me, they were just tired of all the misery.

By the time I reached the infirmary, my heart pounded and my stomach felt as if I'd swallowed a chunk of glacial ice.

"Tom!"

He looked up from Sharyn's bedside, his face haggard. There were bags under his eyes. Elsewhere in the otherwise empty room, Ian and Amy moved to and fro, doing things I could only guess at. They looked exhausted, and I suddenly felt a little guilty for getting some sleep.

"Hey, bro," the Chief said. "You just missed Dave. He

was in here for a long time, keepin' us company. You know, sometimes I don't think I spend enough time with that dude." He gazed down at his sister. "She's hangin' in there. Tough as nails."

Then, after a pause, he added, "Thanks for what you did before, getting Alex and taking care of all that for me. I'm not big on leaning on folks…but right now…"

I marched up to him and held up the cell phone. "I took this from Cavanaugh last night at the funeral parlor," I said. "I forgot all about until just now…when it rang. It was *her*…Cavanaugh…and she was calling from my mom's mobile number!"

From Tom's expression, I knew he didn't need more explanation than that. "Will…" he whispered. "I'm sorry."

But I wasn't interested in sympathy. "I shouldn't have answered it. I know the rules and regs. But when I saw my mom's number on the caller ID, I just couldn't help it. Cavanaugh said one line to me…just one…before I hung up. She said that my mom wasn't available to answer the phone. Then she laughed."

Tom nodded slowly. "It was smart to hang up. But…that means you don't know what exactly—"

I showed him the display. "A few seconds later…she texted me."

The Chief read the words. I already knew them. It was pretty long, as text messages went, but I'd somehow memorized it anyway.

I have your mother and sister. To keep them alive, all the Undertakers have to do is nothing, absolutely nothing, for the next 24 hours. But if one of my people even smells you before then, well, your mother would make a very capable host for me. And the little girl, Emily, would be delicious!

All the words spelled out. All the punctuation there. Capital letters in all the right places. It was an adult's style of texting—and apparently, a Corpse's.

Tom swore. It wasn't something he did much, and the fact he was doing it now seemed oddly comforting. It meant he understood the situation despite his preoccupation with Sharyn.

It meant he was still my Chief.

"Get Katie in here," he ordered. "Tell her I said to stand down. Nobody leaves Haven until this time tomorrow."

"And the governor dies," I said. Then, steeling myself, I added, "We can't do that."

"Will, I'm not going to have your mother and your sister's deaths on my conscience. You've already lost your dad."

"And if we let the Queen get away with this," I told him, "she'll just do it again the next time she wants us out of the way. Heck, she could just start taking hostages and demanding that we give ourselves up to save them." That block of ice I'd swallowed kept getting bigger with every word.

Was I really willing to sacrifice Mom and Emily for the "greater good"? Or was I just playing the tough soldier and hoping Tom would talk me out of it?

I'm pretty sure it was the second one.

Tom said, "No way, bro. We're out. We can cut Ramirez loose. *He* can go warn the governor."

"You said that wouldn't work!" I protested.

He shrugged. "It's all we got now."

"No, it isn't," I said. "We can do what we do. We can rescue my family."

He studied me. "You know where they are?"

"No," I admitted. "But I can tell you where they're *not*. They're not in Cavanaugh's office in City Hall. No way is she keeping them there for a full day without somebody finding out about it."

Tom nodded. "And she can't have them arrested neither. Your sister'd have to go to family services, and your mom would immediately demand for a lawyer. Too easy for the whole thing to blow up in the Queen's face."

"My house maybe? Under guard?"

"I doubt it," he replied. "Too many neighbors. Somebody might come calling. How about Cavanaugh's house? You know…like Booth did when he took Helene."

I said, "Nope. Booth lived out in the burbs. Cavanaugh's got a condo off Rittenhouse Square. Same as my house. Too many neighbors too close by. Somebody might see something. Hear something."

"Then where?" the Chief asked.

"The same place she put her *last* prisoner," I told him. I took a deep, steadying breath. This was a crapshoot, and the stakes were very high. "Eastern State Penitentiary."

Tom considered. "Maybe. It's quiet and easy to guard."

"It might be why the Corpses took over the prison in the first place," I added. "They need a place to put...well...political prisoners, I guess. People they can't just risk locking up in one of the city jails."

"It's solid thinking," the Chief said. "But if you're right, then the Queen's expectin' a rescue attempt. In fact, she's probably countin' on it because it would keep us busy and away from Penn's Landing."

That was something I hadn't considered.

"Then let Katie keep her three teams and her plan. I'll go in and get my sister."

Tom raised his eyebrows. "By yourself?"

"No," I said. "Me, Helene, and the Burgermeister."

"So two rookie Angels and a totally untrained Monkey against who knows how many Deaders?"

"We went up against four at the funeral parlor last night," I said. "Including the Queen. And Sharyn's been giving Dave private lessons."

Tom's eyes strayed to his sister, who lay atop the gurney between us, her eyes closed. She wore the same shirt she'd had on when she got hurt. Ian probably hadn't felt comfortable enough to try to change her: a black shirt turned gray by lots of washing, with the words MOPEY TEENAGE BEARS scrawled across it in big letters.

I'd seen her wear it at least fifty times; wardrobes in Haven didn't tend to be very big.

The Mopey Teenage Bears—a German band.

The same band as on the poster in my room.

Dave's poster.

"I'm gonna have to have a word with him," Tom said to himself.

"Huh?"

"Never mind, bro. You got bigger stuff to do. Get your team together and get ready to hit the prison. You got maybe four hours before dawn, so make it quick. Take whatever stuff you need. And swing by the Brain Factory. Ask Steve 'bout his newest project. Tell him I said you could have it."

"Thanks, Tom."

"Don't thank me, Will. I wish I could go with you. I probably *should* go with you. I owe your dad…and you…at least that much. But I can't leave Sharyn, and maybe more importantly, I can't leave Haven. I've been dropping the ball lately, Chief-wise."

"It's cool," I said quickly. "We all get it."

"That ain't the point. I'm the Chief of the Undertakers first and Sharyn's brother second. These last couple of days, I let that slide. No more. I need to talk to Katie, and you got your own stuff to do. Let's both get to work."

"Yeah."

"But, Will," he said, "be careful. I don't mean your usual 'careful' but *serious* careful. I still might lose Sharyn. I don't know what it'd do to me if I lost you too."

I had no idea what to say to that. Finally, the best I could manage was a hasty "You won't." But by the time I got it out, Tom's eyes had already strayed back to his sister's gurney.

I left him to his thoughts.

After all, I had my *own* sister to think about. And my mom. It was time to go to work.

CHAPTER 33

HAVEN'S LIBRARIAN

The Brain Factory occupied a wide, blind hallway between the infirmary and the Monkey Barrel. Steve Moscova, the Brain Boss, called it a "gallery." It was maybe twelve feet wide and thirty feet deep, with lights strung along the ceiling. A lot of lights. Actually, the Brain Factory was probably the best lit place in all of Haven.

They needed it.

Here was where the chemicals got mixed, the blueprints drawn up, and the gizmos perfected. When the Angels went out into the field to face an army of the walking dead, they did so—*we* did so—with weapons forged right here.

These dudes totally needed to see what they were doing.

There were maybe a half-dozen Brains, and Steve lorded over them, as Sharyn had once put it, "with an iron pocket protector." He had gotten the Sight later than most, almost a year later than his younger brother, Burt. It was a subject he was sensitive about. He thought it made him sound nerdish.

But nerd or not, Steve was a genius.

The genius himself stood at a lab table against the gallery's back wall with Agent Ramirez. Steve seemed to be showing off an assortment of Undertakers gadgetry to the FBI guy: a plastic water pistol, a Super Soaker, a wrist radio. That kind of stuff.

I ran up to them, drawing stares from the other Brains. "Steve!"

They both turned.

"Have you been to the infirmary?" Steve asked. "How's Sharyn?"

"Still asleep," I said.

"Unconscious," he corrected. "Not asleep."

"Whatever," I said.

"There's a difference. REM sleep has an entirely different electroencephalographic signature than coma."

Yep, definitely a nerd.

"Okay. She's still unconscious."

Ramirez remarked, "She should be in a hospital." But the look on his face said he now understood that wasn't possible. He'd come around—a far cry from the outraged adult he'd been yesterday. The world had gotten a bit more complicated for Agent Hugo Ramirez and a bit scarier too.

I knew exactly how he felt.

"Listen, Steve," I said. "I need to talk to you."

But Steve, as was his way, rolled right over me. "I was just showing Agent Ramirez our latest innovation." Then he held up Aunt Sally. I hadn't laid my eyes on the crossbow since Sharyn had used it to shoot a Corpse through the watchtower window at Eastern State.

It didn't look any different.

"I've seen it," I said.

"Not the crossbow. *This*!" He removed the bolt that sat atop the bow. Now I hadn't seen too many crossbow bolts in my life, but even so, I could tell this one was special. For one thing, it wasn't metal or wood but clear plastic. And there was fluid inside.

"What is it?" I asked.

"A Ritterbolt!" he replied proudly.

I groaned. "Oh...come on!"

If the Brain Boss noticed my discomfort, it didn't show. "The bolt is designed to remotely inject a lethal dose of saltwater. The force of penetration drives the plunger in the rear of the bolt forward, delivering all fifteen cc's stored in the syringe. Should work at least as well as a handheld Ritter."

"Should work?"

He shrugged. "Functions as expected on test dummies. But out in the field...well, it *should* work."

I took the bolt from him and hefted it. It was light, lighter than a real crossbow bolt. "How many have you got?"

"Alex is making the shafts out of acrylic based on my design," Steve said. "He just delivered the first ten."

"Ten," I echoed, thoughtfully. "Okay, I'll take them."

Steve blinked. "What?"

"Cavanaugh's kidnapped my mom and sister," I said, working hard to keep an edge of panic out of my voice. "I'm going after them."

"Now wait a minute!" Ramirez exclaimed. "What?"

"Got a text from her. She's taken my family and says she'll...do stuff to them...if the Undertakers don't disappear for the next twenty-four hours."

"She wants us out of the way," Steve concluded.

"That what Tom figures," I said. "I'm guessing they're stashed at Eastern State, so I'm going in to get them."

Ramirez shook his head. "I can't let you do that, Will."

Around us, the rest of the Brain Factory had picked up on what was happening and stopped working. Steve's "gallery" had gone as quiet as a tomb.

I faced Ramirez. He was a head taller than me and at least sixty pounds heavier. But he also had one arm in a sling. "Sorry," I said, meaning it. "But it's not your call. I've already talked to Tom. I'm going."

He opened his mouth and then shut it again. Finally, he said, "I'll go with you."

"Thanks, but you'd just get in the way."

"Will, I'm a trained federal officer."

"With a sprained shoulder and no Sight," I said. "No offense, but I don't think you could help."

"But one...person"—the way he tripped over the word

made me think he'd almost said child—"against God knows how many of Cavanaugh's people."

"Don't call them 'people,'" I said. "Corpses."

"My point's the same."

"I'm going to ask Helene and Dave to come with me."

He shook his head. "So…three against a small army. It's suicide."

I shrugged. "What choice do I have?"

"Let me call my office," he pleaded. "I won't say anything about Corpses. I'll just come up with some kind of story to get some agents to that prison to look around."

"And the minute the Queen gets wind of it, my family dies. They'll never even find the bodies. No way."

"But what are you going to do?" he asked, sounding desperate. "How would you even get in?"

"Over the wall," I said. "Like we did last time."

He frowned, obviously trying to come up with another argument.

But then Steve said, "Won't work."

We both looked at him.

"What?" he added, looking irritated. "You think I can't strategize?"

"Why won't it work?" I demanded.

"Three reasons," Steve replied, and in typical Steve fashion, he ticked them off on his fingers. "One, the first time was in broad daylight, with the Angels using deception to convince any passersby that they had a right to be there. This operation will be at night, and anyone who sees you, human or Corpse, won't be fooled.

"Two, the prison walls are thirty feet high. You'd need a long ladder to get over it, and our only long ladder was used in the *last* prison mission and then abandoned.

"Three, the Corpses know how you got in last time, and they'll be watching for a repeat. Even if you do manage to get over the wall, they'd be on you in a heartbeat…yours, not theirs, because they don't *have* heartbeats."

Then he crossed his arms, looking pleased with himself.

"He's right," Ramirez said.

"I *have* to go in," I said. "They've got my mom and sister."

"We'll find another way."

Then Steve said, "I already know another way. Hey, Kelly! Toss me that book! There…on the lab table beside you."

"Sure thing, Boss!" one of the Brains called. A moment later, a thin paperback was whizzing through the air like a square Frisbee. Steve tried to catch it but missed, so I whipped my hand out and snagged it before it went flying into the shadows.

Frowning, I read the cover: *Escapes from Eastern State Penitentiary.* The cover showed an old black-and-white photo of two guards—or maybe they were policemen—examining a man-sized hole in the dirt.

"Where'd you get this?" I asked.

Steve replied, "The library."

"The Philly library?" Undertakers, as a rule, didn't have library cards—or any other sort of personal identification.

He shook his head. "Haven's library."

"We have a library? Since when?"

"I opened it about two weeks ago. I'm not surprised you haven't heard of it. Word isn't really getting around as quickly as I'd like. So far, we've only loaned out maybe a half dozen books, mostly to Brains and Hackers."

I wanted to ask him where'd he'd found the space to set up such a thing and why he'd even bothered. I mean, I liked books fine, but lately, I'd been too busy fighting for my life to find time for a little reading. And the lighting in Haven being what it was—well, the Brain Factory and maybe the infirmary were about the only places where you could read without going blind.

I almost said all that but then stopped myself. I just didn't have time for another Steve lecture.

"I'll have to stop by," I said.

"Hope you do," the Brain Boss replied. "Open the book to page fifteen."

I did. Across two pages was a drawing, one that had apparently appeared in the *Philadelphia Inquirer* back on April 3, 1945. The caption read, "How twelve convicts escaped by tunnel from Eastern Penitentiary."

I looked at it. After a moment, Ramirez came to my right shoulder and looked at it with me. Then Steve took point on my left shoulder and did the same.

"Most people think the famous bank robber William 'Slick Willie' Sutton planned the escape," Steve said—so cheerfully that, given the circumstances, I almost wanted to hit him. "Actually, Sutton simply found out about the plot and insisted on joining in. The tunnel was really dug by Clarence Klinedinst and his cell mate, William Russell. It took about two years and, when finished, ran a hundred feet from Klinedinst's cell, under the prison wall, and came up in the grass right beside Fairmount Avenue."

"I think I've heard of this," Ramirez muttered.

Steve continued, "Twelve men escaped, including Klinedinst, Russell, and Slick Willie. Every single one was recaptured, many within minutes. They made the mistake of escaping at seven in the morning, when the sun was up, so everyone on the street could see them. Sutton got caught about two blocks away. Klinedinst didn't get far either. Russell actually managed to stay free…until he decided to visit an old girlfriend."

"Great," I said. "But what's your point? I don't have two years to dig my way under the prison wall."

But Steve shook his head. "You don't have to. After the escape attempt, the authorities sealed the tunnel on both ends."

"I'm sure they did," said Ramirez.

"Of course," the Brain Boss agreed. "But the actual tunnel, all one hundred feet of it, is still there! And that's how you can get in!"

CHAPTER 34

FRIENDS

Fifteen minutes later, I walked out of the Brain Factory with Aunt Sally over one shoulder and a sack of equipment over the other. The crossbow came with ten Ritterbolts—ugh!—and ten steel bolts. Inside the sack were three small Super Soakers and six standard Ritters. As Steve had put it, I was armed for bear.

I only wished that bear was all I was after.

Before I'd gone a dozen steps, Ramirez called my name and came jogging out of the Brain Factory after me.

I rolled my eyes.

"Please," I said. "There's no way you're talking me out of this."

But he surprised me. "I get that. I don't like it, but I get it. Being here with you kids…well, I guess it's opened my eyes in more ways than one. I still can't quite wrap my head around everything you've suffered through, but I can't deny that you're capable. I've been touring Haven, just looking around since Sharyn's surgery. Everything I see impresses me."

I guess I was happy to hear that, but I couldn't help wondering at the level of trust Tom was now showing our adult "guest." Was the Chief really all that confident that Ramirez wouldn't make for the nearest exit, regardless of his newfound respect for the Undertakers? Or had Sharyn's condition messed Tom up so badly that he wasn't thinking straight?

Not a happy thought.

The FBI guy said, "But before you head out on this insane mission, I want to ask you one thing."

I shrugged. "So ask."

"Have you ever killed someone?"

For a moment, I lost my tongue. It was there in my mouth somewhere. I felt sure of it, but Ramirez's question had turned it bashful. Finally—and with some effort—I replied, "You know I have."

"Booth," he said.

I nodded.

"But that wasn't face-to-face. You poisoned him."

"So?"

"So…this is different. For you and your friends to have any chance of pulling this off, you must be figuring on shooting someone with that crossbow or stabbing them with those syringes."

At least he didn't call them "Ritters."

331

"Yeah," I said.

"And as I understand it, that won't just incapacitate these…creatures. It'll kill them."

I nodded.

"Ever done anything like that?"

I almost answered no, but then, for some reason, I changed it to "Not yet."

"Ever *seen* it done?" Ramirez asked.

"A bunch of times," I replied. "Over the last couple of days."

"And how did it make you feel?"

I remembered the Corpse that Sharyn had pinned with Aunt Sally and then interrogated. Afterward, she'd killed it with her Ritter.

No, she had Helene do it.

I knew *exactly* how it had made me feel. These were monsters, killers of children. They'd invaded our world with conquest on their minds. They were cruel, ruthless, and completely without pity.

But to kill anything that way, intentionally and without any remorse, it hadn't seemed—

"I didn't like it," I said.

"Why not?" Ramirez asked.

I shrugged.

"Think you can do it yourself?"

Sharyn did it. So did Helene—twice. So did Chuck—to save *me*.

"Yeah. I can do it."

"How can you be sure?"

I met his eyes. "Because it's my family."

"Okay," he said. "Good luck, Will."

He started to turn away, but I called him back. "That's it?" I asked. "No lecture? No speech about deciding whether I'm a killer?"

Ramirez smiled thinly. "If you'd told me you were looking forward to harpooning those...people...then I'd have been worried. But killing to protect for your loved ones... that's another matter."

"Oh," I said, irritated and not sure why.

"Go," he said. "Do what you have to do. Save the day. I wish I could go with you." He held up his one arm, which still hung in its sling. "But since I can't, I'll stay here and do my part."

"And what *is* your part?" I asked.

When he answered, it was without any trace of irony. "I'll be praying."

Grown-ups, I thought.

Then, with a sigh, I headed down the corridor toward my room in search of the Burgermeister.

I found him on his bunk. Better still, Helene was with him. When I came through the curtain, they both looked up at me. Helene's expression was pained. But Dave looked worse. His cheeks were wet, though the instant he saw me, he turned away and wiped his face on the edge of his blanket.

"Hey, dude!" he said in a bright tone that wouldn't have

fooled a three-year-old. "Anymore news from the infirmary? Sharyn?"

"She's hanging in there," I said. "Tom's with her."

The Burgermeister nodded, screwing his face up in a way
that could have been determination or something else.

In that moment, I felt something close to shame. For days
now, I'd been wondering why Dave had been so distracted
and so short-tempered. All this time, he'd been worried
about Sharyn. Not like we weren't *all* worried—but his feelings went deeper than the rest of us.

Like Tom's. Then again, *not* like Tom's.

"She's gonna be okay, dude," I said. "If anybody can survive this, it's her."

"That's what I've been telling him," Helene added.

Helene. Since Sharyn had been hurt and she'd almost died
during the raid on Eastern State, I'd made it my mission to
protect her. I wasn't sure if this had been completely conscious
or just something the back part of my mind had cooked up
without telling the front part. My brain did that sometimes.

Either way, my shame deepened. I'd spent all that energy
trying to keep her out of danger. But here I was, fully prepared to ask her to follow me into the fire, all because my
family was in trouble. What kind of message did that send?
Were Emily and my mom more important than Helene?

For a few seconds, I considered not telling them what I
had in mind. Maybe I could get one of the other Angels to go
with me instead. Or maybe I'd go alone after all.

But, no. These were my two best friends, the two best friends I'd ever had. They'd never forgive me if I left them out of this, no matter what they were going through themselves.

"Listen, guys," I said. "I need to ask you both something."

"Sure," Dave said.

"What's up?" Helene asked.

I told them all of it. Cavanaugh's phone call and text. My talk with Tom. Steve's library book about Slick Willie Sutton's escape tunnel. I even told them about Ramirez stopping me in the corridor and posing his "can you kill?" challenge.

They listened without comment as I explained my plan. At the end of it, I finished up with, "You guys don't have to come. I know it's a lot to ask. And I totally get it if you don't—"

"Oh, shut up, you idiot!" Helene snapped. "Burgermeister, let's do this!"

They both jumped to their feet.

My best friends.

CHAPTER 35

BREAKING IN AGAIN

W e stopped by the Monkey Barrel, where Alex loaned us three shovels with less gripping than I would have expected. "Just make sure to bring them back," he muttered. "They don't grow on trees."

We left on our Stingrays at 2:30 in the morning, Undertakers' prime time. Helene had tied the gun sack to the rear of her banana seat, and I'd done the same with Aunt Sally. The shovels we wore on our backs, fastened diagonally across our shoulder blades by using bungee cords. It wasn't comfortable, but it worked.

We must have looked weird to those few cars that passed us on the narrow streets, but no one challenged us. This wasn't all that surprising because in the city, people carry all sorts of things on bikes. I once saw I guy sporting a battery-powered TV that he'd duct-taped between his handlebars.

Three kids with shovels in the middle of the night barely earned a second glance.

We de-biked on Fairmount Avenue, about a block west of the prison, and went the rest of the way on foot, mindful of the lights around us. Steve had used his computer to pull up a Google Maps view of the prison grounds and, printing it out, had marked where the tunnel entrance and exit had been.

Well, *exit and entrance*, I suppose, given our perspective.

The penitentiary looked like a huge stone cliff face, lifeless and forbidding. No guards and no lights were visible. But inside, I knew, were Corpses—maybe a lot of Corpses—all of them at least half-expecting us.

My mom and sister were in there too.

I hoped.

"See that landscaping wall just past the sidewalk?" I asked, pointing from across the street at the prison frontage. The wall stood about five feet high, tapering down to maybe a foot as it neared the gates.

"Yeah," Helene replied.

"Where?" Dave pressed.

"There! That's where we have to go." The garden area filling the space between the top of the landscaping wall and the much higher and thicker prison wall was maybe twelve feet wide and offered only sparse winter shrubbery to hide us. Fortunately, at this time of night, it was a well of shadows.

True, Slick Willie and his buds had been easily spotted

during their escape attempt. But that had been at dawn. This was the darkest part of the night. It gave us an advantage.

At least that was my theory.

We waited until Fairmount Avenue looked as deserted as it was likely to get and then we crossed the street, moving fast but not running. I looked everywhere at once, watching for movement. Nobody and nothing appeared.

On the sidewalk, Dave boosted us both up to the top of the landscaping wall and then he followed clumsily after us, with Helene and me pulling on his beefy arms. Not a particular graceful technique but one we'd used before.

Within seconds, we stood huddled around an innocent-looking patch of grass.

"How wide is this tunnel entrance?" Helene asked.

"About two feet," I said. To my right, Dave groaned. I tried to ease his mind. "Don't worry. We'll get you through it."

"Except how do you know it's *this* two feet?" asked Helene. "And not the two feet over *there*…or over *there?*" She pointed at the flat grass around us.

"Satellite imaging," I said.

Helene's eyes lit up. "Oh!"

Dave's remained dark. "Huh?"

I replied, "Steve showed me this infrared satellite photo of the prison the Corpses took. Apparently, one of the Hackers found it."

"Infrared," Dave echoed. "That shows heat, right?"

I nodded.

"Why'd the Deaders want a picture of this place that shows off heat? Corpses don't even *have* body heat!"

"Steve wasn't sure. But shut up, that's not the point. When he showed me the picture on the computer, he zoomed into this exact spot. I recognize that old bush right there. On the photo, this area showed up as a little darker because the air below the ground is colder than the ground itself. He's says this is where the tunnel entrance…or exit…is."

"You sure that's the right bush?" Helene asked.

"Pretty sure."

"Good enough for me," Dave announced. Then he pulled the shovel off his back. "Let's do this."

Steve hadn't been certain how far down the tunnel had been filled. We might have to dig through as much as ten feet of frozen ground. I'd mentioned this to Helene and Dave on the way over here, reminding them they could still back out.

Helene had looked thoughtful.

The Burgermeister had just grunted. And now I saw why.

He attacked the ground with his shovel, elbowing us aside. The kid was a machine, his eyes locked on his job and his big arms moving like pistons. For a minute, Helene and I just stared at him.

Finally, I asked, "Um…need any help?"

"Naw," he replied, his breath puffing out in thick clouds of mist. "Spent two summers working for my uncle's company, diggin' pools. You dudes keep watch. I got this."

So we did. And so did he.

It took about twenty minutes, though it seemed like a lot longer. Partway through, he managed to snap his shovel in half on the hard earth. Grunting again, he took mine and continued without complaint.

Helene and I pressed ourselves against the prison wall, bathed in shadows. She watched the street. Cars went by, but not many, and none of them took notice of us.

At the same time, I studied the prison itself, peering up at the watchtowers along the top of the wall. I could see neither light nor movement.

I began to seriously worry that I'd been wrong.

What if my family wasn't in there after all? What would I do then?

But that kind of thinking was pointless. This was the only idea I had, so I might as well follow through.

"I'm through!" Dave whispered. Then he straightened and stretched.

The hole he'd dug was about four feet wide and so deep that he stood in it almost up to his neck. Helene pulled out her little flashlight and, mindful of passing cars, shone it down.

And there it was—a jagged hole about two feet across. "Looks like it goes maybe four more feet," the Burgermeister said, following Helene's light. "Then it cuts off at an angle."

"Scary," Helene remarked casually, as if announcing the weather.

"And tight," Dave added, looking worried. "I sure don't want to get stuck down there."

I didn't blame him. Steeling myself, I said, "I'll go first. Then you. Then Helene. That way, if you get stuck, the two of us can work you loose from both sides." I met Helene's gaze. "That okay with you?"

She shrugged. "It's your mission."

Pulling out my own flashlight and clutching Aunt Sally close to my chest, I hopped down into the newly dug pit beside Dave.

"Careful, dude," he said.

"Yeah," I said.

My mouth felt dry. I was about to go headfirst into a tunnel that a bunch of criminals had dug almost sixty years ago.

What could go wrong?

Then I crouched low and let the cold ground swallow me up headfirst.

CHAPTER 36

THE DIRT TUBE

Ever crawl through a tunnel? I don't mean those cozy little triangles you used to make out of blankets and couch cushions. I don't even mean those trenches you and your friends shoveled out in the park, covered with plywood, and then called "forts."

I mean a *real* tunnel.

The one beneath Eastern State had been dug by desperate men under conditions for which "sucks" would probably have been a step up. The passage was three feet high at its best and barely two at its worst. Some spots were shored up with planks that looked about a thousand years old, but most of the time, the ceiling was only hard-packed ground—thankfully frozen. If we'd tried this in the summer, our very movements might have brought the whole place crashing down.

I'd never considered myself claustrophobic. But I found out quickly that was because I'd never tried scuttling on hands and knees through a cold, dark tube of dirt. The air smelled worse than stale—I'd gotten used to "stale" in Haven. It smelled dead. It smelled of things rotting inside the walls all around me. It smelled of corpses—or Corpses—and I was gripped by the sudden terror that Cavanaugh had anticipated this move and that there were Deader guards hiding in the dark just ahead…their black teeth poised to go right for my face.

I swallowed, pushing back my fear.

Behind me, Dave grumbled and cursed, sounding more angry than afraid. I have to admit, I took a weird kind of comfort in his complaints. Helene, though, felt differently.

"Burgermeister," she hissed. "Keep it down, will ya? This is supposed to be a surprise attack, duh!"

"Right," Dave murmured. "Sorry."

"Keep moving," I told them, though it was the absolute last thing I wanted to do.

A hundred feet, Steve? It feels more like a hundred miles!

The tunnel's downward path leveled off and became slightly wider. My flashlight showed spots where lights had once been hung, their wires rotted away to string by the years. Klinedinst and Russell had been thorough; there was no taking that away from them.

I was cheered by the thought that as we neared the "start" of the tunnel, the going might get easier. Most people, after all, did their best work at the beginning of a long project.

This might not be so bad after all.

But then we hit the stream.

You'd think it would have been frozen. It wasn't, and it didn't flow like any stream I'd ever seen. It didn't come through one wall and then go out the other. Instead, it seemed to rise up from the soil, turning the dirt floor into an icy mud pit.

I found it by literally going into it headfirst. I'd been crawling along on my hands and knees, with the flashlight in my left hand, when my right hand suddenly disappeared in the muck, sinking to the elbow. An instant later, my face hit the mud.

Gasping, I flailed and pulled free, accidentally kicking the Burgermeister in the shoulder in the process. He cursed liberally.

"Sorry!" I gasped. "It's wet here!"

Then, as I tried to shift my weight, my left arm went in, flashlight and all, and my face was once again swallowed up in the brown ooze. And it was worse than just being wet because the sticky mud clung to my skin and clothing.

After another few moments of clumsy struggle, I felt a huge hand close on my ankle and pull me back.

"Chill out, will ya, dude?" Dave exclaimed. "You kick me again, and I might forget we're friends!"

"Everything okay up there?" Helene called.

"I'm fine," I sputtered, wiping the mud from my face. "There's water here, a big patch of it, and it's seriously cold."

Dave shined his flashlight in my face. "Lookin' good,

Will!" he said with a laugh. "See what happens when you play leader?"

"Yeah," I groaned.

"You sure you okay?" Helene asked again, trying to see over the Burgermeister's intervening bulk.

"I'm fine," I repeated. Then, annoyed with myself, I reached across the stream. It wasn't wide, but it was wide enough that I couldn't get my legs past it without soaking them. Gritting my teeth, I pushed forward, continuing down the tunnel a ways before turning and shining my light back the way I'd come to see how my friends were doing.

I witnessed a funny thing.

Dave didn't try to avoid the stream. Instead, he lay down atop it, his chest and belly pressed into the mud, and called back, "Helene, why don't you go ahead and climb over me."

Behind him, she said, "Huh?"

"No sense in both of us freezing our butts off!" the Burgermeister growled. "Just hurry up and do it before I change my mind."

So she did. It was a tight squeeze between Dave and the tunnel ceiling, but the slender girl managed it, and once clear, she crawled up to me with a sheepish smile.

"Thanks, Dave," she said without turning.

I grinned. "He's just looking out for you," I said, giving her a pointed look. "No harm in that, right?"

"Shut up," she said. But the smile stayed there.

Behind her, Dave rose from the muck and shook himself like a waking bear. "Okay," he said. "Let's keep going."

"Yeah," I said. "But don't get stuck. Lined up like this, Helene and I won't be able to do the push/pull thing anymore."

"I'm good," he grumbled. "Plenty of room down here. It's comfier than Haven! Heck, I even got myself a nice warm bath!"

I said, "Save it, dude. I got it worse than you."

"Bet you didn't!" Dave exclaimed.

"Shut up, both of you!" Helene said in a hiss. "Jeez, you guys are grouchy when you're wet." Then, after a moment, she groaned and added, "Ugh! I just broke my watch!"

"What? How?"

"Scraped it against the wall by mistake. The band snapped. I can't even *find* it now!"

I checked my own. It seemed fine. It had even survived the stream, which was surprising; these things broke all the time.

"Dave, how's yours?" I asked.

"My what, dude?"

"Your watch!" Helene said.

"Don't got one," Dave replied. "I ain't an Angel, remember? Besides, I can't even get one of those things around my wrist!"

Helene said. "Come on, Will. Your family's not gonna save themselves!"

True enough, I thought, a little guiltily.

We crawled onward, following the tunnel and hoping the second half would prove easier than the first.

It didn't.

We got to the end without further trouble. But then the trouble turned out to be this: We'd gotten to the end. It just stopped. A wall of dirt. For a minute, I just stared at it. Steve had warned me that the tunnel turned upward at this point. But I'd really been hoping that at least some of that vertical shaft would still be here. It wasn't.

Crap.

Helene squeezed up beside me and touched the wall. Her finger came back coated in fine gray powder. "This isn't dirt," she said, sniffing it. "I think it's ash."

"Steve said something about the guards backfilling the tunnel with ash from the prison incinerators," I said. "Looks like they did a good job of it too."

"How high up does it go?"

"Something like fifteen feet," I replied.

She sighed. "Well…let's start digging. Where's your shovel?"

"Dave's got it," I replied. "I gave it to him back at the start when he broke his. Remember?"

"Yeah."

"Besides," I added. "I've got a Super Soaker and Aunt Sally. Not sure I could've managed all three. How about you?"

"I've got one," Helene replied. "Dave, you got a shovel?"

"Sure," he called from behind us. "Except I can't get up there. You two'll have to do the digging this time."

"Okay," I sighed. "Pass it up to me."

Helene and I dug—if you can call what we were doing

"digging." Is there a verb for stabbing awkwardly at a wall of frozen ash while on hands and knees? If there is, I couldn't come up with it.

After a while, we got into a funny kind of rhythm. I'd chip away at the wall, dislodging big chunks of hard ash. Helene would use her shovel to scoop them up and pass them back to Dave. What he'd do with them I didn't exactly know, though I suppose we'd better leave the prison a different way. Otherwise, we might just have to dig our way through the tunnel all over again!

Fortunately, ash turned out to be a lot lighter than dirt—easier to move. Within an hour, loose clumps of it started to rain down into the space we'd just opened up.

"Found the shaft," I reported.

"Knew you would," Helene said, her tone even. She was putting on a show, staying nice and calm no matter what happened—for my sake.

"Thanks," I said.

"For what?" she asked.

"You know for what."

"Sure," she replied. "They're gonna be okay, you know."

"Yeah," I said.

Helene pressed, "They are!"

More big lumps of frozen ash came free, giving me the room to stab my shovel all the way up into the vertical shaft.

We were getting closer, which meant it was time to start being quieter.

When I answered Helene, it was in a whisper. "I don't even know for sure that they're here. This is a guess." It was the first time I'd uttered the fear aloud.

I paused and looked back at her. Her face was awash in shadows, our flashlights having been propped up as best we could on the tunnel floor. The air was thick with debris, and each of us had wrapped scarves around the lower half of our faces. Even so, I could easily see the ash that layered her cheeks, so thick it almost looked like a mask. She was sweating too, despite the cold air, and had to be bone tired.

But she's here.

"Who's guess?" Helene whispered back.

"Mine."

She nodded. "Then they're here."

"How do you figure that?" I asked, honestly perplexed.

Dave answered from somewhere behind her, his tone impatient. "'Cause she trusts your guesses more'n most dudes' sure things," he droned, as if repeating some litany. Then he added impatiently, "Jeez, I wish you two would just get it over with! Doofuses."

I felt my face flush.

"Keep it down, Dave!" Helene hushed him. Then, in a gentler tone, she added, "Sharyn's gonna be okay too."

For half a minute, no one spoke. Finally, the Burgermeister muttered, "Yeah."

We went back to work.

After another hour, the shaft was wide enough to climb

up into. There'd once been a kind of ladder—or so Steve had said—but it had long since rotted away. Fortunately, the quarters were so tight I could worm my way upward by bracing myself with my shoulders and knees. This left my hands free for the shoveling.

The process was slow, dirty, and painful. But it worked. Three feet. Six. Nine. Twelve.

Fifteen.

Then I came to the bricks.

As more and more ash fell away, more and more of them appeared—a wall of them, blocking any exit from the shaft. I looked at them. They looked back at me, hard and unyielding.

"Found the way out," I whispered down.

"Thank God," I heard the Burgermeister reply. He sounded far away.

"Except it's bricked up."

Helene asked, "We kind of expected that, didn't we?"

Well, yes and no. Steve hadn't been sure. After the escape, the prison officials had naturally sealed up this end of tunnel using concrete, mortar, and chicken wire. But later, in 2005, a team of archeologists had spent two days digging through all that to rediscover the entrance.

Steve hadn't known what they'd done to reseal the hole because by then the prison had become a museum. "It might just be plastered over," he'd told me optimistically.

It wasn't.

Bricks.

Despair gnawed at me.

But no way had we come this far to be stopped now!

Then I noticed that some of the bricks were loose, the mortar between them crumbly—like really old Play-Doh. Unfortunately, the tight shaft made my shovel useless. So I handed it down to Helene, fished out my pocketknife, and went to work hacking and scraping.

Within a minute, I couldn't see. Within two minutes, I could barely breathe.

There was too much dust and too little air.

But I kept at it, trying not to think about the ceiling of dirt—the top of the shaft—that was right over my head. All that weight pressing down, with little more than surface tension to keep it where it was. Plus, it was cold—*very* cold; it felt like lumpy ice pushing against my skull.

I kept hacking.

Ash choked me, making me gag and cough. Helene kept asking if I was all right. Her voice started to sound very far away. Pictures of my mom and sister floated before my eyes.

Are you alive?

You have to be alive!

The first brick came loose. It just popped out suddenly and tumbled down the shaft, bouncing painfully off my knee in the process. The shock of it seemed to focus me, though not as much as when Helene yelped and gave my ankle a hard pinch.

"Watch it, Will! That almost hit me!"

"Shhh!" I said sharply, keeping my voice low. "And sorry…but there'll be more of 'em coming."

After that, I worked the wall with new energy. A few dozen more stabs and a second brick came out. Then a third.

"Getting there," I whispered, still gagging but hopeful. Then, sparing a moment, I eagerly—maybe even a little desperately—shone my flashlight through the newly made gap.

Darkness. Cursing, I reached my free hand in and encountered a hard but smooth surface.

What now?

Then, when I pulled my hand back, I felt the grit on my fingertips.

"What is it?" Helene asked, sounding almost as breathless as I felt.

"Something behind the brick," I replied. "Plaster…I think."

Unless it's concrete.

No, don't think like that.

I don't know how long it took me to clear the rest of the bricks. Ten minutes? Forever? I worked in a haze of claustrophobic misery. Every so often, Helene would ask me how I was and I'd reply fine. Except I wasn't fine. Not even a little bit. Right at that moment—scared, dirty, exhausted, half frozen, and wedged in that tight shaft—I couldn't even remember what "fine" felt like.

But finally, I'd reclaimed just enough elbow room to use the shovel. Helene handed it up to me. I couldn't see her face, but I could sense her anxiety. She and Dave had kept quiet down there, but they were suffering too.

Worse, all the bricks, dirt, and ash we'd moved was now behind us, filling the tunnel at our backs and blocking any retreat.

If I couldn't penetrate this last barrier—assuming it *was* the last barrier—we'd likely die down here.

I twisted my body to give the shovel as much space as possible. Then I steeled myself and rammed its blade through the hole and into the plaster.

It went right through!

I almost cried with relief. But instead, I hit it again. And again. It cracked and crumbled outward, exposing the first light—except for a flashlight beam—that I'd seen in longer than I could remember. A half dozen more hits and a last huge chunk of plaster tumbled away.

I don't think there's any way to describe the feeling of finally squeezing through that jagged, newly made hole and crawling, filthy and sore, into the dark tiny room beyond. Let's just say that cramped old prison cell felt like a four-star hotel and leave it at that.

Helene came next, emerging like a zombie from her grave—pun intended that time. Dave followed, his broad shoulders hammering back the edges, his ash-layered face red with effort.

But he was smiling. We all were. True, this mess of a mission had only just started. And true, our only accomplishment so far had been to break into a crumbling prison populated by monsters who would happily kill us on sight. But we'd made it this far, and now that we had, I could admit—if only to myself—that I'd been pretty sure that miserable tunnel was going to be our tomb.

What I *didn't* know was that in just a few hours, one of us would be the "guest of honor" at our own funeral.

CHAPTER 37

RESCUE

Remember when I said that Eastern State Penitentiary was laid out like a wheel with spokes sticking out from a central hub? Well, the cramped cell in which we'd just emerged sat at the far end of one of those spokes: Cell Block Seven, to be exact.

A tiny bit of light spilled through a small window set high into the back wall. A little more trickled down from the mouth of the corridor beyond the cell entrance. Bottom line, it was almost but not quite completely dark. But compared to the stifling blackness of the dirt tube, it felt positively bright in here.

An ancient toilet stood in one corner. I doubted very much if it had worked in years. Dust and rubble layered the uneven floor. The cell door was completely missing, leaving behind a rectangular opening maybe five feet high and half that wide.

The place stank of damp plaster and wood rot and…something else. I looked at the others and saw that they'd smelled it too.

Death.

There were Corpses nearby.

"Okay," Dave whispered. "We're in. Now what?"

"What time is it?" Helene asked.

I glanced at my watch. "Eight twenty-two in the morning."

"Jeez…" Dave moaned softly. "How long were we *down* there?"

"Too long," Helene said.

"I'm going to scout around," I told them. But as I headed for the door, Helene grabbed my arm.

"Let me do it," she said.

The Burgermeister groaned, but at least he did it softly. "Not again. What *is* it with you two?"

I glared at her, but this time, there wasn't any challenge in her eyes.

"Why?" I asked.

"Because if you see your mom or Emily, you'll just charge right in there," she told me. "You know you will. You've done it before."

I opened my mouth to protest. Then I closed it. I didn't like it, not one bit, but she was right.

"Okay," I said.

Helene nodded and slipped past me, moving like a ghost out through the ruined door and melting into the shadowy corridor.

I blew out a sigh, trying to loosen the knots that our long crawl had left in my arms, legs, and back. Dave and I shared a nervous look.

"Let's arm up," I told him. "Just in case."

I readied Aunt Sally, snapping on one of Alex's crank assemblies and fitting it with the first of Steve's Ritterbolts. When I looked up, I caught Dave frowning at his Super Soaker, which had sprung a leak—probably during our crawl through the tunnel.

With a grunt, he dropped it and instead hefted his shovel. It was the spaded kind, its blade still caked with dirt, with a three-foot wooden shaft that ended in a molded handle.

"This is better anyhow," he muttered.

Despite everything, I felt myself smile. "An Undertaker with a shovel. It doesn't get better than that."

We waited.

Time stretches when you wait. And the more scared you feel, the longer the stretch. During that zillion-year period while Helene was scouting, the apprehension was like torture! At any moment, I expected to hear a distant cry of pain or alarm. Even poised as we were to rush to her aid, this was a big place, and Helene might be dead long before could get to her.

But then, that moment of near panic would pass without anything happening, only to be followed by another. And another.

It was one of longest and most anxious times of my life.

And that's from a guy who just chiseled his way out of a vertical grave.

Finally, a lifetime later, Helene returned, seeming to melt out of the darkness. Her eyes shone, but her face was grim. At least there wasn't a mark on her—except for the purple bruises that still colored her throat from our first visit to this god-awful place.

She said, "I counted eight Deaders, though there might be more patrolling around the prison. They're all wearing those yellow slickers."

"That's gonna make it harder," I said.

"Not for me," Dave added, swinging his shovel.

Helene looked curiously at him. "Don't ask," I said. "Did you see…my mom?"

She shook her head. Then she frowned, as if debating whether to say more.

"What?" I demanded.

"Emily's there," Helene replied. "They've got her in a chair right in the middle of the hub. She's not tied up, but they're guarding her close. She looks like she's been crying, but I don't think they've hurt her"—she paused and swallowed—"too much."

Emily.

My little sister was just a few dozen yards way, alone with those monsters and probably scared out of her mind. The urge to run in there and massacre the Corpses who'd taken her was so strong it almost drove me nuts.

Again, Helene touched my arm. "We got surprise on our side," she whispered. "We go in fast and hard, firing in every which way. They got their raincoats, but the Deaders I saw all had their hoods down. We'll just have to go for headshots. Take down as many as we can. Don't give them time to react."

I nodded. It wasn't a particularly complicated or elegant plan, not the kind of thing that Sharyn would have numbered. But then, the last time we'd hit this prison, we'd tried doing it the smart way and had taken a beating.

"Sounds solid to me," the Burgermeister decided.

I slung Aunt Sally over my shoulder and pulled my out my Super Soaker. Helene reached into her backpack and produced a fistful of colored water balloons. Beside her, Dave lifted his shovel and gave it a little flip—fast and oddly graceful. He reminded me of Sharyn working with Vader.

I wondered again about the "private lessons" she'd been giving him.

I took a deep breath. "Let's do it."

We left the cell and walked three abreast, with me on the right, Helene on the left, and the Burgermeister in the middle. We took it easy at first, not wanting our footfalls to give us away. But as we neared the half-open double doors at the end of the corridor, we slowly and steadily increased our pace, moving in rhythm with one another, keeping our breathing steady, while putting all our senses on high alert.

Undertakers training.

Twenty feet.

Fifteen.

Ten.

Five.

Now!

Dave's foot came up and hit the doors with such force that one of them tore right off its rusted old hinges. An instant later, we spilled into the hub. Helene went left, and I went right. The first thing I saw was a Corpse in a yellow slicker turning toward me, looking as surprised as his bloated purple face was capable of looking.

I shot him with my Super Soaker, catching him right between the eyes. His mouth fell open, and his limbs turned to jelly. He dropped like a sack of hammers.

Behind me, I heard the splash of a water balloon, following by a frantic moan. Then a crash as some helpless, blinded Deader walked straight into a wall. I turned, still firing, and caught another Corpse in the back of the head as he was lunging for Dave; Helene had been right: their hoods were down.

The dude smacked the tile floor—hard.

For his part, the Burgermeister made straight for the chair in the middle of the room. By the time he reached the first of the two Corpses who flanked it, his shovel was already singing through the air. The blow was tremendous, as good as any medieval axeman's, and the Deader's head toppled off her shoulders.

Sharyn thought this guy was too slow to be an Angel?

The second Corpse, probably acting on orders, turned his

attention to the tiny figure seated in the chair, reaching for her with killing hands.

"No!" I yelled. Charging forward, I fired my Super Soaker but caught him on his raincoated shoulder—useless. He gave me a wicked grin as his purple fingers grasped my little sister's slender neck. I heard her cry out in fear.

Then the Burgermeister swung his shovel in a savage arc that buried it in the Deader's chest.

The Corpse went down, flailing like an upended turtle.

Emily's tear-filled face looked up and found mine.

"Will?" she squeaked.

I dropped my Super Soaker and ran to her. Nearby, Helene felled two more Corpses with water balloons. At the same time, Dave planted a huge sneakered foot on the second Deader's abs and yanked his shovel. Then he flipped it over, raised it high, and bought it down with terrific force.

Another head went rolling off.

I barely noticed. Emily's arms were around my neck, and she was crying.

So was I.

There's been a time when my little sister had been more pest than pleasure, when she'd shadowed me annoyingly around the neighborhood, or when I'd been forced to cancel plans with my friends to babysit her. I'd resented her, teased her, ignored her. But I'd always loved her. And right now, the love was all that mattered.

"Will," she whispered into my ear. "I've missed you."

"I've missed you too, Emmie," I choked.

"Is that all of 'em?" Dave demanded.

Helene looked around the room. I forced myself to do the same, lifting my sister up in my arms. Eight Corpses lay around us in various states of injury. The ones Helene and I had salted were down but wouldn't stay there. In fact, the first guy I'd hit looked like he might be trying to get to his feet.

"Burgermeister," I said. "Would you mind?"

"My pleasure," Dave replied. He descended on the recovering Deader like a charging bear. The shovel hissed. And another head rolled.

"Dude," I said. "You're getting good at that."

"Feels great," he grinned. "Like I was born to do it."

"While you're at it," Helene remarked, "how about using your newfound talent on the rest of these guys? They're all salted, but I don't want—"

But before she could finish that sentence, a door burst open behind her and another Corpse emerged.

He was a Type Three, reasonably fresh and very strong. Also, his fancy pinstriped suit and red power tie—barely visible beneath his yellow slicker—were somehow familiar. Instinctively, I stole a quick glimpse at his Mask. Yeah, this guy had been with Cavanaugh in Chang's Funeral Parlor. He was one of the dudes I'd zapped with my bucket trick only to have him transfer into another body and come popping out of a morgue drawer.

Gerald Pierce.

Pierce moved with lightning speed. As I watched in horror, he wrapped one dead forearm under Helene's chin. His other arm snaked around her waist. She uttered a startled gasp as she was yanked right off her feet.

"Hello, Mr. Ritter," the Deader said in English.

I suddenly flashed back to the last time I'd been in this room.

Pierce stood almost exactly where that other Corpse had been, trying to kill Helene now as the other had then. The horror of it hit me like a hammer, but I forced it back down.

I'm not her knight in shining armor, and she's no damsel in distress.

She's an Undertaker.

And so am I.

"Pierce, right?" I said, fighting to keep calm.

"Correct," he replied. "Now drop your weapons, or I'll break this little girl's neck."

The Burgermeister and I exchanged looks.

"Will…" he began.

I gave a very slight shake of my head, and he fell silent.

"Last chance!" Pierce pressed. Then, just to make his point, his arm tightened viciously. Helene kicked, her hands clawing uselessly at his yellow slicker. She tried to say something but couldn't make a sound.

With a curse that would have made a truck driver blush, the Burgermeister put down his shovel.

"Good boys," the Corpse said, grinning. His gums were

black and his teeth clearly loose. His skin was bloating up badly, making his milky eyes sink into their swollen purple-gray sockets.

"Now what?" I asked.

His grin widened. "Now we wait for my associates to recover fully."

In my arms, Emily trembled. "Will?"

"Shhh," I said, rubbing her back. Then I turned to the Corpse and said, "Where's my mother?"

For a few seconds, he just looked at me. Then, as if a lightbulb lit up above his decaying brain, he replied, "Oh, I see! You came here expecting to rescue both of them! How courageous. Unfortunately, Mrs. Ritter isn't here. Ms. Cavanaugh has...other plans...for her."

In Pierce's grasp, Helene's face had gone red. Her struggles became frantic.

Again, panic gnawed at me. I had my knife in my pocket and Aunt Sally on my back. But with Emily on one arm, I couldn't make an effective grab for either of them.

"Ease up!" Dave demanded. "You're choking her!"

Pierce chuckled. "I fail to see your point!" But then he looked around at the other Deaders, three of whom were trying to get up, and his grip on the girl's neck slacked slightly. He wasn't ready to kill her, knowing we'd attack the moment he did.

But within a minute, his buds would be up and about.

We're running out of time.

"Where is she?" I demanded again.

Pierce offered an oddly human-looking shrug. "I fail to see any advantage in telling you that. Not that it matters. My mistress has already won the day."

"Won the day?" Who says that?

But then I caught Helene giving me a look—a look with meaning in it. One of her hands dropped from Pierce's forearm, as if she were weakening. But then, as I watched, it slid into her coat pocket.

I got the message: "Keep him talking."

"We already know most of it," I said. "Cavanaugh wants the statehouse, so she's got this Dashiell guy to help her out. Right?"

Pierce's sunken eyes narrowed. "And how did you come by that knowledge, Mr. Ritter?"

Dave answered, "You wormbags ain't as smart as you think!"

His expression turned thoughtful. Then he said, "Of course. The FBI agent. So…my mistress was right to have him taken. He knew too much!"

Helene's hand came slowly out of her pocket. And it wasn't empty.

The Deaders around us had nearly roused. We had thirty seconds—maybe less.

"Yeah," I replied, keeping my focus on Pierce. My heart was hammering; it was almost painful. "She *was* right. Too bad we got to him before she had the chance to find out for herself."

Ty Drago

"It doesn't matter!" the Corpse hissed. "In moments, you'll be dead!"

Then Helene's fist pumped up and down—hard—jabbing her Ritter into Pierce's forearm and slamming the plunger home.

Startled, Pierce stared at it, more perplexed than angry because, of course, the needle didn't hurt his lifeless body.

"And just what was that supposed to—"

Which was as far as he got before his left arm exploded.

He dropped Helene, who landed badly and stumbled, her ankle visibly twisted. Nevertheless, she gritted her teeth, spun around, and treated her attacker to a savage kick in the midsection, knocking him flat.

As she did, something went flying out of the Corpse's jacket. It skittered across the tile floor and hit my dirt-caked sneaker. I looked down at it. Then I looked back at Dave and Helene.

"Guy's *still* a tool," Helene remarked.

Pierce lay on his back, staring at his arm—or rather, where his arm used to be. "What *was* that?" he exclaimed, his smug tone having turned to sudden terror.

"Dave!" I called. "The others!"

The Burgermeister snatched up his shovel. "I'm on it!"

And he was. The first Deader to recover lost his head before he even knew what was coming. The second raised his arm to block the blow only to have the shovel blade lop it off at the elbow before it buried itself deep in his skull. He went down too—and stayed down.

The last guy regained his feet and turned to fight. I tossed my pocketknife to Helene, who snatched it out of the air, hit the 2 button, and pressed the Taser into the small of the big Corpse's back. He stiffened, his milky eyes going wide, black fluid dribbling from his mouth, nose, and ears.

Then he dropped like a lumberjacked tree, and Dave did his shovel thing a final time.

"What are you doing to the bad men?" Emily asked me, looking around.

My sister wasn't a Seer—at least not yet. Too young. So I couldn't help but wonder what she saw. But I filed that question away for another time—too much to do.

"I have to put you down for a minute, Em," I said.

"Don't leave me!" she cried.

"I won't. I promise. But I need both hands."

She reluctantly nodded, and I lowered her to the floor only to have her cling to my leg, which made it harder to ready Aunt Sally.

Then I glanced over and caught Dave brandishing his shovel over Pierce, who held his free arm up as a useless shield.

"Don't!" I barked. The Burgermeister paused to look at me. So did Helene, who had her Super Soaker out now. She'd limped to the middle of the room and was watching the doors, turning in a slow circle just in case another Deader showed up to the party late.

To Dave, I said, "I want to talk to him."

CHAPTER 38

JUGGERNAUT

With Emily in tow, I went over to Pierce, who looked up at me with fearful, milky eyes. "What did the girl do to me?"

"She stuck you with a needle filled with saltwater," I said.

"We call it a Ritter," Dave added, though I wished he hadn't.

I pointed Aunt Sally at Pierce. "Allow me to demonstrate." Then I shot him in the leg.

For whatever reason, Steve's invention worked faster in limbs than in the torso. Barely a second after the bolt hit and the plunger plunged, Pierce's leg seemed to launch like a rocket off his hip. It skittered across the tile floor before suddenly bursting, painting the nearby wall with Corpse juice.

Even though I knew he'd felt no pain, Pierce acted as if he had. He moaned piteously and threw his remaining arm over his face, as if the world had just become too unbearable to look at. He stayed this way while I loaded another crank assembly onto Aunt Sally.

At my side, Emily asked, sounding confused. "What did you do, Will?"

Instead of answering her, I looked over at Helene. "Are we clear?"

"I think so," she replied.

"Better be sure. Pierce?"

The Deader mewled pathetically and risked a look at me. I pointed Aunt Sally at his chest. "If I shoot you *here*," I told him. "Your entire stolen body will pop like a balloon. Nothing left. And there's no handy substitute. Know what that means, wormbag?"

He nodded.

"Good. Now I'm going to ask you a bunch of questions. The first time you don't answer one or try to lie to me, I'm going to send you to wherever it is *Malum* go when they die. You got that?"

Pierce opened his mouth. His tongue was swollen and black, like there was an eel hiding behind his teeth. "Yes."

"Good. First question: any more of you in the prison?"

"No," he said without hesitation.

"But more will be coming...now that we've dropped your buds?"

"Yes."

"How soon?"

"I...don't know."

"Okay. Now here's a big one. Where the hell's my mother?"

Then, just for emphasis, I pressed the point of the Ritterbolt against the front of his yellow slicker, right about where his navel would be.

Pierce actually trembled with fear. Was this really the same guy who'd threatened Helene with a smile on his face? Did all bullies—and what *were* Corpses if not bullies—when they fell fall this hard?

"She's…with Dashiell."

"Dashiell," Helene echoed. "That's the guy Cavanaugh hired to kill the governor."

At that, Pierce almost smiled.

"What's so funny?" I demanded. Then, when he didn't reply, I shot his other leg.

His smile vanished in a second.

So did his leg.

As Dave guarded the dude with his shovel, I rearmed Aunt Sally. "Emily," I said. "Why don't you go sit in that chair? We'll be out of here in a minute."

"No!" she replied, screwing up her little face into a look that our mom sometimes called Emily Ironnose. "I'm staying with *you*!"

I sighed. "Okay."

Then to Pierce, I said, "I'll ask one more time."

The Corpse was down to just one limb now. He shuddered with desperation. "Please…don't kill me!"

"Pretty cute, coming from you," the Burgermeister growled.

"I just do what I'm told. I follow orders."

"Good. Follow *this* one," I said. Then I moved the point of the Ritterbolt up to his bloated, rotting forehead. Pierce's face twisted in near panic. He looked like he wanted to crawl right down through the floor. If he'd had a working bladder, he'd probably have wet himself. "I *order* you to tell me exactly where my mother is!"

His answer came out in a rush. "She's in City Hall Tower with Dashiell."

Helene and I exchanged looks. "City Hall Tower?" she echoed. "But that's nowhere near Penn's Landing! The governor's giving a speech at Penn's Landing this morning, isn't he?"

I nodded.

Pierce stared in horror at the needle, his milky eyes crossing. "My mistress doesn't want to kill the governor!" he exclaimed. "Get that…thing…away from me!"

"Then who…?" I began.

But the Deader on the floor spilled his guts before I could even finish my thought. "The governor's wife!"

"What?" This came from the Burgermeister, who'd been standing over Pierce this whole time with his shovel poised like a guillotine. How he was able to keep his arms up like that, steady as a rock, was a mystery. But not as big a mystery as what Pierce had just said.

"The governor's wife?" I replied, my "tough-guy interrogator" bit momentarily forgotten.

Pierce nodded, suddenly the very soul of cooperation. "The mistress wants power at the state level. She can't get that by killing the governor."

Which was true. Hadn't we all discussed it back in Haven?

But if the governor's death wouldn't help her, how would the death of his wife—

And just like that, I figured it out.

It happens that way sometimes.

"She's gonna *marry* him," I said, speaking to no one in particular.

"Who's gonna marry who?" Dave asked.

I looked at Helene and could see from her expression that she'd gotten it too. If the Burgermeister hadn't, it was only because he'd never seen what we'd both seen.

The *Pelligog* in action.

"So what's the plan?" I asked Pierce. "She kills the governor's wife, then finds an opportunity to stick a *Pelligog* into the governor, grabs control of his mind, marries him, and then sets herself up as the first lady of Pennsylvania? After that, she runs the state she way the runs the city—from the background. Sound about right?"

Pierce looked from one to the other of us. If it were possible for those dead eyes to appear shifty, he managed it. I glanced down at Emily, who was pressed close to my leg, sucking her thumb. She'd zoned out, which was scary in a way but also probably good—at least in the short term.

Then my eyes fell to my sister's other hand. She held something in it, clutched tightly in her little fist. Reaching down, I took it from her. She gave it up without complaint or comment.

It was the *something* that had come flying out of Pierce's pocket. Some kind of quartz, maybe ten inches long.

It felt...strange. But not bad strange. Just holding it seemed to make me less tired. Rejuvenated. Suddenly, the aches and pains of the night were gone.

"You okay?" Dave asked. "What's that?"

"I don't know," I replied. And I didn't have time to find out. I pocketed the *something*. As I did, I noticed Pierce looking at me. There was something like horror behind his milky eyes, a horror that had nothing to do with the threat of Aunt Sally.

I pressed Aunt Sally's tip down until it almost punctured one of Pierce's shifty eyes. "*Is* that Cavanaugh's plan?"

Pierce whimpered. "If I tell you the rest, will you promise not to kill me?"

"Sure," I said.

"Yes. That's her plan."

"And my mom? Why is she with Dashiell?"

"The assassin is controlled," Pierce replied. "His orders are to kill the governor's wife during her speech in Love Park. Then he's to shoot Susan Ritter through the heart and leave her body in the City Hall Tower before jumping over the rail."

"Jumping over the rail?"

"He's to kill himself," the Corpse explained.

"Would that work?" Dave wondered. "I mean, even with one of those…spider things…controlling you, are you so far gone that you'll kill yourself just 'cause the Queen tells you to?"

I looked over at Helene, who'd gone pale, lost in a really bad memory.

"Yeah," she whispered. "It'd work."

"No witnesses," Pierce added.

"And when's this supposed to happen?" I asked him.

"Nine-fifteen in the morning. Just a little bit into the speech at Love Park."

Helene blew out a sigh. "Then we got some time to warn Haven."

Still keeping Aunt Sally aimed at the trapped Deader, I checked my watch. Eight twenty-two in the morning.

Wait…

Hadn't it been eight twenty-two when we'd crawled out of the tunnel? "Helene! What time do you have?" But she only shook her head helplessly. Then I remembered that she'd lost her own watch back in the dirt tube.

And the Burgermeister, of course, didn't have one.

I quickly scanned the room and noticed an expensive-looking gold watch lying in the dust near to where Pierce had fallen. It was his own, of course, left behind when the arm inside it had exploded.

With a sick feeling of dread, I leaned over and picked it up.

It was 9:03.

"Holy crap!" I exclaimed. "We got twelve minutes!"

Helene gasped. "Oh my God…"

"What do we do?" Dave asked.

My watch had broken back in the tunnel, probably when I'd been fighting with the bricks. But did that mean the radio was busted too? I lowered Aunt Sally and fumbled with it. There *was* a signal, but it seemed messed up, fading in and out. Something wrong with the antenna maybe?

"How's your ankle?" I asked Helene.

She tested her bad foot, putting a little bit of weight on it. Then she winced. With a defeated sigh, she replied, "Hurts bad. I think it's swollen. I can't ride—at least not fast enough to do any good."

I glanced at Dave, who only shrugged. We both knew how good he was—and wasn't—on a bike.

Prying my sister from around my leg, I knelt down in front of her. Seconds were kicking by. Precious seconds. But I forced myself to stay calm. "Emmie?" When she didn't reply right away, I put one hand on her thin shoulder and pried the thumb from between her lips. It was a gesture I'd seen my mother do a hundred times. "Emmie. I need you to look at me, honey."

"Okay, Mommy," she muttered, as if speaking in a dream.

Swallowing, I ignored that.

"This is my friend, Helene." I motioned to Helene, who limped over. "She's gonna take you someplace safe. I'm going to go get Mommy."

Emily looked at me, her eyes clearing. As if suddenly remembering where she was, she asked, "Are you going to save her from the bad men too?"

"Yeah, I am."

"Okay." She hugged me, squeezing hard, as if still afraid I might not be real. Then Helene took her hand and smiled down at her. After a few painful seconds, my baby sister smiled back.

I straightened up, peeling off my watch and tossing it to Dave. "Get outside and use the radio! Tell Haven to send somebody up to the City Hall Tower right now!"

On the floor between us, Pierce—or what was left of him—chuckled. "You'll never get there in time."

I looked at him.

Then I pointed Aunt Sally at his chest.

"Wait!" he exclaimed. "I answered all your questions!"

"Here's one more," I said. I didn't have time for this—I didn't have anything *like* time for this—but I intended to do it anyway. "Whose body are you in?"

"What?"

"That body you're wearing!" I barked. "It belonged to someone once. A person! A human being! Someone with a life…a family. People who loved them and who miss them. Whose body *is* it?"

The Corpse trembled pitifully. "I...I don't know."

"Will," Helene whispered. "Are you sure—"

"Wrong answer," I said.

Then I shot him in the stomach, tossing Aunt Sally to Dave, who caught it smoothly with one hand.

"*Go*, dude!" he told me.

I turned and ran, not back toward the tunnel but straight down Cell Block Nine, heading for the main gate.

Behind me, I heard Pierce screaming. It was an awful sound, but at least it didn't last long.

A few seconds later, he exploded.

And I felt nothing. Nothing at all.

As I neared the double doors at the end of the cell block, I knew I'd thrown caution right out the window. If there were more Corpse guards patrolling the yard between the cell block and the gate, they'd be on me in a second. But I had to take the chance. The dirt tube would be too slow. Love Park was across the street from City Hall, and City Hall was more than a mile away.

Fortunately, there were no guards.

Fairmount Avenue buzzed with morning traffic. I pushed open the prison gate and turned west, running along the landscaping wall and past the hole that Dave had dug about a million years ago. At the corner, I crossed, not bothering about the light, drawing honks from some cars that I completely ignored.

I sprinted another block to the alley where we'd stashed the bikes. I mounted mine, turned it east, and pushed off.

All that took thirty, maybe forty seconds.

I kicked the pedals harder than I ever had in my life.

My heart hammered behind my ears, sounding like shotgun fire. Despite the winter chill, my hands were soaked in sweat. Riding a bike in the city is risky enough at the best of times. But if I wanted to make it to Love Park before Dashiell took his shot, I had to go all out.

I turned down Twentieth Street, ignoring the cars, ignoring the stoplights, ignoring the pedestrians. "Outta the way!" I kept screaming, wishing I had a siren to blare or even a bike horn to blow.

Traffic roared and honked. Curses flooded the air like raindrops. I was ticking off everyone around me, but I didn't dare stop. If I got hit by a car, it was over. If I got knocked down by someone crossing the street, it was over. I still had Pierce's watch, having slipped the heavy thing around my wrist as I'd run out of the prison, but I didn't dare look at it. Second by second, I needed to study the road ahead of me, watching for the next break between cars, dodging the next obstacle.

I hit the Ben Franklin Parkway, the wide thoroughfare that runs from the art museum to City Hall. Traffic was heavier here than on the side streets, but at least it offered a bit more room to maneuver. Better—or maybe worse—I could see the clock in City Hall Tower, still half a mile away. It was getting closer but slowly, horribly slowly. And its minute hand was inching downward. It had just passed the two and was making its way toward the three.

Love Park sat just northwest of City Hall. Lots of events happened there all the time, and it was almost always crowded. But today, with the first lady of Pennsylvania addressing a bunch of urban school kids, the place would be mobbed. There'd be cops around—not as many as around the governor himself maybe but plenty. And because this was Lilith's real objective, I guessed a pretty high ratio of those cops would be of the dead and drippy variety.

I could only hope Dave and Helene had gotten word to Haven and that somebody was already on their way up to the tower. I briefly considered skipping the park and going straight up there myself. I mean, I didn't owe the governor's wife anything, did I? And this was my *mom* we were talking about!

But I'd never get there in time. City Hall Tower was a block farther and five hundred feet higher. The assassin would have taken his first shot, then his second, and have jumped to his death before I even made it to the stairs.

Besides, I was an Undertaker, and I trusted my friends. If they could get to my mother before Dashiell killed her, they would.

If they could.

Twelve minutes after nine.

I pedaled harder.

Ahead, I spotted the bubblegum lights of police cruisers. They'd cordoned off the park with blue sawhorses. Uniformed cops patrolled the boundary. A lot of them. More than I'd imagined. On the far side of the fountain, a dais had been built right behind the big *LOVE* sculpture. As stages went, it wasn't real high, just tall enough to let the people on it be seen by the gathered crowd.

And what a crowd it was. Maybe a thousand people, most of them kids. School buses lined the nearby streets. This event had apparently been turned into a weekend field trip. Heck, if I'd still been an eighth-grade student at John Towers Middle School, I might have found myself here too.

Thirteen minutes after nine.

My eyes flicked up toward the tower. Would I see a glint of metal? The flash of the morning sun off a telescopic lens? Neither. As it happened, the sun was behind City Hall at this time of day, which had cast the whole park in shadow. I wouldn't see a thing. Nobody would. *Pelligogged* or not, Dashiell knew what he was doing.

I reached the edge of the event, still at least a block from the dais. From here, I could see the governor's wife, flanked by men in suits. She wore a heavy beige coat against the morning cold, her blond hair pinned down by white ear-muffs. She was speaking into a microphone. I could hear her voice echoing through the speakers, though I was still too far away to make out any words.

Fourteen minutes after nine.

A police car loomed in front of me. I skirted around it and jumped my bike up over the curb onto the sidewalk, weaving around the people in my path. A cop spotted me. Human.

"Hey!" he called.

Another cop appeared. This one was dead. He didn't say anything at all. He just moved to cut me off.

I pulled a water pistol from inside my coat and shot him in the face. As he fell back, I heard people suddenly shout, "The kid's got a gun!"

Crap!

Another cop lunged at me, human this time. I maneuvered around him, jumped off the curb again, and slipped my bike between two of the sawhorses. I was in Love Park now, skirting the big fountain and pedaling directly through the crowd, only some of whom had so far registered my presence. Those that did backed instinctively away. Those that didn't, I screamed at—"Look out! Watch it!"—until they either jumped or fell clear.

I could hear the woman's words now but didn't bother to listen. I was down to seconds, not minutes, and the cops were closing in on all sides.

That's when I spotted the ramp.

It stood on the right side of the dais and the cordon seemed to flank it, clearing the path that the governor's wife had probably used when she'd arrived and would use again when she left. I made for it, kicking at my pedals with every last bit of my strength.

A dead cop pushed through the crowd on my left and came at me. He caught my arm and would have pulled me down if I hadn't made an awkward, lucky shot with my pistol that crippled him. Another one leapt—literally *leapt*—for my back wheel, but I managed a final burst of speed, and he missed by inches.

Then I cleared the cordon and turned up the open path toward the ramp and dais behind it.

As I did, my eye flitted one last time to the tower clock.

Fifteen minutes after nine.

I'm too late!

No time for warnings. I drove my bike—full speed— along the path and up the ramp, my wheels actually leaving the ground as I did so.

What happened next seemed to happen in slow motion.

The governor's wife turned, her speech forgotten, her eyes widening in shock and confusion. Her bodyguards, if that was what they were, moved in to stop me, but I was already airborne, and stopping at this point just wasn't in the cards.

I kicked one of them in the face. I'm not sure if it was accidental or on purpose.

Then I leapt into the air, pushing off my pedals, leaving the bike behind.

I'm not really sure what I was trying to do. But I think I meant to tackle the woman, to get her out of the line of fire.

I *think*.

But I'm pretty sure I *didn't* intend to take Dashiell's shot in the back.

CHAPTER 39

LIFE AFTER DEATH

I don't remember any pain. I don't even remember hitting the floor of the dais.

What I *do* remember is being cold. Really cold. Like someone had taken my coat and dumped a bucket of ice water over my head. My mind registered that something terrible had happened, but I had no idea what it could be.

I mean, the governor's wife *hadn't* been shot. Lying on my stomach with my head turned to one side, I could see her clearly. She was on the floor too, just a few feet away, with her bodyguards sprawled atop her, shielding her with their bodies—the way I'd tried to.

I did it! She didn't get shot!

But I think maybe someone did.

Everything turned to chaos. People screamed. I could hear running feet. Lights flashed—police cars maybe. A lot of them. Had more shown up? How had they gotten here so quickly?

Somebody yelled, "The kid had a gun!"

Somebody else yelled, "It's just a water pistol!" Then the same somebody added another of those words my mother probably wouldn't have approved of.

Mom.

She was in City Hall Tower with Dashiell. He'd taken his shot; I'd heard it. But he must have missed. Would he try again, or would he just turn his gun on my mom as he'd been ordered? A fresh wave of panic flooded me, making me feel even colder. I opened my mouth to beg for help—not for me but for my mother. But no sound would come out.

"City Hall!" someone yelled. "The shot came from the observation deck!"

Yes! Go there quick! Save my mom!

A woman's voice: "Get off me! Will you men please get off me?"

A man's voice: "You have to stay down, ma'am!"

The woman's voice again: "Get off me, you idiot! This boy's been shot!"

What boy?

Gentle hands touched my face. My vision blurred. I felt so sleepy all of a sudden. I heard the woman's voice again, much closer this time, practically on top of me. She sounded like she was crying.

"Get an ambulance! Now! No, I'm not going anywhere! This child just saved my life! Now get an ambulance!" Then *she* added a word that my mother *definitely* wouldn't have approved of.

On the other hand, under the circumstances, maybe she would.

If she's still alive...

"Hang on," the woman told me. "You just hang on. Everything's going to be fine."

I remember thinking she had a kind voice.

Then everything went dark.

Very dark. And very cold. In fact, the cold was all I could feel. The woman, the wooden dais, even the air seemed to have vanished—which was just as well because I was pretty sure I'd stopped breathing.

Is this what death feels like?

"William?"

A woman's voice but not the same woman. This voice was younger, less panicky. It was also vaguely familiar, like something left over from a dream.

"William?"

I opened my eyes.

I was on a bed, under a white sheet. There was light all around me, though I couldn't see walls or even a ceiling. It was like floating on a cloud. Maybe this was heaven after all.

A blond woman was smiling down at me. She had the face of an angel. In fact, she *was* an angel, one that I'd met once before.

"Can you hear me?"

"Yeah," I replied, and I was surprised by the way my voice sounded. Raspy. Dry. Like I hadn't used it in a while.

"Good," she said. Did I read relief in her smile now? I wasn't sure. "Just lie still. You're going to be just fine."

Then, as if some kind of brain fog lifted, I managed to add two and two to figure out exactly who'd been shot instead of the governor's wife.

"My mom!" I exclaimed. I tried to sit up, but my entire body felt like soft rubber.

The woman put a warm hand on my shoulder and eased me back down onto the pillow.

"It's important that you stay calm, William."

"My mom's in trouble!" I cried, begging. Tears flooded my eyes. "Please! He's gonna kill her!"

"If I show you your mother, will you lie still and calm down?"

What did *that* mean? But I just nodded, mainly because something in her tone gave me hope.

She turned away and spoke to someone I couldn't see. "Point us at the tower."

The world seemed to spin. Instinctively, I closed my eyes, and when I opened them again, the weird white room was gone, replaced by something even weirder.

Now my bed was tucked—wedged really—into the City Hall Tower's narrow observation deck. Ahead stood the open steel door that led to the cramped elevator. To my right ran a curved wall of windows, separated by a waist-high metal railing that ran all the way around the deck. Through them, the city of Philadelphia sprawled outward in all directions five hundred feet below us. Overhead, looking huge and imposing at the building's pinnacle, loomed the famous statue of William Penn.

"What…?" I began.

The woman, who remained beside my bed, touched a warm finger to her lips, pointing with her other hand to two figures standing just a few yards ahead, almost around the curve of the observation deck.

One was a small, thin man wearing a parka. His hood was up, which was probably good because he'd evidently opened a couple of the windows. Winter wind tossed his dark hair and made his hood flap.

In the guy's hands was a long rifle with a ridiculously big scope mounted onto it. Beside him, a woman stood handcuffed to the railing. She wasn't as blond as the angel, but to me, she looked at least as beautiful.

"Mom!" I called.

"She can't hear you, William."

I tried to get up. I tried desperately, but I just didn't have the strength.

"Stay calm."

"But that's Dashiell! He's got my mother, and he's going to—"

"I know. Just watch," she said.

So, helpless, I watched. Dashiell rested the barrel of his

rifle on the railing and peered into its scope. My mother looked terrified. She was wrapped in her winter coat, a long wool beige number that my dad had given her the Christmas before he'd died. I knew it was warm enough, but unlike Dashiell's parka, it lacked a hood. Mom's hair blew every which way.

I could see her shivering.

Then Dashiell took aim at something far below, something well outside my field of view.

Love Park! The governor's wife!

But this had already happened!

When it came, the shot was so loud it made the windows rattle. My mother jumped. Then she started to cry. She always looked so much like Emmie when she cried.

Again, I tried to get up to go to her. Dashiell had taken his shot, only he'd hit *me* instead of his intended target.

And he clearly knew it because he straightened up, cursing furiously. For several seconds, he stood there, as if trying to decide what to do next. Then he looked at my mother. She stared back at him with tear-streaked eyes. She said something, but as she was turning away from me, her words were lost in the wind.

The assassin pulled back the bolt on his rifle, ejecting the spent cartridge. Then he spoke, and *his* words, unlike my mother's, rang through loud and clear.

"Your turn, Susan."

"No!" I yelled.

"No!" someone else yelled.

I turned to see Hugo Ramirez emerge through the open steel hatchway that led to the elevator. His left arm was still in its sling, and his face shone with sweat. He clutched a small black pistol.

Dashiell spun toward him, his face darkening.

"Special Agent Ramirez of the FBI! Lower your weapon and step away from the woman!"

Thank you. Oh God...thank you.

The assassin took perhaps half a second to size up the situation. Then he moved, dropping the empty rifle and ducking behind my mother, pulling her in front of him like a shield until she was yanked hard against her handcuff and cried out in pain.

This time, when I tried to get up, I almost fell off the bed. The woman took my shoulders.

"All this has already happened, William. We're not even really here. There's nothing you can do."

And to be honest, I'd already guessed that. But it didn't matter. She was my mom, and this murdering psycho had her, and I needed to do something about it! I *needed* to! It was a knee-jerk reaction, like putting your hands out when you trip.

Ramirez said, "There's no way out of here, Dashiell. It's over."

But the killer only smiled. Then he produced a switch-blade from his coat pocket, snapped it open, and pressed it to my mother's throat.

I heard a whimpering sound, and it took a moment for me to realize that *I'd* made it.

I had never felt so helpless in all my life.

"Why are you showing me this?" I asked—sobbed, really.

"Just watch…"

"Put your gun down, FBI," Dashiell commanded. "Or I'll slit her throat."

But Ramirez's gun arm didn't waver an inch. "Do that, and I'll shoot you dead before she hits the ground."

"But think of the paperwork, agent," the assassin replied with a laugh. "A dead civilian?"

"This isn't a joke. Let her go, or you're going to die on this observation deck." Ramirez took a step closer, but as he did, the assassin's hand tightened, and his blade nicked my mother neck. She gasped and struggled, but he held her fast.

"Stop it!" I cried, even though I knew it was stupid and pointless to do so.

Ramirez froze again, but his eyes remained locked on the assassin's.

"The mistake you're making," Dashiell told him, "is assuming that I expect to survive this job. I have my orders. I was to kill my target, dispatch this witness, and then make a dramatic swan dive into the city hall courtyard. Just think of tomorrow's headlines!"

"And that's okay with you, is it?" Ramirez asked. "Offing yourself for a client?"

For just a moment, the assassin faltered a little. "It's… necessary."

"Why's that?"

"She…" Dashiell blinked. "She said so."

"Lilith Cavanaugh?"

At the sound of the Queen's name, Dashiell's confusion evaporated. His eyes narrowed. "Are you maybe…recording me, agent? Trying to get me to incriminate my employer? I've never heard of anyone by that name. Sorry."

Then Ramirez did an odd thing. He smiled and lowered his gun. I stared at him, flabbergasted. My gaze switched between the two men, and I noticed that Dashiell seemed every bit as surprised as I felt.

"Actually," the FBI guy said, "I'm *not* recording you. This isn't even a real gun. It's a cheap plastic water pistol…though a little more realistic than most maybe." He squirted it into his open mouth and made a sour face. "Saltwater."

"A bluff?" Dashiell asked, looking confused and wary.

Ramirez's smile widened. "Nope. Just wanted to keep you talking long enough."

"Long enough for what?"

In that instant, a figure dropped from above, crashing down onto the assassin through an opening in the roof of the observation deck.

The strike was so perfectly landed that it split Dashiell and my mother apart. She fell to the deck floor, groaning in pain as her manacled wrist was twisted again. The assassin tumbled away but recovered his feet almost instantly, the knife still in his grip.

Then he whirled around to face the new threat.

Tom Jefferson blocked the width of the walkway, a human barrier between my mother and her would-be killer. His face was like stone, his expression colder than I'd ever seen it.

"Who are *you*?" Dashiell demanded, brandishing his switchblade.

"I'm an Undertaker," the Chief replied in a toneless voice.

The assassin sneered. "I've heard of you kids. She said you might try to get in the way. But I admit I didn't expect anything like this! Just where did you come from?"

Tom nodded upward. "While Ramirez was keepin' you busy, I came up the stairs, climbed out onto the roof of the deck, and worked my way around."

"Clever," Dashiell admitted. "But you must be freezing without a coat in this weather. Careful, kid…you'll catch your death."

Tom didn't smile. On the contrary, I didn't think I'd ever seen him so pissed. He took a step toward the assassin, who held up his blade, turning it this way and that in the morning light, like a little kid on show-and-tell day. "Think twice, boy? I'm armed, and you're not."

The Chief took another step forward. "I saw you take your shot," he said flatly. "I was too late to stop it…but I *saw* it." For a moment, a shadow seemed to cross his face. Then he added, in a tone much colder than the biting February air, "You missed."

Dashiell shrugged. "Unfortunate but not disastrous. Once I'm out of here, I'll arrange a new opportunity."

"You're not *getting* out of here."

The assassin chuckled. "A handcuffed woman and two unarmed men? I've faced much longer odds that than, Undertaker. In a minute, you'll all be dead, and I'll be on the stairs."

Tom didn't seem to have heard the threat. "I'm a soldier," he said. "But I've never killed a human being before."

"Well, don't worry, kid. You're not going to be starting today."

Tom just went on talking. "You missed your target. But you hit someone else."

"I know. I saw it. Some kid on a bike."

The Chief of the Undertakers surged forward. Seeing this, Dashiell reacted by lunging with his switchblade. I expected Tom to dodge. He was great at hand-to-hand; I'd never seen anyone better. But he *didn't* dodge. He didn't even try to parry. He simply grabbed the blade, wrapping his big left hand around it and clamping down like a bear trap.

Dashiell stared at Tom's closed fist and at the blood that had already begun to ooze from between his fingers. He tugged at the knife handle, but it didn't budge.

Tom's eyes were stone. If he felt any pain, he offered no sign of it. Instead, he slammed his fist into the killer's face with devastating force. I actually heard the crunch as the man's nose broke.

Dashiell released the knife and staggered back, blood pouring over his mouth and jaw. Tom stayed with him, hitting him again, a haymaker that spun the killer around and drove him into the observation deck railing. There he floundered, visibly stunned.

Tom advanced, opening his left fist and letting the switchblade fall to his feet. I could see the deep gash that crossed his palm. Blood dripped steadily down to the deck's metal floor.

Ramirez was already coming forward. "Tom…that's enough. Stand down."

But the Chief ignored him.

As we watched: me, my mom, the angel, and the FBI guy, Tom grabbed Dashiell's collar and twisted him around until they were face-to-face again.

"You missed your target," Tom repeated, his voice like ice.

Then he reached one hand down, grabbed Dashiell's leg, and heaved the smaller man right off his feet, holding him aloft as if he weighed no more than a child.

Through his gritted teeth, I heard Tom say, "But you killed my *brother*."

Then Tom Jefferson, the Chief of the Undertakers, threw the struggling assassin out the open window, over the railing, and into empty air.

Dashiell screamed. He seemed to scream for a long time, until, finally, very abruptly, he stopped.

So…that's how long it takes to fall five hundred feet.

Ramirez arrived at Tom's side a second later. He looked over the railing. Then he looked at the Chief, who met his eyes with challenge and not an ounce of remorse. "You gonna arrest me, agent?"

The FBI guy looked shaken to his core.

That made two of us.

"I don't think I could if I wanted to," he replied.

But Tom shook his head. "That ain't no answer."

Ramirez's shook *his* head. "No, I'm not going to arrest you."

"Why not? I just killed a man."

"Yes, you did," the agent told him. "But this is war…and you're a soldier."

Tom nodded. Then it was as if the fury that had been driving him suddenly bled away. His shoulders slumped, and the cold mask he'd been wearing disappeared.

"Will's dead," he whispered in so soft a voice that I almost didn't hear it. "And now I gotta tell his mom."

CHAPTER 40

RESURRECTION

The world changed again, turned white. I barely noticed. What Tom had said—what he'd *done*—rang in my ears and burned in my memory like fire. A hundred feelings roiled around in my head, wrestling for control. Shock. Horror. Guilt.

And pride. Oh yeah, that was there too.

The Chief of the Undertakers, the best man aside from my father I'd ever known, had just killed someone. And he'd done it for *me*.

What an impossible, incredible, terrible thing!

"William?"

We were in the white room again. No walls. No ceiling. Just the angel, her gentle voice and her strangely familiar face.

"William? Are you all right?"

"No," I said.

She nodded, as if this were the right answer.

"What happens now?" I asked.

"Now you go back."

"But…I'm dead."

She smiled, and I was surprised by the warmth and affection I saw in that smile. "No, you're not…though it was a close call."

"Who are you?" I begged.

"I wish I could tell you," she said, and from her tone, it was clear that she meant it. "And one day, I will."

"Well," I said, feeling suddenly impatient. All this mystery, especially in the wake of my own shooting, my mother's near murder, and the awful spectacle of Tom's revenge, was getting tiresome. "Is there anything you *can* tell me?"

"The rules are the same as last time," she replied. "You may ask one question."

"Except 'Who are you?' Right?"

"I'm sorry."

I sighed. I was still tired, very tired. But I suddenly noticed that I wasn't in any pain. Hadn't I been shot like ten minutes ago? Shot by a big rifle that used big bullets? It was one thing to have survived that but to not even *feel* it?

I remembered the first time this angel had paid me a visit. I'd just botched a rescue attempt at Fort Mifflin, outside Philly. I'd been body slammed by a Corpse and come away with a concussion and a broken arm. Except I hadn't. Instead, I'd had a dream like this one and woken up completely healed.

If this angel could do that, then what else could she do?

And just like that, I knew my question.

"Can you save Sharyn like you saved me?"

The woman smiled gently. "No, I can't. But you can."

"What does that mean?"

"At the prison, you picked up something. When you wake up, you'll find it under your pillow. Take it to Sharyn Jefferson. Touch it to her head."

"And that'll fix her?"

She nodded.

"What is it?"

"I'm sorry, William. No more questions. But you'll learn the answer to that one in time." Then she leaned closer, her tone more grave. "But William, listen to me. After you were injured, the Queen acted quickly. She had her people arrive on scene almost at once with an ambulance. Then she had you declared 'dead' while on your way to Jefferson Hospital."

"So...everybody thinks I'm dead?

For a second, I thought she'd fall back on the one-question rule again. To my surprise, she didn't. "Yes. What you did was witnessed by thousands of people in Love Park and has been replayed on television many times. The official story is that your body was rerouted to the medical examiner's office. But that's a lie."

"Where am I then?" What can I say? I love pushing my luck.

"Chang's Funeral Parlor. The Queen has given her

subjects orders to treat you, to keep you alive. Then, later, once you're stable and conscious, she intends to torture you for information."

My throat went dry. "Fantastic," I muttered. "Any chance you might help me out?"

"I've helped you all I can," she replied. "But I have faith in you. When you awaken, more than twelve hours will have passed since the shooting, and you're going to be in far better condition that the Corpses imagine. You can escape on your own."

Nice words—except that for the first time, I thought I read real worry in the woman's eyes. It didn't make me feel all warm and fuzzy.

"Thanks," I said.

"You're welcome," she replied. "Until next time…"

And then she and the white place we shared faded away, returning to whatever dream world they'd come from.

I opened my eyes.

Chang's Funeral Home. The basement morgue room.

Only this time, *I* was the one stretched out on the metal table. The lights were dim, and the door to the outer room stood closed. I was alone. The only sound was my own ragged breathing mixed with the steady beep of a nearby machine.

I still had my pants and shoes, though my coat and shirt were gone.

I tried to sit up but got myself tangled in a web of tubes. One was sticking into the back of my hand—an IV drip running from a hanging bag of who knew what. Two more went up my nose. But the worst one was the one down my throat. It was *wide* and held in place by several strips of tape.

Gagging a little and fighting a sudden panic, I ripped off the tape (which hurt) and then pulled out the tube (which *really* hurt). Then I sat there, gulping air. Oddly, whatever they were shooting up my nose helped with this; I could already feel my heart steadying. Nevertheless, I also yanked out the nostril tubes before I went to work on the IV. That came out easier than I'd have thought, though it stung something awful when I pulled the needle from my vein.

I winced but didn't dare cry out. Quiet was the name of the game right now. There were bound to be Corpses nearby, maybe monitoring my condition.

There was a bandage around my chest. A big one. It ran from just under my armpits to just above my navel and had been wrapped around me a half dozen times. This wasn't surprising because I'd been shot. Maybe they'd done emergency surgery or something to get out Dashiell's bullet.

I decided to leave it alone—for now.

That left the sensors. These were stuck to my chest in a half dozen places and plugged into a machine that monitored my heart rate with a display of tiny spikes and the *beep beep* sound I heard earlier. Would I trigger an alarm if I peeled these things off? Would the Corpses figure I'd had a heart attack and come running with one of those paddle things that zaps you back to life?

Not good.

I looked around for my shirt and coat, but they were nowhere to be seen. That made me panic all over again, afraid my pocketknife would be gone. But then I remembered tossing it to Helene back at the prison. She had it, which meant it was safe.

Thinking of my pocketknife sparked another memory, and I reached under my pillow. It took me a few seconds to find it: a jagged piece of what looked like quartz less than a foot long.

Touching it had a strange effect. I felt suddenly stronger—more focused.

There's some kind of power in this thing!

I would have liked to keep holding it. It felt strangely *good* to have it in my hand. But there were things to do. So I shoved it in my pocket and slid gingerly off the table. There I stood, thinking furiously. I was tethered by the sensor wires to the heart monitor, so I couldn't go far without removing them. And removing them would almost certainly alert the Deaders.

Now what?

I worked my way around to the IV stand and read the label in the dim light: "B Braun Saline 0.9% Sodium Chloride Injection 1000ml IV." As I unhooked it from its pole and tugged the tube out of the bottom of it, I could only hope the big words meant what I thought they meant.

Finally, I checked out the beeping machine. It seemed to

have a thousand controls, most of which—if they had labels at all—were marked with meaningless initials.

Well, I can't stay here all night!

So I just yanked out the electrical plug.

The moment the machine went dark, I listened for some kind of alarm to sound. None did. I hurried over to the door and took a spot behind it. Then I went to work peeling off the sensors.

I'd just finished when the door pushed open. A voice said in English, "The mistress will tear us limb from limb if we've allowed him to die!"

Two dead men, both wearing funeral director suits—very formal—stepped into the room. A couple of Type Threes but the kind who liked to take care of their host bodies. These were clean and surprisingly well groomed. They still squished inside their shoes when they walked, but they didn't smell half as bad as most of the Threes I'd met, and there wasn't a beetle or maggot on them.

As they stared at the empty bed and the tubes and wires strewn about, I slipped around behind them and darted out the door. The smaller outer room stood empty. I crossed it at a run and climbed the basement stairs two at a time, pushing the heavy door at the top wide open—and running right into a third dead guy.

This Corpse wore a cop uniform, and he scooped me up in his arms like a favorite uncle or something. The stench of him hit me first; I felt my stomach roll over. He was a ripe

Type Two, not yet dripping fluids but layered in them, as if he'd slathered his purple skin with *Lotion du Putrid.*

"*Got. You. Boy,*" he said in Deadspeak, grinning a triumphant, decaying grin.

I suddenly wished I were Dave—strong enough to grab the guy's head and twist it all the way around as he had done to the Queen back in Chang's Funeral Parlor. Sadly, I just didn't have that kind of muscle.

Instead, I squirted the bag of IV juice right into his face.

And yes, the words meant what I'd thought they'd meant.

He went down, taking me with him. With some effort, I squirmed free of his flailing arms, struggled to my feet, slipped in the saltwater, fell, and then struggled to my feet again. Behind me, I could hear wet footsteps on the basement stairs.

Dead Mortician One and Dead Mortician Two were ascending, coming fast.

I took off for the back of the house. The front was probably closer, but it was also uncharted territory, and I couldn't afford to make a wrong turn and find myself cornered. So I dashed past the kitchen, through the mud room—still with its yellow slickers on their pegs—and tore open the funeral parlor's back door.

The winter air hit me like a wall.

Ignoring a biting wind that seemed to blow right through me, I barreled down the stoop stairs and turned into the narrow alley, squeezing my way along to the street. I made it just as Chang's front door opened and Dead Mortician One appeared.

He saw me. I saw him.

Then he started down the steps.

I sprayed him with the rest of the IV bag. It wasn't much. But it was enough. The well-groomed Type Three walked right into a lamppost and seemed to get stuck there, stepping back, walking into it again, stepping back, walking into it again. You get the idea.

It might have been funny if I hadn't been freezing to death.

But because I was, I turned and bolted up the street in the direction of City Hall.

CHAPTER 41

EULOGY

They looked for me.

Not just the funeral director Deaders but others. Over the next few minutes, it seemed like every Corpse in town had shown up for the party. They scoured the streets, shining flashlights in every nook and cranny. They even banged on a few doors, waking the neighbors and telling them God knew what.

But call it skill or luck, I managed to stay one step ahead of them. Maybe I'd just gotten used to being hunted and, like any city rat, knew how to go unseen.

That said, it was a pretty miserable journey.

The cold was like a swarm of wasps, everywhere at once, attacking and stinging me from all directions. The bandage around my chest helped a little but not much—and by the time I squeezed through the fence beside the abandoned printing house, the top half of my body felt like a side of frozen beef. My face had gone numb, and my ears burned as if held over a charcoal grill.

Getting through the unlocked cellar window by myself proved painfully awkward, and I ended up overbalancing and tumbling into the building's basement. I landed hard on my back. For a few minutes, I just lay there, panting and groaning. Then, steeling myself, I rolled over and climbed to my feet on exhausted, trembling legs.

I stumbled down the stairs to the subbasement and from there to the sewer. By the time I reached the maintenance door, what little strength I had left seemed to have drained away. I fell heavily against the cold metal, grasping the knob and trying to work up the energy to turn it.

But then it turned by itself.

Before I could react, the door yanked open so abruptly I nearly tumbled in. But instead, I caught myself and looked up into the broad, expressive face of Dave Burger.

"I *knew* it!" he shouted, pumping the air with one huge fist.

Then he hugged me.

Usually, I hated this. Usually, I squirmed like an eel to escape his hugs as quickly as I could. But this time, I didn't. I wish I could say it was friendship that kept me in his arms. I wish I could say it was relief to be back in Haven.

But if you want the truth, it was the body heat.

When he finally let go and looked at me, his smile flipped over. "You look like crap!"

I smiled thinly. "Nice to see you too."

"I *told* them you weren't dead! No way is Will Ritter dead, I said. I don't care what thousands of people saw on television! There was just no way! Helene kept calling it denial."

"Burgermeister—"

"I think she's mad at me," he rambled on. "I think she's ticked off at me for not accepting. But I couldn't. I just couldn't! That's why I'm here instead of going to their stupid memorial."

"Dave!" I snapped.

He jumped a little, as if my outburst had startled him. "What?"

"Emily and my mom…where are they?"

"Here, of course! Helene and I brought your sister in, and Tom and Ramirez showed up with your mom a few minutes later. Hey, dude, I've been meaning to ask you: where'd you get that red hair? I mean, your mom's blond, and your sister—"

"Do you know where they are now?"

"Who?"

I sighed. "My mom and my sister."

"They're at the memorial! Where else would they be?"

"And where's that?"

"In the rec room." Then his grin returned, wider than ever. "Come on! I'll take you!"

As we ran, I was surprised at how empty the corridors seemed. Dave explained to me that every Undertaker—all of them—had come to my memorial, even the Schoolers who were out on assignment. Nobody had been saying much since it all went down, and between Sharyn, who still hovered on the edge of death, and me taking that bullet—well, Haven just hadn't felt much like a haven lately.

"Who told you all I was dead?"

For a moment, the Burgermeister looked taken aback. "Who told us? It's all over the news, dude! They don't know your name, of course. You're just this mysterious kid who took a bullet for the governor's wife. They're calling you a hero!"

"Great," I muttered.

Dave didn't seem to have heard me. "Then Tom and Ramirez came back. Tom saw you get shot. The look on his face. The look on your *mom's* face. Nobody had any doubt that you were gone…except me, that is!" Then he stopped in his tracks and looked me over, really looked me over, for the first time. "Um…didn't you get shot?"

"Yeah," I said. "It's…complicated."

He sighed heavily. "With you, it always is."

We went back to running, my head flooding with images of my mom. I hadn't seen her in more than four months, unless you counted that whole top of City Hall Tower thing, which had already begun taking on the fuzzy, unreal quality of a dream.

On the other hand, hugging Emily back at Eastern State had been like taking that first drink after crossing a desert. Not that I've ever crossed a desert, but you get the idea. What would it feel like to have my mother's arms around me after all this time, especially because both of us had just come so close to dying?

It sounds sappy, but I couldn't wait to find out.

But then I remembered Sharyn and realized that I *had* to wait—if only for a little while.

I mean, what if she *died* while my mom was hugging me.

"Hold up," I said, screeching to a halt in one of the empty corridors.

Dave overshot me by about ten feet, his size thirteen shoes kicking up dust as they hammered to a stop. "What?" he demanded.

"How's Sharyn doing?"

At the mention of her name, Dave's enthusiasm melted like fried ice. "The same," he replied unhappily. Then he seemed to rouse himself. He gestured down the hallway in the direction of the rec room. "Dude...your mom! She thinks you're *dead*!"

"I know. Believe me, I know. But we gotta stop at the infirmary first."

"What for?" His smile faded a little. "You hurt?"

Well, yeah, I was. In fact, I was hurting all over. But right now, that wasn't even a blip on my radar screen. "I'm fine. There's just something I have to do."

The infirmary was empty accept for Ian, who had apparently skipped my memorial to watch over Sharyn. At the sight of me, he visibly paled, and I saw him grab at the brick wall to steady himself.

I went over to the gurney and looked down at Sharyn's comatose form.

Slowly, I reached into my pocket and pulled out the quartz—and felt instantly better.

All pain seemed to melt away, taking all exhaustion with it. My face and ears no longer felt numb.

What is this thing?

"Will?" Ian asked. The medic looked at me as if I were a ghost. "How?"

"Wish I knew," I said. "But...for what it's worth...I'm back from the dead bearing gifts!"

Then, as he and Dave watched, I touched the quartz gently to Sharyn's forehead.

"What's that?" both boys asked at once.

"No idea," I replied.

"Where'd you get it?" Dave asked.

"An angel gave it to me."

They both gawked.

Finally, Ian replied, "Cool."

I kept the quartz in full contact with Sharyn's skin. She didn't move. "Come on," I heard myself say. "Come on, Sharyn. We need you!"

Dave said, "Maybe it needs batteries. I could—"

"Hey!" a voice demanded. "What the heck happened to my hair?"

Sharyn sat up, pushing me and the strange quartz aside. She rubbed one hand over her bald head. Her fingers found the tube that Alex had inserted in her skull, and before any of us could protest, she pulled it out and tossed it casually across the room.

"Ow," she muttered.

Then, as she touched the small round hole in her head, I watched it close. Completely close. No scar.

"That's...impossible," Ian whispered.

"Hey, little bro!" the Boss Angel said to me, smiling. "You been keeping out of trouble?"

I tried to reply, but no words came. That had been happening to me a lot lately.

Dave cleared his throat.

Sharyn looked at him. He looked back at her.

"Hot Dog?" she whispered, and I was surprised to hear her voice crack a little.

Without a word, Dave came forward and hugged her fiercely.

Ian and I stood rooted to the floor, side by side, watching in astonishment.

A minute later, the four of us hurried down the rec room corridor. Sharyn was moving on her own power, though she still seemed a little bit weak. On the way, I'd given her the SparkNotes version of the events during her "absence." She'd seemed disoriented at first, then incredulous, and finally *really* annoyed.

"You mean I missed all *that*?" the Boss Angel had exclaimed.

As we neared the rec room entrance, I started hearing a voice. I knew it at once, though it had an unfamiliar quality. Gone was the quiet confidence, the calm leadership that I'd come to rely on. The owner of this voice sounded grief-stricken, world-weary—defeated.

"He didn't always do the smart thing," Tom intoned. "But he always did the *right* thing. Sometimes, it didn't seem that way at first, but every time, that was how it worked out…every single time. Amy here is with us today because of Will's recklessness and courage, and yesterday, that same recklessness and courage saved the life of another person, the first lady of our state.

"In both situations, Will never hesitated. He never stopped to worry over his own skin. He just acted. That's a virtue that I've ever only seen in two other people. One is my sister, Sharyn." His voice choked a little. "And the other was Karl Ritter, the founder of the Undertakers…and Will's dad."

We reached the doorway. Inside, the rec room was packed. Rows of chairs had been set up facing the room's far wall, where an old school picture of me had been blown up, framed, and somehow mounted to the crumbling bricks. The chairs were full, and there were kids lining the walls and crowding every aisle.

Most were sitting in stoic silence. A few were crying. And all had their collective attention fixed entirely on Tom.

The Chief said, "Sitting right here in the front row, we got Susan and Emily Ritter, Will's mom and sister. Both of them are trying…like we all are trying…to deal with the grief and pain. And as much as my heart goes out to his family…and believe me, Undertakers, it does…at the same time, I gotta keep reminding myself that he's really and truly gone."

Sharyn and I stopped in the threshold, side by side, with Ian and the Burgermeister behind us. We looked at each other. I opened my mouth to say something. I'm not sure what—announce our presence maybe. But Sharyn put a finger to her lips. Then she winked at me.

Yep. She's back.

"I went through the same thing with Karl. One minute, he was there, and the next, he wasn't, and it just didn't seem possible that such a man could be so completely gone. Like his son, he seemed too…alive…to ever die. I once told Will that, even weeks after he'd been killed, I kept expecting Karl to come strollin' back into Haven, wearing a big smile and quotin' Mark Twain…"

I looked at Sharyn.

She nodded sagely.

My cue.

Then I stepped through the doorway and into the back of the room and said at the top of my voice, "News of my death has been greatly exaggerated."

Silence didn't fall; it *hammered* down—so suddenly and so completely that I thought I'd gone deaf. Every head—and I mean *every* head—turned my way as if pulled by a common string. At the front of the room, Tom actually staggered back a step, his eyes wide. His tear-streaked face was a mask of utter and absolute shock.

Suddenly, I sort of *got* Sharyn's sense of drama.

Then, into this thundering silence, Dave "the Burgermeister" Burger declared, "Told ya so!"

A figure stepped in front of me. Helene's face was pale, and her eyes were red from crying. She seemed a little shorter than she had been twelve hours go, which was weird but unimportant. The girl stared at me as if I'd just slapped her, and for a horrible moment, I thought she meant to slap *me*.

But instead, she threw her arms around my neck.

And for the first time, I let her. If fact, for the whole of that hug, I gave as good as I got.

At the same time, I saw Tom come forward. His face crumpled as he looked first to Sharyn, then to me, then back to Sharyn. His strong arms opened—one hand, I noticed, was bandaged and probably stitched—and closed around his sister, pulling her into a tight, wordless, desperate embrace.

"Whoa, bro!" Sharyn gasped. "Get a grip!"

"How?" I heard him whisper.

"Ask Will," Ian said. "He did it."

Helene pulled back and looked me over. I took the crystal out of my pocket and held it up for everyone to see. "A present from Lilith Cavanaugh," I said. "Something I bet Steve would love to sink his teeth into."

Tom, Helene, and the others absorbed this. By now, the rest of the Undertakers had abandoned their chairs. They crowded around us, pushing close. FBI special agent Hugo Ramirez stood among them. He was regarding me with an odd expression, shaking his head and smiling thinly.

"His father's son," I heard him mutter. It was maybe the nicest thing anyone had ever said about me.

I grinned at him, at all of them, though at the same time, I was scanning their ranks, looking for—

"Will?"

A slim figure came forward, pushing kids aside as if they weren't there. As she emerged into the open and stopped in front of me, I noticed that, like Helene, she looked somehow shorter than I remembered. Older too. Her blond hair had a few strands of gray mixed in.

Emily hung onto her pant leg as she had to mine. Her face had been washed, and somebody had found her fresh clothes. They looked about four sizes too big.

But at least she was smiling.

"Will?" my mother said again. She was staring at me, as if absorbing the sight of me like a sponge.

"It's me, Mom," I said, choking a little on the words.

"You…" Her voice broke. After a moment, she swallowed and tried again. "You've gotten taller."

Then she threw her arms around me and began to sob.

I'd wondered what those arms would feel like. Now I knew.

They felt like *home*.

CHAPTER 42

THE EYES OF THE ENEMY

The Queen of the Dead bathed in the camera flashes. She stood smiling atop the dais, the very same dais whereupon her carefully laid plans had been ruined by a single teenage boy. Now she had to start all over again, come up with a new way to advance the *Malum* cause. Months of work destroyed in a single moment by a display of ridiculous heroics.

She'd lost Pierce, and far worse, the anchor shard had been taken from her. Getting another would be costly and difficult in the extreme. Her only consolation was that, try as they might, no possible way existed for those—whelps— to determine the nature and potential of the treasure they'd stolen.

They lacked the wisdom.

The Queen said into the microphone, "Two days ago, a young boy…who has yet to be identified…made a daring and dramatic appearance on this very spot, throwing his body in the path of an assassin's bullet. His heroism and sacrifice is an inspiration to young people everywhere and a shining example of the integrity and strength of spirit of the good people of Philadelphia."

But the most galling part of the latest Undertakers debacle was having to be *here*, with the governor and the governor's wife beside her, saying these words:

"What exactly happened in the hours after this brave boy was rushed to the hospital may never be fully explained. By all accounts, he was declared dead en route only to disappear when the ambulance reached the medical examiner's office. The circumstances of this disappearance remain a mystery and seem, in many ways, as miraculous as his appearance had been.

"Personally, I would like nothing more than to see this young hero come before me just for a few moments so I could shake his hand and thank him for his selflessness and courage.

"However, as that isn't possible, the governor, first lady, and I have invited back some of the children who were present two days ago. As witnesses to the mystery boy's amazing feat of bravery, they are here to act as surrogates of sorts...and to shake our hands in his stead."

With that, Lilith stepped to the edge of the dais and reached down to take the first of the waiting palms. One by one, she and her two distinguished guests moved along the line of middle school children, smiling for the cameras and shaking hand after hand.

Oh, how she loathed them! How she longed to rip their little arms from their little bodies, tear into their slender throats with her teeth, to taste their blood and flesh. But instead, she smiled and posed and went from boy to girl to boy to girl to—

At one of the boys, she stopped. He was slender, his head covered by a heavy hoodie. But there was something familiar about him. Something about the look in his eyes.

It can't be!

Will Ritter, his face expressionless, offered his hand up to the Queen of the Dead, who paused in her tracks, glaring at him. For several long seconds, she had to fight to control herself, to prevent her fingers from locking around the wretched boy's throat. Too many cameras. Too many witnesses. And he *knew* that. That was why he'd come. He knew she couldn't touch him!

But she *could* speak to him.

Lilith accepted the offered hand and squeezed hard. Will winced but not much—not nearly enough. But she didn't dare apply more pressure, didn't dare break his hand.

Using the Ancient Tongue, she spoke directly into his mind. He was an Undertaker, so he alone would hear her words. It wasn't much, but it was the only weapon she had.

"You. Won. The. Day. Boy," she said, locking her eyes on his. *"But. I. Am. Not. Booth. I. Am. Still. Here. Do .You. Understand. Me. Boy? I. Am. Still. Here!"*

She knew he could See her as she truly was, See the rotting

Corpse who clutched his hand. She waited for the terror to shine in his face, waited for him to pull away in panic. And she would let him go; after all, what choice did she have? But at least she could savor that reaction, revel in the horror that must be burning into him, consuming every corner of his child's brain.

But it wasn't there.

No terror. No revulsion. Instead, Will Ritter met her hard gaze with one of his own, filled with a confidence beyond his tender years. There was strength there. And determination.

And wisdom.

"So am I," he said.

Then, with a slight smile, he withdrew his hand from hers and melted into the crowd.

The Queen of the Dead looked after him, the expression he'd worn burning into her, consuming every corner of her stolen body.

And for the first time in her long existence, she was afraid.

ACKNOWLEDGMENTS

I do a lot of research. I'd like to thank the city of Philadelphia for its cooperation and for helping me stand where Will Ritter stood and see things through his eyes. A particular thank-you goes out to the good folks at Eastern State Penitentiary, Philly landmark and prison-turned-museum, for answering my many questions. Their kind patience allowed me the freedom to poke around, soak in the mystery, and let my imagination soar.

On April 3, 1945, twelve prisoners actually *did* escape from that formidable place by digging a hundred-foot tunnel under the prison walls. The tunnel has since been sealed at both ends, though at one point it was reopened and a robotic camera sent in to have a look. Bottom line, I may have taken some liberties with the details, but the tunnel, my friends, is still *there*.

It's difficult to express the depth of my gratitude to Ann

Behar, my amazing agent, whose steadfast belief in the Undertakers warms a writer's heart. My thanks and affection also go out to Kay Mitchell, the Sourcebooks publicist who has done so much to get the word out about the Undertakers and their adventures.

To my wife, Helene (the *real* Helene Boettcher), you are a joy and an inspiration. It goes without saying that none of this would have happened without you.

And last but never least, to MTB—four of the best friends any writer ever had. To say that you guys rock doesn't even begin to express it.

ABOUT THE AUTHOR

Ty Drago is a writer, editor, publisher, husband, father, business analyst, shaven Sasquatch, born Quaker, old guy who looks good in hats, friend to all, enemy to none, and—by nature—a storyteller.

His published works include a YA historical mystery called *The Franklin Affair* published by Regency Press in 2001; *Phobos*, a science-fiction noir published by Tor Books in 2003; and of course, the *Undertakers* series. He is currently busy with the third book in the series, *The Undertakers: Capitol Corpses*.

In addition, he edits and publishes *Allegory*, www.allegory ezine.com, a premiere online magazine that features short stories and articles from around the world.

The proud parent of two grown children, he makes his home in South Jersey with his wife, Helene.